IN THE
FULL LIGHT
OF THE
SUN

Clare Clark

virago

VIRAGO

First published in Great Britain in 2019 by Virago Press
This paperback edition published in 2020 by Virago Press

1 3 5 7 9 10 8 6 4 2

A CIP catalogue record for this book
is available from the British Library.

ISBN 978-0-349-01080-9

Typeset in Goudy Oldstyle Std by M Rules
Printed and bound in Great Britain by
Clays Ltd, Elcograf S.p.A.

Papers used by Virago are from well-managed forests
and other responsible sources.

MIX
Paper from
responsible sources
FSC® C104740

Virago Press
An imprint of
Little, Brown Book Group
Carmelite House
50 Victoria Embankment
London EC4Y 0DZ

An Hachette UK Company
www.hachette.co.uk

www.virago.co.uk

For Clare A, with love

I undertook to enlighten him ... From that day on
my van Gogh made astonishing progress: he seemed
to have an inkling of all he had in him, hence that
whole series of sunflowers on sunflowers in the full light
of the sun.

Gauguin, Avant et après (1903)

JULIUS

Berlin 1923

I

Julius took the night train back from Paris. He slept fitfully, a thin sleep threaded with whistles and the jolting clatter of wheels. It was still dark when he rose. In the dining car a yawning waiter brought him a cup of weak coffee. With its teak panelling and glass-shaded lamps, the diner was all that remained of the elegant Nord-Express which had run this route before the war. Julius stared out of the window. There was no moon. The passing telegraph poles sliced the blackness into squares.

He supposed he should feel anger, grief even, but all he could summon was the weariness of defeat. His marriage was over and the end, like so much about Luisa, was both tawdry and unutterably banal. The pair of them writhing and grunting in her tumbled bed, their frozen horror as he switched on the light. He gave them one minute to get out of his house before he called the police. Frau Lang covered her face with her apron as they fled down the stairs, their clothes bundled in their arms. He should have done the same. *I worship the nude like a god*, Rodin once said, but there was nothing godlike about their nakedness, their shrivelled cocks, the skinny white shanks of their legs.

And later Luisa, oblivious Luisa in the bottle-littered drawing room, her make-up smeared and her dress falling off one shoulder, her arm around Lehmbruck's *Kneeling Woman*, a silver straw between her fingers like a cigarette. Her contemptuous smirk as she leaned down, eyes glittering, and snorted cocaine from the sculpture's cast stone thigh. When he told her he wanted a divorce she laughed, shrill and sharp, like glass breaking.

'I'll drink to that,' she said and, hoisting a champagne bottle by the neck, she put it to her lips. The wine ran out of her mouth and over her chin.

The train slowed. Above the dark curve of the hills a grey dawn was breaking. Quicksilver balls of rain rolled diagonally down the window. Julius closed his eyes, his fingertips kneading the back of his neck. Though it troubled him to admit it, he was as much to blame as she was. Such a weakness you have for beautiful things, his old friend Bruno said drily when Julius first introduced them, and Julius only laughed. He was fifty-three, recently demobbed and dizzy with desire. Luisa was twenty-four. In the bleak, broken-down months after the armistice her loveliness was a kind of miracle. He could not get enough of her. In her arms the past grew hazy, shedding its horrors, and the future was ravishing and new. He thought she would heal him, that he could wash himself clean in the clear, cool stream of her. By the time he understood that he was wrong, that her exquisite face masked a crude, incurious mind and what he had taken for innocence was nothing but ignorance and lack of imagination, she was already his wife.

Five years, three of them more or less wretched. They were neither of them what the other had imagined them to be. Their arguments, once fiery, grew bitter, hard with disappointment. There were no more passionate reconciliations, only silences, brief distrustful breaks in the bombardment. Like opposing armies they dug into their positions. Julius returned to his bachelor habits,

4

burying himself in his work. Luisa shopped and danced and shrieked till dawn.

He was ashamed, that was the truth. He had built his reputation, his whole life, on his ability to see, not only with his eyes but with his heart. In *The Making of Modern Art* he had railed against an establishment blinded by the seductions of technical virtuosity, urging them to seek instead the heroic struggle that was the soul of great art, and yet, confronted with Luisa, he had made all the same mistakes. He had succumbed to the surface of her, mistaken her physical perfection for a purity of spirit, for something transformative and true.

A couple came into the dining car. The woman was short and dark with sleepy Modigliani eyes. She smiled at Julius and wished him a good morning, her German heavily accented with Russian. Julius nodded in return. He would do the decent thing. Since the Kaiser, with characteristic compassion, had deemed insurmountable aversion insufficient grounds for divorce, it was necessary for one side or the other to take the blame. Adultery was cleanest. In cases of proven adultery, divorce was granted automatically. The newspapers might still take an interest, but there was none of the public scandal that dogged a contested hearing. He would talk to Böhm this afternoon, have him make the necessary arrangements. In Berlin there were plenty of women who would pretend to have fucked you for a fee.

He would pay for his principles, of course. Only guilty husbands paid alimony. And while a part of him raged against financing any more of Luisa's extravagances – for the bourgeois daughter of a money-doesn't-grow-on-trees bank manager, she had always displayed a staggeringly can-do attitude to prodigality – a larger part was glad. An honourable man paid for his mistakes. He took his punishment, however harsh. There was a kind of purification in it, a humility that was almost grace. And it was not as if he did not have the money. The van Gogh book had proved a runaway bestseller, not only in Germany but in France and Britain too. America beckoned. The royalties would have left him comfortably off even without the recent collapse in the value of the mark. With exchange rates as they were he could afford to be generous. Besides, there was the child to think of. People would gossip, they always did, but he would not have anyone say he had mistreated the mother of his son.

In Berlin the rain was falling steadily. It was the busiest hour of the morning. People jostled and pushed on the pavements, umbrellas raised like shields as the trams clattered past and the omnibuses sent up arcs of dirty water. It was nine thirty when the taxicab finally pulled up outside the villa on Meierstrasse. Julius paused on the pavement, gazing up at the house's elegant façade. It was a long time, he thought, since he had looked forward to coming home.

A red-faced Frau Lang greeted him at the door. She did not meet his eye as she took his coat and hat. His breakfast, she said, was already in the dining room, it would be getting cold. She made it sound like it was his fault. When he said he was not hungry, that all he really wanted was a bath, she hardly seemed to hear him. She scowled at the floor, her fingers working the sleeve of his coat into pleats.

'And some coffee,' he added. 'The swill they served on the train was undrinkable.'

Still Frau Lang did not move. Julius felt a twinge of irritation. He could not think what had contrived to provoke her so early in the day. No doubt it was another trivial altercation with the nursemaid. The two of them were as territorial as bears.

'The bath, if you please,' he said crisply. 'Or do I have to draw it myself?'

The housekeeper's face crumpled. For a terrible moment Julius thought she might cry. Then, bundling his coat against her bosom, she scuttled away towards the stairs. Julius sighed. Frau Lang had come to work for them when he and Luisa were married, Luisa had insisted on it. She told Julius that Frau Lang had worked devotedly for her parents for years, that they would never have survived the war without her. Had Julius known his parents-in-law then, he would not have been so quick to count that in her favour.

Wearily he rubbed his forehead. The smell of trains clung to his clothes and his eyes ached. From the morning room he could hear the muffled tap-tap of the typewriter. He would ask Fräulein Grüber to telephone the lawyers and make an appointment with Böhm. There was nothing to be gained from putting it off. Above him, in the arch made by the twin staircases, the Vuillard panel gleamed, a riot of sunlight and pink roses. He tilted back his head, breathing in the sweetness of it, the play of colour and texture that was at once as simple and as complex as nature itself. Then, crossing the hall to the morning room, he opened the door.

'Good morning,' he said. The typist started, her hands flying up from the keys to cover her mouth.

'Herr Köhler-Schultz, you're back,' she said. Her voice was bright, artificial. 'Did you have – I mean, ah – is there anything you need?'

'I need to change. Half an hour, then we'll go through the letters. I assume there's nothing urgent?'

Fräulein Grüber bit her lip. 'I didn't know – your appointment this morning with Herr Rachmann—'

The dealer from Düsseldorf. Julius had forgotten all about him. 'That's today?'

'Half past ten. I'm so sorry, I would have cancelled him, but he didn't leave an address in Berlin and I wasn't sure – that is, if you'd rather not see him – in the circumstances, I mean – I can ask him to come back another day. If that's what you'd prefer.'

Julius hesitated, half tempted to agree. The last thing he wanted was some insolent young Turk from the provinces sprawling in his study with his hands in his pockets, drawlingly addressing him with the familiar *du*.

'The boy has verve,' Salazin had said with a shrug. 'Perhaps he'll bring you something marvellous. And if he doesn't, well, it's an authentication, not an adoption. At worst he'll remind you how blessed it is no longer to be young.' Hugo Salazin, who at sixty still had the instincts of a pickpocket and the smile of a Prussian sphinx. No wonder his gallery was one of the most successful in Berlin. With a sigh, Julius shook his head.

'No, I'll see him,' he said. 'Dealers are like cockroaches. If you don't get rid of them immediately, they multiply.'

The typist laughed politely, showing her teeth. When the telephone rang Julius gestured for her to answer it and went upstairs. There was little danger of running into Luisa this early in the morning, it would be hours before she deigned to surface, but all the same he steeled himself a little as he crossed the galleried landing. His rooms were on the east side of the house, hers on the west. Reflexively, uneasily, as he passed it he glanced down the wide passage towards her door. To his surprise it stood open. A wedge of pale light gleamed on the parquet.

Slowly, reluctantly, he walked along the passage and looked in. Usually Luisa abandoned her bedroom in a chaos of discarded clothes and magazines and torn-open letters, a tray of half-finished tea and toast congealing among the bedclothes. This morning the bed was neatly made, the table in the window bare but for a bowl of flowers. There was a sudden hurried scuffle of footsteps on the landing.

'Frau Lang?' Julius said, turning, and like a rabbit caught in the headlamps of a car she froze. 'Where is my wife?'

The air went out of her. She subsided on to the stairs, one hand clutching at the banister.

'She went,' she said. Something choked her throat, she could hardly get out the words. There had been no warning, Frau Lang would not even have seen them go, Wednesday was her afternoon off, only she came back early and there they were, the mistress and the nursemaid under umbrellas on the pavement outside the house and the baby swaddled in blankets and screaming fit to bust as the cab driver tried to cram the heaped-up luggage into the boot of the car. So much luggage, Frau Lang said, she could not think who had packed it or how they would manage. When the mistress saw her she pushed the nursemaid into the taxi. They had to hurry, she said to Frau Lang through the window, they were late for their train. She did not say where they were going, only something about her parents and having the rest of their things sent on. Frau Lang had supposed it was an emergency. She could still hear the baby screaming as they drove away.

'This was yesterday?'

The housekeeper nodded unhappily. She did not look at him.

'And did she say when she'd be back?'

There was a long silence. 'She left a letter,' she said at last. 'In your study.'

Julius went downstairs. His chest was tight, cramped with foreboding. Luisa would not have taken the baby, not if she meant to come back. His study looked just as he had left it, the books on his desk neatly ordered, a fire blazing in the grate. Taking the room in four strides he flipped through the sheaf of letters on his blotter, discarding them like playing cards. Nothing from Luisa. He turned to the mantelpiece, pushing aside the Rosso head.

Nothing there either. Nothing but an unnatural blankness in the corner of his eye. A coldness came over him, the blood shrinking from his limbs. It was not possible. It could not be possible. Dizzily he turned.

It was gone. Julius stared at the blank wall, the grey line where the frame had marked the paint. At the envelope impaled on the empty nail. His skull was full of noise, a shrill hissing nothingness like an untuned wireless. He stumbled forward, his hand searching the wall as though he might still find it there. As though the absence was nothing but a trick of the light. The wall was cold. Blindly he grabbed the letter, ripping it from the nail. It was nothing. A mistake. A prank to frighten him. His face was stiff, someone else's face. His fingers too. He could hardly tear open the envelope.

A scrawl. Something about his deficiencies, her boredom and unhappiness. A gap. And then.

Of course I couldn't leave without my Vincent. Just having him with me makes me feel safer, protected somehow. What a comfort it is already to look at him and think of you.

The anger was like pain, so complete he could hardly feel it. With a howl he hurled himself against the bare wall, smashing it with his fists. There was a fire in his chest, in his skull, smoke-thick and acrid. He could not breathe for the choke of it. The empty nail caught the side of his palm, the sharp metal slicing the skin. He closed his hand around it, jerking and twisting at it as though he would wrench it from the wall. Blood bloomed, ran down his wrist. He closed his eyes but her voice wormed into his ear, over and over like a gramophone record with the needle stuck.

'He gives me the creeps. Those piggy eyes ogling us when we

make love, and where's his other hand anyway? I mean it. It's disgusting.'

And he had laughed. She did not mean it, she could not mean it, she was teasing him. She was young, he would teach her. How had he not seen that she was unteachable? *It's disgusting.* The painting that for thirty years had turned over his heart.

There was blood on the wall. A smear of red and a faint grey line. An empty nail. The air blue somehow, as though the painting had left behind its stain. *My Vincent.* A fresh fury burst like a shell inside him, knocking the air from his lungs. Wheeling round, he kicked out at the low stool behind him, upending it with a crash. There was a lamp beside the armchair, a pile of books. He flung the lamp against the wall, then the books, handfuls of them, as hard as he could, but the rage kept exploding and exploding, thundering in his ears, so he turned to the bookshelves, tearing the books out by their spines, hurling them to the floor. His arms moved violently, mechanically, like pistons. Wildly he turned towards the mantelpiece. The Rosso head gazed at him, her blank eyes impassive.

'She looks like me,' Luisa had said once. He had not seen it then. He saw it now. Her faint smile was full of mockery. He had never hated someone so absolutely. Snatching up the head, he hurled her at the window. The glass smashed.

'Ohhh.'

It was not so much a word as a catch of breath. Julius turned, his hands held up in front of him. Fräulein Grüber stood in the doorway. There was a young man with her. He was slender, fine-boned, with pale skin and coppery hair. Under one arm he carried a painting wrapped in brown paper. For a dazzling, impossible moment Julius thought it was his van Gogh, that she had sent it back. The young man looked at the broken window, at the lamp and the books, splayed and broken on the floor.

'I – I'm so sorry,' the typist stammered. 'We'll – I'll come back.'

Her face was stricken as she fumbled for the door handle. The young man said nothing. He looked at Julius. His gaze was steady. Then, bowing his head, he stepped backwards. The door closed. Julius looked down at his blood-streaked hands, the emptiness inside them. A cold breeze blew through the broken window and stirred the pages of the books.

Later he remembered those eyes, the extraordinary milky green of them, like sea glass.

II

As always, Frau Lang made the necessary arrangements. The glazier arrived promptly the next morning, before Julius had finished his breakfast. The housekeeper took him out into the garden to inspect the damage. Their voices drifted up through the dining-room window. The hoodlums these days, the glazier said, they'd smash us all to pieces in our beds. There were still fragments of glass on the flagstones. The morning sunlight caught them, making them flash.

Julius had found the Rosso under a euonymus bush, half rolled out of sight like a lost football. Her face was undamaged. She gazed at him as he crouched to reach her, a smear of earth on one pale cheek, the faint smile still on her lips. It was only as he picked her up that he saw that the back of her head was shattered, the finely worked wax split to reveal the plaster cast inside. Julius thought of Rosso in his studio, the way his fingers seemed to summon her from air and light, and his heart shrank. To wantonly destroy a work of art, to want to destroy it: he had not imagined himself capable of such barbarism. He cradled the head in his hands, his fingers folded over her gashed skull. Then, taking an ironed handkerchief from his pocket, he wrapped her gently in it and carried her back into the house.

In the hours since then his shame had grown hard, a stone in his throat. It made it difficult to swallow. Julius pushed away his coffee cup. In the hall Frau Lang tutted to herself as she brought his coat and hat.

'The glazier's boarding up the window now,' she said. 'I told him it wouldn't do, that you couldn't be expected to work boxed in like that, but he says there's nothing for it. The glass is too large, it has to be ordered.'

Julius took a taxicab to his lawyer's office. Slow-moving hand-carts obstructed the roads and the sun glared in shop windows. By the time he reached Invalidenstrasse the hatred was in his bones. He sang with it like a struck glass. Brushing aside Böhm's pleasantries, he thrust Luisa's letter into his hands. The lawyer read it, then frowned at Julius over his spectacles.

'So the painting isn't hers?' he asked. 'You didn't give it to her?'

'Of course I didn't,' Julius raged. 'Why would I? She detested it.'

Böhm soothed him. A wife could not simply appropriate her husband's assets. A sternly worded letter to Luisa's lawyers might be enough to ensure its safe return. And if not, legal steps could be taken.

'As for a divorce, I would advise postponing a decision until the matter of the painting is resolved,' he said. 'Perhaps she'll come back.'

'Not if I have anything to do with it.'

'All the same. There is nothing to be gained from provocation.'

Reluctantly Julius allowed himself to be persuaded. Luisa was impulsive and unpredictable, God knows what she might do just to spite him. In the lift, as the uniformed attendant worked his levers, he leaned heavily against the brass rail. It tormented him to think of his painting propped carelessly in a corner of his father-in-law's overheated house, discarded among the brown slabs of faux-medieval furniture, the brassy knick-knacks that crowded every surface. Behind Julius's closed eyelids the painting was as vivid as if it were in front of him, Vincent three-quarters turned, his pose recalling the great self-portraits of Rembrandt, his palette and his brushes in his hand, his eyes burning in his exhausted face as all around his head the canvas thrummed with a frenzied cacophony of violet-blue swirls and dashes. The artist and the madman, staring into one another's souls.

The elevator bumped to a stop. Of all the portraits he had made of himself, Vincent had written to his brother Theo, it was this one that caught his true character. In the thirty years Julius had owned it, he had bought and sold dozens of other paintings. He abhorred the modern habit of stockpiling art as though it were pig iron or petroleum, hoarding it in warehouses against future appreciation. Julius looked at a picture until he could find nothing new in it and then he let it go. As van Gogh's prices spiralled, he could have sold the self-portrait for ten times what he paid for it, then fifty, then a hundred and more, but he did not sell. He never wanted to stop looking. In the starkness of Vincent's fear, in the savage honesty of his scrutiny, there was something Julius could only describe as heroism.

He went directly from Invalidenstrasse to the Hotel Adlon. In Pariser Platz people strolled in the sunshine. Foreigners of course, a plague of tourist-speculators. With the mark sinking ever further on the exchange markets, they swarmed over the city like locusts. Above the columns of the Brandenburger Tor, winged Victory whipped up her horses, celadon green against the bright blue sky. There was nothing Julius wanted less this morning than to see Salazin's young man, but he knew it had to be done. He had seen the expression on the dealer's face when Fräulein Grüber opened the door, the shock that was at least half fascination, the gleam in his eyes that might have been calculation but could just as easily have been glee. Dealers these days would do anything to get ahead. Young Rachmann was Salazin's man. He would not have either of them thinking they held the advantage.

He could have invited Rachmann back to Meierstrasse, there were enough rooms with unbroken windows, but Julius had no intention of allowing the young man back under the skin of him, of inciting him to remember. The music room at the Adlon was the preserve of favoured customers of the hotel. With its Bechstein grand piano and painted stucco ceiling, it was the embodiment of restrained luxury. In the music room Julius could be his public self, Germany's pre-eminent art critic, composed, cultured and authoritative, a man garlanded with the privileges of lifelong success. A man above violent outbursts of emotion, as incapable of screams and smashed windows as a would-be dealer from the provinces was of paying the Adlon's astronomical bills.

Julius slid a note into the waiter's palm and asked him to bring coffee. 'When my guest arrives, please ask him to wait. I'll see him at midday.'

The meeting was scheduled for half past eleven. Julius settled himself at the table, spreading books and papers around him. He drank coffee, first from one cup and then from the other. A little after noon, the waiter showed Rachmann in. Frowning up from over his spectacles, Julius raised a finger and continued to write. He wrote for several minutes. When at last he capped his fountain pen, Rachmann put down the painting he carried. He pressed his hands to his heart, then extended them to Julius, the fingers uncurling in apology and appeal. There was a delicacy to the gesture, a grace even, that made Julius think of Degas.

'I've kept you waiting,' the young man said. 'I'm so sorry.' He spoke in a light, low voice, his consonants coarsened by a faint but unmistakable Düsseldorf accent. Julius glanced at the ormolu clock on the mantel.

'Well,' he said coolly. 'You're here now.'

'I was here then, but they wouldn't let me see you. I don't think they believed me when I said you were expecting me. But then I'm not sure I would have believed me either.' His smile was warm and unfeigned. 'I've admired you for a long time, sir. It's a great privilege to meet you.'

Over the years Julius had grown accustomed to the obsequies that accompanied these encounters – his endorsement could add several zeroes to the value of a painting – but there was something different about this boy, he thought, less sycophantic calculation than a kind of unguarded candour. He would have to toughen up if he was to survive as a dealer. A man without wiles would not last long in Berlin.

'Coffee?' he offered. 'We'll have them bring another cup.'

'Thank you. And thank you for seeing me. I'm so grateful. Truly. Overawed, really. When Herr Salazin suggested – I'm talking too much. I do that when I'm nervous. I'm sorry. And I'm still talking. Please tell me to shut up.'

Julius smiled. He rang for the waiter. 'Why don't you show me what you've brought,' he said. 'Who knows, perhaps I'll be grateful too.'

The painting was an impressionistic still life of flowers and apples, and unmistakably a Schuch, the muted palette applied with the artist's characteristically square brushstrokes. Pretty enough, if, like many of Schuch's canvases, a little overworked. When Julius confirmed his attribution to Rachmann, the young man smiled to himself, a small, fierce smile that creased his eyes, and touched a corner of the canvas with the tip of one finger. He had a pianist's hands, Julius thought, or a poet's. Most painters had hands like peasants.

'Is it true that, like van Gogh, Schuch sold only one painting in his lifetime?' Rachmann asked as Julius wrote out his certificate of authentication.

'It's true except that, unlike van Gogh, Schuch chose not to sell. He despised the circus of it, he said, and besides he came from money. He could afford a little disdain.'

'I don't know,' Rachmann said. 'Perhaps it was Schuch's disdain that muddied his colours. Perhaps, like Fou-feu, he'd have been better off with poverty and passion.'

Startled, Julius glanced up at the young man. Fou-feu, Crazy Fire, was the sobriquet Julius had imagined for van Gogh among the whores of Arles. The book's sniffier critics had derided such flourishes as mendacious, figments of Julius's overheated imagination, but what then were Vincent's purple fields, his yellow skies? *What I do may be a kind of lie*, Vincent had written to Theo, *but only because it tells the truth more plainly.*

Rachmann smiled awkwardly. '"The storm in his breast and the fierce sun in his heart." Your book, I – it changed everything for me. The way you wrote about van Gogh's life, his pictures. All my life I had looked at paintings, but when I tried to read about them there was nothing there of what I saw, what I felt. I thought it was because they were not something you could explain out loud. And then I read your book and it was as though you had thrown open all the windows and suddenly the air and the light and the music came flooding in and it was not just Vincent who was alive. His paintings danced. Your words made them dance.'

There was a silence. Julius had never imagined *Vincent* would become a bestseller. When he wrote it, he had sought only to write as van Gogh painted, discarding the old rules and instead setting down the truth as he felt it, intensely and in a fever of colour. Naturally the art establishment had derided the book as trivial and unscholarly, as 'vulgar melodrama'. They favoured academic monographs, dry-as-dust texts that stifled their subjects as assuredly as if they had pressed a pillow over their faces, but Julius was not writing for them. He wrote for the Rachmanns, as van Gogh painted for the ordinary working men, to open their eyes and their hearts. To make the paintings dance.

'Thank you,' he said simply and, as he scrawled his signature, something in him softened.

Julius thought of the young man often in the weeks that followed. One evening, leaving the Philharmonie, he was sure he saw him standing on the corner of Potsdamer Strasse. The smile was already on his lips when the young man turned and Julius saw that he was not a man at all, but a bob-haired girl in a man's suit, her stiff-collared shirt unbuttoned to the breastbone, her mouth a bright slash of scarlet. As he hurried away she put two fingers in her mouth and whistled. The harsh noise seemed to tear the night in two.

Berlin was changing. For all their mordant brashness, Berliners were notoriously hard-working, measuring out their days in marks, but as money slipped its moorings a kind of hysteria gripped the city. It had always had its private clubs and smoky basements, hidden places promising forbidden pleasures, but now the bars and the dance halls spilled their lights across the streets and the pavements teemed with people. Suddenly, it seemed, everyone was for sale: skinny boys in sailor trousers, their cheeks lurid with rouge; girls, breasts barely covered, in negligees, in hitched-up gymslips, in high leather boots. Couples kissing hungrily, brazenly, under streetlamps. As though, with no certainty of tomorrow, there was nothing to be done but to give oneself up to today.

At home Frau Lang let Julius in sleepily, swallowing a yawn. A single soft lamp lit the hall. No one played music at top volume or shrieked on the stairs or spilled champagne over the balustrade of the gallery. Luisa and her friends had strewn themselves through the house like dolls leaking stuffing, their trails marked by discarded furs and empty glasses and flimsy shoes tipped drunkenly on their sides. Without her, without her screeching cronies, the villa was returned to itself, hushed and immaculate.

Frau Lang had lighted a fire in the study. She did not need to be asked, she knew his habits. In the light of the flames the wall danced, orange-tinted, and the empty nail grinned at Julius, a gargoyle sticking out its tongue. Then he switched on the lamp and it shrivelled, shrinking back into the wall. Böhm had written to Luisa's lawyer as he had promised, requiring the immediate return of the van Gogh, and had received a bland evasion in reply. Since then several more letters had been exchanged. One of them, dictated by Julius, included meticulous instructions for the painting's care, the necessity of keeping it in appropriate conditions, away from direct light and protected from extremes of heat or cold, of dryness or humidity, that might cause harm to the delicate surface of the paint.

Luisa's lawyer's reply was brief. *You may rest assured*, he wrote, *that my client fully appreciates the value of her asset.*

The glazier had finally replaced the study window. The lamp's reflection gleamed in the black glass, a van Gogh swirl of yellow-gold. Julius stared at the blank white wall and the rage that filled him was a kind of company.

It was late April when Rachmann wrote to ask if Julius might be willing to meet with him again. On Meierstrasse the cherry trees were in blossom, clouds of pink and white, and a three-mark loaf of bread could not be found for less than fifteen hundred. Beneath his careful politeness the dealer sounded shaken. A bookseller friend of his father's in Düsseldorf had taken his own life, his widow had no choice but to sell his stock. Among the piles of books Rachmann had discovered a sheaf of drawings. He wondered if Julius might be willing to look at them. He had promised the family he would help them if he could.

Please excuse my presumption, he wrote, *but perhaps tomorrow afternoon, if you can spare the time?*

Julius's diary was already unpleasantly full, a meeting of the prize jury he chaired, followed by another with Geisheim, editor of the *Tribüne*, for whom he wrote a regular arts column, but he told Fräulein Grüber to reschedule the latter for the following day. Newspaper editors were accustomed to the vagaries of circumstance. He would meet with Rachmann at five.

'At the Adlon?' the typist asked but Julius shook his head. Since the Japanese had joined the frenzy of foreign acquisition, the Adlon had grown unbearable.

'Here,' he said and the thought of it lifted his spirits.

Rachmann was already waiting when he arrived home from his meeting.

'Half an hour early,' Frau Lang said disapprovingly. 'I put him to wait in the morning room. I only hope he hasn't been distracting Fräulein Grüber from her work.'

She brought him to the study. Julius watched as the young man looked around him, taking in the Pissarro with its shimmer of silver birches, the Munch drawings in their black frames, the little Claudel he had brought down from his bedroom to replace the Rosso on the mantelpiece.

'Such beautiful things,' Rachmann said.

Isn't that why you wanted me, another exhibit for your fucking museum? Luisa's voice was so sharp in Julius's ears it was as though a crack had opened in time. Discomfited, he gestured to the young man to bring his drawings to the desk, but Rachmann had turned away towards the blank wall and did not see him.

'Tell me you still see it,' Rachmann murmured and the shock of it was like stepping into space, nothingness where there should have been solidity. He stared at the young man, who smiled, as though it were ordinary to lift a man's skull and look inside. 'Tell me that you never forget to look, that this room still moves you every single day.'

Julius shrugged. He should have realised the young man meant only the works that were there, the ones he could see. He felt both foolish and obscurely disappointed. 'I still look,' he protested and Rachmann nodded, an amused scepticism pulling at his mouth. Again Julius had the unsettling sense that the young man could read his thoughts precisely. 'Though perhaps not as often I should,' he conceded.

Rachmann's smile softened. 'Actually, I'm glad you stop looking sometimes. If you didn't, you would never be able to write.'

Julius had Rachmann spread the drawings on the desk. Most were insignificant. One, an unsigned sketch in red chalk, caused his heart to leap. A male nude in the classical style, his weight in his right haunch, the curve of his muscled stomach mirroring the jut of his right buttock, the quintessence of careless virility. Julius could no more have mistaken it than his own reflection.

'Marées,' he said, unable to conceal his pleasure. 'Without question. A study for the *Hesperides*. Flawed, a little – there is an overworking here, do you see? He seems unsure of the angle. But otherwise very fine, very fine indeed.'

Rachmann let out a breath, pressing his knuckles to his lips. 'Thank God.'

'You suspected?'

'I hoped. Frau Schmidt has endured so much.'

Julius looked at the drawing, the exquisite economy of the marks on the paper, and he thought of the widow in Düsseldorf, her husband, their business, everything wiped out in a single stroke. The inflation had made a mockery of Germany's stolidly prudent middle classes, magicking lifetimes of painstaking pension payments into handfuls of dust. In Berlin, it was said, a man killed himself every single day.

'You should get a decent price even now,' he said. 'That the drawing is a study for so beloved a work will add considerably to its value.'

'It's wonderful, isn't it? I only wish I could afford to buy it myself. The thought of parting with it—' Rachmann shook his head ruefully. 'I'm afraid I have all the wrong instincts for a dealer.'

'On the contrary. If it doesn't break your heart to part with a work you have no business acquiring it in the first place.'

Reflexively Julius looked across the study to where the afternoon sun struck the white wall and for a moment he saw it, Vincent's haunted, haunting face fixing him with his unblinking stare. Then the light shifted and he was gone. Julius looked back at the drawing. The nude figure stood astride, his feet square, exposing his naked body with all the blithe confidence of youth, but his face was turned away, his eyes closed and his arms bent at the elbows as though the emotion that seized him was simply too powerful to contain. In the garden a bird sang, a rushing trill of notes.

'Are you familiar with Charles Blanc?' he asked. 'He was director of the École des Beaux-Arts in Paris after the February Revolution. He claimed that drawing was the masculine art and paint the feminine one, that, while drawing can show us what passes in the mind, it is painting that illuminates the secrets of the heart. I would only have had to show him this drawing and his thesis would have crumbled into ash.'

'You feel it too.'

He used the familiar *du* but there was no insolence in it. He spoke quietly, trustingly, as a son might speak to his father. Julius smiled.

'How could I not?' he said.

Julius bought the Marées. He paid five times what it was worth. He did not look at Rachmann as he handed him the money order, just as he did not look at the beggars in their army greatcoats when he dropped the folded notes into their outstretched hands. He did not want to see the transaction reflected in the young man's eyes, the excessiveness of the sum and its insufficiency. He thought of the widow in Düsseldorf and he knew it changed nothing. A vast swirling drain had opened in Germany, sucking everyone down. A man could throw every last pfennig he had into a hole like that and make no difference at all.

It was not how they had imagined it. When the war had come, they had greeted it with rapture, the artists and the writers, the poets and the musicians. They had imagined a great purification, the fiery cleansing of a corrupted, philistine world, from whose ashes would emerge a new, pure Germany. A natural work of art, Karl Scheffler called it. Too old to fight on the front line, Julius had volunteered as an ambulance driver, a soldier in a sacred struggle that he believed would deliver the world to a new state of grace. The horrors of the war had changed him from the inside out, but they had not completely extinguished that hope. Month after endless month, sick with fear and exhaustion, his clothes stiff with other men's blood, Julius had thought of Dostoevsky, that unwilling soldier who had understood what all soldiers come to understand, that men are not gods, that the only hope of redemption was for every man to accept his share of the guilt and shame and horror of living and to endure it together, a spiritual family bound by frailty and forbearance. On the battlefields of Flanders it was impossible to imagine a return to the unthinking venality of the old Germany.

And still it had come. Five years later the new Germany was more venal than ever, a cobbled-together nation of collaborators and spies: shopkeepers selling under the counter for foreign currency; black marketeers paddling policemen's palms with one hand and pocketing their profits with the other; fur-swaddled farmers' wives licking the cream from their fingers at the Kurfürstendamm cafés while starving children rummaged in the rubbish bins for scraps.

And Julius was one of them.

III

Three months were to pass before Julius saw Rachmann again, three dizzy months that spun Germany faster and faster, prices spiralling upwards so fast it was impossible to guess from one week to the next the cost of a cup of coffee or a taxicab or a ticket to the Philharmonie. No one knew where it would end. Before the war a man waving a thousand-mark note might have expected to attract attention. By the middle of June, when Rachmann wrote to ask if he might bring a Trübner landscape for Julius's authentication, housewives were using thousand-mark notes as spills to light their boilers. The hundred thousand note, hastily introduced in February, bought half a dozen eggs, if there were any to buy. To meet the demand for money, the banks had thirty paper factories and nearly two thousand printing presses working around the clock. The production of banknotes was one of the country's few remaining profitable industries.

Julius wrote back to Rachmann by return, suggesting a meeting the following Monday. He felt a thrill of anticipation. A Trübner was in a different league from works on paper, even works by Marées, if it were not that in recent months the trading of treasures had become commonplace. These days there was no guessing what people would part with and for what.

He wrote to Luisa too, his anger stoked by brandy and lawyerly prevarication. Afterwards he could not recall precisely the accusations he had made. By the time he came down the next morning, heavy-limbed and headachy, Fräulein Grüber had already sent out the post.

Böhm had moved premises. The elegant nineteenth-century building with its large lobby and uniformed lift attendant had given way to a featureless concrete block on a dismal shared courtyard near the Criminal Court. Böhm's office was on the first floor, a once-large room clumsily partitioned to create two cramped offices and a tiny waiting area. It was only when he saw URSCHEL & BÖHM ANWÄLTE painted on the glass panel in the door that Julius was sure he had come to the right place.

Böhm looked older, his clever face lined and grey. When Julius asked how he was, he shrugged. 'We must change with the times, must we not?' he said. 'Luisa has made you an offer.'

'What offer?'

'If you consent to a divorce, agree to accept responsibility for said divorce and continue to provide financial support, she will return the van Gogh. The terms of the support are set out here.'

Julius stared at the piece of paper. Beneath the exorbitant sum a note was printed in capital letters. DUE TO CURRENCY FLUCTUATIONS ALL PAYMENTS SHOULD BE MADE IN FRENCH FRANCS.

'But that's extortion,' he hissed.

'It's a negotiation. A question of what compromises you are willing to make.'

'No,' Julius said. His hands were shaking but his head felt very clear. If it was war Luisa wanted, then war she would have.

'There will be no compromise. We file for divorce. Adultery. My wife's. No financial support, not a sou, until I have my painting. And my son.'

Böhm was silent. Then he picked up his pen. 'You have evidence, I suppose?' he asked. In the twenty years Böhm had been his lawyer Julius had never once lied to him. He took care not to lie now. When Böhm asked if he had discovered Luisa in flagrante, Julius shook his head.

'But there were clear signs of sexual congress?' Böhm pressed. He did not ask between whom. Julius laughed grimly.

'There was a naked man in my wife's bed,' he said. 'Do you have another explanation?'

'Do you know this man's name?'

'It wasn't exactly the moment for formal introductions. But he was one of her crowd. It won't be hard to find out.'

'Perhaps. Although in these situations people tend to close ranks.'

'Not Luisa's friends. They'd sell their grandmothers if there was profit in it.'

Böhm frowned, sitting back in his chair. 'Very well then, perhaps you should make some enquiries. We have time. We can file a preliminary petition without a name and, as things stand at present, with all the backlogs, there's no chance of a hearing before the summer recess. Perhaps in the autumn, if things improve—?' He shrugged wearily. 'Might she attempt to deny the allegations?'

'It's Luisa. She'll deny everything.'

'Then we'll need proof. Without it the courts will decline the petition.'

Julius thought of Frau Lang, the horror on her face as she covered her eyes. 'There was a witness. My housekeeper. She saw everything.'

'Excellent,' Böhm said and Julius nodded, stiff with triumph and self-disgust.

Rachmann looked tired and thin, his slenderness ground to something harder and more delicate. The sharp line of his cheekbones emphasised his startlingly green eyes, the Botticelli fullness of his mouth. In the study he glanced towards the bare wall.

'A van Gogh self-portrait,' Julius said. 'Perhaps the finest he ever painted.'

'It's on loan?'

'Something like that.'

Rachmann shook his head. 'You'll think me foolish, but somehow I'd convinced myself the Marées would be here. Convinced myself so thoroughly that just now, when I walked in, my first thought was that it had been stolen.'

Stolen. The word hung in the sultry air. 'You miss it, the Marées?' Julius asked.

'Horribly. Ridiculous, isn't it?'

'You'll get used to it.'

'And I had hoped for a happy life.'

'As a dealer? Not a chance.'

Rachmann laughed. It was early, but outside it was already getting dark. A storm was coming. Against the looming thunderheads, the trees were van Gogh-vivid, thick swirls of white and emerald green.

'So did you keep it?' he asked, attempting casualness. 'The Marées, I mean.'

'Of course.'

'I'm glad. I was suddenly afraid you might have sold it weeks ago.'

'I didn't sell it. It's in my dressing room upstairs.'

Rachmann nodded and fiddled with the straps of the portfolio he carried. He said nothing. He did not have to. Julius could almost hear it, the low hum of longing like a bee in a flower. It was too much to ask, of course. There was no room in the house as privately his as his dressing room. *Jesus, Ju, why do you always have to be such a gimlet?* Gimlet, just one of Luisa's slang words for bore. She had hundreds: bluenose, fire extinguisher, flat tyre, old fogey. Old anything.

'Perhaps you'd like to see it?' he said suddenly.

Rachmann stared at him. 'Please, you don't have to, that is – you wouldn't mind?'

'Not at all.'

He led the young man up the stairs. At the top he paused, a little out of breath. Rachmann stopped beside him, taking in the high-ceilinged gallery, the exquisitely inlaid double doors that led to the drawing room. When Luisa had been here this had been her friends' favourite place to congregate, leaning over the balustrade as music blared from the gramophone, their laughter and cigarette ash spilling into the hall below. These days the doors were kept locked. Julius had not been into the drawing room since she left.

The dressing room smelled of leather and soap, and, faintly, unmistakably, of himself. As they stood in front of the Marées, Julius was pricklingly aware of the battered leather slippers under the chair, the splay-bristled toothbrush in the cup by the sink, the silk dressing gown on its hook on the back of the door. In her silver frame his mother smiled shyly, her head on one side. Dressed in an evening gown with diamonds in her hair, she looked young and awkward and absurdly beautiful. He saw Rachmann glance at her, the smile deepening in his sea-green eyes, and it was as if he had let the young man climb inside his skin.

Back in his study Julius felt the intimacy of the dressing room moving like a current between them, altering the shape of the air.

He wanted to ask Rachmann if he had enough money, enough to eat. He wanted to confide his loneliness, his fear of growing old, the bitter hatred he felt towards his wife and the man she was making him become. Instead he gestured at the carefully wrapped painting.

'Tell me about this,' he said.

Rachmann took the package on to his lap and frowned at it. 'I bought it in Cologne. Not a dealer. A man on the street. You know.'

Julius did know. These days there were men like that on every corner in Berlin, women too, shabby in once-respectable clothes, their family heirlooms laid out on bits of sacking and traded for sausages and coal.

'He told me that his father and Trübner were friends,' Rachmann said. 'That they met in Karlsruhe. His father had kept it in his study all his life. I didn't want to take it from him, it felt all wrong, but he was so grateful, so desperate. He said I was helping him. Of course he had no paperwork for the painting, no provenance as such—'

Julius shook his head. 'Provenance counts for a great deal less than the bean counters would have you believe. Attribution is not a matter of accountancy.' He put his spectacles on, then gestured towards the window. 'Bring it over here. We need all the light we can get.'

A fake. Julius knew it the moment he saw it, or rather he felt it, the familiar tightness in his throat, the clammy chill under his skin, the seasick roil in his stomach as if the floor was pitching. As though the wrongness of the painting made it pitch.

He closed his eyes, leaning on the back of his chair. The dark behind his eyelids was dizzy with silver. His mouth was dry. He licked his lips. Slowly the queasiness receded. He did not look at Rachmann. Instead he took off his spectacles and, taking a handkerchief from his pocket, carefully polished them. The steadiness was coming back into his hands. He worked the handkerchief into the corners of the lenses. When he was sure they were quite clean, he put them back on and looked again. Trees, sky, a glimpse of Italianate façade, all in Trübner's characteristic style but without his instinct for colour, his play of light and shadow. A vision of nature reduced to a view, decorative and dead.

He steepled his hands, steeling himself to say the words.

'It's not a Trübner, is it?' Rachmann said very quietly.

'No. It's not. I'm sorry.'

Most disappointed dealers grew defensive, belligerent even. They disputed his conclusions, demanded he reconsider. The young man clasped his hands together and said nothing. Only the whiteness of his knuckles betrayed him.

'You could always take it to someone else,' Julius said. 'Get a second opinion. Walter Ruthenberg is reliable, do you know him?'

'Might he disagree with you?'

'It's possible.'

'But if he did he would be wrong?'

'In my opinion, yes. I'm afraid so.'

Rachmann was silent, staring at the painting. Julius wanted to put a consoling hand on the young man's shoulder. Instead he waited. When Rachmann finally looked up at him his face was soft and sad as a child's.

'I have no right to ask you this,' he said. 'You've already given me so much. But might you be able to tell me why? It's just – if I could only understand what it is you see, how you know, then perhaps – perhaps I wouldn't feel like such a fool.'

'You're not a fool. I know many more experienced dealers than you who would have made the same mistake.'

'But I can't be like them, don't you see? I couldn't bear it. If I'm to do this, if I'm to make it count, I need to see as you see, with my heart.'

Julius could not remember the last time someone had spoken to him so openly, as though there was nothing to be lost by speaking the truth. 'A man who feels as you do is already halfway there,' he said, but Rachmann only shook his head.

'I wish that were true, but it isn't. It sounds fanciful, I know, but I saw the way the painting passed through you, the wave of it. As if in that moment it was part of you. As if you were part of it. Look, I'm sorry, I should go.' Hurriedly he fumbled the painting into its wrappings. 'Thank you, sir, for your time and your honesty. I am very grateful for both.'

Julius put a hand on the young man's arm. Rachmann hesitated. 'Then stay,' Julius said. 'Stay and I'll tell you what it is I see.'

Gently he took the painting from Rachmann and set it on the desk. Then, scanning the shelves by the window, he pulled out a heavy book, leafing through it until he found a colour plate of Trübner's *Monastery on Herreninsel*.

'Trübner was the most painterly of painters,' he said. 'He believed that the true beauty of a painting lay not in its subject but in its composition, the colours, the texture of the paint. In art for art's sake. See here, in your painting, where this tree has been reworked? A bodge like that would have been unendurable to him.'

Rachmann frowned, his determination to master his feelings clenching him so tightly it might almost have been anger. 'That's how you knew, because of that tree?'

'Not immediately, no. Yes, the tree is important, the flawed perspective here too, once you see them you know that Trübner could never have made this painting, but that comes later. At first it is something else, something more – instinctive. Imagine you meet an old friend on the street. He looks just as you remember him, he smiles and speaks as he always has, but it is not him. You know it. Later perhaps you will be able to say why, his voice was too high, his nose too long, but in that instant all you know for certain is that you are being deceived. You feel it in your gut, your bones. Whoever he is, this man, he is not your friend.' Julius sighed. 'I'm sorry. I wish it were otherwise.'

'I know. Thank you.'

A sudden flash of lightning lit the room, followed, a moment later, by the rumble of thunder. The air had the metallic tang of rain. Julius slid the window shut.

'A drink before you go?' he asked, but Rachmann shook his head. There was somewhere else he had to be, if he did not leave soon he would be late. Reluctantly Julius rang for Frau Lang. Rachmann took his hat and umbrella from her with a bow. His gallantry was lost on Frau Lang. As he turned away she puffed her lips, rolling her eyes to the ceiling. When Julius glared at her she subsided like a soufflé.

Rachmann looked down at the painting in his arms, then, with a sardonic twist of a smile, held it out to Julius. 'I couldn't interest you in an almost-Trübner before I go, could I? Something for that empty nail in your study?'

It took a particular type of courage, Julius thought, to make light of catastrophe. 'I'm sorry it turned out this way,' he said. 'I hope it isn't too damaging a setback.'

'Me too.'

There was an awkward silence. Then Rachmann shook his head. 'Perhaps I shouldn't admit this to you, but there's a part of me that wishes I had the nerve to brazen it out. All those scavenging vultures out there picking off German treasures for small change. It would be worth something, wouldn't it, to get one over on them?'

'Something, yes. But not half of what it would cost you to do it.'

'Ah, scruples,' Rachmann said and his laugh was nine parts sigh. 'What would we do without those?'

'What indeed?'

Frau Lang opened the door. The wind blew rain into the shallow porch, printing dark circles on the stone. Rachmann stepped out and opened his umbrella.

'Good night, Herr Köhler-Schultz. And thank you.'

'I only wish there was anything to thank me for.'

'Everyone told me that in Berlin no one would give a greenhorn like me the time of day. But your generosity, your wisdom, a man of your eminence—'

'Eminence, dear God, you make me sound a hundred years old.'

Rachmann winced. 'Flattery will get me nowhere, is that it? Those damned scruples. Though, for the record, it isn't flattery when it's the truth.'

The young man turned away. *You take compliments like a pawnbroker takes a watch*, Luisa had told Julius once, *as though the favour's all yours.* He started down the steps towards Rachmann and caught, just for a moment, his expression, a bleak grimace of frustration and defeat. Julius wanted to call him back. Instead he watched as he walked away down the path. The raindrops struck his umbrella and flew apart, silver streaking the black.

'Look at you, getting all wet,' Frau Lang tutted, bustling him back into the house. 'Right then, you'll be wanting that tea.' She hurried across the hall. As she pushed open the servants' door, Julius caught a glimpse of the baby's black perambulator.

'If the petition is successful you will of course get custody of your son,' Böhm had said the day before. 'Though perhaps not immediately. Guilty or not, most courts these days prefer to leave a child with his mother until he is at least four years old.'

The boy and the nursemaid had occupied the top floor of the

35

house, their days marked out by a brisk, unchanging routine. Julius was not sure what exactly had occupied their time. He had not been encouraged to take an interest.

'I want my son,' he had told Böhm belligerently, and for the first time he wondered if it might be true.

IV

The storm that swept through the city that night was the fierc-est to hit Berlin in decades. By evening the rain was a solid wall of water, hammering the sun-hard ground and lashing the flowers in their borders. At the Staatsoper, where Julius had gone to hear Strauss's *Elektra*, the thunder rolled like timpani through the spaces in the music. By the time he got home, doubled up and dashing from the taxi to the front door, the storm seemed to have taken the house inside itself. The walls shook and the windows rattled in their frames. In his study Julius poured himself a glass of cognac and watched as the trees in the garden pitched and tossed, dark against dark. When the lightning split the sky, it lit the blank wall like a flash lamp.

It was almost dawn when the wind finally dropped, though the rain continued to fall. On the wireless the news announcer spoke of flooding, blocked roads, damage to buildings from lightning and from falling trees. An S-Bahn train had derailed when a tele-graph pole had fallen across the line. The extent of the casualties was not known. Julius stood in his pyjamas at his dressing-room window, looking down into the garden. A branch had been torn from the largest of the lindens. It jutted, raw-stumped, from the lawn, rose petals scattered around it like confetti.

Julius stood at the window for a long time. Then he went up to the nursery. It surprised him a little to find the room exactly as he remembered it. He sat down on the chair in the corner and looked at the cot with its wooden bars, the rocking horse, the painted train on its circle of track. There was still a pile of picture books on the night table and the silver-framed studio portrait taken when the child was only a few months old. The photographer had propped him in a wheeled wooden cart, his starched white dress bunched up around him. His pale hair was neatly combed. Beside him a toy dog stood guard, its felt tongue lolling from its mouth. It was a syrupy composition, sentimental in the Victorian style. Julius had always disliked it.

He picked it up. His son squinted up at him anxiously, his little hands clinging like starfish to the slatted sides of the cart. Julius had never expected to have children. Luisa had not wanted them any more than he. He was too old to ruin his life, she said, and she too young. There was a doctor fashionable among her friends who dealt with things like that. Julius was glad. In that first heady year he could not bear the thought of sharing her. As time passed the savagery of their arguments found its echo in their lovemaking, desire and anger eliding in brief, fierce couplings, Luisa bucking and biting beneath him, digging her nails into his back. Her announcement that she was pregnant was to him just another act of war. Her ripening body had the heart-quickening eroticism of Titian's *Venus of Urbino*, but Julius could not bring himself to touch her. It seemed impossible that together they had created a child, that symbol of innocence and incorruptibility. Instead he could imagine only the tumours he had seen preserved in jars at Virchow's museum at the Charité, misshapen clots bristling with hair and teeth, fury and embitterment made flesh.

And yet when he came, he was a baby all the same. It changed nothing. Luisa continued to cram the house with her empty-headed friends. Julius continued to write, to lecture, to travel. Someone had to pay for the flowers and champagne. In their private fiefdom on the top floor the baby and the nursemaid followed their own obscure rituals and routines.

'Excuse me, sir, I'm very sorry, I didn't—'

Startled, Julius looked up. The housemaid stood awkwardly in the doorway, her broom clutched in both hands. It was a matter of pride to Frau Lang, the silence with which her girls moved around the house. She knew Julius could not endure the clatter of feet when he was working.

'It's all right, come in. I'm not staying,' he said, but the housemaid shook her head, backing away on to the landing. She bobbed a curtsy as he passed her, her ears scarlet. It was only as he fumbled for his watch that Julius remembered he was wearing his pyjamas.

In his dressing room the wireless was still on. Rain dripped from the gutter and ran in fat rivulets down the window. Julius put the photograph of his son on the chest of drawers.

'According to the Berlin Meteorological Office, the barometer will rise by nightfall, bringing clear skies,' the wireless announcer said. 'Milder conditions are forecast.'

Was it in that moment that something in Germany broke? There was no other explanation, not that Julius could see. The inflation had been bad for months, for years, but always there had been a shape to the crisis, a structure that, to Julius at least, made sense. However abysmal, the world continued to be bound, just about, by the basic laws of economics, of physics. Banknotes circulated. Wages were paid and goods purchased, even if the prices were scandalous. The mark remained a mathematical unit possessed of an absolute value, even if that value changed with every passing week. Though no one knew exactly on any day what it would buy, it was still, till then, a measure of something.

And then, abruptly, it was not. *Milder conditions are forecast.* With that confident pronouncement the world broke its moorings, smashing everything to smithereens. Within weeks the inflation was a fever dream, senseless and unstoppable, and Julius was rich. Not rich as his father had been with his factories and his stocks but obscenely, unutterably rich. In Europe sales of *Vincent* were faltering, the royalty cheques were starting to dry up. American sales had proved disappointing. In Paris or New York he would barely have been comfortable. In Berlin he was a maharajah. By mid-August a single dollar, worth eighteen thousand marks a month before, was worth a million. By September it was a hundred million. It was like riding in an elevator sheared from its couplings, a helpless frozen hurtle towards the smash, except the smash did not come. The elevator only fell faster, one hundred and fifty million, two hundred million. Every zero was another jewel around Julius's neck. He could hardly lift his head for the weight of them.

One night, at the theatre, he was cornered in the interval by a banker acquaintance. The banker told Julius he was part of a syndicate acquiring whole streets of property in Berlin. Buildings which a year ago might have sold for fifty thousand marks were now changing hands for less than five hundred dollars. He urged Julius to invest.

'You'll make a killing,' he said, but Julius turned him down flat. Decent men, he said icily, no longer had the stomach for slaughter. He did not mention the exquisite little Seurat nude he had recently picked up for next to nothing in a private sale. Works of art were not like bricks and mortar, they had no intrinsic, objective value. On an April afternoon nearly thirty years ago

Julius had ambled into Ambroise Vollard's gallery on rue Lafitte in Paris. The *Self-Portrait* had felled him, splitting him open like an axe, but Vollard only shrugged and hauled it off the wall as though it were a Rive Gauche daub. He had had enough, Vollard said morosely, of lost causes. He sold it to Julius for six hundred francs. A painting was only worth what a buyer was willing to pay.

Julius did not hear from Rachmann. He thought of him often, hoped he was managing to stay afloat. The Trübner had come at a very bad time. Every day more businesses went bankrupt. There were no jobs. A single egg cost one thousand million marks. A milliard, they called it. The word no longer merited remark. On the outskirts of the city farmers patrolled their potato fields with guns. Julius was supposed to be working on a new book. Sometimes, as the day faded and the shadows draped the corners like cobwebs, he looked up and for a moment, before he remembered, it was there still, that haunted, haunting face, fixing him with his piercing, unblinking stare. Sometimes the setting sun washed the whiteness to a pale rose pink and the empty nail gleamed like an eye.

Buoyed up by foreign buyers, Hugo Salazin's gallery was one of the few that had not closed its doors. Julius did not know which depressed him more, Salazin's artists or his clients, but when he received an invitation to the opening of his newest exhibition he accepted immediately. The gallery was already crowded when he arrived. He pushed his way through the cacophony of chatter, scanning the crowd for Rachmann's coppery head, but, though he passed through the rooms several times, Julius did not see him. Disappointed, obscurely anxious, he lingered, one eye on the door. Most of the pictures around him appeared to have been sold. It did not seem to matter that they revealed nothing of themselves but their surfaces, like mirrors. Perhaps, Julius thought gloomily, that was the secret of their success. The Dadaists might be fools and charlatans, but in their destruction of all artistic enterprise they had hit upon one immutable truth: a society gets the art it deserves.

And still Rachmann did not come. At last, weary of waiting, Julius pushed through the crowd towards the exit. Walter Ruthenberg was standing near the door. He shook his head at Julius, rolling his eyes.

'Monstrous racket, isn't it?' he said over the din. 'In more ways than one. I'm surprised you're here. I thought you hated this sort of thing.'

Julius shrugged. A professor at the university, Ruthenberg's academic monograph on van Gogh had been published at the same time as Julius's *Vincent*. Julius had felt sorry for the man until he realised that Walter felt exactly the same way about him.

'Actually, I was hoping to run into you,' Ruthenberg said. 'Do you have a minute?'

They went out on to the pavement where it was quieter. Beyond the spill of light from the gallery the street was very dark. The city no longer lit the streetlamps, they could not afford the electricity. Ruthenberg took out a pipe and a pouch of tobacco. 'Sent by a forbearing friend from Amsterdam. Most things I can take or leave, but this?' He took a tiny careful pinch and pressed it into the bowl. 'I have something that might interest you. A rather lovely little Corot. I gather you're in the market.'

Julius knew he meant the Seurat. He should have known that there was no such thing as a private sale in Berlin.

'Provenance is murky, but then, when isn't it with Corot?' Ruthenberg said. Striking a match, he put it to his pipe, sucking on the stem to make it draw. 'A young dealer I know picked it up in Hamburg and brought it to me for authentication. I told him to hang on to it or, better still, take it to Paris, but if you were interested ...'

Julius frowned. If he was interested Ruthenberg would take a fat commission. Most dealers with a Corot would not consider that good business. 'Which dealer?' he asked. 'Do I know him?'

'Rachmann, he's called. The Gemäldegalerie put him on to me. Clever boy, but very green. He'd want francs.'

Julius stared at Ruthenberg. Then carefully, casually, he shrugged. 'I suppose I could take a look. Is he still in Berlin?'

'What are you two gossiping about out here?'

Julius turned round. Salazin stood in the doorway, his pouched eyes glittering.

'Walter was telling me about your friend Rachmann,' Julius said. 'I hear he's flourishing.'

'Of course he's flourishing,' Salazin said. 'Men of his kind always do.'

'His kind? If anything, he struck me as rather too principled for your game.'

Salazin laughed. 'My dear Julius, that boy'll be the last man standing. Grew up with nothing, of course. Father was a blacksmith, had his sons hawk firedogs in the streets to keep the family from destitution. Believe me, behind that pretty face young Rachmann is as tough as old boots.'

Rachmann telephoned the next morning. He arrived at Meierstrasse just as it was getting dark. He seemed uneasy. When Julius shook his hand his smile flickered nervously, his gaze sliding sideways towards the floor.

'It's good to see you,' Julius said. 'It's been a while.'

'Yes, well. I've hardly been in Berlin.'

'You managed to see Ruthenberg,' Julius said, more sharply than he intended, and a flicker of surprise passed over Rachmann's face. Awkwardly Julius gestured at his slim leather briefcase. 'Don't tell me you squeezed a Corot in there?'

Rachmann hesitated. That was why he had come, he said at

last. He wanted to tell Julius in person. The Corot was sold. A businessman. He wanted to remain anonymous.

'In Berlin?' Julius retorted. 'Fat chance.'

'A foreign businessman.'

'Is there any other kind these days?' It was a joke of sorts but Rachmann did not smile. 'I wish I'd seen it. I hear it was delightful.'

Rachmann bit his lip. 'I should have brought it to you.'

'Well. They sent you to Ruthenberg.'

'Except they didn't, they sent me to you, but I – I couldn't. I just couldn't.'

'I don't think I understand.'

'Don't you? When there are more fake Corots in circulation than there are originals? He's the most forged artist of modern times. After the Trübner, how could I bring you a Corot? How could I be sure? It didn't matter what Herr Ruthenberg thought of me, not really, but you? How could I take that chance?' He glared at Julius, distress flushing his pale cheeks, then covered his face with his hands. All this time he wanted to come back, Julius thought, and the gladness burned his throat like brandy.

'Did you really think I'd blame you for the Trübner?' he said.

'Didn't you?'

'Of course I didn't. Every dealer will have his Trübners. You should never be afraid of taking risks. Only of cupidity and ugliness.'

The young man shook his head. 'That risk, that mistake, it nearly finished me. I thought I was finished.'

'But you're not. Look at you. You're still here.'

Rachmann looked at Julius. His eyes were very green. 'I couldn't have borne it,' he said simply, and again Julius's throat burned.

V

Julius waited for Zelma Staub outside the theatre where she worked on Bülowplatz, a seedy-looking establishment with a crumbling façade. She had been a friend of Luisa's during the war and had gone on coming to her parties, even when Luisa's affections had waned. She had been the one who gathered up the dirty glasses, who nodded sympathetically as men talked of other girls. Her coat was shabby, her dyed hair grey at the roots. She did not know that Luisa and Julius had separated. When Julius asked if he could buy her lunch she hesitated.

'You knew her,' he said. 'It helps.'

They went to a nearby café. Zelma ate quickly, her hands cupping the plate as though she was afraid someone would take it away. Her face softened as Julius talked about the old days.

'That night of Luisa's birthday, do you remember?' he said. Luisa had told the story so often he could almost believe he had been there. 'When that friend of hers played the Spanish guitar and that other man sang? God, what was his name?'

'Pieter Placzek. Someone told me he sings on the wireless now.'

'Placzek, that's right. He serenaded Luisa and everyone cried, do you remember? Everyone except that friend he hung around with: tall, sandy hair, boyish features—'

'The writer?'

'I can't remember his name either. Don't get as old as me, Zelma, whatever you do – everything goes. Conrad something, was it?'

'The only writer I remember was called Harald.'

'Harald, of course. He used to say that one day he'd be more famous than Mann, do you remember? Perhaps he is and we just haven't heard. We should look him up. What was his surname again?'

'Baeck, Harald Baeck. Though I don't think he ever published anything.'

Harald Baeck. Julius took a gulp of his watery coffee, swallowing his shame. 'I'm not surprised,' he said. 'That man had a heart of stone.'

That evening he sat for a long time in his study. *What would life be*, Vincent wrote to his brother, *if we had no courage to attempt anything?* Julius was weary of the blank wall, of the deep ache that it roused in him, but he could not keep himself from looking. The details of the painting pressed down on his memory: the feathered curl of Vincent's unkempt beard, the green line down the length of his nose, the blue smudge of shadow under his eyes that matched exactly the frenzy of overlapping brushstrokes around his head. He had tried to hang the Seurat in its place. The nail was the right height for it, it would not have to be moved, but, though his fingers fumbled with the wire across its back, he could not do it. In the end he rang for Frau Lang and told her to take it away. She peered at it, bulging her eyes.

'For Christ's sake, it's a nude, not the devil incarnate,' he snapped at her and the housekeeper had picked up the painting and marched out of the room, her arms held stiffly out in front of her. As though it were a tray of faeces, Julius thought with a familiar surge of exasperation and remorse. When Frau Lang had first come to them he had pleaded with Luisa to let her go, but Luisa had only laughed.

'You wouldn't be so cruel,' she teased. 'Don't you know she worships you?'

He knew nothing of the sort, but over the years he had grown accustomed to her and her compendium of grimaces. She was short-tempered and small-minded and stubborn as a donkey but she knew his habits and his preferences. She understood, as Luisa would not, the importance of his work, the impossibility of distraction or interruption. She was reliable and she was loyal. After Luisa left, Julius had asked her if she wanted to go back to Munich but she shook her head.

'My place is here,' she said firmly. 'With you.'

According to Fräulein Grüber's typed report, Harald Baeck lived in an apartment in Friedrichshain. He was not on the telephone. He was listed in the Berlin directory as an employee of the Siemens factory in Spandau.

'A factory?' Julius said doubtfully. 'You're sure he's our man?'

'I telephoned to check,' Fräulein Grüber said. 'He's worked there for three years. He writes instruction manuals for electrical appliances.'

A single ticket to Siemensstadt cost 150,000 marks. When Harald Baeck saw Julius standing beside the policeman at the turnstile he went grey. He turned and tried to force his way back through the throng of passengers, but it was leaving time and the crush was too great. Julius pressed a banknote into the policeman's open palm. Then, pushing his way through the crowd, he put a hand on Baeck's shoulder.

'You and I need to talk,' he said.

They went to a bar near the station. Julius bought them both a brandy. Baeck drank his in a single swallow. Julius thought of *The Brothers Karamazov*, Mitya protesting to Rakitin, *But if God does not exist, that means everything is permitted,* and Rakitin's laughing reply: *Surely you know everything is permitted to the intelligent man?* Julius did not believe in God. He believed in beauty and in the beautiful exalted struggle of the human spirit. Or he had, once.

'I have a proposal for you,' he said.

Baeck did not protest. The next day, as agreed, he went to Böhm's office and signed a statement admitting that he had had sexual relations with the respondent at her marital home on the night of 9 February 1923. Böhm told Julius that, except to confirm his name, Harald Baeck had not said a single word.

Newspaper presses were requisitioned to print banknotes. There was talk of paper rationing, of walk-outs and strikes. Geisheim summoned Julius to a meeting at the *Tribüne* offices and told him he was cutting the number of pages, just till things improved. Julius did not protest. No one bought newspapers any more anyway. He walked home slowly, a headache like a hatband tightening around his skull. Frau Lang banged open the front door.

'He just barged in,' she hissed, taking Julius's hat. 'I told him you were out and he barged straight in like he owned the place.'

Julius sighed. 'What are you talking about? Who barged in?'

'I'm afraid she means me.' Rachmann stood in the doorway of the morning room. 'I should have telephoned, I know, but I go back to Düsseldorf tomorrow and I wanted to say thank you. For all the kindness you've shown me. I wouldn't have waited, only Fräulein Grüber said she thought you might – but of course if it's inconvenient I quite understand. I'm not usually the barging-in type.' He smiled at Julius and, despite his headache, Julius smiled back. There was something so fresh about the boy's eagerness and his embarrassment, his inability to dissemble. Beside him Julius felt used up, shop-soiled.

'Then I'm glad you made an exception this time,' he said. 'Some coffee, Frau Lang, if you please.'

'Of course.' Frau Lang smiled dutifully, but Julius saw how she narrowed her eyes at Rachmann as though he was an unruly guest of Luisa's, liable to vomit on the stairs or make off with the silver.

'And cake,' Julius added pointedly. 'We have cake, don't we?'

The cake was glossy and golden, topped with overlapping slices of apple. As Frau Lang deposited it without ceremony on the table, Rachmann's eyes widened like a child's. There was no cake in the bakeries in Berlin, not any more. Julius cut him a slice and watched as delicately, precisely, he ate every crumb.

They talked about art. Rachmann was untutored but his passion was prodigious and unfeigned. It was in the port city of Häarlem, he told Julius, that he had fallen in love for the first time and twice over, with the portraits of Franz Hals and the smell of the sea. He had been eight years old.

'Though I realise I shouldn't admit to Hals,' he added. 'Not if I wish you to think well of me. I should lie and say it was Rembrandt.'

Julius smiled. 'Perhaps, but I should know that you were lying. Rembrandt is the greater artist, it's true, but there is a darkness in his work, he shows us the shadow of mortality. Whereas with Hals it is all about life, vitality, the impetuosity of his brushwork like a burst of laughter. Naturally the child chooses Hals. It is a matter of key, Hals the treble and Rembrandt the bass.'

'But that's it,' Rachmann said, laughing delightedly. 'That's it exactly.'

Julius had not known until that afternoon that he could feel nostalgia for something that was yet to happen. That afternoon, for the first time, he saw his son sitting where Rachmann was sitting, his young face rapt, his mind bursting with the ideas that Julius had carefully planted and cultivated. He had toyed with the notion when the boy was first born, the collection of places and pieces that might best stimulate a child's imagination and shape his aesthetic sensibilities. He took down the animal pictures Luisa had chosen for the nursery and hung in their place two Pissarro watercolours, a peasant woman in a blue apron and another woman braiding her hair.

'Why do you even care?' Luisa said, but he insisted. A child was a plastic creature after all, clay to be moulded. He would not allow his son to be coarsened by what was brutal and witless and ugly.

What hope did the boy have now, holed up with Luisa's parents in Munich? Together they would teach the child to be provincial in the Bavarian style, smothered by Böcklin reproductions and lederhosen and violent outdoor games. Julius had grown up with boys like that. He had despised them all.

He was showing Rachmann van Gogh's drawing of the girl in the striped jacket, the one Vincent had called *La Mousmé*, when Frau Lang knocked at the door. He had not realised it was so late. Rachmann put the drawing down reluctantly, as though he could hardly bear to let it go.

'Barge in again soon, won't you?' Julius said as he bade him good night and it charmed him to see the pleasure in the young man's face, his unconcealed delight. Julius was attending a concert at the Philharmonie that evening, he knew he should go upstairs to change, but he lingered in his study, one hand on the back of the chair Rachmann had sat in. On the table the apple cake glistened, spilling buttery crumbs. Julius wished he had thought to give it to Rachmann to take with him. He should have had Frau Lang pack up a basket. He should have pressed money on him, should have slipped a note or two covertly into the pocket of his overcoat. A single dollar would have sustained him for weeks. Instead he had allowed the boy to leave empty-handed, Julius, who grew richer like Midas every day without touching anything at all.

He went to see Böhm. A light snow was falling, the first of the winter. Shivering, Julius hailed a horse cab. Until recently horse cabs had been a relic. Now, suddenly, they were back. The cab was old and rickety, the horse hardly more than a skeleton, but Julius was glad of it. Berlin was no longer safe. Every day new rumours sent angry mobs spilling out into the streets: the government was stopping unemployment relief, farmers were stockpiling food, the sausage in the meat market was made from human flesh. They blamed the politicians, the shopkeepers, the Jews. As the grandson of a Jew who had converted to Protestantism thirty years before he was born, Julius knew how Jewishness could mark a man out – his disparagement of German art had long provoked more-or-less veiled slurs from his critics – but still it shocked him, the depth and violence of the hatred. In the Jewish quarter men in beards and high-crowned hats were routinely stripped of their clothes and beaten bloody.

The fire in Böhm's office was unlit, the room so cold that Julius could see his breath. He did not take off his coat. The lawyer apologised, the civil courts were still impossibly clogged, no date had been offered even for a directions hearing, but Julius had not come to discuss the divorce. He told Böhm he wished to make provision for his son, a capital sum to be held in trust until he came of age.

'A financial settlement?' Böhm said doubtfully. 'Money?'

Julius nodded. Almost no one used money in Berlin any more. The prices were meaningless – a single match for nine hundred million marks – and they changed six times a day; no one ever had enough. At the cinema near Böhm's office the sign in the window of the ticket booth read *Admission – two lumps of coal*. Berlin's most eminent doctors demanded their fees in food.

'One thousand American dollars,' Julius said. 'I want him to be free.'

'Then buy him a house. Buy him two houses. A tangible asset that will appreciate and generate an income.'

'Steal from my comrades, you mean? I can't do that. And anyway, why would I take such a risk? Do you know how fast the dollar is rising? They say tomorrow it will pass seven hundred milliard marks.'

Böhm gave a choked little laugh. 'With respect, Julius, your son is not yet a year old. You think this can go on until he is twenty-one?'

The newspapers went on strike. On street corners the newsstands stood empty, shuttered against the cold. The headlines had been bleak for months, Julius could hardly bring himself to read them, but the words had imposed order, the chaos confined to paragraphs and columns. Without them the madness mushroomed, spreading like gas. Nobody knew what was happening. It's not the end of the world, his father had barked when Julius wept over some trifle as a boy. It felt like it now.

He was having breakfast when the telephone rang. Fräulein Grüber knocked on the dining-room door. It was Herr Böhm, she said, he said it was urgent. When Julius picked up the receiver Böhm's voice was hoarse. He asked Julius if he was listening to the wireless. The Reichsbank had finally intervened in the foreign exchange markets. The new *Rentenmark* had been stabilised at 4.2 marks to the dollar. In a single stroke the bank had wiped twelve zeros off the exchange rate. No one could say if it would hold, but if it did, the inflation was over. When Böhm hung up Julius stood in the morning room, staring at the floor.

'Is everything all right, sir?' Fräulein Grüber asked.

'I don't know.' He looked down in confusion at the receiver in his hand, then handed it to Fräulein Grüber, who replaced it on its cradle.

'You don't look well,' she said. 'Perhaps you should sit down.'

Julius shook his head. He could hardly believe it was possible. It seemed so simple, so improbable, like something from a fairy tale. A pen waved like a magic wand and, just like that, the madness was ended. If it held. He looked at the fire in the grate beside Fräulein Grüber's desk, the coal glistening in the coal bucket. If it held he was no longer a rich man.

He went out. He did not know what else to do. He walked to the canal, then west towards the zoo. On a November day just like this one, five years ago, Germany had signed the armistice that ended the war. It was very still. The grey buildings looked like paper cut-outs against the flat white sky and the canal was a strip of metal, reflecting the bare black branches of the trees. It was like a photograph, Julius thought, no colour anywhere, and he was filled with the sudden certainty that none of it was real, that he was a character in a film, walking towards a destiny that someone else had already written for him.

He crossed the bridge. On the other side two men were walking towards him, deep in conversation. The taller of the two was talking intently, gesturing with his hands. The other looked like Rachmann. As they drew closer Julius saw that it was indeed Rachmann and, as he quickened his pace to meet him, Rachmann looked up and caught his eye. Julius smiled but Rachmann turned his head, muttering to his companion, who glanced at Julius before hurrying away down a side street. Rachmann waited until he was out of sight. Then, turning back to Julius, he held out his hands and smiled. 'Herr Köhler-Schultz, what a pleasant surprise. You'll excuse my brother, I hope. An urgent appointment, he couldn't wait.'

'Of course.'

The two men stood side by side, looking down into the dark water of the canal. 'It's impossible not to remember, isn't it?' Rachmann said softly. 'Another ending, five years ago?'

Julius nodded. There was a lump in his throat. 'I know.'

'It's strange, I was just thinking of you. But then I always think of you when I walk here.'

Neither of them wanted to go back to work. They walked back along the canal towards Meierstrasse.

'Is this the end?' Rachmann asked. 'Will it hold?'

'Who knows? We can but hope.' According to Böhm, the newly issued banknotes bore the word *wertbeständig*, constant value, as though anyone in Germany still believed in such a thing, and Julius felt a sudden giddy urge to laugh. '*Hope means hoping when things are hopeless*. Who said that? Not a German, certainly.'

Rachmann grinned and the strange elation that had seized Julius grew stronger. 'I think we should celebrate,' he said. 'Before the madness begins again.'

At home he had Frau Lang bring up a bottle of the vintage Billecart-Salmon. No one had drunk champagne in the morning at Meierstrasse since Luisa left. The housekeeper set out the ice bucket and glasses in silence, and stalked from the room. Julius burst into laughter.

'You're a malign influence,' he told Rachmann. 'In Munich Frau Lang was a pillar of the Temperance Society.'

'And here in Berlin?'

'Does such a thing even exist in Berlin?' Still laughing, Julius peeled the foil from the bottle and twisted the cork free. He poured two glasses and handed one to Rachmann. 'A toast. To constant value, whatever that may be.'

'To constant value. And to you, Herr Köhler-Schultz, for your faith in it.'

'Please, call me Julius,' Julius said, surprising himself.

Rachmann smiled. 'Matthias,' he said. Leaning forward, he touched the rim of his glass to Julius's. Matthias, Julius thought as he drank, the apostle chosen to replace the traitor Judas Iscariot, whose name meant gift from God.

'Though I have to say,' Matthias added teasingly, 'mine seems the better end of the arrangement. Herr Köhler-Schultz is quite a mouthful.'

Julius smiled. 'My fault, I'm afraid. I was plain Köhler growing up. I took the Schultz when I left for university, in memory of my mother. My father was mortified, which was, I'm ashamed to admit, a large part of the point.'

'You were young when your mother died?'

'As young as it is possible to be. She died in childbirth.'

'I'm sorry. That is a heavy responsibility.'

Julius was silent. How was it, he wondered, that a blacksmith's son from Düsseldorf could see into the furthest corners of his heart?

'My older brother's wife died from puerperal fever,' Matthias said. 'It was during the blockades and there was no food, no medicine. The child lived. Erich loves him very much but there is still blame. All these years later he still cannot quite forgive.'

Julius thought of his own father, an industrialist for whom the world was only ever a balance sheet, money in and money out. He had wanted Julius to be a mechanical engineer. 'I suppose there will always be things for which our parents cannot forgive us. Which we will not forgive our children.'

'Alas, I have no children to forgive,' Matthias said. 'But you do, I think?'

'One. A son.'

'What is his name?'

'Konstantin. His name is Konstantin.'

'And are there things you cannot forgive Konstantin?'

Julius thought of the photograph on his dressing table, his son's dimpled hands and anxious expression. 'Not yet. But then he's not yet a year old. There's still plenty of time.'

Matthias smiled faintly, staring down into his glass. 'Perhaps, though, we should not wish for our parents to forgive us. Perhaps it is the striving for their forgiveness that spurs us to live good lives.' He hesitated. 'I did not fight. In the war. I was called up in 1916, I joined my regiment, but I had a – I went to pieces. Battle shock, they called it. I can't remember much of it. There was an offensive and then later a hospital. My father thinks I am a coward. He does not say so, but I know. He thinks – he thinks I failed him. That I failed our country. I carry that with me always. It is there always, driving me on. That perhaps if I can make him proud, I will make it up to him. That he will forgive me.'

'Is it your father's forgiveness you are seeking or your own?'

Matthias was silent. 'My father's, I think,' he said at last. 'Though I have little hope of either.'

'You were ill. Many good men were. It was not your fault.'

'Being born wasn't yours. It does not stop either of us from taking the blame.'

It was dark when Matthias finally left, and very cold. Julius did not go back to his study. He stood in the empty hall beneath the Vuillard, his thoughts swirling and settling like fresh snow.

VI

The new mark held its value. The streetlamps came back on and suddenly everything was available, not just eggs and bread and potatoes but gingerbread and Glühwein and dates and crystallised fruits and piles of bright oranges with glossy green leaves. In the windows of the Wertheim department store, huge Christmas trees winked with hundreds of coloured electric lights, gaily wrapped boxes heaped beneath their branches.

Julius had not set foot inside the place for years. The monumentally columned and frescoed atrium glittered with illuminated cabinets displaying hats and musical instruments and porcelain figurines. Huge faux-Greek sculptures loomed in lit recesses along the walls, Dionysus leering over a bunch of grapes, a scantily clad Artemis brandishing her bow and arrow as though demonstrating it for sale. Between the sweeping staircases that led to the upper floors, a colossal gold clock in the shape of a sun hung like a gigantic altarpiece, counting down the minutes until closing time.

He took one of the store's eighty elevators to the toy department. The shelves were crowded, the sheer range overwhelmed him. He could not imagine what a child of Konstantin's age would like. He was relieved when a uniformed shopgirl came to his rescue and suggested a rather elegant Noah's Ark. He waited while she wrapped it up. Behind her on the wall, the shop's name was spelled out in letters decorated with flowers. Julius thought of the painting of almond blossom that van Gogh made for his newborn nephew. By then Vincent was very ill. He told Theo that the boy was all the years that would never be theirs, that he would flourish and grow and do the things that his weak and foolish grown-ups had left undone. Between his seizures Vincent painted madly, whole canvases in a single day, but he wrote to Theo and his wife Johanna that it was better to make children than pictures. He was angry when they christened the baby Vincent. He did not want the child to be cursed with his name.

The Noah's Ark was startlingly expensive. The shopgirl handed him the package with a smile. 'Your grandson is a lucky boy,' she said, and he nodded and wished her a happy Christmas.

Some months before, Julius had been invited to Munich, where the university wished to bestow some honour or other upon him. He had refused to attend. He was too busy, he told his publishers, and besides, the award was specious, academic ceremonies interminable and Munich infested with cretinous fascists. Reluctantly his editor had agreed to receive the honour on his behalf. Per Peritz was a shy, bespectacled man with a bald spot and a habit of stammering over his Ps. Introductions were a torture to him. When Julius telephoned to tell him he had changed his mind, that he meant to go to Munich after all, Peritz's relief was palpable. They'll be so pleased, he said. *Pleased* took a long time to say.

It was not how Julius had wanted it. He had written to Luisa with painstaking civility to ask if, with Christmas coming, she would consent to allow Konstantin to stay with him for a few days in Berlin. Whatever their difficulties, he was still Konstantin's father, the house on Meierstrasse still the boy's home. Konstantin could travel with his own nursemaid or a suitable replacement engaged to collect him; either way, Luisa would not be inconvenienced. Frau Lang, he added, was already buttering her cake tins.

The reply came from Luisa's lawyers. Frau Köhler-Schultz sent her apologies, but arrangements had already been made for the festive season. The afternoon post brought a scrawled note from Luisa. The spikes of her letters slashed the page so that the words seemed to cross each other out.

> You bastard. All this time and suddenly you want to play the Weihnachtsmann? But of course you do. The only things you've ever wanted are the ones you couldn't have.

The train pulled into Munich's Hauptbahnhof a few minutes before seven in the morning. Otto Metz had sent a car to collect Julius and drive him the twenty miles to his house at Würnsee. The morning newspapers lay folded on the back seat beside a wicker hamper: hot buttered rolls wrapped in a napkin, a Thermos bottle of coffee, a flat silver flask of what Julius discovered was excellent cognac. As the proprietor of Germany's largest publishing house, Otto Metz took the comforts of his successful authors almost as seriously as he took his own.

'There's something I need to do in town first,' Julius told the driver. 'It shouldn't take long.'

Julius had forgotten how small Munich was and how relentlessly picturesque. The winter dawn stained the snow a rosy pink and tipped the roofs with gold. They crossed the river and abruptly they were in the suburbs, the houses hidden between high walls and stands of trees. The citizens of Haidhausen liked to keep themselves to themselves.

The Noah's Ark was cumbersome, the pavement slippery with ice. Julius stepped cautiously out of the car. The night in the train had left him stiff. Where there had once been a wicket gate, a heavy iron contraption had been installed. It was locked. Julius peered through it at the house and, shivering, rang the bell. When no one came, he rang again. In an upstairs window a light came on.

The front door opened. A maid peered out, a pale slip of a thing in a thin black dress. Wrapping her arms around her for warmth, she hurried down the path. A key on a leather loop dangled from one hand.

'Are you Herr Behne?' she said. 'Only Herr Aust says to tell you he specifically asked that you come round the back.'

'My name is Köhler-Schultz. I am here to see my son.'

She flinched. 'I didn't – that is, we was expecting Herr Behne.'

'You need to let me in. The child is here, isn't he?'

The girl looked unhappily back towards the house. 'If you wouldn't mind waiting, sir, I'll fetch Herr Aust.'

Julius remembered Aust, an officious little man with pink eyes and an oily manner. He had served with Julius's father-in-law's regiment during the war, a regular soldier who somehow contrived to attach himself to Walther Draxler as his batman. Walther always called him Putzer, the cleaner, a piece of derogatory slang straight from the front. He said it was an old joke between them. It was accepted in the Draxler family that Aust's devotion knew no limits.

'I have no intention of waiting for anyone,' Julius snapped. 'I have travelled all night to see my son. Now open the gate.'

The maid twisted her hands together, her ears scarlet. 'I'm sorry, sir, but I can't do that. Herr Aust—'

'Hilde? What on earth is going on?' Aust stood in the porch. Dipping a clumsy half-curtsy, the maid fled gratefully back towards the house. Aust frowned at her, then walked unhurriedly up the path, his mouth stretched in a bland smile.

'Herr Köhler-Schultz,' he said. 'What a surprise.'

'I need you to open this gate. I will not be stopped from seeing my son.'

Aust tutted regretfully. 'I'm sorry, sir. I wish there was something I could do, but unfortunately Frau Köhler-Schultz and the child are not presently at home.'

'Do you think I'm a fool? Unlock this gate, Aust, or I swear I'll break it down.'

'You'll understand, sir, if I ask you to leave now. I will of course let Frau Köhler-Schultz know that you called.'

'Don't turn your back on me, come back here!' Furiously Julius banged on the gate, rattling it noisily in its frame, but Aust was already walking back towards the house. As he closed the front door Julius banged the gate one last time, half-heartedly. He wondered if Konstantin heard the echo of it, chiming like a clock in the frigid air.

That afternoon Julius sat with Otto in his winter garden. They talked about the new coalition government, about the appointment of Stresemann as Foreign Minister and the chances of fiscal stability. Against the snowy landscape the jungle of tropical plants was a vivid poison green, the leaves fleshy as tongues. A fountain splashed. Julius's mind kept circling back to the light in the window of the Draxler house. He could not shake the sense that there was something else he should have done.

'So, come on then,' Otto said. 'Who's the next van Gogh?'

Julius shrugged. 'Let's say I'm considering my options.'

'Good. Well, consider fast. The public may have bought *Vincent* by the yard, but the public has the memory of a goldfish. Peritz has had a rather wonderful idea, by the way. Did he tell you?'

'Fortunately for us both, Peritz has always left the ideas to me.'

'Michelangelo!' Otto said triumphantly. Perhaps, Julius thought, it was the secret to Metz's uncommon success, that he only ever heard the things he wanted to hear. 'Apparently the greatest artist of all time was a repressed homosexual who lived in squalor and smashed up his sculptures when they wouldn't speak to him.'

'Fascinating. Just not a story I'm interested in telling.'

'So tell it your way. Do what you did with *Vincent* and treat the record with the disdain it deserves. Only a fool lets the facts get in the way of a good story.'

'"Art is a lie that helps us see the truth."'

'You or Vincent?'

'I thought you just said it didn't matter.'

'It doesn't, but any man who quotes himself deserves to be boiled alive like a lobster.'

'In that case it was him. Unquestionably.'

Otto laughed. 'I'm looking to buy another, actually, a portrait, Nadine's always hankered after one of those, but so far no joy. I even had Cornelius go directly to the brother's widow – they say she's got a few still stashed under the bed – but he claims she won't bite. You know her, don't you?'

'Johanna van Gogh? A little. I visited her once or twice before the war.'

'She must adore you, I mean, *Vincent*? You couldn't buy the publicity.'

'On the contrary, she took great umbrage. I had the temerity to remember that she pushed Theo to stop giving Vincent money. In her version her devotion knew no bounds.'

'So she wouldn't be inclined to do you a favour?'

'Not even slightly.'

'Pity. Of course, there's always your *Self-portrait*. I hear an ex-wife can leave a man open to negotiation.' He was only half joking. When Julius gave him a narrow look Otto snorted. 'I know, you'd rather cut your wrists, blah, blah. Let's hope for my sake the lovely Luisa bleeds you dry. Till then, you'll let me know if you hear anything, won't you, usual commission and all that?'

The usual commission was ten per cent. Julius nodded. 'I'll see what I can do.'

He stayed for the weekend. Nadine Metz insisted. Among the dozen or so guests, she told him, there was someone she particularly wanted him to meet. Recently widowed, Elvira Eberhardt was elegant and intelligent. They talked of Schiller, so fiery and volatile, and his long friendship with the chilly, taciturn Goethe. When she was a girl, Frau Eberhardt said, her father would summon her downstairs in her nightdress to sing 'Ode to Joy' to his guests before dinner.

'He was like Goethe, my father. The impression he gave was always of coldness. I never once saw him show affection, not even to my mother, but Beethoven made him cry like a child.'

Her own daughter was almost grown up. 'She's being finished in Switzerland. If she doesn't finish with them first. It is the finest school of its kind in Europe, but my daughter abhors it. She's like a dog in a cage, barking and barking to be set free. Do you have children, Herr Köhler-Schultz?'

'One, a boy, and nowhere near being finished. So far he is barely begun.'

'You are lucky. Boys are easy. Emmeline – well, you'll meet her tomorrow.'

'She's here?' Julius said, surprised.

'It's not what anyone wished for. Otto and Nadine have been

very understanding.' She sighed, then forced a smile. 'I thought we might walk around the lake tomorrow. Perhaps you might accompany us, if you're not joining the skaters?'

'I'd be delighted.'

When he rose late the next morning, however, there was no sign of mother or daughter. It was a crisp, fine day, the sky a brilliant blue. He breakfasted alone, then took his coffee to the winter garden. He had imagined it a pleasant place to read the newspapers, but the humid air was heavy and oppressive and the glare of sun on snow gave him a headache. He saw the girl by chance, as he rose to leave, turned away from him and half hidden amongst the thick foliage. She was curled in a wicker chair, her dark hair tumbled about her face, her knees pulled up to make a kind of easel of her legs, on which she had propped a sketchbook. She sat very still, her pencil poised above the paper, her gaze fixed on something Julius could not see. He held his breath, matching her stillness with his own.

Suddenly, decisively, she began to draw. She did not look down at the paper. Her pencil moved swiftly, so certain of its marks that Julius found himself almost on tiptoes, craning to see what she had made until, as abruptly as she had started, she stopped. She glared at the sketchbook and, with a howl of vexation, hurled it to the floor. It landed face down, its pages bent. She kicked out at it with one foot, sending it skidding across the tiles, and threw her pencil after it. Then, pulling a cushion into the crook of her neck, she squirmed down in the chair, her legs pulled up so that her bare feet rested on the arm, yawned wide and pink like a cat, and closed her eyes. Within a moment she was fast asleep.

Cue curtain and house lights, Julius thought. Little wonder she was a trial to her mother. Turning to leave, he accidentally knocked an iron plant stand, sending a pot crashing to the floor. The girl yelped, startled, and sat up.

'I'm sorry if I frightened you,' Julius said. 'I didn't see you there.'

The girl shrugged, stretching sleepily. Her fingernails were bitten and dirty, almost as dirty as the soles of her feet. 'No, well, I was hiding.'

'I see.'

'If my mother finds me she'll make me go for a walk.'

'You don't like walking?'

'Not with my mother. There are only so many improving homilies a girl can take before she stabs someone in the eye.'

Julius raised an eyebrow. 'Ah. So you must be Fräulein Eberhardt.'

'My fame precedes me.'

'I sat next to your mother at dinner last night.'

'Splendid. So you already know what a disappointment I am.'

'On the contrary,' he protested. As the girl grimaced, blowing dismissively through her lips, he felt a flare of sympathy for her immaculate, exhausted mother. 'Well, I won't keep you. Good day, Fräulein. And happy hiding.'

'Fat chance. You're Herr Köhler-Schultz, aren't you?'

'That's right.'

'You wrote *The Making of Modern Art.*'

'I did,' he said, gratified. He sometimes wondered if the success of *Vincent* had wiped every other word he had ever written from the public memory. 'And still am, God help me. A new edition comes out next year.'

'So you've changed your mind?'

'Not exactly. But the world moves on and we move with it, willingly or not. One sees new sides to things when one's standing in a different place.'

'Tell that to my mother,' she said, tilting her head at him, and he thought of Renoir's portrait of the actress Jeanne Samary, her dark eyes and flushed cheeks, the luminous cream of her skin.

Samary's father had been a cellist so obsessed with cleanliness that he washed his hands thirty times a day. Fräulein Eberhardt's fingernails would have driven him to nervous collapse.

'You do realise that she's looking for a husband,' she added.

Julius frowned. 'Now, really—'

'It's true. The inflation did for us completely, every penny. She only came here because of you.'

'That's enough.'

'She is after someone rich and famous and you are rich and famous, aren't you? Enough for her, anyway. She doesn't even care if you're divorced. She's very modern that way.'

'I said, that's enough!' Julius snapped and, snatching up his newspaper, he stalked away into the house.

'Fine,' Fräulein Eberhardt called after him. 'But don't say I didn't warn you. She pretends she's sweet as honey but she's not. There's nothing sweet about her at all.'

Julius returned to Berlin that afternoon. An urgent business matter, he told Nadine when she remonstrated with him. No peace for the wicked. He was grateful for the distraction of the returning skating party. Suddenly there were servants everywhere, bustling around with glasses of whisky and jugs of Glühwein, and the drawing room was noisy with laughter.

He was at the car when he heard her calling his name. Reluctantly he turned. She had changed out of her painting clothes into a silky black sweater that emphasised her narrow waist, the curve of her breasts. Julius looked away. She was a child, he rebuked himself, a silly, importunate child. The chauffeur opened the car door.

'Fräulein Eberhardt,' he said coolly. 'Is something the matter?

'You left without saying goodbye.'

She was much smaller than he had realised, her head barely

reaching his shoulder. She wore a necklace that dipped over her collarbones, a thread of gold hung with a tiny golden key.

'You should go inside,' he said. 'It's too cold to be out without a coat.'

'You sound like my mother.'

'Do I? Then perhaps you should listen to her.' Nodding at the chauffeur, he climbed into the car. 'Good day, Fräulein.'

'Wait,' she said, and she put a hand on the door. 'You don't have to go, you know.'

'Actually I do. In fact, I'm already late.'

Fräulein Eberhardt hesitated. She was shivering, her lips blue-stained. 'The things I said to you, that's not why you're leaving, is it?'

'Your self-regard is striking but no, child, I am not leaving because you insulted your mother.'

'I am not a child.'

'No? Then perhaps it is time you stopped behaving like one. Now if you'll excuse me, I need to catch my train.'

Fräulein Eberhardt was silent. 'She's not like that, you know,' she said in a small voice. 'The things I said. Here.'

Digging in her pocket she pulled out a folded piece of paper and thrust it at him. Confused, he took it. As the chauffeur slammed the door she ran back towards the house. Julius saw the door open, the outline of her slight figure against the blaze of light from the hall. Then the door closed and she was gone.

The car glided along the wooded road that led to the lake, its headlamps twin tunnels of light in the deepening gloom. Pale trees loomed out of the darkness and disappeared. Julius turned the square of folded paper in his hand, feeling the sharpness of its corners against his fingers. On the seat beside him the Noah's Ark gleamed in its shiny wrapping. He sighed. Closing his eyes, he dropped the note unopened into his coat pocket.

VII

In the weeks after Julius's return from Munich, Matthias was frequently in Berlin. Business, he said vaguely, and Julius did not press him. He was glad that the young man made it a habit to drop by. He no longer bothered to make an appointment, preferring to call in on his way from a meeting or en route to dinner, and, although Frau Lang made no secret of her disapproval, Julius was charmed by his impulsiveness. He was right, he was not the barging-in type. On the contrary, he seemed to possess an infallible instinct for the right moment, the evenings when Julius's appointments finished early, when he was dining alone. Several times he brought a painting for Julius to authenticate. Often he did not. He had a way of leaning forward when he listened, as though he absorbed the words through the surface of his skin.

'You do promise you'll send me packing, won't you, the moment you're tired of me?' he insisted, and though Julius laughingly assured him he would, there was never an evening, as the young man rose to leave, when Julius did not wish he might stay a little longer. He thought of the vacuous gaggle of men that crowded Luisa's parties, Matthias's age, most of them, as squealingly fearful of silence as children playing Musical Chairs. In their youth Julius and his friends had stayed up all night, drinking, of course, but mostly talking, talking, talking, not the frenzied empty chatter of cocaine but the meticulous, miraculous unfurling of ideas, of literature and philosophy and art. They had wanted to understand everything, to feel everything. Matthias was the same.

In the Yellow House in Arles, van Gogh had dreamed of creating a community of artists. *If only ten people could be found in every country to come together with the simple intention of working for good, the world would blossom like a flower,* he wrote to Theo. His own strength was failing but art would endure. *To the horizon, an infinity of beautiful things.* Though perhaps those words were Julius's. He could no longer exactly remember where Vincent ended and his imaginings began.

He was putting in his cufflinks when Frau Lang knocked at his dressing-room door, outraged and out of breath.

'It's Herr Rachmann, he's here. I told him quite plainly you were going out, but he insisted. Apparently it can't wait, though why I couldn't say.'

Snatching up his coat, Julius hurried downstairs. Matthias was standing in front of the fire. He turned as Julius came in, his face shining with excitement.

'I'm sorry, Julius, I'm interrupting you, I know, I should have telephoned but I go back to Düsseldorf first thing tomorrow and I couldn't leave without telling you.'

'Without telling me what?'

'We're opening a gallery.' His grin was so wide it split his face in two. 'My brother and I, here in Berlin. Hardly a gallery even. A room. A cupboard. A cupboard on the third floor of a building with no elevator that isn't quite in the gallery district. Moltkestrasse 98. We signed a lease this afternoon.'

'But that's wonderful news,' Julius said. 'Congratulations.'

'Thank you. I can't really believe it. Of course it's all thanks to you.'

'I hardly think so.'

'I'm serious. Don't you remember, the very first time we met, I told you that all I wanted was to be taken seriously and you said that if I was serious about art I had to be in Berlin. So here I am.'

'Then I'm delighted I said it. What I remember is you saying that you wanted a happy life.'

'And perhaps, thanks to you, I'll have one. Where else can a man be truly happy but here?'

The gallery would be called the Old & New Art Gallery Ltd. There was so much of Matthias in the name, Julius thought, in its blend of artlessness and awe. Matthias's brother would deal in antiquities, Matthias in modern art.

'We should celebrate,' Julius said. 'Stay for a drink. Better still, stay for dinner.'

'But you're going out.'

'A dinner I haven't the slightest desire to go to. Frau Lang will telephone and tell them I've been taken ill. An occasion this momentous cannot go unmarked.'

Matthias protested. It was an imposition and much too late and besides he had only the suit he stood up in, but Julius insisted. He had Frau Lang decant a bottle of the 1900 Château Margaux and watched with pleasure as Matthias took his first sip, savouring the wine's tannic sleekness, its long, lush finish.

'Oh my God,' Matthias said, laughing. Julius laughed too.

'To the Old & New Art Gallery,' he said, raising his glass. It was only when the wine was all drunk that Matthias confessed that he and his brother were already in dispute about the future of the business. Gregor had recently secured a profitable contract to supply decorative antiquities to a large Berlin department store, he was confident others would follow. He wanted Matthias to give up on modern painting and work with him. Julius thought of Matthias flogging amphorae amid the faux-Hellenic monstrosities of the Wertheim atrium and shook his head, aghast.

'But that's unconscionable. You'd be nothing but a glorified encyclopedia salesman!'

Matthias shrugged. 'Gregor has had enough of being poor. To follow one's heart when there is an easier way, he thinks it's a kind of madness. Maybe it is.'

'You don't think that.'

'No. But perhaps in time I can learn to.'

'Or perhaps you could find yourself another partner. A partner who would support you, who wanted what you wanted.'

'You make it sound as though such men are everywhere.'

'There are enough of them, if you know where to look,' Julius said. He leaned across the table. 'I know a lot of people, Matthias.'

Matthias shook his head. 'You're very kind,' he said stiffly. 'But I can't impose on you like that.'

'Why not? I'm not in a position to invest myself, not presently, but I have friends, collectors, wealthy men who are always looking—'

'Stop. Please.'

'I don't understand,' Julius said, bemused. 'I want to help.'

'I know that and I'm so grateful, but I can't, don't you see? I admire you so much, I don't want to be your protégé, your – your good cause. I want to earn your respect. I want, if I can, one day to be your equal. Oh, I know what that sounds like, the arrogance of it, but that's not what I mean, I just want – I want to do it myself, I want you to know I can do it myself.' His face was stricken. 'Please tell me I haven't offended you.'

'Of course not,' Julius said softly. 'Forgive me. It was I who spoke out of turn.'

Later they went to the Hotel Eden for a nightcap. Julius could see no reason to leave Meierstrasse but Matthias insisted. He ordered vintage cognac.

'The best you have,' he told the waiter and grinned at Julius. 'We always drink your wine but tonight, for once, it's my turn. Thank you, my friend. To you. To us.'

Julius returned to Meierstrasse very late and more than a little drunk. Frau Lang tutted as she let him in and he laughed at her and kissed her loudly on the cheek.

'Heavens, Frau Lang, didn't your mother ever tell you not to frown like that in case the wind changed?' he asked and, seizing her by the waist, he spun her in a clumsy waltz.

Once Matthias moved to Berlin Julius hoped he would see him more often. Instead his visits dwindled. The new gallery seemed to take up all of Matthias's time. He still dropped in, brought paintings for authentication, but too often he had hardly taken off his coat before it was time for him to leave.

'Stay for a drink,' Julius said every time, but Matthias always declined, always had somewhere else he had to be. Perhaps it was Berlin's breakneck pace or its famously bracing air but, despite his relentless schedule, he never seemed to tire. It made Julius feel very old sometimes to see his excitement, the exhilaration that lit him like a lamp.

'It's not a girl, is it?' he asked one evening, saying goodbye.

Matthias shot him a startled sideways glance. 'A girl? No, of course not.'

'Well, I hope it's not business at this time of night.'

'Actually, I'm dining with Walter Ruthenberg.'

It was Julius's turn to be startled. He had not known that Matthias and Ruthenberg continued to work together, still less that they were on first-name terms. 'Are you indeed?' he said with a brittle laugh. 'In that case you should eat first. Ruthenberg's frugality is legendary.'

'He doesn't serve wine like yours, it's true.'

So it was not the first time. Julius wanted to ask when and how often. Instead he forced a smile. 'Then dine here tomorrow. We will redress the balance.'

Matthias bent over his painting, his face averted. For a strange, brief moment Julius was afraid he was laughing at him, but when he looked up his expression was warm, even tender. 'I'd like that,' he said. 'I'd like that very much.'

Matthias arrived early. Julius saw him from the gallery, leaning in the morning-room doorway, his hands in his pockets. He smiled over his shoulder at Julius as he hurried across the hall.

'I've kept you waiting, I'm sorry,' Julius said.

'Not at all. The lovely Fräulein Grüber has been keeping me entertained.'

'The lovely Fräulein Grüber should have gone home an hour ago.'

The typist blushed, bundling her coat into her arms. In the study Julius mixed Negronis and gave one to Matthias.

'So how was Ruthenberg?' he asked. 'How was dinner?'

'He was very hospitable. The dinner was – simple.'

'As plain and stodgy as his prose,' Julius said. He expected Matthias to laugh. Instead he shook his head.

'I'm sorry, Julius, I know he's your great rival, but I rather admire his work. It has integrity.'

Galled, Julius put down his drink. He could not recall Matthias ever disagreeing with him so directly. 'Integrity, really? Is that what you think?'

'Actually, yes. He writes with such obvious care, such precision.'

'He writes like a schoolboy. He writes as though art can be explained, as though it can be contained within the constructs of the rational intellect, but art is not like history or science, it cannot be reduced to facts, to formulae. There is no integrity in reason, in weighing one side and then the other. Paintings are not potatoes. To write about art you must speak as art speaks, passionately and directly to the soul.'

There was a silence. Matthias looked at him, his green eyes unreadable. Then slowly he smiled. 'I know,' he said, and he clasped his hands together as though he meant to catch Julius's words in the cup of his palms.

Matthias was in high spirits. Somehow he had convinced his brother that it would be imprudent to rely too heavily on the department-store trade, that with circumspection and careful management modern paintings might yield a second steady stream of income. If Matthias had once been prepared to gamble with borrowed money, the Trübner had taught him a valuable lesson. He was not in the business to get rich. He wanted to establish a new gallery of modern art that would be taken seriously, respected by artists and buyers alike. He would build the business painting by painting, learning a little more with each step.

'There is one thing you were wrong about, though,' he said as they lingered over coffee.

'Not Ruthenberg again?'

Matthias smiled. 'On that point I'm convinced. I meant when you told me it was impossible to have a happy life as a dealer.'

'I think I said parting with beautiful things would break your heart.'

'You did. And I was afraid you were right. When I was growing up my father was a servant in—'

'I thought your father was a blacksmith.'

Matthias flinched. Too late Julius remembered it was Salazin who had told him about Matthias's father. It was quite possible that Salazin was wrong, possible too that Matthias resented Julius prying in his private affairs. He was wondering whether to apologise when Matthias shrugged.

'Yes, when I was very small. But then there was the accident, his hand, and he became a servant. I used to sit in the kitchen with him sometimes while he polished the silver and I told myself when I grew up I would own beautiful things. I used to look at paintings in museums and want so badly for them to be mine, but in the last few months that urge to acquire, to own, it's gone. I sell a work but I don't lose it. Its beauty, its power, they are still mine because its essence, its spirit and mine – I can't put it into words, not like you. But I think of a wall after a hot day, the warmth that stays in the bricks even as the air cools . . . ' He trailed off, his cheeks flushed. 'I can't explain it. Tell me to shut up before I make it any worse.'

Julius was silent. He thought of the van Gogh, the fierce exultant longing that had filled him when he saw it, the passionate desire to possess it, to absorb it inside himself, like falling in love. He thought of Luisa's exquisite disdainful face, the way she had looked at him as though he was every mistake she had ever made. *Isn't that why you wanted me, another exhibit for your fucking museum?*

Matthias drained his coffee cup and put it back in its saucer. He smiled crookedly at Julius. 'Ah, high-mindedness. It's so wonderfully affordable.'

In the chiaroscuro candlelight his face was the face of a Caravaggio.

VIII

'He goes through your diary.'

Julius gaped at his housekeeper. 'What did you say?'

'Herr Rachmann, when he comes here.' Frau Lang twisted her handkerchief in her hands. There was something stubborn about her, even as she struggled not to cry. 'He makes Fräulein Grüber tell him things, what you're doing, who you're with. It's not right.'

Julius thought of Matthias laughing in the doorway of the morning room, the way Fräulein Grüber blushed when he bade her good night. Angrily he shook his head. 'That's enough, do you hear me?'

'Ask Fräulein Grüber if you don't believe me.'

'I said that's enough! You will show every one of my guests the proper respect or we will both have to think hard about your position here, do you understand?'

Frau Lang's face crumpled. Silently, stumblingly, she backed out of the study. Sighing, Julius took off his spectacles and rubbed his eyes. Frau Lang had always been impossible but he had not thought her capable of such baseness. Her hostility towards Matthias was intolerable, nothing but a toxic admixture of jealousy, snobbery and ill temper. His humble background, his youth, his openness, even his impeccable manners had damned him from the start.

And yet her accusations clung to him, he could not shake them off. One morning, as Fräulein Grüber hurried from the study with her shorthand pad, he called her back.

'There's something else,' he said. 'Is it true that you share private information about me with Herr Rachmann?'

Fräulein Grüber's cheeks flamed. Suddenly Julius wanted very badly not to know. He crossed his arms, his fingers gripping his elbows. 'Is that a yes, Fräulein Grüber?'

'I'm so sorry, sir. I know I shouldn't have done it, only—'

'Only what?'

She flinched, staring wretchedly at the floor. 'It's just, when he asked me, it was right after Frau Lang accused him of barging in right in front of you – maybe you don't remember, but Herr Rachmann, he was completely mortified, he was afraid you wouldn't want him to come back, that if he did you'd be too polite to turn him away but all the time you'd just be waiting for him to leave. He said he didn't know what to do, when he asked me I thought it wouldn't do any harm, that I was helping.' Her voice shook. 'It was wrong, I see that now, I should never have – I'm so sorry.'

Julius thought back over the evenings Matthias had dropped in to Meierstrasse, the curious knack he had for picking nights when Julius was sure to be at home, and he laughed softly to himself. He would never have guessed that Matthias's considerateness was at least one part cunning.

'I suppose – I suppose you'll want me to pack up my things,' Fräulein Grüber said, not looking at him, but Julius shook his head.

'I don't want any such thing. If Herr Rachmann is so determined not to inconvenience me, why on earth would I wish you to stand in his way?'

Fräulein Grüber frowned doubtfully. 'So you're not angry?'

'On the contrary, you have my permission to tell Herr Rachmann whatever it is he wants to know. His scrupulousness is a credit to him, whatever Frau Lang may think to the contrary.'

Böhm telephoned. After months of delay a date had finally been set for the preliminary hearing. The court would hear the petition and statements would be shared with the defence. Nothing would be settled, except a date for the hearing proper. Julius was not required to attend. It did not stop Harald Baeck's face from rising like a moon in his dreams.

Böhm came to Meierstrasse to take Frau Lang's statement. She perched awkwardly on her chair like a schoolgirl, her knees pressed together. Böhm was gentle. Taking a cardboard file from his briefcase he opened it and handed it to her.

'I'd like you to look at this photograph and tell me if you recognise the man in it.'

Frau Lang grimaced. She looked at the photograph and quickly away. 'Yes,' she said. 'That's him.'

Böhm took her through her testimony. As she gave her answers her neck turned red, then a deep purple. When Böhm had finished he smiled at her.

'You've been a great help, thank you. Is there anything else you would like to add, anything you think we've forgotten?'

The housekeeper shrugged. 'I don't know if it's any use, but there was a brown mark, dark brown, on his – his—' She dug her thumb into her right thigh.

'A birthmark? You're sure?'

When Frau Lang nodded Böhm smiled at her and made a note on his pad. 'Thank you, Frau Lang. You've been very helpful.'

'Although now I think about it,' she said, suddenly uncertain, 'it might have been the other one.'

'I think that's everything, don't you, Alfred?' Julius said hurriedly. 'Frau Lang, stay here please. I'll see Herr Böhm out.'

In the hall he shook Böhm's hand. 'You won't – that is – I'm sorry about Frau Lang's confusion. It's just that Herr Baeck, well, he wasn't exactly the first.'

He did not meet Böhm's eye. In the study Frau Lang was sitting where he had left her, a handkerchief crumpled in her hands.

'I'm sorry,' she said. 'About the birthmark.'

'It's all right, I've explained things to Herr Böhm, there's no harm done. But we do have to be careful. One man, remember? The man in the photograph. No one else.'

Frau Lang stared at her lap and said nothing.

'You're a good woman, Frau Lang, a Christian woman. I would never ask you to lie. Herr Baeck has signed a statement admitting his part. All we have to do is corroborate his story. The rest, well, that's nobody's business but ours. We have to think of Luisa's parents, of little Konstantin. The scandal, if it got out, it would destroy them. For their sakes, if not for Luisa's, we must find it in our hearts to be merciful.'

The day before the directions hearing a typed envelope arrived for Julius with a Munich postmark. Inside there was no letter, only a photograph of Konstantin standing by a lake. Konstantin could stand. He had shed his baby plumpness, he was all angles, and his silken hair was thick and curly. Julius stared at the boy his son had become, a stranger grown stranger still, and the loneliness opened inside him, a crack so deep and sudden that it made him dizzy. When he closed his eyes Luisa's voice seemed to come from inside him.

You'll open yourself up to a painting or a slab of stone, you'll let it break your bloody heart, but a real person, a living breathing person with their fear and their weakness and their failures, then you run a fucking mile, it disgusts you. When Konstantin was born the ferocity of her feelings for him shocked them both. Julius had watched her with the child and, despite everything, he felt both awe and a kind of yearning. He could not fathom what it would do to someone, to be loved like that.

He looked at the photograph for a long time. His coffee grew cold. When Frau Lang came in to clear his breakfast, he went upstairs. The Noah's Ark was still on the table in the nursery. Julius touched the shiny paper, then, ripping at it, tore open the parcel. One side of the painted ark slid off to reveal the pairs of animals stored inside. Lowering himself to his knees, Julius tipped them out on to the floor. The carpet was thick and the animals wobbled but he set them out in a long line, smallest first, all the way from the brightly coloured birds to the elephants and the long-necked giraffes. When the animals were lined up he placed Noah and his wife side by side at the top of the gangplank. Noah smiled broadly into his beard. He did not look like a man readying himself for catastrophe. Beneath her red headscarf, Mrs Noah's eyes were round and very blue.

Julius knelt until his feet were alive with pins and needles and he could no longer endure the soreness in his hip. Limping a little on numb legs, he picked up the torn wrapping paper and screwed it into a ball. He did not pick up the animals. He left them where they were, waiting patiently, two by two.

That night Matthias called in unannounced. Julius half considered sending him away, he was in no mood for company, but, to his surprise, he found himself grateful for the distraction. They did not talk about the divorce. Julius had not mentioned the hearing to Matthias. He did not want Matthias asking questions he did not want to answer. He was glad when the young man asked him about the paintings recently acquired by the Wallraf-Richartz museum in Cologne. It was well known that their new director of modern art had been on a buying spree; the man was a master of self-promotion and knew precisely how to stoke the interest of the newspapers. One painting in particular, he told reporters, was certain to cause a sensation, though they would have to wait for the grand unveiling before Germany's great and good to find out which. It was rumoured that he had beaten London's National Gallery to van Gogh's *Sunflowers*.

Matthias had seen one of the *Sunflowers* paintings in Munich after the war. He did not know that van Gogh had intended the paintings as part of a triptych, two sunflower canvases, one with a yellow ground, the other turquoise, flanking a portrait of Augustine Roulin, the wife of his friend the postman, rocking a cradle. It was Mme Roulin who took care of him when he was ill.

'He saw the sunflowers as lamps,' Julius said. 'Candelabra illuminating his secular madonna. It was extraordinary, in those few weeks in Arles it was as if a kind of magic took hold of him, his brush only had to touch the canvas and it sprang to life. Two complete triptychs in a matter of weeks, maybe more. Imagine it, the blaze of those paintings against the whitewashed walls of the Yellow House.'

Matthias smiled. '*The sunflowers are mine.* Isn't that what he wrote to Theo?'

'And they were, they are and always will be, whatever that slippery bastard Gauguin might try and claim to the contrary. You don't know that story? Gauguin wrote later that Vincent only made the paintings because Gauguin told him to, that it was Gauguin's idea to paint "sunflowers on sunflowers in the full light of the sun". By then, of course, Gauguin was destitute and dying and terrified no one would remember him. Better to take credit for someone else's masterpieces than not to be credited at all.'

'Vincent made many, many weak paintings but his great works, they unman you,' Julius said later. By then he was drunk, the words soft-edged and heavy in his mouth. 'Yes, there is agony in them, but somehow no disillusion, no bitterness. Just the brush dipped again and again in his beating broken heart.'

'What do you mean, weak paintings?' Matthias asked.

'Vincent was self-taught, impatient, in thrall to the wrong artists. Many of his early works are clumsy. But even then he painted completely, with every part of himself.'

And later still, in his study with a bottle of cognac, 'The van Gogh that used to hang there, my wife stole it. She took it with her, when she left me.'

'She loved it that much?'

'She detested it but she took it anyway. A hostage. She wanted to make sure I would be generous.'

'She didn't need to take a painting to know that.'

Julius thought of Harald Baeck's face in the crowded station, the colour draining from his skin. 'How can you say that?' he said bitterly. 'You don't know what cruelties I am capable of.'

'I know that you are a good man.'

'Except that I'm not. I'm not a good man.' The way Matthias looked at Julius then made Julius want to weep. 'I have a son but it's the painting I can't live without. What kind of a man chooses a painting over his own son?'

'But you haven't chosen. Not yet.'

'Not out loud maybe. But whatever I say, whatever my lawyer claims for me in a courtroom, I know differently. I've chosen.'

Matthias shook his head. 'You're wrong. We don't choose the deepest desires of our hearts. Our only choice is whether to act on them. Whether the hurt we cause . . .'

He broke off unhappily, but Julius had drunk too much to feel anyone's pain but his own. 'You think that helps?' he demanded. 'You think knowing you can never change, that the rottenness is too deep-rooted in you, that it's part of who you are, you think that makes anything better, that it stops the guilt, the shame?'

'No, I don't think that.'

'How can you know anything about it, a man like you, a man who wants nothing from life but its beauty?'

'You think I don't have secrets, that I'm never ashamed of who I am?'

Julius laughed bleakly. 'You're young. Everyone wants to have secrets when they're young.'

'It's not like that, not for me.'

'Isn't it? Then tell me. Go on, tell me your shameful little secrets.'

Matthias's jaw hardened, his hands clenched as though he was steeling himself to say something. Then abruptly he stood and walked out of the room.

'Wait, where are you going?' Julius protested. 'For Christ's sake, Matthias, come back.' Staggering to his feet, clumsy with drink, he knocked his glass to the floor. A puddle of cognac spread across the parquet.

The front door banged. Julius stood unsteadily in the doorway of the study. He hardly knew what had happened. He rubbed his forehead, his fingers pressing into his temples, but the cognac made it hard to think and neither his hands nor his face felt like they belonged to him. He pressed harder, pushing his fingers through his hair, and let his head drop back against the jamb. In the firelight of the study the empty wall glared at him, triumphantly blank.

Frau Lang found him the next morning, sitting in the armchair in the nursery. She eyed his dishevelled dinner suit, the animals scattered around the Noah's Ark, no longer two by two, and brought him strong coffee with two aspirin on the saucer.

Downstairs someone had cleaned up the broken glass in his study. There was a vase of snowdrops on the table, the first flowers of spring, and the room smelled of beeswax and lavender. He asked Fräulein Grüber to arrange for the Noah's Ark to be sent to Konstantin in Munich.

'I want it sent today,' he said. Scrawling a line on a piece of paper, he slid it into an envelope. 'This needs to go with it.' A single line, *Thinking of you always, your loving Pappi.* Any more and he would never be able to stop. He told the typist to arrange for a taxicab. He had an urgent appointment in town.

'And have Frau Lang bring up Herr Rachmann's coat and hat for me, would you?' he added. 'I'll drop them at his gallery on my way.'

He waited for the taxi in his study, his hands in his pockets, staring out into the garden. Mrs Noah fitted neatly into his palm. He took her out, turning her over in his fingers. She stared at him beadily with her round blue eyes. Then, opening his desk drawer, he dropped her in and went out.

The street was narrow, cobbled in the old style, the brick buildings leaning conspiratorially towards one another to block out the sky. Most housed small shops, an ironmonger's, a barber's shop, a tobacconist, its narrow window stained yellow with cellophane. Their signs were weathered, the paint peeling. Several were boarded up. Halfway down the street a coalman unloaded sacks from his cart into an open cellar. His horse eyed Julius impassively as he passed. Raising its tail, it expelled a slow, sloppy stream of manure.

At 98 *THE OLD & NEW ART COMPANY LTD* was written on a card tacked to the bell second from the top. The card was warped and smudged with rain. Julius felt inexplicably nervous. He took a breath, smoothing Matthias's coat over his arm, then pressed the bell.

No one came. Three floors was a long way to come down when one was not expecting anyone. He rang again, keeping his finger on the bell. He could hear the muffled rasp as it rang inside the building. Still no one came. Julius stepped away from the door. Perhaps Matthias was out. Or perhaps, he thought uneasily, he had heard the bell and did not want to see him. Perhaps he was still angry, upset. Perhaps he was waiting for Julius to go away. As he stood looking up towards the third-floor windows, it occurred to Julius that, for all his excitement about the new enterprise, Matthias had never once suggested that Julius visit him in Moltkestrasse. The thought was like a shadow passing over him; he felt the shiver of it. When he heard the clatter of footsteps from inside the building he wanted to run. Instead he forced his mouth into a smile.

The door opened. A tall, thickset man scowled at Julius. He wore a shirt without a collar, none too clean, its sleeves rolled up to reveal strong forearms furred with dark hair. Julius supposed he was Matthias's brother, though they looked nothing alike. He had imagined a salesman, smooth manners and a suit, but this man looked like a hoodlum. He smelled of cigarettes and turpentine.

'What?' the man demanded.

Julius looked down at the coat and hat in his arms. 'I was – I was hoping to see Herr Rachmann. I have some things of his. Are you his brother?'

The man's scowl deepened. 'Who's asking?'

Julius stiffened. Perhaps they were brothers. He had Matthias's way of puckering his mouth as though he were sucking on the insides of his cheeks, only where Matthias seemed always to be biting back laughter, his brother looked ready to throw a punch. There was a denseness to him that seemed to suck what light there was from the grey afternoon.

'My name is Köhler-Schultz,' Julius said coldly. 'I am an associate of Matthias's. A friend.'

Something changed in the man's expression. He leaned forward, his lip curling in mockery and contempt. 'His friend? Fuck, you really are an arrogant fucking prick.' Sneering, he hawked up a bubbled gob of spit on to the pavement by Julius's foot. Then, stepping back, he slammed the door.

'Who the hell do you think you are?' Julius shouted, and he pressed the bell again and again until the rasp of it rang in his teeth but this time no one came.

He took Matthias's coat and hat back to Meierstrasse. Matthias could collect them the next time he came. When the telephone jangled he jumped, hurrying out to the morning room. Fräulein Grüber looked up, startled, and handed him the receiver but, instead of Matthias, it was Böhm's voice that greeted him. He sounded sombre. There had been an unexpected hitch. Not only had Luisa's lawyer denied the claims in Julius's petition, he had applied to the court to issue a counter-petition, citing Julius as respondent.

'But that's impossible,' Julius said furiously. 'Dishonourable conduct, for God's sake? What does that even mean?'

'We won't know until we see their petition. Of course, there's always a chance they're playing games, delaying the process to force a negotiation. I'm sorry to have to ask this, but is there a possibility that she might have something, anything at all?'

Julius pushed away the thought of Harald Baeck and let a bitter anger run into the space it made. 'You know what she has. She has my child and my painting.'

Matthias did not come to Meierstrasse that evening. Julius took the slim bundle of Luisa's letters he had never quite been able to throw away and dropped them one by one into the fire, but it was not enough. In the flames he saw Matthias, his stricken expression as he stumbled out of the study. The brother's words echoed in his skull, savage with contempt. *You really are an arrogant fucking prick.* Dishonourable conduct, he thought, and his stomach churned, a curdle of discomfiture, fury and guilt.

IX

It was Geisheim at the *Tribüne* who insisted Julius go to Cologne. The Köhler-Schultz name was synonymous with van Gogh, he said, ignoring Julius's protestations. If the Wallraf-Richartz had scooped the *Sunflowers*, and all the *Tribüne*'s sources suggested that they had, Geisheim wanted Julius breaking the news.

'Call in your copy from Cologne,' he instructed, already half-way down the corridor to his next meeting. 'It's not often art makes headlines. We need to be first.'

Outside the newspaper offices the grey sky closed over the city like a lid. It was bitterly cold. The Berlin winter, provoked by the first stirrings of spring, had struck back. Julius had meant to go home. Instead, shoulders hunched, he walked eastwards along Leipziger Strasse. On the Jungfern bridge he stopped, staring down at the dark shape of himself on the inky water, then past the boarded-up restaurant on the corner towards Moltkestrasse. The thought of bumping into Matthias was at least as uncomfortable as it was irresistible, and still he lingered on the bridge, hoping and not hoping for a glimpse of him. The icy pavement leaked its chill through the soles of his shoes.

A sharp wind sliced between the buildings, cutting through his coat. Julius put his gloved hands to his mouth, feeling the heat of his breath through the leather. He thought of Konstantin in Munich, opening his Noah's Ark. He wished he had been there to see it. The wind made his eyes water and his nose stream. As he fumbled a handkerchief from the pocket of his coat, a folded square of paper fell to the ground.

Stiffly he bent to pick it up. It was a drawing in pen and ink, the paper jagged along one side where it had been torn from a sketchbook. Like a picture in a dream it was at the same time utterly familiar and disconcertingly wrong, van Gogh's *Self-Portrait with Bandaged Ear*, only the face was not Vincent's. Instead a young woman stared out from beneath Vincent's fur-trimmed cap, her lips pursed. She reminded Julius of someone, although for a moment he could not place her. He frowned at the drawing, sifting his memory.

And then it came back to him: Fräulein Eberhardt, the daughter of the Schiller widow, the troublemaker with the tattered nails. He thought of her pale face in the gathering darkness outside the house at Würmsee, the curve of her breasts beneath her black sweater. Beneath the drawing, in capitals: A MOMENT OF MADNESS. It had been made in haste but somehow it captured the spirit of van Gogh's original, not just his style but his emotional desolation, his bleak acceptance of blame. On the wall behind her head, where in his portrait van Gogh had placed a print of Mount Fuji like a lost paradise, Fräulein Eberhardt had drawn tropical foliage around a small stone fountain, a sweep of snow-capped mountains in the background: Otto Metz's winter garden.

In the bottom right-hand corner of the paper there was an arrow drawn in pencil. Julius turned the page. Under her address in Switzerland, Fräulein Eberhardt had scrawled a message in pencil.

*I'm sorry. Sometimes I'm vile. I wish I
wasn't but I can't seem to help it.*

*Write to me, won't you? Just so I know you
forgive me.*

I shake your hand, EE

I shake your hand, Vincent's characteristic farewell when he
wrote to his brother Theo. Julius's yearning for the *Self-Portrait*
came so suddenly that it winded him. He leaned on the bridge's
parapet, the paper trembling in his hand. In the asylum at Saint-
Rémy the doctors had forbidden Vincent to paint. They said it
was painting that brought on the seizures, but for Vincent the
not-painting was worse, a kind of torture. Julius did not know if
the girls at Fräulein Eberhardt's finishing school were given lessons in drawing and painting or if they were taught only to smile
and nod and sing the songs of Schiller, their hands neatly folded
in their laps. He tried to imagine Fräulein Eberhardt arranging
flowers and discussing menus but he could not do it. He thought
instead of Vincent who, confined to his room without brushes
or canvas, had eaten his paints, scooping them from the palette
with his fingers.

The afternoon was growing dark. The streetlamps came on.
On the far bank a heavy-set man stopped, looking over the black
water towards Julius. His heart thudding, Julius hurried home.

That night he wrote to Fräulein Eberhardt. An apology like
that deserved acknowledgement, even several months after the
fact. He wondered if she had been waiting for his absolution all
this time, her hopes flaring like a match with each morning's post.
He rather hoped so. Remorse was worth nothing if it did not sting.

It was possible, in Berlin, to forget that parts of Germany were still
under enemy occupation. At Versailles the French had insisted

on a buffer zone, a demilitarised Rhineland to protect themselves against German aggression, and the Allies had carved up
the territory like greedy boys at a tea table. A few miles outside
Cologne, a troop of British soldiers boarded Julius's train and
made their way through the carriages, checking the passengers'
papers. There were military checkpoints at the bridges, army
lorries in the streets. At the crowded museum reception, British
officers mingled with the bigwigs and bankers and bootlicking
artists who made up the city's crème de la crème.

The breezy normality of it made Julius feel nauseous. Further
south, in the Palatinate, the occupying French army was known
to be encouraging the separatists, actively supporting the creation
of an independent Rhenish state. Five years after the armistice
the war was not over, far from it. Having humiliated Germany and
forced her into bankruptcy, Clemenceau and his like now sought
to break her into pieces.

The new director of the museum had done his homework.
Sidling up to Julius before the speeches, he suggested they slip
down to the exhibition before the other guests. A critic of Julius's
eminence, he murmured, should not have to fight for a front-row
seat. He led Julius directly into the main gallery. A heavy velvet
curtain some twelve feet wide hung from ceiling to floor, obscur-
ing most of the far wall, a theatre awaiting an audience. With a
bow, the director gestured for him to go first. Julius felt a thrill of
anticipation run through him: he could almost see it through the
velvet, Vincent's *Sunflowers*, primitive and exalted, blazing with
faith and the fiery dazzle of the Provençal sun.

He stepped behind the curtain. A single painting hung on the
wall, lit by a row of electric lights set into the ceiling, but it was
not the *Sunflowers*. Vast, violently coloured, it was perhaps the
most nightmarish painting that Julius had ever seen. A trench
in a shattered landscape, a bloody sprawl of slaughtered soldiers,

their limbs blown off, their heads smashed open, their bellies spilling fresh snarls of intestine. Around them, the decomposing remains of corpses exhumed by the explosion. Rotting flesh, alive with maggots. A pair of putrid hands pushing up from the mud in supplication. And above the carnage, a uniformed corpse impaled on twisted wooden stakes, his wounds gaping, his sightless eyes staring at the sky, and between his legs, obscenely, the jut of a bayonet blade, the handle of a knife.

Julius closed his eyes, pretending to look for his spectacles. He dreamed of it still, the shells exploding round his ambulance, the soldier who disappeared in a fountain of blood. The bodies piled three deep in a ditch, the springiness of flesh beneath his boots as they searched for the living, the crack of bones like breaking sticks. He swallowed, steeling himself. Then, putting on his spectacles, he moved closer to the canvas until the maggots resolved into marks of paint.

'Devastating, isn't it?' the director said. 'A vision of suffering to rival Grunewald.'

'On the contrary,' Julius snapped. 'Grunewald finds beauty in anguish. This painting is a sickening mess.'

'It tears the scales from our eyes. Otto Dix was a war hero, he won the Iron Cross, but this painting tells the terrible truth. War is not heroic. War is unutterable hell.'

Julius thought of the red-faced British officers upstairs, with their polished buttons and their perfect German. Until the occupation, the citizens of Cologne had never in their history been required to carry identity papers.

'You have to take it down,' he said.

The director raised an eyebrow. 'Because you dislike it?'

'Because it isn't art, it's propaganda. For God's sake, man, do you think when they see this the British aren't going to be rubbing their hands with glee? A painting like this, at this moment, isn't just a blow to German morale, it's a pistol against our country's head. An invitation to let them help themselves.'

'I'm interested you see it that way. For me it's a cry of pain from a decorated military hero determined to show us the truth about war. Would you prefer him to lie?'

'I don't give a damn if he paints himself blue and hangs upside down from the rafters. History will not remember him. But you, Herr Direktor, have a responsibility to your country. Yes, war is brutal. It is also sometimes necessary if we are to protect ourselves against those who would destroy us.'

The director smiled serenely. 'I would not censor Otto Dix, Herr Köhler-Schultz, any more than I would seek to censor you. I shall read your column with interest.'

People were coming. Julius could hear the surge of voices as guests moved through the first room. Without a word he turned and marched out of the room. He would not be a part of this repulsive circus. In the crowded foyer he waited impatiently for his coat. He wanted to be alone, in the darkness, scoured by the frozen Cologne air. When the attendant held up his coat for him to put on Julius snatched it and, bundling it into his arms, forced his way towards the exit. It was only by chance that he saw two men standing near the staircase. One wore a dark beard and a frogged evening coat of plum velvet. The other was Matthias.

Julius felt a stab of gratitude so sharp it stopped his throat. He called Matthias's name but the hall was noisy, it swallowed the words. As he pushed through the crowd towards him, Matthias leaned close to his companion and murmured in his ear.

'Matthias!' Julius called again and this time Matthias looked round. Julius smiled, his heart full, but Matthias only frowned at him furiously, shaking his head.

'Don't,' he said, or at least that was what Julius thought he said, because before he could be certain Matthias was gone, swallowed up by the throng.

Julius returned to Berlin on the dawn train. He cabled Geisheim from the station, three words: NOT THE SUNFLOWERS. Back at Meierstrasse he told Fräulein Grüber to telephone the editor's assistant. His piece would be ready for collection at four o'clock. Till then he was not to be disturbed. An hour later the typist knocked softly at the door.

'What is it?' he demanded angrily.

'I'm sorry, but Herr Rachmann is on the telephone. I said you were busy but he insisted. He says it's urgent.'

Julius looked down at the sheet of paper in front of him. WHAT IS BAD ART? was written in heavy capital letters at the top. Everything else on the page was crossed out. 'Not now,' he snapped.

Fräulein Grüber closed the door. Julius glared at the page, then crumpling it into a ball, hurled it towards the fire. In all his years on the newspaper he had never once faltered over a column. He had known always what he wished to say and how best to say it, how to balance erudition and accessibility, the superficial shimmer of the surface with the depth of the long view. The sentences spooled from him like spider's silk, reflexively, their patterns pre-ordained. Not this time. This time words were tangles of sticky hair, clumping and clotting in his head. He closed his eyes to try to see them better, but all he saw was Vincent, green-faced and gaunt, and, reflected in his relentless stare, the corpse of Dix's crucified soldier.

All afternoon Julius wrote words down and crossed them out. When the messenger from the Tribüne came at four o'clock, he sent him away. Geisheim telephoned. Julius did not take the call. It grew dark. Fräulein Grüber tapped on the door and asked cautiously if he had anything for her to type. He told her to go home. He heard her leave a few minutes later, the brisk tap of her heels on the parquet, the heavy clunk of the front door as it closed behind her. Rising from his chair, he stood in front of the fire. Balled-up sheets of paper littered the grate. Tomorrow he would go and see Geisheim and tell him it was not the business of German newspapers to promote the imperial ambitions of their enemies. He turned his head, looking at the nail in the wall, the ghostly shadow nail beneath it. Böhm had left a message while he was in Cologne. It was almost over. The courts had given Luisa's lawyers two weeks to submit their counter-petition. If, as he suspected, they had nothing, Böhm would push the courts for a hearing. He would have his divorce, his painting and his son.

Wearily Julius rubbed his neck. He supposed Matthias had telephoned to explain but he was no longer sure he cared for his explanations. He did not have time for childish histrionics, not if they unsettled him like this and distracted him from his work. He had had enough of that with Luisa. Sighing, he touched his finger to the empty nail. Vincent had written once to Theo that there was nothing more artistic than to love people. It was non-sense, of course, at least for him. Van Gogh's work drew its power from his loneliness. His genius lay in his longing, in his terrible inexhaustible hope. He painted pictures because they were the best substitute for human beings that he could find.

Suddenly Julius could not stand to be sealed up a second longer. He flung open the study door, shouting for Frau Lang to bring his coat. Then he stopped. Fräulein Grüber stood in the hall, clutching her handbag. Next to her, cold-pinched and coatless, stood Matthias. 'It's not Fräulein Grüber's fault,' he said. 'She just opened the door.'

Julius shook his head. He felt old suddenly, and very tired. 'I was just going out.'

'Of course, I understand, I'm sorry, I wouldn't have come, only I – I wondered if you might let me have my coat. It's the only one I have.'

His coat. Nothing else. He sounded even wearier than Julius. Julius nodded heavily. 'Frau Lang will fetch it for you.'

'Or I can get it?' Fräulein Grüber offered. 'It won't take a minute.'

'That would be kind. Thank you.'

There was an awkward silence as she hurried away, the door banging shut behind her. Then Matthias sighed. 'Forgive me,' he said.

'I'm sure Fräulein Grüber is happy to help.'

'Not the coat. The other night, when I left—'

'Forget it.'

'I can't.'

'Look, it's my fault, I was rude.'

'No, you were honest,' Matthias said quietly. 'I wasn't. I wanted to tell you, I tried to, but I couldn't. I was afraid, if you knew—'

'If I knew what?'

The servants' door swung open and Frau Lang bustled into the hall, Fräulein Grüber in her wake. She eyed Matthias warily. 'Did you call for me?' she asked Julius. 'Only Fräulein Grüber seems to think you're going out.'

'I'm not sure,' Julius said. 'Maybe later,' but Matthias shook his head. Taking his coat from Fräulein Grüber, he put it on.

'It's all right,' he said. 'I'm leaving.'

'Then I'll need my coat too,' Julius said to Frau Lang.

They walked together along the canal. Below them the dark water gleamed, gilded by streetlamps. It took a long time for Matthias to find the right words. That night, he said, when Julius had challenged him to tell his secrets, he had wanted to speak out but his courage had failed him. He had fled because he was afraid, afraid of Julius's disapproval or, worse, his disgust, afraid that the truth would change everything and destroy what for Matthias had always been precious and pure. It was only in Cologne that he had understood it was lies that destroyed things, even if they were never spoken out loud. He did not want to lie any more.

'You asked me if I had a girl, do you remember?' he said. 'I said no, but it was not the whole truth. There is someone.'

Suddenly, irrationally, Julius thought of Luisa. 'So who is she? Do I know her?'

'Not her. Him.'

Julius was silent. Perhaps he should be shocked, scandalised even, but instead it was like a lamp coming on in a familiar room; he saw that he had known it all the time.

'I can't tell you who he is,' Matthias said. 'I gave him my word. He's afraid of trouble, the police, his family knows nothing, that's why I couldn't speak to you in Cologne. He was with me.'

'The man in the velvet coat.'

'I told him it was safe, that no one would know us. I wanted him to see the sunflowers. We'd talked about it so much. Sunflowers on sunflowers in the full light of the sun. And it wasn't even there. There was only that – that horrible—'

'I know,' Julius said gently. And then, 'Do you love him?'

Matthias did not answer. It was only when he stopped and buried his face in his hands that Julius realised he was crying. Tentatively he touched Matthias's back. It was a long time since he had felt such deep and simple tenderness.

'It's all right,' he murmured. 'Everything's going to be all right.'

A shudder ran through Matthias's shoulders and into Julius's hand. Without thinking Julius slid his arm around the young man and pulled him close. Despite Matthias's confession there was no awkwardness in it, no suggestion of sexual charge. Wherever it had come from, the restless yearning that had drawn Julius to the Jungfern bridge was gone, and in its place a wordless intimacy that warmed his chest like cognac, a sweep of honeyed fire.

X

Julius's condemnation of Dix's painting was public and unflinching. In the horror of war, he wrote in the *Tribüne*, great art found humanity and hope. But the Dix was not great art. It was its opposite, an ill-painted, ill-conceived obscenity. Corpse pornography, he called it, an orgy of the grotesque. It made him want to puke.

The day they published his column he wrote to the board of the Wallraf-Richartz, holding each and every one of them responsible, then sent his letter to the editor of the *Kölnische Zeitung*, calling for a citywide boycott of the museum. He lobbied the directors of all the major art museums across Germany, urging a combined effort to compel Cologne to take the picture down. He despatched furious articles to influential newspapers and art magazines. He even wrote to Dix, lambasting him for his horrifying failure of judgement and demanding that he withdraw the picture and provide another in exchange.

It was Matthias he wrote for, Matthias who spurred him on. The painting had reawakened the terrors that tormented Matthias during the war; suddenly he was afraid to sleep, afraid even to close his eyes. Hour after hour he woke bolt upright and pouring with sweat, roused by his own screaming. Sometimes he soiled himself. He told Julius everything, there were no longer any secrets between them. Julius had only to think of Matthias and the words poured from his pen.

But, despite his efforts, the painting was not taken down. A few critics supported Julius's position, Ruthenberg among them, but many more took the museum's side. The assaults were vicious and personal. Julius was mocked for his snobbery, his bigotry, for being small-minded and old-fashioned and old. His opponents pointed to his lifelong advocacy of French Impressionism, his disdainful denunciations of the great painters of Germany, and accused him of a plot against German art. One or two even exhumed the ancient Langbehn line that a Jew could no more become a German than an apple become a plum. Julius had been raised a Protestant and his antipathy to Dix was surely the opposite of unGerman but that was the thing about stories, the more they were told, the more true they became. Julius was dragged into lecture halls and radio broadcasts. He spoke to newspaper reporters, gave interviews for the newsreel.

It changed nothing. At the Wallraf-Richartz the queues stretched round the block. It was, the director acknowledged, the most successful show in the museum's history.

Julius did not know how he would have survived those turbulent weeks without Matthias. It was bad enough when the painting was in Cologne, but when Gustav Stemler at the Nationalgalerie announced that they would be bringing the Dix to Berlin the controversy reached a new, more vitriolic climax. Overjoyed at the opportunity to slam their long-time detractor, the artists of Germany came out against Julius in force. They ignored his careful arguments. Instead they lumped him in with the octogenarian Prussian generals, the National Socialist thugs who smashed shop windows for fun and claimed it would make Germany great again. In public Julius shrugged off the criticism, but at night, alone and exhausted, his certainties crumbled. Their gibes echoed in the darkness: *Yesterday's man. A dinosaur. Perhaps once a critic of consequence but now little more than a peddler of fatuous pseudo-biography for the masses.* Would this be how he was remembered, not as the iconoclastic *enfant terrible* he had been for so long, but as one of the die-hard reactionaries Dix parodied so savagely? He was almost sixty. He was running out of time.

'Relics,' his friend Bruno had said to him last time they met. 'That's what we are. The more or less insignificant remains of a culture that no longer exists.'

Julius had ignored him, putting the remark down to an excess of whisky and self-pity. Now it haunted him. When his publishers informed him that they were postponing the third edition of *The Making of Art* he reacted furiously, even though it was he who had failed to meet their deadline. Luisa's lawyers still had not submitted their counter-petition. Böhm said that he was pushing to have their application to postpone overturned but that it might still be months before they got to court. He asked if Julius might be willing to consider a negotiation. There was the boy to think of and the painting. Perhaps it was time to settle.

Julius might have considered it. It was Matthias who urged him to hold steady. He could not let Luisa blackmail him, he could not let her win. Besides, he had enough to worry about with the Dix. Julius knew he was right. The interruptions were ceaseless. Even on those days that the telephone did not ring off the hook he found it hard to concentrate. Sleeplessness upset his digestion. He suffered from headaches, a faint persistent feeling of nausea. When a dealer acquaintance of Matthias's brought him a Friedrich for authentication he could hardly make sense of what he was looking at. *I put my heart and soul into my work,* Vincent wrote to Theo, *and I have lost my mind in the process.* It terrified him.

'I looked and I didn't know,' he confessed afterwards to Matthias. 'It was like there was a fog inside me, noises with no meaning. I couldn't feel it, I didn't know. Friedrich, for God's sake! How could I not know Friedrich? I've been looking at his work for forty years.'

'You're tired, that's all.'

'I'm exhausted and it's killing me! Do you have any idea what this is doing to me, to my reputation? They want to finish me, Matthias, and they're winning. Perhaps I should let them win.'

'No!' Matthias grasped his arm, digging in his fingers. 'We can't stop now. We're going to fight with everything we have and for as long as it takes. There'll be time enough for Friedrich when this is over. This is what matters now.'

Only Matthias's conviction kept him from giving up. He was Julius's confessor and his consolation, his younger, surer, bolder self. He fortified Julius's failing courage, urged him to greater efforts when he flagged. When Julius was shouted down, it was Matthias who pushed him to shout back. Forced on to the defensive, he urged him to attack, audaciously, aggressively.

Worn out, Julius fell ill. He developed a persistent cough, some days it was all he could manage to get out of bed, but Matthias came every day, urging him to hold steady. When Julius heard a rumour that Stemler had spoken to Geisheim about replacing him with a younger critic, it was Matthias who proposed that Julius use his column in the *Tribüne* to denounce Stemler's erratic record in championing modern art, his weakness for cheap publicity, his tendency to run the public Nationalgalerie as though it were his own private fiefdom, and demand his dismissal.

'Surely it will only fan the flames?' Julius protested but Matthias was adamant.

'If it runs in the *Tribüne* it will look like Geisheim's idea,' he insisted. 'Like he's taking your side.'

Julius was right, his piece did fan the flames, articles appearing in rival newspapers as an enraged Stemler did his best to smear Julius in return, but, as Matthias pointed out, by then it was too late. A man defending himself always looked defensive. There were times, Julius thought, when Matthias sounded just like a divorce lawyer.

No one had ever shared themselves with him as Matthias did then. As the months passed, the intimacies ran between them like a thread, stitching them together. Matthias told Julius about his estrangement from his violent father, the lingering war hysteria that ran through his veins like mercury, his brief career as a dancer in Paris and Amsterdam and Vienna. He spoke of his lover, who was Russian and could not stay in Berlin, not now Lenin was gone and the city was full of spies. Soon he would leave for Switzerland. Matthias wanted him to go, he was afraid for his safety, but he was also afraid for himself, afraid the man would not come back, that he would forget him.

'You love him,' Julius said and this time it was not a question.

'Perhaps I do,' Matthias replied, and Julius felt his own heart open like a hand.

As for Julius, he told Matthias things he had never before said aloud. He talked of the gnawing dread of getting old and dull-headed and obsolete, of being discarded and forgotten by a world that had once held him in such great esteem; he confided his fears about not writing, the sudden pressures of money, his terror that he might have to sell his art to meet his debts; he spoke of the wretched unhappiness of his marriage, the painting whose loss tormented him every day, the child he had not wanted and feared he would never know.

'She was so beautiful,' he said. 'I thought I would never tire of looking at her. That I would forgive her anything.'

'I'm boring you,' Julius said sometimes but Matthias shook his head.

'Never,' he said. 'I want to know everything.'

And so Julius told him everything or nearly everything. He did not tell him about Harald Baeck, a man who could be blackmailed because his desires broke the law. A man like Matthias.

XI

On a rainy Sunday afternoon in May, Julius walked to the polling station on Budapester Strasse and cast his vote in the federal elections. The main streets were noisy with lorries, supporters hanging over the sides, throwing pamphlets and jeering at one another like opposing sides at a football match. Squares of discarded paper littered the wet pavements. Flags flapped from tailgates. Amongst the black-white-red stripes of the Second Reich Julius glimpsed the occasional blank black frown of the swastika. The extremist parties were set to do well. The inflation might be over, but most Germans failed to see bankruptcy as a notable improvement.

Luisa had withdrawn her cross-petition. After interminable obstructions and postponements a court date for the divorce hearing had finally been confirmed. In less than a month the court would grant his petition and he would be free of her. The courts would mandate the return of his painting and the future custody of his son. He could begin again. It was weariness, he told himself, the terrible grind of it, that lowered his spirits. He had expected exhilaration.

A truck lurched through a puddle, flinging up an arc of water that hit Julius full on the legs. He gesticulated furiously, pointlessly. The truck roared on, impervious. Julius squelched home. He was exhausted and, though he could hardly bring himself to admit it, afraid. The previous week, he had lunched with Helmut Werner and outlined his proposal for his next book. Werner had nodded politely, but the next morning he received a summons from Otto Metz. They met that evening at his publisher's club.

'Tell me they've made a mistake,' Metz said, gulping whisky and soda. 'Seriously, Ju, Dostoevsky?'

'Absolutely Dostoevsky,' Julius said firmly. He told Metz about Dostoevsky's arrest for revolutionary activities, the execution by firing squad that was commuted to hard labour only as Dostoevsky stood blindfolded in front of the guns, the convulsive fits he suffered ever after. 'You wanted another tortured genius, didn't you? Well, here he is.'

'No, Ju. What we want is another *Vincent*. Do you know why your book was a bestseller? Because, for all the ear-cutting craziness, van Gogh was essentially a child and the public like children. They like van Gogh's paintings. They're cheerful and easy to understand. A field is a field, even if the sky is green and the sun is spinning in circles. But a Russian novel? How many people do you think have ever actually finished a Russian novel? *Crime and Punishment* – the clue is in the title.'

Metz had a dinner and could not stay. He told Julius to come and visit, that Nadine would love to see him. He did not mention Werner's advance, but Julius knew he had not forgotten. If he chose to write the Dostoevsky book Julius would have to pay the money back. The only problem was he no longer had it.

'You mustn't listen to them,' Matthias said. 'What does the money matter in the end? You are a visionary, you must write what springs from your soul,' and the words were a rallying cry, driving Julius onward, but he could not stop the panic rising in him like vomit, the sour terror that he was finished, that he would never write another word.

Back at Meierstrasse Frau Lang fetched him a towel and dry socks and shoes. She wanted him to change out of his wet trousers but he told her not to fuss.

'I'm sorry,' she said. 'I thought it peculiar you hadn't mentioned it, but she said it was all agreed. I put her in the morning room. I didn't know what else to do with her.'

The girl was curled in a chair in front of the fire, her shoes kicked off and her knees pulled up against her chest. She was drawing. Her possessions were strewn across the floor and over the fender stool. On the side table, amidst a scatter of pencil shavings, a half-eaten apple lay discarded, its pale flesh shadowed with brown. When he cleared his throat she twisted round, throwing down her sketchbook and tugging the sleeves of her high-necked sweater down over her hands. Her expression was wary, defensive. She did not stand up.

'Fräulein Eberhardt,' Julius said coldly. 'What a surprise.'

'I should have written, I know, and I was going to, only . . . ' She broke off. 'You said if I was in Berlin. In your letter. I thought – they took my pencils away. I didn't know where else to go.'

'Why are you here at all? Aren't you supposed to be at school?'

'I left.'

'Left or ran away?'

She chewed her thumb and did not answer. Her nails were still a disgrace.

'Does your mother know where you are?' he demanded. When she still did not answer he turned and crossed the room towards the telephone.

'Don't,' she said. 'Not yet. Please?'

'She must be out of her mind with worry.'

'Then she shouldn't have sent me back there. You don't know what it's like, it's like prison. Like a long slow death. I couldn't breathe.' When Julius lifted the receiver she leapt up, tugging his sleeve. 'Don't, please, I beg you. She'll make me go back.'

'Of course she will. What else do you expect her to do? Yes, a Munich number—'

Furiously Fräulein Eberhardt jammed her finger on the cradle, cutting him off.

'You lied to me,' she hissed. 'You said you understood, but you lied.'

'Now listen to me, young lady—'

'No, you listen to me! In *The Making of Art* you wrote about going to see a famous art collection, thousands of paintings, only not one of them was hung, they were just stacked in a warehouse above a railway station with men there whose only job was to hold them up for you to look at, only you didn't look at them, you couldn't because all you could think of was the madness of it, all those treasures hidden away in that silent, suffocated place with trains screaming in and out, and you were so angry, so blindly angry, that all you wanted was to destroy it, to burn it to the ground. You can't write that and then tell me I have to go back, don't you see? That's what it's like for me every day. A part of me dies in that place every single day.'

'Really, child, these histrionics—'

'I was wrong. I should never have come here. I thought – but what does it matter? It was all just words, stupid, empty words.' Digging in her pocket she pulled out a crumpled letter and thrust it at him. His own handwriting. She jabbed at a line. '*You have something. Don't waste it.* You should have been more specific. Don't waste it by expecting anything of me. I write pretty sentences but surely you're not so naïve you believe I mean what I write? All I care about is flogging books and getting fat on the proceeds. With respect, *child*, the rest of it is hardly my concern.' She glowered at him, furious spots of pink flaring in her cheeks, as he burst into laughter. He could not help himself, she caught him exactly.

'Don't you dare laugh at me,' she said.

'I'm not. I'm laughing at myself.'

Unmollified, Fräulein Eberhardt scowled at the fender stool. Then, shoving her feet into her battered ballet slippers, she snatched up her bag and began to stuff things inside. She was half caterpillar, half butterfly, Julius thought as she scrabbled on the floor, caught between cocooned self-involvement and the first damp-winged intimations of sexual power. He wondered how long it would be until she bobbed her hair and bound her chest, until she looked like the other girls in their drop-waisted dresses and their cloche hats and their strings of pearls, their lipsticked mouths all stretched in the same empty O of delight. He supposed it must come, though he could not imagine it, the lipstick or the emptiness.

'Where will you go?' he asked.

'That's none of your business.'

'Your mother will doubtless feel differently. What am I to say to her?'

'You'll think of something,' she said, already halfway to the door. 'Making stuff up is what you do, isn't it?'

Julius picked up her sketchbook from the table. 'You've forgotten this.'

'Keep it. It's all used up anyway.'

'As you wish.'

'You can look at it if you want, I don't mind.'

'Is it any good?'

'You're the critic, aren't you?' She glared at him. Julius regarded her evenly. Fishing his spectacles from his pocket, he opened the sketchbook. The pages were a jumble of drawings and studies: hands and heads, household objects, house flies and beetles. In words strung together like a necklace, A DRAWING IS A LINE GOING FOR A WALK.

Fräulein Eberhardt sidled closer. 'The real stuff's at the back.'

Julius turned to the back of the book. A pen-and-ink portrait of Elvira, harsh lines, a harsh likeness.

'She's getting married again, did you hear?' Fräulein Eberhardt said. 'He's in the government. Hordes of screaming children and the most disgustingly hairy ears. Truly, like he's stuffed them with spiders.'

Julius had heard that Elvira Eberhardt was to remarry. Jacob Vidler was a widower, a distinguished diplomat and a decent man, but Fräulein Eberhardt was right, his ears were disconcertingly hairy. Swallowing his smile, Julius turned the page. Some pencil drawings, a handful of hastily executed watercolours, landscapes mostly, jammed between the pages, more or less successful, more or less ordinary.

The nude took him by surprise. It sprawled over the page, knees angled, back arched and head thrown back, one hand between the legs, the other on the belly. A spent, surrendered body, but one undone by sexual release or simply used and abandoned? It was not clear. The graphic composition drew the observer inside the image, made him complicit, but was he lover or predator, intimate or paying client? The ambiguity was unsettling and unsettlingly erotic. He supposed she must have copied it from somewhere. There was something of Schiele about it, the late work when the Austrian finally abandoned his pose of pornographer, and after all, what finishing school would give its girls the chance to draw like this from life?

And then he saw it. The nude was her. She had drawn herself. Hurriedly he shut the book and put it on the table.

'Well?' she demanded. 'Is it any good?'

'Some of it has – something, yes.'

'You really think so?'

'I do, yes,' Julius conceded. 'You're untutored, of course, but—'

'That's why I'm here. I want to go to art school. Here, in Berlin.'

'And your mother?'

'She'd listen if you told her. We could telephone her now, tell her I'm here, that you think I have something. Something worth something. Will you tell her?'

Her excitement reminded Julius of Matthias, the night that he announced he was opening his own gallery. He sighed. Then he nodded. 'All right. Yes, I'll tell her.'

'Thank you!' she cried, flinging her arms around his neck. Her hair smelled of trains. 'Thank you, thank you, thank you, thank you.'

Julius disentangled himself. 'I can't promise it will make any difference.'

'She'll listen to you, I know she will.' Laughing exultantly, Fräulein Eberhardt turned a wild pirouette. 'I knew you were a good man, Herr Köhler-Schultz. I knew it from the first moment I saw you.'

Elvira Eberhardt was adamant. Art school was out of the question. Emmeline was to complete her education in Switzerland. She asked that Julius arrange for her to take a train to Bern, where a member of the school staff would collect her.

'I should be grateful if, in future, you could desist from encouraging my daughter in such foolishness,' she said coldly. She did not thank him for telephoning. Perhaps, Julius thought as he hung up, Fräulein Eberhardt had been right about her mother all along.

She had no luggage, only her satchel and a dog-eared portfolio. As the taxi driver stowed them in the boot she pleaded with Julius, begging him to change his mind, but he only shrugged. Without her mother's authority there was nothing he could do. She stared at him through the rain-spattered window as the cab pulled away, its red tail lights smeared like paint on the wet tarmac.

An hour later the doorbell rang. A sodden Fräulein Eberhardt stood on the doorstep, her portfolio in her arms, tails of hair plastered across her forehead.

'You can't make me go back there,' she said.

He made her speak to her mother. He could hear her shouting through the wall of his study. When she called him to the telephone he took the receiver reluctantly. Elvira Eberhardt apologised. Her voice was strained. With the elections, she said, there was no possibility that she could be in Berlin before Wednesday. It was an imposition, she knew, but might Emmeline be able to stay with him until then? Startled, Julius reminded her that Luisa was with her parents, that aside from the servants he lived alone, but she only laughed a little too loudly and said something about the old proprieties seeming so silly these days. He could hear the rumble of voices in the background, the clink of glasses.

'Forgive me, I have to go,' she said. 'You'll keep her, then?' and when, against his better judgement, he agreed, she thanked him briskly and hung up.

At breakfast the next morning he found an envelope propped against his coffee cup. Inside he found a sketch of a glowering Frau Lang and, underneath, in heavy capitals, WHAT IS IT NOW? *This is it*, Fräulein Eberhardt had written on the back. *Wish me luck. I shake your hand, EE*

She returned in the late afternoon. Julius told Frau Lang to send her down to his study when she had changed. She would dine with him and Herr Rachmann.

'Changed into what, exactly?' the housekeeper huffed. 'She's not brought a stitch with her, nothing but the clothes on her back and those hardly respectable.'

'Then find her something. There must be something of Luisa's that would do.'

Matthias was in high spirits. 'A mystery woman,' he teased. 'What a dark horse you are, Julius!'

'Please, she's a schoolgirl,' Julius protested. 'And frankly nothing but a nuisance. I'm only helping the child because I feel sorry for her.' He told Matthias that he had spoken to the painter Lovis Corinth, who ran a prestigious private art school for women, and that Corinth had agreed to look at Fräulein Eberhardt's portfolio. 'After that I can send her back to her cold-hearted mother with a clear conscience.'

'Knowing that same cold-hearted mother will never forgive you.'

'There is that consolation,' Julius admitted, and Matthias laughed.

'What's funny?' Fräulein Eberhardt asked.

Julius turned. She stood in the doorway, the evening sun slanting behind her. She wore a coral silk-chiffon dress that Luisa had bought on impulse and never worn. The sunlight lit the fabric like a candle flame, imprinting it with the outline of her slender body. Julius thought of Rembrandt's half-clothed woman bathing in a stream, her chemise hitched up over her thighs, and he felt a reflexive shimmer of desire.

'Fräulein Eberhardt,' he said. 'Come in. Have a drink.'

She stepped into the room, awkward in her borrowed heels, and immediately the spell was broken. She had put on make-up, rouge and powder, bright coral lipstick. The result was lurid, cartoonish. Julius frowned. He had wanted Matthias to see her as he had seen her the first time, bare-footed and bare-faced. He almost sent her back upstairs to wash. Instead he handed her a drink.

'Gin sling all right?' he asked. 'How was your day?'

Fräulein Eberhardt shrugged, twisting the glass in her fingers. 'I'm not sure. Hopefully it was all right.'

'Fingers crossed,' Julius said drily.

'I won't know for sure till they've seen everyone. But they said they liked it.'

'Am I allowed to know what you're talking about?' Matthias interjected.

'The Berlin Academy.' Fräulein Eberhardt gulped her drink. 'That's why I'm here. I had an interview there today.'

Julius blinked. 'You never said you'd applied to the Academy.'

'You never asked.'

There was a silence. Matthias looked from Julius to Fräulein Eberhardt and a smile spread across his face. 'In that case, I think you'd better start at the beginning.'

XII

Matthias could argue again and again that theirs was the side of righteousness, but he did not have to live with the consequences. On the day that the Dix was unveiled in Berlin Julius lunched with Geisheim. Outside the restaurant the road was being dug up. Every few moments the hum of conversation was broken by the angry shriek of hammer drills. They did not talk about Stemler. Perhaps over coffee, Julius thought, but as soon as their plates were cleared Geisheim signalled for the bill.

'I'm sorry, I'm going to have to run. Summons from management.' He signed the chit the waiter brought him and shook his head at Julius. 'Our generation was idiotic enough to believe that the primary purpose of newspapers was to report news. I am now reliably informed that the *Tribüne* is an advertising hoarding. The stories are just there to fill in the gaps.'

'It's not that bad, surely.'

'It's every bit as bad. I've tried to fight it but it's a losing game. Our costs are too high, we don't turn in the profits. If we don't modernise they'll fold us.'

'Modernise how?'

'Younger readers. Younger writers. Less serious analysis and more of what those on high nauseatingly insist on calling zing. Less serious anything. Less art.'

Julius stared at him. 'You're sacking me.'

'I'm telling you how things are. You're the one who's been kicking up a fuss all year. And weren't you just telling me you've no time for the new book? Well then. Perhaps this is the perfect moment to spring your bonds.'

It was Stemler. Julius knew it. He had known it when Munich's Neue Pinakotek withdrew their invitation to write the catalogue for their new exhibition of Impressionists, just as he had known it when the chairman of the most illustrious art prize in Germany suggested that it might be time for both of them to step down. The same chairman had just accepted a seat on the board of the Nationalgalerie.

When Frau Lang greeted him on his return home with the news that a pipe in Julius's bathroom had burst, causing water to come through the morning-room ceiling, he had to fight the impulse to summon the police and lodge a charge against Gustav Stemler for malicious criminal damage.

The water brought down a section of the plaster, smashing a side table and ruining the smaller of the two sofas. When Matthias saw it he whistled. 'It must have taken quite a performance to bring down the house like that,' he joked.

His flippancy infuriated Julius. 'Do you think this is funny?' he snapped, and felt a twinge of remorse as Matthias winced. He was being unfair, he knew it, but the chaos drove him to distraction. With the morning room out of bounds, Fräulein Grüber had moved her desk and the telephone into the hall. All day long the not-so-muffled bell shrilled and the clattering typewriter played a counter-melody to the thump-whine of hammers and saws. There were days when, unable to work, unable even to think, Julius was certain he would lose his mind.

Upstairs, meanwhile, the floors were taken up to repair the pipes. Julius had no choice but to move into Luisa's rooms. Her dressing room was still full of her clothes.

Sometimes, late at night, Julius opened the wardrobes and ran his hand over the soft furs, the brightly coloured silks. Most of them he had chosen himself. He had a good eye and was willing to spend a great deal, almost as much as she would have spent on her own. Luisa adored it at first, their trips to Paris had been among the happiest times they had shared, but, as things soured between them, she accused him of controlling her. He did not want a wife, she said, only a mannequin, a clothes hanger to show off his impeccable taste. Julius had retorted that she should be glad, that it was only because of her beauty that he could forgive her banality, the intolerable emptiness of her head. There was nothing but hate in him by then, hate for the impossible hope she had fired in him, for her failure to heal him, to make him the man he had always hoped to be. Hate for his inability to stop falling, helplessly and hopelessly and again and again, in love with beautiful, intoxicating things. Pitiless and precise, he hurled his pain at her like rocks. It had not occurred to him that she might hate him for precisely the same reasons.

It was evening when the telephone rang. Fräulein Grüber had gone home and Julius sat in his study beside the open window, looking out over the garden. The blaze of the day had burned down to a molten pinkish-gold and the air was sweet with lilac. Only Matthias would call at such an hour. Smiling, Julius rose and went into the hall, picking up the receiver just as Frau Lang opened the door from the kitchen. He waved her away. 'Hello?'

'Ju?'

'Luisa,' he said stupidly. He had the disorienting sense that he had summoned her, that, by thinking of her, he had somehow imagined her into being.

'I hope I didn't disturb you. You weren't still working, were you?'

'Actually I was.'

'I'm sorry. Perhaps I should try again later?'

'What is it you want, Luisa?'

She hesitated. 'I know this is out of the blue, but I have to be in Berlin in a few days' time. I thought we might – I wondered if we could meet.' Her voice was husky, uncertain. *You love me*, she had once said to him in the same voice. A lifetime ago when neither of them had been able to believe their luck.

'Why?' Julius said tersely. 'Will you have the painting?'

'Don't be like that. Half an hour, that's all. We need to talk.'

'Will you bring Konstantin?'

'Konnie? No, of course not.'

'Then the answer's no. There's nothing left to say.'

Another silence.

'Please, Julius. Aren't you tired of us always being our worst selves?'

Julius hesitated. He could feel the downward tug of it like a weight in his chest, the lure of letting go, of finally telling the truth. Then he thought of the empty wall, the empty crib in the nursery, and he shook his head at Luisa's nerve, at his own suggestibility. When, in all the years he had known her, had Luisa ever wanted to make peace? This was not an olive branch. It was her last desperate throw of the dice.

'Talk to your lawyer, Luisa,' he said brusquely. 'I'll see you in court.'

Matthias's apology was half-hearted at best. 'It's not so terrible, surely. Of course if you really can't bear it you could always emigrate. Or I could fake my own death.'

Julius sighed. He knew Matthias intended it as a kindness, a distraction from Luisa, from Geisheim, from the Dix dogfight that refused to die, but, grateful as he was, there was little Julius wanted less than to dine with Fräulein Eberhardt.

'I'm just not sure why you thought of it,' Julius said. 'Why you've been writing to her at all. She isn't your problem.'

'You don't think a girl like her becomes everyone's problem in the end?'

Julius could not deny that Matthias had a point. Fräulein Eberhardt had written to him several times, first to tell him that the Academy had offered her a place and after that seemingly just to let off steam. Chaotic and exuberant, crammed with sketches and sharp asides, her letters reminded Julius of Vincent's letters to Theo, and not only because she always signed off in his style: *I shake your hand, EE.* Like Vincent, she wrote with a blend of acuity and self-absorption. Like Vincent, she seemed incapable of feeling something without saying it. She raged about the dullness of her lessons, the inedible meals, the unbearable tediousness of her classmates.

> We speak the same language and yet I swear I don't understand a word of what they say. Who cares about bloody raccoon coats and Rudolf Valentino? I bite my cheeks to keep myself from screaming & say it over and over: Berlin.

Her fourth letter was a torrent of fury and distress. Her mother had changed her mind. She was forbidden to attend the Academy. Her life was over. Julius thought of his own father's unyielding autocracy, the grim years he wasted studying engineering before he escaped to Berlin, and he was suddenly furious. His letter to

Frau Eberhardt was icily civil and concluded with Schiller: *No emperor has the power to dictate to the heart.* A fifth letter from her daughter arrived two days later. THANK YOU THANK YOU THANK YOU THANK YOU ran across a whole page, the words strung with bunting and balloons. A barrage of fireworks lit the margins.

They release us from this hellhole on Friday and we come straight to Berlin. I'm coming to Berlin! THANK YOU THANK YOU THANK YOU. Elvira says that if I come to any harm she will hold you personally responsible (I hope you're afraid!) but what harm could I possibly come to in BERLIN?! I will never forget this, NEVER. You are my saviour. You have literally SAVED MY LIFE.

'What does she mean, she'll hold me personally responsible?' Julius asked, but Matthias only laughed.

'Now you see why I had to ask her to dinner,' he said. 'She worships the ground you walk on. We have to stick together, your little band of protégés.'

They ate in the dining room, the candle flames like feathers in the fading light. To Julius's relief Matthias was the perfect host, pouring wine, putting Fräulein Eberhardt at her ease. Within an hour they were all on first-name terms. Matthias talked about art, about a new exhibition of paintings at Fleicheim's by the Spanish artist Picasso.

'We should go together,' he said to Emmeline. 'There's no point in asking Julius to come, he considers Picasso a charlatan, but we must do our best to like some things that Julius does not like, don't you agree? We are not entirely his creations, after all.'

He told stories too, stories Julius knew but some too that he had not heard before, of Matthias's years as a dancer, when he called himself Rodrigo Villalba and danced bullfights and ghost stories and unrequited love and the fierce, lonely life of the gaucho on the Argentine pampas.

'And still I've never set a toe in Spain,' he admitted. 'Let alone Argentina.'

Emmeline laughed and drank more wine. Whatever the finishing school had managed to teach her, it was not how to dress for dinner. In her draped velvet jacket and wide-legged silk trousers she looked as though she was wearing her pyjamas. Julius wondered what her mother would say if she could see her, but he had to admit that in the candlelight she and Matthias made a striking pair, her with her hair loose and kohl smudged around her eyes, him with his pale cheeks flushed with wine. Looking at them Julius felt old, suddenly, and excluded, not by them – already they were talking about him, Matthias remembering something Julius had said to him the very first time they met – but by the gulf of years that separated them. The world looked quite different when everything one wanted was still to come.

'Do you still dance?' Emmeline asked Matthias when dinner was almost over. She sat on her chair with her feet tucked up under her like a fakir, her elbows on the table, her chin resting on her clasped hands. Julius wondered if she was not a little drunk.

'I don't perform any more, if that's what you mean,' Matthias said.

'I bet you were wonderful. Was he wonderful, Julius?'

'Sadly I never had the opportunity to see him,' Julius said. 'I wish I had.' He smiled at Matthias, who smiled back, raising his glass in a silent toast.

'Dance for us tonight,' Emmeline said suddenly, untangling her legs. 'In the hall: wouldn't that be something? Under that beautiful chandelier?' Matthias shook his head, amused, but she had already turned to Julius, one hand on his arm. 'Wouldn't that be perfect? Rodrigo Villalba in a special performance just for us? Oh, please, Matthias, say you will.'

'Fräulein Eberhardt, Emmeline, I hardly think ...' Julius protested but Matthias smiled, his head on one side. He looked towards Julius, then back at Emmeline.

'Very well,' he conceded. 'I'll dance. But only if you dance with me.'

Emmeline laughed. 'But that's ridiculous. I can't dance to save my life.'

'Of course you can,' Matthias said. 'Everyone can dance. You just need the right music. Julius, I hate to ask, but since this is a very special occasion, do you suppose we could persuade you to unlock your gramophone?'

Julius glanced at him, startled he would ask, but Matthias only went on smiling at him as though it was a perfectly ordinary request. Perhaps it was. Matthias who knew everything and would never do anything to hurt him. Slowly he rose, gesturing for the others to follow.

Julius had had the drawing-room light switches moved out to the landing when he first took the house. He did not want anything to mar the perfect plainness of the room. He flicked them on. Then, turning the key, he pushed open the double doors. Huge and high-ceilinged, the room was austere, softened only by three sets of French doors opening on to narrow balconies. A pair of enormous mirrors hung on either side of the fireplace, reflecting a pair of simple grey Rietveld sofas, a low glass table. There were no paintings. Instead a row of white plinths displayed sculptures by de Fiori and Maillol. Emmeline stared.

'Julius, my God,' Matthias gasped, laughing in disbelief, and the pleasure tasted sharp and hard in Julius's mouth, like an unripe fruit. He followed as they walked slowly through the room, gazing around them. The gramophone squatted in a corner, its over-wrought marquetry an affront to the spare beauty of the space. A leather box of discs stood beside it. Matthias bent down to look through them, then slipped one from its paper sleeve and placed it on the turntable.

'You're not really going to make me do this, are you?' Emmeline asked. Matthias smiled and lowered the needle. In the empty crackle that followed he held out his hand. Helplessly she took it and he pulled her towards him, sliding her hand into the crook of his elbow, taking her other hand in his.

Chopin's Waltz in C sharp minor, arranged for orchestra. The first of only a handful of records Julius had given to Luisa, back when he wanted her to love what he loved. As the first deli-cate bars spooled from the gramophone's horn, Matthias drew Emmeline close, then as the orchestra took up the melody he began to dance, taking Emmeline with him. He danced with a fluid, effortless grace, the music shaping itself to him and he to it, one completing the other. A sculpture, Julius thought, and he thought of Rodin, his hands caressing the soft flesh of his models, memorising them with his fingers. Matthias danced and in his arms Emmeline softened, her body melting against his until there was no space between them, their bodies moving as one, and, as with Rodin, there was beauty not only in the perfection of form but in the charge of the moment, the raptness of erotic desire.

It startled him when the music stopped. Matthias turned Emmeline in a final sweep to end the dance, but she did not step away from him. Her body seemed hardly hers. Blurred and breathless, she gazed up at him like someone woken from sleep.

'You see?' Matthias said softly. 'You can dance.' Taking her hands, he led her back to the sofa where Julius was sitting. Gently, as though he was giving him a present, he put her hands in

Julius's. Then, cupping their joined hands in both of his, he kissed her gently on the cheek. His hair brushed Julius's face. 'Now all you have to do is to teach Julius.'

There was a dazed silence, as though the dancing had cast a spell over them all, as though somehow it had melted their edges, blurring the three of them into a single being. As though it had reduced the world to this one perfect room.

'I have to go,' Matthias murmured. 'But you two? You should dance.'

He slipped away silently. Emmeline smiled dreamily at Julius, her hands still in his. 'We should dance,' she said.

Her voice was liquid, an invitation. Julius looked at her dark eyes, her white throat, the curve of her breasts beneath the shimmer of velvet, and, discomfited, he rose and crossed the room to the French windows. Outside on the balcony the night air was cool, soft indigo, the moon no more than a sliver of silver. Below him in the darkness the trees drifted, cloudy with blossom. It was very quiet. Then, softly, a single cello began once again to pick out the first chords of Chopin's waltz.

'Van Gogh was right, night is more alive and richly coloured than the day.' Emmeline leaned against the balustrade beside him, her arm brushing his. Then, twisting around, she levered herself up to sit on the curved iron rail.

'Be careful,' he said. 'You'll fall.'

'I won't. Not unless you push me. You're not going to push me, are you?'

'Accidents happen.'

She laughed softly, her fingers playing with the key that hung around her neck. As the music drifted through the open window she curled her bare feet around the balustrade to steady herself and, holding on to the rail with both hands, leaned backwards, tipping back her head to stare up at the stars. Julius's gaze trailed like fingers from her chin to the dent at the base of her throat, along her delicate collarbones to the deep V of pale skin between her breasts. His breath quickened.

"'I dream of painting and then I paint my dreams",' Emmeline murmured. 'Do you think there really are pink stars like van Gogh says?'

'There are when he paints them.'

Her smile deepened. Pulling herself up, she looked at him. Her dark eyes gleamed. Then, with a small push of her hands, she slipped down from the balustrade, her body against his, her hands sliding up to press against his chest. Julius told himself he should step away but he moved closer, inhaling the smoky clove-and-cinnamon scent of her. He had not known he was so full of yearning. He wanted to devour her, to cram her into himself until she filled up the raw hole inside him. His fingers found her neck, pushed up into her hair, his thumbs caressing the line of her jaw. She arched herself against him. In the darkness she was not a child. Bending his head, he kissed her, tentatively at first and then ardently, greedily, his teeth grazing her lips, and as she reached her arms around his neck he crushed her against him, one hand against the slippery silk of her coccyx, the other cupping the back of her skull, until there was no space between them, nothing but the dance and the star-spattered dome of the sky.

XIII

His hands on the mantelpiece, Matthias stared into the empty grate. Julius felt sick. He could not understand it. He thought of the way she had slowly unfastened the buttons of her jacket, her Correggio smile as she slipped it off her shoulders and let it fall. Underneath the jacket she wore nothing at all.

'Perhaps I should go and see her,' he said, dry-mouthed. 'Talk to her.'

'Absolutely not,' Matthias snapped. 'That's the very worst thing you could do. She's very upset. These accusations – if she is serious about contacting your wife's lawyers she could do terrible damage. We have to be very careful.'

Julius sank his head into his hands, his fingers pressing against his closed eyes. He tried to recall a moment when she had resisted him, when she had hesitated, but all he could remember was her abandon, her head thrown back as though he was a god or a ghost, a force she could not see.

'It wasn't like that,' he whispered. 'Why would she say it was like that?'

'She's seventeen, Julius. You're the first man she has ever kissed.'

'She told you that? Then she's lying. Surely you see that she's lying?'

Matthias said nothing and the realisation was like gooseflesh, shrivelling Julius's skin. Matthias did not believe him.

'It's not true,' he insisted. His voice was shrill. 'You have to believe me, I could never – if she had asked me to stop, if she had said anything, I would have stopped, but she didn't. It was what she wanted.'

'She's a child, Julius. How could she possibly know what she wants? Look, it was a telephone call, that's all. She was barely coherent. I've agreed to go and see her later at her hotel, I'll talk to her, all right? In the meantime, she's promised not to do anything stupid.'

He did not turn around. He cannot look at me, Julius thought, and he put his hands over his face so that he would not have to see.

Matthias returned to Meierstrasse the next afternoon. He refused tea, refused even to sit down. His expression was grim. He told Julius that while Emmeline Eberhardt had not yet written to Luisa or her lawyers, she had refused to promise that she would not. There was less than a fortnight till the divorce hearing.

'I don't understand,' Julius said wretchedly. 'Why would she make these kinds of accusations? What can she possibly stand to gain?'

Matthias's face hardened. 'She showed me the bruises, Julius.'

Julius stared at him. 'What bruises?'

'The bruises on her wrists from where you held her down.'

'But that's impossible. I never hurt her – I couldn't. You have to believe me.' When Matthias said nothing Julius grabbed his shoulder, pushing it roughly. 'Jesus, Matthias, why aren't you listening to me? I didn't do it. She's lying, can't you see?'

'Let go of me, Julius,' Matthias said coldly. Immediately Julius dropped his hand, pressed it against his forehead.

'I'm sorry, I – I just can't believe this is happening to me. I mean, bruises? Jesus.' He looked pleadingly at Matthias, who looked away. 'She's making it up, don't you see? I don't know why she is but she's making it up.'

'Right.'

'Don't say it like that. You know me better than anyone, you must know that I could never do something like that. Christ, Matthias, you have to listen to me.'

'No.' Matthias wheeled around, his eyes hard. 'For once, Julius, you have to listen to me. This is what you are going to do. You are going to write to Fräulein Eberhardt and beg her forgiveness—'

'For what?' Julius cried. 'How many times do I have to tell you? I didn't do anything! It was her, she was all over me!'

'For God's sake, shut up and listen. You will beg her forgiveness. You will make her a gift of the van Gogh drawing you keep in your desk drawer, the girl in the jacket. You will insist she keeps it, as a token of both your esteem for her and your profound regret. You will swear never to see her again.'

'Or what, she goes to Luisa's lawyers? That's blackmail, Matthias.'

'No. It's contrition.'

'But that drawing – I can't . . . '

Matthias stared at him stonily, his mouth thin. 'Can't what?'

'It was her,' Julius stammered. 'She started it. She wanted me.'

'So you say. But she says she did not. You want her to tell her story in court?'

Julius leaned dizzily against the back of a chair. He had not thought it was so simple a matter to tip the world off its axis.

'And if I do it you'll help me?' he asked. 'You'll talk to her?'

'I'll help you. But only this way, is that clear? Leave the letter and the drawing with Fräulein Grüber. I'll send someone to collect them this afternoon.'

'You can't stay?'

'I already told you, I have to be somewhere.'

'You'll come back tomorrow, though, won't you? Once you've spoken to her?' Julius could hear the whipped-dog abjectness in his voice but he could not help himself. He could not let Matthias walk away from him like this, as though everything was finished. Matthias shrugged.

'I'll write,' he said.

'If you're busy I can come to you.'

'I won't be in Berlin tomorrow. I'm going away for a while.'

'What do you mean, a while?'

'Two weeks, maybe three. Does it matter?'

Julius stared at him. 'But I thought, with the hearing—'

'Jesus, Julius, it's not my fucking divorce.' The anger was sudden and startling, like something breaking. 'I've got to go.'

'Wait!' Julius stumbled after him into the hall. 'Matthias, wait.'

For one swooping nightmarish moment, before he caught his arm, Julius thought he saw Matthias smile. Then he turned, shaking Julius off, and his eyes were hard.

'I didn't rape her,' Julius said in a choked voice.

Matthias's expression did not soften. 'I looked up to you, Julius. I trusted you. I thought you were the finest, the most principled man I had ever known.'

Julius's shoulders shook. He was weeping. He put his hands over his face, but he could not stop it. He was filled with a terrible certainty that if Matthias walked out now he would take the last of what was good in Julius with him.

'I'm telling the truth,' he whispered. 'I swear it.'

'Just as you'll swear in a court of law when you divorce your wife?'

Julius let his hands fall. Matthias was staring at him, a terrible kind of triumph in his gaze. 'How can I ever believe you now?' he demanded and, turning, he walked out of the house.

XIV

Julius wrote the letter, enclosing the drawing as Matthias had instructed. There was something almost calming in the pain of it. He did not know how it was that Matthias knew about Harald Baeck, or even if he knew; when he tried to recall Matthias's face in that moment he could not summon it, but he knew that this was his punishment, that even though he was innocent of the crimes Emmeline Eberhardt accused him of, he was guilty. When he closed his eyes he saw Baeck's grey face, the shake in his hand as he swallowed his brandy. He gave the letter to Fräulein Grüber and told her she could go home. He waited until he heard her leave. Then he locked the door of his study and got steadily, determinedly drunk.

The next morning when he stumbled downstairs the study was immaculate, all traces of the previous evening wiped away. The whisky decanter was full, the drawers of his desk neatly arranged.

The wall, however, they had not managed to clean. He had wanted colours, had hunted for them frenziedly, tipping drawers out on to the floor, searching for cobalt blue and its opposite orange, for the thick deft line of seasick green that defined the bridge of Vincent's long nose, but in the end he had had to make do with a fountain pen and, when that refused to flow, a stub of charcoal pencil. He had made a poor fist of a likeness. His Vincent was lopsided, his features clumsy and ill-proportioned. The nose was too small and too high. The eyes, by contrast, were much too big, their round irises gleaming pewter where the pencil was thickest, layers of it, over and over. They squinted blankly, unfocused, unseeing. Deranged. The hair and beard were wild scrawls.

At some point he supposed he must have tried to rub it off. He could see the pink streaks of the India rubber where it had smudged the charcoal into smears. Julius stared at the mess he had made and the too-big eyes stared back at him, into him. A mad self-mutilating messiah, a nail piercing his forehead.

Julius closed his eyes. His head was splitting. He could smell the sweetish stink of himself, the sweat sharpened by the stale reek of alcohol. Sinking into a chair he thought of Vincent, exhausted and grim, painting himself for the first time as a madman in defeat. By then there was no hope left. He had fought with all his strength but the illness was stronger than him. The fits would only grow more violent, more frequent. He knew it and it terrified him. He could see the fear when he looked at himself, in his eyes and in his skin, sucked back against the bone, so he painted it, and he painted the courage too because what greater courage was there, to want with all one's heart not to see and still to go on looking?

The next day a letter arrived from Matthias. It was brief and formal. The matter was taken care of. There were only two conditions: that Julius promised never to contact Emmeline again and that he say nothing to Elvira. As far as Emmeline's mother was concerned he was still *in loco parentis*. There was no address, only a postmark on the envelope: Lörrach, a city near the Swiss border.

Julius wrote back to the gallery on Moltkestrasse. He did not know what else to do. He said that he accepted the conditions, that he would be forever grateful to Matthias for what he had done. *I know I am not the man you believed me to be. I will be sorry for that as long as I live. I wish I deserved your forgiveness.*

He did not know if the letter was sent on. Matthias did not reply. The days grew hotter, the nights hotter still. One morning he received a cutting from the *Frankfurter Zeitung* sent anonymously in the post. In the article Walter Ruthenberg expressed his full support for the Dix. *I was wrong*, he wrote. *However hard it is to face, we cannot and must not hide from the truth.* Julius tore it up. That night he lay on the bed that had been Luisa's, the window thrown open to the stifling darkness, and stared up at the ceiling. A tomcat had taken up residence in a nearby garden. All night it howled at the moon, all its desires distilled to a spine-shrivelling high C. In the morning Julius asked Fräulein Grüber to cable Luisa in Munich and tell her he had changed his mind. He would meet her while she was in Berlin.

'The Tiergarten,' he said. 'The boating lake. She'll know.'

He saw her before she saw him. She was wearing a pale green linen coat and a little straw hat that perched above her right ear. She had cut her hair. As he walked towards her she turned, a gloved hand shielding her eyes from the sun. She looked immaculate, plaster-smooth, like a mannequin in a shop window.

'Julius,' she said. 'I'd begun to think you weren't coming.'

Julius forced himself to smile. He knew as well as she did that he was exactly on time. 'You look well,' he said.

'Thank you. You look exhausted. But then you always did work too hard.'

'I'm fine.'

They stood side by side at the water's edge. On the other side of the lake a boy in wire-rimmed spectacles was carrying a magnificent wooden boat. Even with its sails down it was almost as big as he was. Julius thought of the Noah's Ark, Noah and blue-eyed Mrs Noah standing together at the top of the gangplank.

'There's something I have to tell you,' he said.

'What a coincidence. There's something I have to tell you too.'

'I'd rather hoped you would allow me to speak first.'

'As usual, you mean? Well, go on then. I'm all ears.'

'I'm dropping the petition.'

Luisa jerked her head round to stare at him. 'What?'

'The petition, I'm dropping it. It will mean a delay, the hearing will have to be postponed, but I've spoken to Böhm, he'll move things as quickly as he can. If you agree, the process is quite straightforward. We won't even need to be there.'

'You mean you'll plead guilty, you'll accept adultery?'

'It's the simplest way.'

Luisa was silent, looking out over the water.

'I don't understand,' she said at last. Her voice was wary. 'Why now?'

'Because in two weeks it will be too late.'

'I thought you thought you were going to win.'

'I'd rather lose than win that way.'

Luisa laughed disbelievingly. 'Seriously? A conscience, after all this time?'

'Isn't it time one of us had one?'

Luisa did not answer. In the shade of the ice-cream kiosk the boy put his boat on a bench and began carefully to raise the sails.

'Of course there would have to be conditions,' he said.

'What conditions?'

'I want to see Konstantin.'

'On what terms?'

'Alternate Christmases and a month in the summer. Longer if

he wants it, when he's old enough to decide for himself. I want to know him, for him to know me.'

Luisa pursed her lips. Then slowly she nodded. 'Very well.'

'It would have to be in writing. A binding commitment.'

'And the van Gogh?'

'It goes to him. A trust in his name. You won't be able to touch it.'

'You'd give Konnie the van Gogh?'

'I hope he'll decide to keep it, but he can sell it if he wishes, once he's of age. My father's money allowed me to live as I chose. I want my son to have that too.'

Luisa gave a stunned laugh. 'I'm speechless.'

'As for alimony, my current financial situation is – awkward. You would have to consent to limited support, at least for the present.'

He expected her to protest. Instead she nodded. 'All right.'

'If you consent to proceed on those terms, we have an agreement.'

'My goodness.' She laughed again, then shook her head. 'I'm sorry, I shouldn't. It's just – this isn't exactly how I expected things to turn out.'

On the other side of the pond the boy lifted his boat, the sails like white wings against the brilliant green of the trees. Then, kneeling, he set it in the water.

'Just one more thing,' Julius said. He fumbled in his pocket. 'This belongs to Konstantin's ark, it got left behind somehow. Perhaps you could take it back for him.'

Luisa glanced at Mrs Noah without interest and slipped her into her handbag. Then she frowned. 'You're serious about this? It's not some kind of trick?'

'It's not a trick.'

'Only you should know that I've made certain arrangements. Should you consider changing your mind.'

'I'm not going to change my mind.'

'So you say.' She tucked her handbag into the crook of her elbow. 'Still, I think I'll wait to tell Mazur he won't be wanted, just until everything's final.'

'Mazur?'

'Come on, Ju, you can't have forgotten Tarmo Mazur. Tall, Estonian, beautiful eyes. You met him the night of that party, remember, with Harald Baeck? From what I understand you got a pretty good look at him.'

Tarmo Mazur. The other man in Luisa's bed. The one Julius refused to remember.

'That was why I wanted to see you,' Luisa said. 'To tell you about Mazur's decision. Not that it matters now, of course.'

'What decision?'

'He agreed to testify.'

It took a moment for the words to sink in. Julius shook his head. 'That's – that's impossible. The man would have to admit in court that he's a homosexual. Sodomy's a criminal offence, Luisa. He'd get five years. Baeck too.'

'If anything was proven. Which it might not be, given that by then the sole witness would have been exposed as a blackmailing perjurer.' She shrugged blandly. 'Mazur seemed to think it was worth the risk.'

'Worth it for what? What the hell is there in this for him?' He stared at her. 'You wouldn't.'

'It's a painting, Julius, and a creepy one at that. What else is it good for?'

The boat idled in the shallows, its sails slack. The boy watched it. Then, tugging off his shoes, he waded into the water and gave it a push.

'It doesn't matter now anyway,' she said. 'Not any more. I just thought you should know. I wouldn't want you to have second thoughts.'

The anger was ashy in Julius's mouth, its fire burned out. He told Luisa he would have Böhm send the paperwork to her lawyer, and watched as she walked away across the park. He would do as he promised, he would drop the petition and accept the part of the guilty husband, but there was no distinction in it. It was not self-sacrifice but justice. He might be able to fool Konstantin for a while, he was too young to know better, but he would not fool Matthias. He would not fool himself. For all his peacock display of honour he was just the same as her. The boy's boat drifted in the middle of the lake, marooned and out of reach.

XV

Neurasthenia, the doctor called it. Nervous exhaustion as a result of overwork. He prescribed rest and, when Julius was sufficiently recovered, a cure, a month at least in Baden-Baden or the Swiss Alps. At Julius's age, he said sternly, a man could no longer take his strength for granted.

Julius took the sleeping draughts he offered. The sleep was dense, a viscous blackness that sucked him down. A sleep that clung to him even during the short periods of wakefulness, clogging his head, his thoughts so mired in its gluey tar that he did not have the strength to reach them. Night and day blurred. When he woke to find Matthias standing by his bed he closed his eyes again, too woozy even to wonder at the dream that put him there.

'The doctor said no visitors. But I suppose if you don't stay long—'

'I won't. I promise.'

It took all the strength Julius had to open his eyes.

'Hello,' Matthias said softly. 'Thank you, Frau Lang, you've been very kind.'

'I'll be just outside the door. If he needs anything.'

'Thank you.'

The door clicked shut. The faint breeze was sweet with lilacs.

'Julius, listen to me.' Matthias spoke urgently. Something was wrong. A sting of alarm pierced the fog in Julius's head. He tried to nod. 'Oh God, Julius, is this my fault? I'm so sorry, so sorry. I never should have believed her.'

Julius touched his tongue to his lips. His eyelids were made of lead. He raised them with an effort. 'Emmeline?' he managed.

'It was the drawing,' Matthias said, clasping his arm. 'She sent it back, she said she couldn't keep it. It turned out she – it was none of it true. I should have known, I should have trusted you, and instead . . . ' He looked down at Julius, his grey unshaven face on the creased white pillow. 'I'm so very sorry. You needed me and I failed you. Forgive me.'

Shakily Julius put his hand on Matthias's. 'Of course. Always.'

Matthias put his free hand on top of Julius's, squeezing it. There were tears in his eyes. 'Do you believe in miracles? Only I think I do now. While I was away – no, I'm going to do this all wrong if I try and explain. Words, they – they say the wrong things by mistake and in the wrong order. But pictures . . . '

Julius had never seen Matthias so agitated. He watched groggily as the young man hoisted a battered suitcase on to the bed and fumbled with the clasps. Inside was a moth-eaten picnic blanket. Matthias lifted it out, unfolding it to reveal a package wrapped in brown paper.

'Here, let me help you sit up,' he said. His nervousness was contagious. Julius propped himself up on his elbows, letting Matthias arrange the pillows behind his back. When he was propped up Matthias handed Julius his spectacles, then set the package in his lap. A painting, framed from the feel of it, perhaps twenty inches by ten.

'I should have waited, I know, you're not well, Frau Lang tried to stop me, but I couldn't. I couldn't bear it, for you or for me. Ever since I saw it, ever since I started hoping, all I've thought of is you. Of bringing it to you. Sharing it with you.'

'What is it?' The words were clumsy in his mouth.

'I don't know.' Matthias shook his head. 'Not for certain. Perhaps it's nothing. It could be nothing. I've made so many mistakes before. But I want you to know that if it isn't nothing, if it is what I think it is, it's because of you. It found its way to me because of you. If it is what I think it is we – you and I – oh God, Julius, just open it.'

He pushed the package towards Julius, who fumbled with the string. Matthias tugged at it, pulling it free. Under the brown paper there was a layer of yellowed newspaper. Like a children's game, Julius thought. He could not think of the name. The newspaper was in Russian, the Cyrillic script at once exotic and familiar. Since Lenin's death, a second wave of artworks had found their way out of Russia to Berlin, many of them master-pieces unseen in Europe for decades. Julius's heart jumped in his chest. Struggling to sit up straighter, he tore at the paper. Another layer, an old length of white fabric that might once have been a sheet. He could hear Matthias breathing, the rapid rasp of it. He unfolded the sheet.

White noise. A sudden joltingly accelerated heart rate. The medicine did that to him sometimes. He inhaled slowly, deliber-ately, and tried to listen to himself but his head was thick and, instead of a clear note, he heard only a discordant cacophony, as though his mind was playing a dozen different pieces all at once. Closing his eyes he felt the churn in his stomach, a fermented bubble of excitement. Or was it apprehension? He could feel the throb of his pulse in his temples, at the base of his throat. The bed seemed to tilt.

Catching his breath, he opened his eyes and made himself look again at the painting. A still life of almost monastic simplicity. A shallow wooden bowl of bread rolls on a bare table, in composition not unlike the study of potatoes Julius had seen in The Hague before the war, and painted like the potatoes in muddy Flemish browns.

'*I see paintings in the dirtiest corners,*' he had written to Theo from the Borinage. '*And the force that drives me towards them is irresistible.*'

Matthias's hand found Julius's shoulder, his fingers digging into the flesh, then abruptly let go. He kept his face resolutely blank, but Julius could sense the pull of his longing like the draw of a magnet, north to south. He had come back. He knew Julius was innocent and he had come back. They could begin again. He glanced up at Matthias, who gazed back at him silently, his eyes burning, his fists clenched so tightly together that the knuckles shone white, and the love that pierced him was pure and fierce.

He looked back at the painting. He felt clearer suddenly, the queasiness dissipating like an early-morning mist. Yes, one of his, surely one of his. The brushwork crude in places, of course. No meat, no wine, no brilliant colour or play of light. No lightness at all but that would not come till Paris and the transformative influence of the Impressionists. A brusque, unkempt, inelegant painting, its dirty palette unleavened by the copper-and-gold luminosity of later works.

'It's been in Moscow,' Matthias murmured. 'No one has seen it for thirty years.'

His voice was unsteady, hoarse with hope. Julius let his eyes run over the dimples and ridges of the paint. Medication and exhaustion had dulled his instincts. It was his, of course it was. He was there in every brushstroke as he always was, all of his roughness and his rage, and all of his raw faith too. The painting might lack finesse, back then he still had much to learn, but it was a truthful painting all the same, as blunt and plain as the coarse bread it portrayed. A painting that was both a howl against the bitter hardship of the men who worked the earth and a love song to their dignity and courage, their forbearance and humanity.

Leaning closer, Julius saw that on the right side the rim of the wooden bowl was awkwardly executed, the shadow overworked. The flaw touched him deeply. Vincent had sent his work to Theo with instructions to destroy anything he considered a failure. But, though the canvases crowded his apartment, piled on top of wardrobes and under tables and beds until there was barely an inch of space left, Theo had destroyed nothing. He had understood what Julius had always understood, that the heaviness, the clumsy doggedness of some of his early work was as much a part of the man as the frenzies of lyricism that possessed him in Arles. That the true nature of his brother's genius lay not in the paintings themselves, which sometimes failed, but in his vision, that, whatever he painted, successful or otherwise, van Gogh only ever painted himself, the stroke-by-stroke portrait of his trial-and-error soul.

Julius took a long slow breath in, holding the certainty tight inside him, letting it harden. And, as his heartbeat steadied, he felt it, the faint familiar warmth along the underside of his ribs. A flawed painting, certainly, marred by haste and inexperience, but by God it was gloriously, violently alive.

'Yes,' he said. 'My God, yes.'

Matthias gasped, sagging against the bed as though the news had knocked all the strength from him. 'You're sure,' he said, his voice choked. 'It isn't signed.'

'Most of the Nuenen work wasn't.'

'But he has been copied, hasn't he? His friends in Paris, other artists – I've heard some of the copies are good.'

'That may be so. But this is not a copy.'

'You're sure.'

'I'm absolutely sure,' Julius said and the joy of it broke something open inside him, flooding him with peace.

Matthias put his hands over his face. Then, reaching out, he took Julius's hand. They stood like that for a long time, or perhaps it was only a few moments. Julius felt the throb of his pulse beneath his fingernails. Then Matthias pulled away.

'There are more,' he said. 'Lots more,' and his laugh was high and wild.

'My God.'

'Yes.'

'In Moscow?'

'In Switzerland.'

'How many?'

'Six, seven? Possibly more. I don't even know.'

'But where do they come from? Who owns them?'

'Everything? It's a long story.'

The sun was setting, a blaze of coral pink above the trees. Matthias switched on the bedside lamp. In the soft light the painting had a glorious simplicity, the gold frame casting its warmth over the humble table just as Vincent had known it would. Julius smiled and it was as though they stood together, breathless, at the crest of a hill, the future unrolling like a landscape towards the blue of the horizon.

'Go on,' he said.

EMMELINE

Berlin 1927

I

Perhaps it was the airlessness, the cram of people and cigarette smoke. Perhaps it was the cognac or the vodka or the flashing coloured lights or the fact that Irina's mouth tasted faintly but distinctly of pickled herring. Whatever it was, the nausea burst inside her like a firework, hot streaks of ice shooting through her so that she barely had time to twist her face away before the vomit was in her throat, her mouth. Her body juddered violently as she clutched the edge of the banquette, letting the sour gush of it splatter into the ice bucket in its silver stand. For a moment Irina's hand hesitated between her thighs, the tips of her fingers brushing the skin at the top of her stocking. Then, with a sharp turn of her wrist like pulling a tooth, she extracted it.

'For fuck's sake,' Irina snapped. Her German was idiosyncratic, a mishmash of idiom and slang, but she always swore in Russian. German curses were like the German people, she said, stolid and lacking in flair. In Russian the words threw anger to the ground and stamped on its face. Irina was not afraid of anger. Her rages had a grandeur to them, a pure and magnificent violence like an avalanche or a tidal wave. Unlike Emmeline, Irina never wondered what to feel.

Slumping against the banquette Emmeline wiped her mouth with the back of her hand and closed her eyes. Her legs were trembling. One of the straps of her dress had slipped from her shoulder but she did not pull it up. She sat very still, floating on an emptiness that was almost euphoric. The trumpets and the saxophones and the low thump-thump of the double bass washed in and out and over her, their syncopated rhythms distilled to a low roar, like the sound of the sea. She could feel the sticky prickle of the banquette through her stockings, against her bare shoulders. I'm in a train, she thought, leaning her head against the upholstery, a train that will take me far away, and she could almost hear the shriek of it, the rattle of the wheels.

Irina had not wanted to come. She liked the working-class dives in the north of the city where the tomboyish girls turned up in their Sunday best, all stiff collars and ties, and someone banged out tunes on an upright piano. Emmeline thought she was mad. Those places were full of salesgirls and typists, tired dumpy-looking girls with darned stockings who worried about politics and wrote down every pfennig they spent in little notebooks. What was sexy about that? At Zanzibar, the windows were blacked out and the sign on the door read *CLOSED FOR PRIVATE PARTY*, and downstairs girls in dinner jackets and see-through dresses kissed luxuriously as Lola the six-foot proprietress sang husky French love songs and drank brandy from a champagne saucer. Lola was actually a Polish refugee called Ludmilla who had fled her village when the communists tried to burn it down, but she never talked about that. At Zanzibar no one was the person they were by daylight.

Emmeline could feel the nausea rising in her again. Swallowing carefully, she opened her eyes. Irina leaned against the edge of the table. She had taken off her dinner jacket. Her pale silk camisole emphasised the narrowness of her back, the sharp jut of her shoulder blades. She drew on her cigarette and tipped her head back, a ribbon of smoke unspooling from her lips. Emmeline knew that other women were looking. There was something about Irina, not just her beauty but her careless defiance, as though it had nothing to do with her. Men always stared at her mouth, her full red mouth with its exaggerated bow, like a fruit about to burst, they panted at the promise of it, their tongues out like dogs, but then men were pitifully simple machines, only three moving parts according to her friend Anton, and he had devoted his whole life to the subject. A man would never notice the whorl of a girl's ears, the heart-breaking arch of her eyebrows. Irina was maddening, impossible, but she had the sexiest eyebrows Emmeline had ever seen.

She was going to be sick again. Pins of sweat pushed up through the powder on her forehead, her upper lip. She tried to breathe lightly, sipping the thick, used-up air, but she could still taste it at the back of her throat, the stale clog of cigarette smoke and face powder and perspiration and the greasy dust of the banquette. Fighting the urge to gag she sloshed a shot of vodka into the glass in front of her, knocking it back in one swallow. *Zhizinnia voda*, Irina called it, the water of life. The straw-scented hit of it like hot wires through her chest, behind her eyeballs. The holy drink, that was the other name for it. Courage before battle and afterwards an anaesthetic, a disinfectant, a healer of wounds. As the shock of it cooled, she poured another and gulped it down. In Russia in the Middle Ages, Irina said, vodka was used to make gunpowder. Emmeline could taste the cordite on her tongue.

With the third shot the swirl in her stomach gave way to a steady warmth. She felt a little better and then, abruptly, exultant. Suddenly all she wanted to do was dance, to slide herself in among the bodies on the tiny dance floor and move with them, against them, their bare flesh kissing hers. She slid to the edge of the banquette, her dress riding up further around her thighs, showing the tops of her stockings. A group of men and women in evening dress were sitting at a table across the dance floor. One of the men was watching her. There were always men like him in places like this, tourists there for the show. His companion said something to him and he nodded and sipped his drink, but he did not look away. His eyes were dark and greedy over the rim of his glass.

Emmeline knew he was watching as she slid out from the banquette. She twined her arms around Irina's neck, pressing herself hard against her, her hands caressing her waist, the curve of her buttocks. The thought of the man's excitement excited her.

'Dance with me,' she murmured, her mouth against Irina's ear, but Irina only frowned and pushed her away.

'You're drunk.'

'Of course I'm drunk. I'm having fun. You should try it.' She kissed Irina hard on the mouth, then threw her head back and began to sway. In the crush a red-haired girl was dancing. Her sequinned dress was cut away at the back almost to her buttocks and when, languidly, Emmeline ran her fingers down the crest of her spine, she turned, laughing, and slid her arms around Emmeline's neck. They kissed, their tongues coiling, before the girl pulled away. She was still laughing. Emmeline laughed too and turned back to Irina, the music moving through her body like a wave.

'Come on, Ira,' she slurred, tugging at her hand. 'Don't be a drag all your life.'

'For fuck's sake,' Irina said again, only this time it was not a boot stamping on a face but a glass wall between them, impervious and ice cold. Crushing the stub of her cigarette beneath her heel, she pushed away into the crowd.

2

Emmeline looked at the invitation card. Dove grey and expensively engraved, it was as thick as a slate and almost as heavy. *To celebrate the opening of the Rachmann Gallery, Viktoriastrasse, 13.* On Viktoriastrasse chauffeurs kept their own chauffeurs and even the trees were a more expensive shade of green.

'What do you mean, maybe?' Anton protested. 'I thought you adored van Gogh.'

'I did. I do.'

'Then come. You'll like it. There'll be champagne and scores of bankers just aching to drape you in diamonds. Seriously, darling, just look at this dump. Isn't it time you snared yourself a chic little pied-à-terre on Ku'damm?'

Emmeline glanced around at the stained and peeling wallpaper, the window she stuffed with newspaper to keep out the draughts. 'I like it here.'

'You don't. You couldn't.'

'Anyway, I told you, I'm finished with men.'

'Nonsense,' Anton said, propping his feet on the arm of the broken-down sofa and stretching out. 'You're a magpie. You'll take anything as long as it glitters. Still, every magpie needs a nest, and this would be business, not pleasure. The older and vainer and more preposterous the better.'

An exhibition of van Gogh's drawings and aquarelles. The invitation was edged in pewter. 'You make it sound irresistible.'

'Well, I know you. It's not as though you don't have form.'

'Ha bloody ha.' She swatted him half-heartedly with the invitation, then dropped it on his stomach. Laughing, Anton picked it up.

'Go on, say you'll come,' he coaxed. 'He's your old friend, you can introduce us.'

'He probably won't remember me. I haven't seen him for years.'

Not since the morning he had come to plead with her to stay away from Julius Köhler-Schultz. She remembered it distinctly, his distress, the way he stared at his feet and shook his head and said that Julius was a wonderful man but weak, so terribly weak, that he had already made so many mistakes, hurt so many people. Emmeline had not understood what he was talking about. It was only when Matthias said something about a secret fiancée that she realised he was warning her off, that Julius was genuinely afraid that after one faintly regrettable fuck she would be flexing her claws and dreaming of happily ever after.

'How can Julius be engaged?' she asked Matthias. 'Isn't he still married?'

'He's getting divorced. They'll marry then. I'm sorry.'

'What is there to be sorry for?' She laughed, rolling her eyes. 'Seriously, you have to stop looking as though someone died. We drank too much and screwed, that's all. It happens. Sometimes it's even fun.'

She thought Matthias would smile then, but he only grew more agitated. 'You don't understand,' he said. 'I'm asking you to stay away from him.'

'But that's ridiculous. So he's engaged, so what? Does he really think I'm going to hunt her down and tell her everything? I'm hoping to forget it myself.'

'It's not that simple.' Matthias grimaced, raking a hand through his hair. 'Look, I'm sorry, I wish there was an easier way to say this, but he never wants to see you again. He's asked that you don't try to write to him or telephone.'

Emmeline gaped. 'But he can't do that. What about me, my future? Elvira only agreed to art school because he said he'd act as my guardian. If he refuses now I'll lose everything.'

'Perhaps you should have thought of that before you dropped your knickers.'

'Perhaps Julius shouldn't be such a fucking hypocrite,' she retorted furiously. 'It was one night, Matthias, one stupid night. So he regrets it, so what? That's no reason for him to ruin my life.'

Matthias clenched his fists. 'Except she's pregnant.'

'And?'

'For God's sake, don't you see? He's terrified. If she was to find out about you, if there was even a possibility – Julius has already lost one child. To lose another, it would break him.'

She argued. It was only when Matthias produced the van Gogh drawing that she understood that it was already decided, that Julius would never change his mind. Van Gogh was his checkmate, there were no moves left after that. So she agreed. She would go back to Munich and she would never contact Julius again. Her only condition was that Julius did not tell Elvira, that when Emmeline returned to the Academy he continued to pretend that he was acting *in loco parentis*. As for the drawing, she refused to accept it. Julius, she said tartly, could save his pieces of silver for his luckless fiancée.

Afterwards the drawing was the only part she regretted. She could still summon every detail of it, the young girl in the striped jacket with the faraway expression and the sprig of flowers in her lap. *La Mousmé*, van Gogh had called her, the Japanese girl; he had painted her in Arles, Emmeline had looked her up. Julius's drawing must have been a preparatory sketch, though it hardly looked like one. She should have kept it. Instead she had given it back to Matthias. If you ever need anything, anything at all, he said as he put it back into his briefcase, and he handed her his card. After he left she tore it in half and dropped the pieces into the wastepaper basket.

That was the last time she had seen him, though like everyone else she read about him in the newspapers. His van Goghs had made him a celebrity, the impoverished blacksmith's son from Düsseldorf who had turned an impoverished Dutch madman into the most expensive artist in German history. That the paintings had been smuggled out of revolutionary Russia, the property of a mysterious Russian prince-patron whose name Rachmann refused to divulge, only added more delicious intrigue to the tale. The newspapers gobbled it up with a spoon.

'All right,' Emmeline said to Anton. 'I'll come. But only if you swear you won't abandon me the moment we get there like you always do.'

'I've never done that. Well, maybe once or twice, but only in extremis. When my entire future happiness is at stake.'

'Your entire future happiness until you wake up and can't remember his name.'

'Hark at you,' Anton retorted. 'One on-again-off-again girlfriend and you're the patron saint of monogamy?'

There was a silence.

'I need a drink,' Emmeline said. The vodka was Irina's, bought from the Russian shop on the corner. Irina always pretended to be German when she went in there, she said it was the only way to avoid the hand-clutching, the incontinent reminiscences.

Emmeline rinsed two mugs and poured them both a large slug.

Before Irina the only Russian women she knew were Chekhov's, bolt upright in their corsets and aching for Moscow. Irina never ached for Moscow. She said Russia would never change, that however many times the Bolshevists turned the country upside down and shook it, it would cling to its history like a baby monkey clinging to its dead mother. There were far too many Russians for Irina in Berlin. She wanted to go to America.

Anton peered into his mug, wrinkling his nose, then downed the vodka in a single gulp. 'Where is the *Kuckuck*, anyway?' he asked. The cuckoo, his nickname for Irina from the start. She's the kind of girl who lays her eggs in other birds' nests, he said with a shrug when Emmeline asked why, but the provocation was plain, the German idiom old-fashioned but still familiar. *Weiss der Kuckuck!* God only knows.

'She's out,' she said crisply. 'What do you care anyway?'

'I care. You like her, even if I don't.' He held out his mug and Emmeline sloshed more vodka into it. She had heard nothing from Irina since their last terrible argument, but the flat was still scattered with her things: a scarlet woollen scarf by the bed, an open book face down beside the sofa, a splay-bristled toothbrush in a jam jar by the kitchen sink. Emmeline had left them where they were. That way it was easy to pretend she was coming back, that any moment the bell would ring and Irina would be there, smelling as she always did of patchouli and cigarette smoke, and they would get drunk and go to bed and for a few hours, as darkness narrowed the world to the width of a sagging bed, Emmeline would know exactly who she was.

It had to be Irina who came back, though. Emmeline would not be the first to crack.

She had known it would be sumptuous, it was Viktoriastrasse after all, but the palazzo splendour of the Rachmann Gallery still took

Emmeline by surprise. The rooms were huge and high-ceilinged, papered in a discreet pewter, one leading to another through a series of archways so that the space appeared to go on for ever. As she followed Anton through the crowd the carpet yielded beneath her feet like moss, absorbing the babble and jostle of the guests so that, despite the crush, the overall impression was one of expensive hush. Against the smooth dark gleam of the walls, the drawings seemed to float, picked out in soft circles of light.

Primed by Anton, Emmeline had expected bankers and businessmen. Instead the party was a roll call of the Berlin art establishment. She saw Hugo von Habermann and the sculptor Fritz Klimsch and Max Liebermann who was also president of the Academy. It was only when you saw them all together that you realised how antique most of them were. In his speech at Emmeline's graduation Liebermann had made a point of declaring himself a modernist. He did not seem to realise that his modernism was already ancient history.

Girls in grey silk offered trays of champagne. She took a glass. Beside her Anton talked to a man she did not recognise. In the years since art school Anton had scraped together a living as an assistant in a small avant-garde gallery on Friedrichstrasse but he meant to be famous and he made it his business to know everyone. He had loathed the Academy, loathed the classical teaching technique, the relentless copying of Old Masters, hundreds of them, over and over again. He said the professors were relics from the Middle Ages, that their solitary aim was to stifle their students' creativity. Anton thought drawing was dead. He spent his time in the darkroom, splicing images, inverting negatives, manipulating the developing process so that some parts of the photograph were deliberately obscured or damaged. He said that truth lived in the spaces that technology opened in the imagination. The pictures he made were stark, off-kilter, stripped of sense or context.

Emmeline thought some of them were beautiful, but she did not know what they meant.

At least Anton was making art. Since the Academy Emmeline had not completed a single large work. Half-finished canvases crowded the apartment, their faces to the wall, each one differently and disastrously derivative, a failure of courage and imagination. She tried new subjects, fresh compositions, but each time the work of other, better artists forced its way up through the paint, burning off the tentative haze of her own ideas like the harsh summer sun.

'Munich and Switzerland and the Berlin Academy and you wonder why you have nothing to say?' Anton said. 'You need to live.'

So she lived. She took a job as an illustrator at a fashion magazine, part time and badly paid, and she drank too much and ate too little and went to bed with people she did not know, both men and women, and she held it all close, the hunger and the hilarity and the humiliations and the hangovers, because an artist was the sum of her experiences and how could great art be forged without great heat, in the fire of a life lived without limits?

It felt strange to be at a party without Irina. Emmeline had grown accustomed to the way people turned to stare at the two of them hand in hand, the double jolt of shock and admiration. Alone, she felt smaller, less visible. She tried to squeeze through the crowd towards the drawings but the crush was too dense, it was impossible to move. A man knocked her elbow, slopping champagne down her dress. He did not apologise. Fat and sleek, he looked like a seal in a wing collar.

'Good evening, ladies and gentlemen, and welcome to the Rachmann Gallery.'

An exquisitely tailored Matthias smiled down from a dais at

the end of the room, his voice sliding out of the walls and from underneath the cornices, unrolling like silk. As he embarked on a laundry list of thank yous, Emmeline let her gaze wander around the room, over an actress she recognised and the artist Emil Nolde to a tall figure with a shock of thick grey hair. Julius Köhler-Schultz, she realised with surprise. The grey was new. A diminutive woman stood beside him, her hand in the crook of his arm. So that was the second Frau Köhler-Schultz. Elvira had written to tell her about the wedding, before she stopped writing altogether. Emmeline had been startled, it was two years by then since Matthias warned her off and she had assumed him long married already. Her mother had not mentioned a child.

On the stage Matthias held his hands out to the crowd. 'Van Gogh himself believed that drawing was "the root of everything". Even in the wildest ecstasies of painting, he stayed true to the line. May we all learn from this extraordinary artist. May we all stay true to the line.'

Matthias moved through the room like a medieval king, magnificent and blithe, his long fingers lightly touching sleeves and shoulders as the crowd parted to make way for him. Slipping away from him and from the Köhler-Schultzes, Emmeline took refuge in the rearmost room. In one corner a peasant woman gazed impassively from beneath her hood, her dark eyes quiet with despair. Emmeline had not brought her sketchbook but she rummaged an old envelope from her bag, a stub of pencil. She drew quickly, with firm strokes.

'Impressive,' a man said, peering over her shoulder.

Emmeline folded the envelope. 'It's nothing. I see better when I draw, that's all.'

The man nodded and proffered an open cigarette case. He was dark, powerfully built, his neck encased in a stiff collar a size too small. When Emmeline shook her head he extracted one for himself and lit it, inhaling deeply as he studied the peasant woman. The tip of the cigarette crackled.

'Cantankerous old crone, isn't she?' Emmeline was silent, willing him to go away. Though the lines were mainly pen-and-ink, van Gogh had used a pencil for the fretwork of wrinkles on the woman's cheeks. The effect was oddly tender.

'Be careful what you wish for, isn't that the old curse?' the man said. 'Better a life of Nuenen mud and potato-eaters than the lap of luxury with one of this lot.'

Emmeline blinked at him, surprised. He did not look like a man who would know about van Gogh. 'I thought they weren't for sale,' she said.

'Then you plainly don't belong here. In this world everything's for sale. The artists most of all.'

The intensity of his gaze unsettled her, the heat of it, like photographic lights. 'So what about you?' she asked lightly. 'Do you belong here?'

The man shrugged, exhaling a slow streak of smoke. His cigarette between his lips, his eyes on hers, he tugged his bow tie undone, then twisting the stud from his collar, pulled it off and jammed it in his pocket. As Emmeline laughed he leaned towards her, his arm brushing hers.

'It's van Gogh who doesn't belong here. He would have hated this circus,' he said softly, so close she could smell the musky scent of his skin under the smoke. 'Come on, let's get out of here.'

'But I've hardly seen anything.'

'Then come back. Tell Matthias I sent you.'

'How can I do that? I don't know who you are.'

'Come with me and I'll tell you. There's a place near here where we can get a proper drink. You'll like it.' Taking a last drag he dropped the butt of his cigarette, grinding it into the carpet. His hand was on the small of her back, warm and certain, she could feel the throb of blood through her skin where it pressed against her. She wondered if he could feel it too.

Matthias Rachmann stepped in front of her. She glimpsed the fleeting shadow of a look between the two men before he smiled at her. 'Emmeline Eberhardt, my goodness, what an unexpected pleasure. How long has it been, three years, four?'

'Something like that.'

'Well, you look radiant. No wonder my brother has been monopolising you. Gregor, would you mind?'

Gregor shrugged, crossing his arms. As Matthias steered her away, Emmeline thought of the cigarette ground out into the silk carpet. She wondered how long Gregor Rachmann would wait before he attempted to reclaim her, whether she would consent to be reclaimed. She smiled without enthusiasm as Matthias introduced her to a man with a receding hairline.

'Herr de Vries has devoted the last decade to putting together the first *catalogue raisonné* of van Gogh's work,' Matthias said. 'A comprehensive list of every work van Gogh ever made. Hercules would have baulked, but this man has pulled it off.'

He turned, grinning, as a bearded man clapped him on the shoulder. 'Do you know Paul Gachet?' he asked Emmeline. 'His father was van Gogh's doctor in Auvers, several of the drawings here are from his collection.'

Paul Gachet nodded without interest at Emmeline and, turning to de Vries, launched into a stream of French. Another man sidled up beside Matthias and pumped his hand before drawing him into a group of women who laughed brightly, showing their teeth. The party was beginning to break up, waitresses moving through the rooms with trays of dirty glasses. Emmeline could not see Gregor Rachmann. In a corner a girl in a black dress scribbled frantically in a notebook, one foot twisted out as though her shoe pinched.

There was something familiar about her, though Emmeline could not think why. Perhaps she was one of the hundreds of writers on the dozens of magazines in her building. Her shoes were cherry red with a red-and-gold T-strap and a pattern of three gold leaves on the toe. Somewhere in Berlin, Irina was talking, drinking, laughing. Snatching a half-drunk glass of champagne from a passing tray, Emmeline drained it in a single swallow.

3

There was something reassuring about drawing for money, and not just because she was good at it. Everyone in the illustration department at *Zuerst* magazine was an artist-in-waiting, just as all the writers in the room next door were poets and novelists and playwrights, whether they had written something or not. It was not just a matter of paying the rent. It was the way the world worked nowadays. They talked all the time about Grosz, now a world-famous artist who had drawn for magazines before the war, about Brecht who had had a hit play and still wrote advertising copy and the cover notes for gramophone records, and they curved their lips, their smiles camera-ready, because someone was always getting famous and next time it might just be them.

Emmeline drew for the advertisement pages. The advertisements were commissioned by companies who paid the magazine to promote their products and the magazine had a strict system for how this was done. On her first day Emmeline was given a manual that ran to nearly twenty pages. Every product, from clothes to face powder, was modelled by the same stylised female figure.

They called her the *Zuerst* girl. The *Zuerst* girl changed her hairstyle and her outfits – sports clothes mostly, the readers of *Zuerst* were young and energetic – but the girl herself never changed. She stood always in precisely the same pose, one leg slightly in front of the other, her head turned and her right hand raised, her features so simply realised it was as though she hardly had a face at all. Sometimes there were six of her on the same page, sometimes only two, but week after week Emmeline drew her, again and again and again, her little finger curling away from her raised hand always at precisely the same angle, distinguished only by her PrimaDonna brassiere or her Völkl ski suit or her chic silk pyjamas from the new line at the KaDeWe department store on Tauentzienstrasse.

Page after page, dozens of her, knees bent like a chorus line, ready to kick.

Emmeline was fumbling in her handbag for her door key when she heard voices coming from one of the upper floors. A door banged. Footsteps clattered in the stairwell behind her. She did not turn round. It had been a long day and no one expected neighbourliness in a building like this. Her hands were so cold she could not feel her fingers. She groped again in the bottom of her bag, sifting through used tram tickets and jumbled change, but the light was out again on the landing, she could not see anything. With a growl of irritation, she squatted and upended the bag on the concrete floor. Her compact skittered to the wall. No key.

'Is everything all right?'

Emmeline turned, scrabbling her things back into her bag. The girl on the stairs was her age, maybe younger. She wore a man's overcoat and a battered felt hat pulled down over her ears. 'It's just, if it's your key, you might want to look inside the lining? Mine slips in there sometimes, the seams wear through and if there's a hole . . . ' The girl shrugged, twisting her body so that her weight was all on one leg, and suddenly Emmeline remembered. The girl at Matthias's party. She lived in one of the upstairs flats. Sometimes Emmeline saw her crossing the road on her way to the tram in the mornings.

'You,' she said. 'Of course.' The cherry-red shoes, that was what had thrown her. Why would someone with shoes like that live somewhere like this?

The girl blinked at her, confused. 'I'm sorry?'

'It was you, at the party the other night, the Rachmann Gallery opening. I saw you there.'

'Did you? I didn't see you.'

'There were a lot of people.'

'Quite something, wasn't it? The paper gave it a whole page, they never do that.'

Emmeline had seen the newspapers. They had declared the exhibition a landmark show and Rachmann's gallery a salon of the first rank. 'You write about art?'

'I wish. I work on the social column. For now.'

'Sex and intrigue.'

'Absolutely never. Look, I'm sorry, I have to go. I hope you find your key.'

'Me too.'

'I'm Dora, by the way.'

'Emmeline.'

'Glad to meet you, Emmeline.' She flashed a grin over her shoulder as she clattered away down the stairs. Emmeline hesitated. Then, sliding her hand inside her bag, she felt along the seams of the lining until she touched a hard, flat shape. Her key.

'Thank you,' she murmured and downstairs the front door banged, as though in answer.

*

Emmeline waited for something to happen, but nothing did. There was no word from Irina, no word either from Gregor Rachmann. She was not sure if she wanted him to find her, but it irked her that he might not even try. She went to work and came home again. She ate boiled eggs and sometimes sausage she bought from the stand near the office. At night the *Zuerst* girls bent their knees and stared blankly into the darkness, replicating themselves inside Emmeline's head like cut-out paper dolls.

One evening she met Anton for a drink at a new bar that had just opened on the Kurfürstendamm. The bar was crowded: young men with slicked-back hair, sharp-faced girls in see-through dresses. Anton brought his latest boyfriend, Kurt, who designed the window displays for KaDeWe. Kurt told Emmeline that shop windows were the modern equivalent of frescos in Renaissance churches and that KaDeWe was the Sistine Chapel of department stores. Emmeline bit back her laughter and tried to catch Anton's eye but he only gazed at Kurt, idiotic with admiration, so she left early and went to Zanzibar, where she drank gin and kissed a girl in a backless dress made of embroidered Chinese silk. She did not ask her name. She knew as soon as the girl held out her hand for a cigarette, her manicured fingers parted just so, that she was the *Zuerst* girl, impeccably attired for a future that would never come.

On Sunday morning she bumped into Dora lugging groceries up the concrete stairs. She looked tired. She told Emmeline her grandmother had been ill.

'She lives in Berlin, your grandmother?'

Dora looked surprised. 'She lives here in this building. We live together.'

She asked Emmeline up for a cup of coffee, but Emmeline said she had to go out. She had no intention of wasting her precious day off on an ailing old lady.

'Of course,' Dora said. 'Another time.'

Emmeline went back into her flat. It was very cold. In the tiny kitchen she lit the gas ring, leaning back as it burst into a sudden blue chrysanthemum of flame. She held her hands over it and then her face, savouring the scorch of it against her skin. Her grandmothers had both died when she was small. She remembered them only from photographs, her father's mother little and sweet-faced, her mother's stiff as a waxwork in black bombazine. When she died Elvira had a lock of her mother's hair made up into a brooch, its intricate weave edged with little pearls. Emmeline had liked the shuddering feeling it gave her to touch it, the jolt of fascination and disgust.

Filling the kettle, she set it on the ring. It was nearly two years since she had seen her mother, her last year at the Academy. Elvira and Jacob had come to Berlin and, because it was Emmeline's birthday and there was a ten o'clock curfew at her boarding house, they took a second room at the Adlon for her.

At dinner Emmeline drank too much. It was the only way she could endure it. Naturally she and her mother argued. They were very good at it by then, the themes refined: the unsuitability of the artistic life, the degeneracy of Berlin, Emmeline's rapidly increasing age and declining marriageability. Ingratitude and lack of respect. Afterwards, when Emmeline said she was going to bed, Elvira followed her up to her room, her face stretched tight with fury, demanding to know what was wrong with her, a girl who had been given every privilege and never wanted for anything. The clichés were counted out: she was a mortification, a disgrace, she had embarrassed Jacob, humiliated Elvira, degraded herself. Elvira was ashamed she was her daughter.

Emmeline waited until Elvira had finished. Then she went back downstairs.

He was twice her age, and handsome in a much-handled way.

He said he was in Berlin on business. She said her name was Käthe. They danced a little and drank a good deal. It was bad luck that, unable to sleep, Elvira took an early-morning walk, returning to her room at precisely the moment he stumbled out of Emmeline's. The hefty bill from the Palm Bar did nothing to improve matters. Elvira and Jacob went back to Munich. The next day a letter arrived from her mother. It was plain, Elvira wrote, that Emmeline had not the scantest respect for her or for Jacob. She could only assume that she had no need of their money either. Emmeline would receive her allowance for the rest of the month. After that she would have to fend for herself.

Through the grimy slice of window Emmeline could see the fat woman who lived on the other side of the courtyard pegging out laundry on her tiny balcony. Her hands were very small, a child's hands, plump and red. When she had hung up all the wet clothes she stood staring into the distance, her heavy arms clasped against her stomach, while beside her the wind fattened the cups of her enormous brassiere, lifting it on its thick elastic straps, and her grey-pink girdle danced.

Reaching for a pencil, Emmeline began to draw. When the kettle shrieked, jolting her out of herself, she looked at the paper. She had wanted to capture the woman's tenacity, the ancient, pagan heaviness of her, but all she had made was pastiche, modern misery in the classical style. Not pathos but satire, a cheap cartoon. Ripping out the page impatiently, she balled it up and threw it at the wall. The sketchbook fell to the floor, scattering its stuffed-in cargo of postcards and cuttings and loose sketches.

A folded envelope caught her eye. Van Gogh's peasant woman in her hood. Without her allowance Elvira had presumed she would be forced to return to Munich, her tail between her legs. And she would have, had she not received a letter from Jacob in which he offered to continue to support her on two conditions.

One, that you never tell your mother of our arrangement, he wrote, *and two, that you take responsibility for your talent and your own unhappiness. Your anger is powerful, Emmeline, but it is not a strength. The damage it inflicts is mostly to yourself. There are few lonelier places than in the embrace of a stranger.*

Emmeline had no qualms about taking his money – a difficult stepdaughter in Berlin was preferable to a difficult stepdaughter under Jacob's own roof – but when she moved out of the boarding house she did not give him her new address. Jacob was a politician, manipulation was his business, and she did not want him springing any surprises on her. If he wanted to reach her, she told him, he should use the poste restante at the Berlin Post Office. Occasionally he did. His letters were surprisingly amusing, filled with affectionate anecdotes about her mother. She knew what he was trying to do but she still read them. There was something both familiar and strange about his version of Elvira, like the reflections in a house of mirrors.

'For fuck's sake,' Emmeline muttered in Russian to the peasant woman on the envelope. Then, snatching up her sketchbook, she went out.

A bitter November wind whipped through the streets. She walked fast, her head down, letting the scraps of her thoughts blow away behind her. She walked for a long time. By the time she reached Viktoriastrasse it was starting to rain. Light spilled out from the shop windows and the bare trees gleamed with silver lanterns. Emmeline tried the door to the Rachmann Gallery, but it was locked. A small silver-framed sign in the window read *Weekdays 10–6, Sundays 12–4*. It was a little after one in the afternoon. Twisting her hair into a hasty knot, she tucked it inside her collar and pressed the bell. A young man opened the door.

'Is Matthias here?' she asked, summoning Elvira's impatient imperiousness. 'Never mind, I'll wait.'

The galleries were half empty, people murmuring together quietly as they looked. Emmeline hardly noticed them. There was only the drawing on the wall and her hand on the paper, her eyes and her pencil and the eyes and the pencil of a tormented virtuoso nearly forty years dead. As the work he had made passed through her into her fingers, she knew what it was like to be someone else completely.

She was in a wheat field in the midday sun when Matthias touched her shoulder, making her jump. He gestured at the sketchbook.

'May I look?' he asked and reluctantly she handed it to him, watching as he leafed through the pages. 'My assistant is under the impression you have an appointment.'

'Does he? With whom?'

Matthias's lips twitched. 'Has anyone ever said no to you, Emmeline Eberhardt?'

'Only always.'

'I struggle to believe that. However, I am going to have to ask you to leave now.'

'But why? Your brother told me I was welcome to come whenever I wanted.'

'Welcome to look. Not to copy. Our clients do not wish to fall over art students and all their paraphernalia.'

'But these are van Goghs. Van Gogh copied everyone all the time.'

'Perhaps so. But it's a question of priorities.'

'And money always comes first?'

She expected Matthias to protest. Instead he frowned, tapping his fingers on the cover of her sketchbook.

'Wait here a moment,' he said. His assistant was talking to a sleek couple by the door. Matthias greeted the couple, then, taking the assistant to one side, murmured something in his ear. The assistant nodded, glancing at Emmeline, and followed Matthias out of the room.

A few moments later Matthias returned with the exhibition catalogue.

'Perhaps this might help,' he said, holding it out to her. The frontispiece showed a self-portrait of van Gogh at his easel, a painting, not a drawing, quite unlike any of the self-portraits Emmeline had seen before. Van Gogh looked thin and ill, his faded red hair cropped close to his skull, the yellow-grey background the same queasy colour as his skin. He eyed his canvas uneasily, as though afraid of what he might summon there.

'One of yours?' she asked.

'Not any more. It's going to Amsterdam.'

'Pity.'

'There are others.'

'Not in Berlin. No van Goghs in a public collection, not one.'

Matthias smiled. 'I'm doing my best. The Cornelius Gallery has six of our paintings in their retrospective next month, some of which may even be for sale. We must hope that this time the Nationalgalerie will not be able to resist.'

Emmeline turned the page. *Edited by Julius Köhler-Schultz*, the title page read, *with an introduction by Pieter de Vries*.

'I was wondering,' she said. 'What happened to Julius's baby?'

The question took Matthias aback. He frowned at her, confused, then shook his head. 'Tragically she – they lost it. She broke off the engagement shortly afterwards. Julius was devastated.'

'So Amelia wasn't the secret fiancée?'

'Absolutely not. And you're never to mention it to her either, do you understand? Amelia has no idea Julius was engaged before, let alone about the baby. As for Julius, if he ever found out that I'd told you—'

'Relax, Jesus, why would I say anything to anyone? It's ancient history.'

Matthias nodded, his lips pressed into a line, and gestured to the catalogue. 'Can you manage with that, do you think? It's been in the office so it's a little battered, but still good enough to copy from, I hope.'

'I can borrow it?'

'You can keep it. A reward for keeping your side of the bargain.'

Emmeline grinned. 'Well, all right then. Thank you.'

'My pleasure. Now get out before one of my real customers complains.'

Emmeline hurried to the tram stop, the catalogue clutched against her chest. The night was overcast, there was no moon, but Potsdamer Platz was ablaze with light. It streamed from the streetlamps and the advertising columns and the huge illuminated clocks and the yellow windows of the bars and cafés and the headlights of the automobiles, spilling and sluicing across the rain-slicked pavements. Twenty feet up, the traffic lights on their tower turned green, then amber and red, and green again while, above the square, huge electric billboards proclaimed the names of Kodak and Lux soap and Coca-Cola in scarlet and gold and blue and the Wrigley's Spearmen with their pointed hats turned somersaults along the buildings, trailing their green banner, *THE FLAVOUR LASTS.*

As the tram rattled north into the darkness Emmeline remembered that Matthias still had her sketchbook.

4

The *Zuerst* girl was not only disgustingly peppy, always about to go riding or cycling or ice skating or out for a drive, she was also a stickler for accuracy. Every piece she wore had to be copied with mathematical precision: the exact position of a dart or pocket, the angle of a collar. Like artefacts in a museum the clothes were numbered, item by item, and carefully checked in and out. When a drawing was complete, the details of the illustration were checked against the original, the appropriate form signed and the clothes carefully boxed for return. If a mistake had been made the whole thing had to be done all over again.

The very existence of the *Zuerst* girl would have baffled Emmeline's professors at the Berlin Academy of Art but they would have had to admit that their pupil had learned their lessons well. Emmeline had learned to look, to see. She drew the *Zuerst* girl over and over until she hated the sight of her, hated her vapid face and her raised hand and every stitch of every article she ever wore, but she made very few mistakes.

Emmeline's predecessor had not been so meticulous. Rummaging listlessly through her desk one dismal afternoon in

January, Emmeline discovered a cache of unfinished drawings. They could not have been more than a year old, *Zuerst* was hardly older than that, but already the clothes were out of date, the heels too high, the hemlines too low. Several of them were scribbled on or torn.

In one the *Zuerst* girl was drawn only from the waist up. She held out her hand, compliant as always as she leaned forward in half a brassiere, her other breast as blank as her undrawn face. Idly Emmeline sketched in her missing underwear. It seemed only proper to cover the girl up. She added a short tight skirt and the glossy high-heeled riding boots that were the particular uniform of the girls who touted for business in clusters along the stretch of Tauentzienstrasse near the zoo. In her outstretched hand Emmeline placed a vicious-looking whip.

THE WORKING ZUERST GIRL, she wrote in capital letters underneath the image, and slid it between the pages of her *Zuerst*-girl manual. She did not show it to anyone else. The other illustrators were friendly enough, but Horst ran the department like a drill sergeant, conversation was not encouraged. Of the six of them there was only one other woman, Olga, who was in charge of incidental illustration. Olga was fat and industrious and always left exactly on time because she had to get home to her children. She kept a blurry snap of them on her desk, two dark-haired little girls standing hand in hand. Whoever had taken the photograph had held the camera too low, cutting off the top of their heads and leaving a wide expanse of grass in the foreground. Dressed in Sunday best the girls squinted at the camera, eyes screwed up against the sun. Their bare knees were as sharp as knives.

The men sat together at two tables on the other side of the room. At precisely midday every day, the four of them rose together in silence and left the room. Emmeline did not know where they went. Precisely one hour later they came back and resumed their work. Olga brought sandwiches in greaseproof paper, which she ate at her desk. In the afternoons the room smelled of pickled cucumber and liverwurst.

The next time work was slow Emmeline drew the *Zuerst* girl in the lace stockings and feathered headdress of a chorus girl; the time after that as the Kaiser in spiked helmet and extravagant moustache. The habit grew compulsive. She drew her in Charlie Chaplin's suit and bowler hat, in Josephine Baker's infamous skirt of bananas. She jotted down ideas as she jolted to work on the tram. It cheered her to imagine fresh insults for her victim, new humiliations. She drew her as a wrestler, as Maria the machine-human from *Metropolis*, as the vampire Count from *Nosferatu*, her extended hand curled into a claw.

One day, driven to screaming point by a spring coat in a fiendishly fiddly paisley, she drew her naked. She gave her Irina's mouth, Irina's high breasts with their pointed nipples, her lush triangle of pubic hair. She had seen Irina only once since they broke things off, one evening on Jägerstrasse. Irina was with two other girls, both of them strangers, and Emmeline, who was by herself, had talked too much and tried to tease Irina, who pursed her lips and said goodbye while Emmeline was still laughing at her own jokes.

The *Zuerst* Irina had the blank stare of an addict. Emmeline scribbled in her cropped black hair, her heavy eyebrows, then added several black hairs on her chin. It was Irina's shameful secret, the hairs she plucked from her chin. Then, working quickly, she added a thickset male figure leering over her shoulder, one hand on Irina's breast, the other between her thighs. Irina always said that the idea of sex with a man disgusted her. A speech bubble over Irina's head bulged with Russian obscenities.

Emmeline never knew who told Horst, though she suspected Olga. When he thrust a pile of drawings at her, demanding to know if they were indeed her handiwork, she thought she detected the translucent gleam of greasy fingerprints on the edges of the paper. Later it occurred to Emmeline that perhaps he had not meant to sack her, that if she had apologised he would have let her off with a reprimand, but by then things had been said that could not be taken back and she was already nearly home.

Someone was hammering at the door. Groggily she sat up. The light was on and she had no idea what time it was. The bottle of vodka she had bought to replace the one she and Anton had finished lay empty on its side on the floor amidst a sea of torn-up self-portraits. She had taken her sketchbook and a mirror to bed, she had wanted to see herself clearly, without Irina, to understand what she looked like when she was really alone, but the flat was too cold and the mirror kept falling over and it was hard to hold a pencil and a pad and a bottle all at the same time.

'Who is it?' she shouted, fumbling out of bed, but she already knew who it was. No one but Irina knocked like that, as though they meant to break the door down. Emmeline wished she knew what she was feeling, whether she should be angry or conciliatory or aloof. Perhaps she should cry. Irina never knew what to do when she cried. The bedroom was so cold she could see her breath.

Another barrage of hammering, so loud it might have been coming from inside her skull. Pulling her dressing gown around her, Emmeline kicked the empty vodka bottle under the bed. Irina drank like a fish but she never showed it and despised people who did, she thought they were weak. No doubt she would think it was weak to be sacked too, though it was not weak, Emmeline thought resentfully, her brain aching with the effort of it, it was the opposite. She had been courageous, she had made a stand, had refused to be turned into some automated drawing machine, and besides, the drawings were funny, Irina would think they were funny, though of course she did not have the drawings any more, Horst never gave them back, and Irina did not always laugh at what you expected, she was so Russian that way—

She opened the door. Dora stood on the landing, her bag clutched in her arms.

'You're here, thank God,' she said frantically. 'It's my grand-mother. She's – I have to go for the doctor.'

Emmeline blinked at her stupidly. 'All right.'

'I can't leave her alone. I'm sorry, I've woken you, I know, but I didn't know who else to ask. If you could only – I've left the door open. Just till I get back.'

'You want me to go up there?'

'Would you? Thank you, I can't tell you—' Before the sentence was complete she was already halfway down the stairs. 'Tell her I'll be back as soon as I can.'

Dora's apartment was smaller than Emmeline's, with lower ceilings, but it was warm. It smelled of coffee. There was no plasterboard partition between the kitchen and the living room, just a curtain held back by a nail on the wall. Pots and pans were piled beside the stove. A shabby brown armchair took up most of the room.

The bedroom door was open. Emmeline peered in. The room was narrow, barely wide enough for the bed. Dora's grandmother lay hunched beneath the blankets like a broken umbrella. Emmeline could hear her breathing, the rapid shallow rasp of it like a plane against wood. A chair by the bed was crowded with the clutter of the sick room: bottles of pills, a jug of water, a thermometer in a glass, a half-drunk cup of coffee. The room smelled sour.

In the kitchen Emmeline drank two cups of water. There was

a coffee pot on the stove so she drank what was left of that too, looking down over the dark courtyard. The view was the same as hers, only higher. The light from the caretaker's room drew a stripe of yellow-white on the snow.

The coffee quickened her pulse, crackling along the filaments of her brain. She did not know what the time was, when Dora would be back. She thought about going downstairs for her sketchbook but instead she sat on the brown armchair and listened to Dora's grandmother breathing. She tried to match her breath to hers, in and out. When Dora finally returned with the doctor she went back downstairs to bed.

The next evening Dora brought her a cake in a white cardboard box. 'To say thank you for last night,' she said. 'I hope you like chocolate.'

'What kind of a person doesn't like chocolate?'

Dora smiled faintly, burying her hands in the pockets of her coat. She looked cold and tired, dark smudges under her eyes. 'Good night, then.'

'How's your grandmother?'

'She – they took her to hospital.'

'I'm sorry.'

'No, it's probably for the best. They can look after her there.' She tried to smile but her mouth did not seem to be working.

'Would it help to have some chocolate cake?'

'Not really.'

'How about vodka?'

Dora gave a gasping sort of laugh and wiped her face with her fingers. 'Vodka.'

'Russian medicine. Apparently it expels bile.'

'Well, in that case.'

Emmeline stepped back to let her in. Dora did not seem to notice the mess. She sat at the table looking at her hands while

Emmeline fetched the bottle. A new one, bought that morning from the Russian shop on the corner. Pouring two shots, she pushed one across the table to Dora.

'To expelled bile,' she said, raising her glass.

'Better out than in,' Dora answered and they drank.

Dora's grandmother was in hospital for two weeks. Dora worked most evenings, covering parties and openings, but on the nights she got home early she banged at Emmeline's door and they sat together on the floor, drinking vodka and talking.

Dora's mother had died when she was little so she had gone to live with her grandmother, her father's mother. Her father had been a writer and critic. When he went to war he told Dora he would be home before she knew it, but he was captured by the Russians and sent to a camp in Siberia. He never came back. Dora's grandfather had been rich, she and her grandmother were left amply provided for, there was always money until the inflation wiped out every penny.

Dora was obliged to abandon her studies and find a job. The editor at the *Merkur* had known her father. When he offered her a post on the social pages she took it gratefully because it was experience and she needed the money, but what she really wanted was to work on a news desk, not at the *Merkur* whose readers, the editor told her, did not much care for politics, but at a proper newspaper, one that mattered. Emmeline did not say that she had never cared much for politics herself. She knew about the demonstrations in Berlin, of course, the street fights between the communists and the nationalist Nazis, and there were always elections, flags hanging like washing across their street, the politicians seemed unable to govern for more than a few months without going to the polls, but no one ever won, not properly, and nothing really changed. Dora's anger surprised her,

her frustration with what she saw as Germany's blindness and docility. Dora believed that newspapers should be shouting from the rooftops, that there was no point in democracy if people did not know or care what was happening, if they could be frightened or bored into voting for the wrong people. In her spare hours she wrote impassioned articles, about the rise of anti-Jewish rhetoric, and the militarisation of German youth groups, and the dangers of conflating moderation with weakness, and sent them off to rival newspapers. She never heard back. She told Emmeline that she knew she should submit her work under a male pseudonym, that she would stand a better chance if they thought she was a man, but somehow she could not bring herself to do it.

'It doesn't seem the right way to start,' she said. 'With a lie.'

Emmeline did not admit to Dora that she had already lied to her several times. She wished she had not but by then it was too late to go back. She liked Dora. She did not want her to know that she was not like her, that she had no clue what it felt like to have nothing, to work at something you hated because you did not have a choice. She did not want her to know that she lived in a ramshackle apartment building with rising damp and a stairwell that smelled of cats not because she was penniless but because she hoped other people's poverty would inspire her to paint. When Dora asked to look at her pictures she shook her head. They were none of them finished, she said. Dora could see them when they were done.

'How long?' Dora asked.

'Soon.'

That was the biggest lie of all.

5

A nton told her being sacked was a blessing. 'Any longer, darling, and they'd have got you too. Imagine it, stuck like this for ever,' and he put one leg in front of the other and held out his hand until she laughed and agreed that it was all for the best.

'Nature over nurture,' Anton said. 'They can manipulate your mind but they'll never get their hands on your artist's soul. You literally drew yourself out of jail.'

Emmeline supposed he was right. She wanted him to be right. So why, then, did she miss it, the wet-dog fug of the crowded morning trams, the reek of Olga's liver sausage? She stretched and primed canvases but she did not paint. She brewed coffee she did not drink and stared out of the window. The windows on the other side of the courtyard stared back at her. Her mind was blank. When she leafed through her old sketchbooks she felt nothing but a rising sense of panic.

She went out. She walked around the city until she could not feel her feet, then sat in cafés, watching people scurry past outside. She drew a little, other customers mostly, sometimes her cup or her own cold-roughened hands, but her drawings bored her. She bored herself. Her allowance came in as always, she had enough to live on but, once the rent was paid and the gas, there was nothing left for distractions. She refused to do what other girls did and put on lipstick and a smile and wait with her skirt hitched for someone to buy her a drink.

She needed another job. There were magazines launching all the time and advertising companies too but Horst had declined to provide her with a reference and it was not easy to get a foot in the door. Several times she was told that she was not qualified, that they wanted someone who had studied advertising art or commercial illustration. A degree in fine art from the Berlin Academy counted for nothing against a year spent perfecting the glint of chrome on a brand-new automobile, or designing book plates and the borders on menus and college diplomas.

She thought of asking Anton for help but she could not face the lectures. As for Dora, she had enough on her plate and besides it was too soon. Emmeline did not want to change things between them by begging her for a favour. Instead she wrote to Olga and to Matthias Rachmann. Did they know of someone who might need someone? She did not expect either of them to write back.

With her grandmother home from hospital Dora called by less often. She worried about leaving the old woman alone. Frau Becker on the ground floor, who did the laundry, came in for an hour at midday to check on her and stoke the stove and give her the lunch Dora had prepared before she left in the morning, but she was busy and did not linger. The bathroom for their apartment was across the landing. Dora tried to persuade her grandmother to use a commode but the old woman declared that the day she used such a contraption would be the day she put a pillow over her own face.

'And not just because of the stink of it, either,' she added. In the evenings Dora took the stairs two at a time, afraid she would find the old woman sprawled on the landing. In the winter the stairwell was freezing and as slippery as ice.

'It's not fair to expect you to do it all,' Emmeline said. 'What about the niece who visited her in hospital, couldn't she take her for a while?'

Dora pulled a face. She had been to a party for the newspaper, the opening of the new van Gogh exhibition at the Cornelius Gallery, and the red lipstick she wore made her teeth look yellow. 'I couldn't do that to Oma, she'd go mad within a week. I'd always thought it was grief – Hilde lost her fiancé at Ypres – but Oma says she was always a bitch, even when she was a baby.'

Emmeline grinned and poured more vodka. Dora gulped gratefully. At the party she had persuaded Matthias Rachmann to be photographed next to one of the pictures he had loaned, a portrait of a Zouave.

'I hope it comes out,' she said to Emmeline. 'Nils claims he caught Rachmann with exactly the same uncomfortable expression as van Gogh's soldier, as if neither of them could wait for the whole performance to be over.'

'I can't believe you got to see the van Goghs before I did.'

'Who says I saw anything? The two on loan from Rachmann were pretty much the only ones I laid eyes on all evening.'

'Only two?' Emmeline asked, surprised. 'I'm sure he told me he was loaning six.'

Dora shrugged. 'It was incredibly noisy; perhaps I misheard. How anyone converses at these things I don't know. I had to get everyone to say everything twice.'

The next morning, at the Cornelius Gallery, the queue stretched down the street.

'They'll only let in a certain number at a time,' the round-faced man in front of her told her, blowing into his hands to warm them. 'We have to wait our turn.'

Emmeline waited, stamping her feet to keep the circulation going. In the shop window beside her a velvet display proffered delicate gold watches like the one Elvira used to wear. Emmeline remembered the diamonds that framed the face, the case that swung open on a tiny hinge. As a little girl she had been transfixed by that watch. She had made her mother open it over and over again, until Elvira told her sharply she would break it and took it away. Viktoriastrasse was full of objects like that, she thought, expensive playthings for people who had forgotten how to play. On the other side of the street women strutted like pigeons, puffed up in pale pillowy furs, their tiny dogs trotting beside them. Her fingers itching, Emmeline fumbled in her bag for her sketchbook but it was not there. She could not think what she had done with it.

'I don't suppose you have some paper, do you?' she asked the round-faced man, but he only looked at her oddly and shook his head. Helplessly she scanned the street. What hope was there of finding a sketchbook on Viktoriastrasse that did not cost a week's rent? The sign for the Rachmann Gallery caught her eye and suddenly she remembered: Matthias still had her sketchbook.

'Would you be an angel and save my place?' she said to the round-faced man. 'I'll only be a minute.'

On the pavement outside the gallery two men were talking, their breath chalking the air. As she drew closer the taller one turned and she saw that it was Julius Köhler-Schultz. He did not look pleased to see her.

'Hugo,' he said reluctantly to his companion, 'do you know Fräulein Eberhardt?'

'I don't believe I've had the pleasure.'

'Fräulein Eberhardt, Herr Salazin.'

Salazin bowed. '*Enchanté*.'

There was an awkward silence. Then Emmeline stepped forward and pressed the bell. Julius frowned. 'You're here to see Matthias?'

'Is that a problem?'

'I don't believe it. If he's here, why is he—'

'We should go, Julius,' Salazin interrupted smoothly. 'Good day, Fräulein Eberhardt.'

'You too,' Emmeline said and rang the bell again.

The young man had got fat, or perhaps it was just self-importance. The gallery was closed, he told her, and Herr Rachmann away on business. If she wished to see him she would have to make an appointment.

'I don't want an appointment,' Emmeline said. 'I'm just here for my sketchbook.'

'Your sketchbook?'

'I left it with Matthias last time I was here and now I need it back.'

'No one has mentioned a sketchbook to me.'

'Then perhaps you could look? I mean, I could always telephone Matthias and ask him, but isn't it your job to make sure he isn't bothered with things like that?'

The young man glared at her and instructed her to wait in the vestibule. As soon as he was gone she slipped into the gallery. To her surprise the drawings had been taken down. In their place hung three paintings. Three fishing boats on a beach; haystacks in a field; a sower in a straw hat. The spotlights had still to be adjusted – light flared against the pewter spaces between the frames and smudged darkness like soot between the thick strokes of paint – but even badly lit the canvases were unmistakable. A fourth, dark cypresses against a tumbled purple sky, was propped on a pallet against the wall.

In the middle of the room, a lectern displayed a large book. Emmeline stepped closer. It was a copy of de Vries's *catalogue raisonné*, the definitive record of every work ever made by van Gogh, opened to show the painting in front of her. Beneath the colour plate, de Vries gave its title, *Boats at Saintes-Maries*, and a brief description of the work along with its assigned catalogue number, V583, and its provenance: *Collection privée suisse*.

'Don't move.'

Emmeline turned. Gregor Rachmann stood in the doorway of the gallery, a drawing board propped against his hip.

'I said, don't move,' he said sternly, his eyes on her as his pencil moved across the paper. She shifted self-consciously, unsure of her expression, of how to be. She was not used to being the one who was looked at. Unhurriedly Gregor Rachmann considered his drawing, then propped the board, paper inwards, against the wall. Emmeline wanted to ask to see it, but she said nothing. She could feel the fingers of electricity moving through her as he crossed the gallery towards her, tracing a path upwards through her stomach and into her chest, quickening her pulse.

'I'm going to move now,' she said but he shook his head.

'Don't do that,' he said softly. He stood very close to her, his eyes on the book, his elbow grazing her arm. She could feel the burn of him through her sleeve.

'I didn't know you drew,' she said.

'There are lots of things you don't know about me. Yet.'

'Tell me one I'd never guess.'

'All right. I paint the boxes for a taxidermist. Thanks to me, the dead pets of spoiled wives frolic in ersatz Monet gardens for eternity. Don't laugh, it's true.'

'Seriously?'

'Tragically. Your turn. Tell me something I don't know about you.'

That I want to touch you, Emmeline thought. That I want you to touch me. She blushed. 'I didn't know Matthias was showing paintings.'

Gregor Rachmann looked at her. 'I think we both know you're going to have to do better than that.'

'I asked you to stay in the vestibule.' Matthias's assistant stood in the doorway. 'This gallery is closed. No one is allowed in here.'

Rachmann rolled his eyes. 'Fuck off, Zedler. She's my guest – if I say she can stay, she can stay. Not that you can see a fucking thing in this shithole. At least at the Cornelius there is light, air, the work can breathe.'

'I'm going to have to insist,' Zedler said stiffly. 'Herr Rachmann's instructions were very clear.'

'As clear as mine? I said fuck off, Zedler. Do you know what that means? Fuck off back to whatever filing cabinet you crawled out of and leave us in peace.'

Zedler's ears were scarlet. 'I work for your brother, not for you. Fräulein, if you would like to follow me?'

'I said get the fuck out of here, you maggot!' Rachmann hissed, his face contorted, spittle flying from his mouth as he raised his fists. The effect was both frightening and crude, and instantly the swirl of arousal in Emmeline's belly curdled to distaste.

'It's all right,' she said to Zedler. 'I'm leaving.'

'Don't let that fucker tell you what to do,' Rachmann snarled. Emmeline recoiled, noticing his dirty shirt, the oily coarseness of his skin, and it was as though a magnetic force had been inverted, she wanted only to get away.

She went back to the Cornelius Gallery. The round-faced man had gone and she had to join the back of the queue. A frozen sleet was falling. By the time she was finally admitted, her teeth were chattering and she could no longer feel her feet.

And then she was inside and she forgot the cold, forgot everything but the paintings, the sheer chromatic shock of colour. She thought of the final pages of Julius's famous book, the colours crowding into Vincent's cramped room to pay tribute to the artist on his deathbed: Orange garbed in fire, Carmine and Geranium Red like wide-winged butterflies, Yellow, his almond-eyed mistress in her oriental robes, she had copied whole passages into her journal, but all of Julius's verbal virtuosity could not capture the emotional power of van Gogh's pictures, the prodigality of feeling in every brushstroke. She walked around the gallery in a daze, stunned by the paintings' urgency, their feverish insistence on a God, not in church or in the Bible but in skies and trees and mountains, in the flaming ball of the sun.

She did not miss her sketchbook. In the face of such paintings a pencil did not stand a chance. Instead she stared and stared. She wanted to be able to remember them for ever. In the second room she found the *Self-Portrait at the Easel* that Matthias had used for the catalogue of his exhibition, the one bound for Amsterdam, and, on the opposite wall, another self-portrait, again at the easel, only this one showed van Gogh against a background of brilliant blue, the paint laid down in overlapping brushstrokes like the plumage of an exotic bird. The label identified it as a loan from Julius Köhler-Schultz. Beside the dazzling colours of Köhler-Schultz's painting, Matthias's van Gogh looked washed-out and evasive.

Two women came and stood next to her. 'You heard Bruno Cornelius killed himself last year?' one was saying. 'Ghastly business, signed his divorce papers at the lawyer's office, then stepped outside and shot himself in the hall. It's the lawyer I feel for, think of the mess . . .'

Emmeline wanted to cover her ears. She wished there was a rule of silence in galleries, gags tied around every chattering mouth so that people would finally stop talking and just look. She glowered at the women but they were on to van Gogh's sliced-off ear and did not give her a second glance. Slowly, reluctantly, Emmeline made her way towards the exit. A woman in spectacles stood at the sales desk, a copy of the exhibition catalogue open in front of her. As Emmeline turned the pages a picture caught her eye. Three fishing boats drawn up on a sandy beach. She peered closer. Under the title, *Boats at Saintes-Marie*, was the number assigned it by de Vries, V583, and the attribution, *Collection privée suisse*.

'Excuse me,' she said to the woman behind the desk. 'This painting, *Boats at Saintes-Maries*, is it in the exhibition?'

The woman glanced at the page and shook her head. 'Ah, no, not that one, I'm afraid. A last-minute withdrawal, the catalogue had already gone to print.'

'Right.' Emmeline searched through the catalogue. Beneath a plate of haystacks in a wheat field she found the same attribution, *Collection privée suisse*. 'And this one?'

The woman eyed her warily. 'Might I enquire as to the nature of your interest in these particular paintings?'

'I'm curious, that's all.'

The woman pressed her lips into a line. Then, turning away, she smiled at a man in a green overcoat. 'Herr Professor, a pleasure to see you again.'

Emmeline had been at boarding school for long enough to know when she was dismissed.

6

Olga replied to Emmeline's letter. Had Emmeline thought of registering with an illustration agency? She included the address of a place an acquaintance of hers had recommended.

Emmeline made an appointment. She was glad to have something to do. The shapelessness of her life had begun to unnerve her. She drank too much, to silence the voices in her head, to celebrate getting to the end of every day. Drunk, she drew more easily, the images moving from her eyes to her fingers without getting snarled in the brambles in her brain. She woke, gritty-eyed and nauseous, in a tangle of blankets, her sheets speckled with ink spots and pencil shavings.

Everyone else was busy. Dora was always rushing off somewhere, to the newspaper office or a party or the public library. She was working on a story about politics and fiction, she thought she might know someone who would be interested in buying it. When Emmeline suggested having an extra key cut so she could look in on her grandmother from time to time, Dora shook her head. She would give Emmeline a key for emergencies, she said, but her Oma was proud, she refused to be a charity case. It did not occur to either of them that the charity might be all the other way.

As for Anton, he was in love. He and Emmeline still met occasionally but he was usually late and once he failed to turn up altogether. He expected her to understand. He took her to KaDeWe so they could look at Kurt's windows.

'Aren't they extraordinary?' he said, stroking the glass with his fingertips. He was not interested in anything but Kurt. Kurt liked to juxtapose the everyday and the strange. Kurt was inspired by the evening gowns his mother wore when he was a child. Kurt believed that every window should tell a story.

'He completes me,' he said, dazed with the wonder of it. 'Until I met Kurt I didn't know how to be me.'

His elation left Emmeline dried out and empty, a skin abandoned by its snake. One evening, after Anton had vanished, rapturous and too early, into the neon night, she went to Zanzibar. They had taken down the red Chinese lanterns and hung strings of white fairy lights in their place. Perhaps that was why the women on the dance floor looked faded and faintly dusty, like exhibits in a provincial museum. The paint was peeling from the walls, so that the naked ladies wearily spreading their legs seemed to be suffering from impetigo. On the stage a bottle blonde in a red dress was singing one of the old American songs from before the war.

> Beneath the banyan parasol, she couldn't talk my talk at all,
> But, Oh, how she could Yacki, Hacki Wicki, Wacky Woo!
> That's love in Honolu-lu

The lights rolled over the stage, catching the corner booths. Two girls sat close together. One was a skinny scrap in a turquoise negligee, her knobbly spine puckering the silk like a badly sewn seam. The other was Irina. Her hair was shorter than Emmeline remembered, she did not know if she liked it. She looked both unfamiliar and heart-stoppingly the same. Emmeline had almost decided to go over when she saw Irina gesture angrily at the turquoise girl, spreading her hands wide, then bringing them down in fists on the table. The gesture was so familiar to Emmeline it was as if her own body had caused it to happen and she was flooded with a kind of homesickness she had not felt since her first day at boarding school, the grief that comes not from the loss of something precious but from the realisation that there was nothing precious to lose.

Abruptly all she wanted was to be somewhere else. As she forced her way back through the crush a plump girl caught her arm. She was dressed like an Egyptian belly dancer in diaphanous chiffon with a sequinned brassiere, and her hair was carrot red. Pouting seductively, she swivelled her hips at Emmeline, one hand on the pale swell of her stomach, the other drawing patterns in the air. Her eyes were outlined in heavy black kohl, the lids painted a bright metallic green that only served to emphasise their lashless pinkness, the pink-brown splatter of her freckles.

'Dance with me,' she shouted, her accent pure Saxon bumpkin, and Emmeline did not know whether to laugh or to burst into tears. The Saxon Salome put her arms around Emmeline's waist, pulling her close. Emmeline thought of the Russian curses Irina had taught her and, extracting herself, shook her head.

'Sorry,' she mouthed above the music. 'Maybe next time.'

Salome curled her lip. 'Next time you may not be so lucky,' she said and, raising her arms above her head, she gyrated haughtily away.

Balz Inc. was on the fourth floor of a building at the wrong end of Friedrichstrasse. Aside from a harassed-looking typist in an alcove on the landing, Herr Balz appeared to be the company's sole employee. His desk was in the middle of the room, a cluttered clearing in a forest of filing cabinets. Drawers gaped, battered papers and cardboard files pushing up through the gaps like weeds, and portfolios of every size were piled in towers on top of the cabinets and wedged into the narrow spaces between them.

'We file by style,' Balz said airily. There was a large smudge on the right lens of his glasses. 'What is your style?'

'I don't really have one. I can do anything your clients want.'

'Which would be fine, only most of them only know what they want when they see it. That's your job, to dramatise the possible.' He leafed unenthusiastically through her portfolio. 'The Modernist style is very now. Bold shapes, bright colours. Think picture-book illustrations for grown-ups. Do you have anything like that?'

'No, but I can do it. Tell me what you want me to copy and I'll copy it.'

'My dear girl, we don't "copy" here. We provide our clients with innovative advertising solutions. Of course the Belle-Époque is always popular. A touch of French glamour.'

'I could do Belle-Époque.'

'I suppose at *Zuerst* it was mostly the New Woman, was it? Some of our clients are very hot on the New Woman.'

'You mean like this?' Taking a torn envelope from Balz's desk, Emmeline sketched a *Zuerst* girl in a tennis dress on the back. Balz looked at it. Then, sighing, he took off his glasses and rubbed them with the end of his tie.

'I can deal with no references, you're not the first,' he said. 'But no drawings?'

Emmeline thought of Horst, tearing her drawing of the police officer snorting cocaine from the *Zuerst* girl's outstretched hand into tiny pieces. 'They keep all the drawings,' she said.

Balz sighed. 'Six months at *Zuerst* magazine?'

'That's right.'

He drummed his fingers on the desk. Then, yanking open a drawer, he extracted a clutch of crumpled papers. 'You'll need to sign this.'

Emmeline stared at the mimeographed form. 'You're taking me on?'

'I can't promise anything. But *Zuerst* magazine, it's new. People like new.'

'But that's – thank you.'

Balz shrugged. 'Don't thank me yet. We'll keep your portfolio. If there's any interest we get in touch, you do some preliminary sketches – gratis, of course – and the client considers his options. If you get the job we negotiate your fee, you deliver the artwork, if the client's happy you get paid. Minus our commission at forty per cent.'

'Forty per cent?'

'Artists are two a penny in Berlin, Fräulein. Without the know-how your picture's just a pretty piece of paper.'

She signed the form. As she walked away without her portfolio she felt uneasy, incomplete, but as she turned on to Unter den Linden the sun came out from behind a cloud and her spirits lifted. All along the wide street the trees were hazy green and studded with the scarlet nubs of new buds. She stopped, look-ing up, and for the first time in months the sunshine was warm on her face.

Emmeline had never really noticed how many advertisements there were in Berlin. Not just in the night-time dazzle of flashing logos and slogans but all day and at every turn, painted on the sides of buildings and pasted on to trams and buses and stuck up in the windows of shops and on the sides of telephone boxes and clock towers and the illuminated advertising pillars on almost every street. You could not cross a road in central Berlin without falling over the Nigrin chimney sweep or a person-sized box of soap flakes or a man in a sandwich board declaring that the suits were better value at Weitz's. Everywhere you looked someone was trying to sell you something.

And yet at the same time it was as if none of it was there at all. Opposite Emmeline's building, near the bus stop, there was a billboard on a blank wall. The poster was changed regularly but the latest one showed a blond woman baring perfectly white teeth. FOR A CONFIDENT SMILE, the poster declared, and underneath, in bigger letters, REINWEISS DENTAL CREAM. It was a busy corner, people walked past it all the time, but no one seemed to see it. Their eyes slid over the poster as they slid over the streetlamps or the edges of the pavement, keeping them steady, but their faces stayed folded up, as though everything that mattered was happening inside their heads.

One morning, sitting on the tram, Emmeline found herself drawing the Reinweiss woman. She worked quickly, catching the tilt of her head, the neat waves of her blond hair, then, clamped between the woman's perfect teeth, she drew a toothbrush, the handle jutting from her mouth. She drew white foam spilling from between her lips and dribbling down her chin and, peeking from between her clasped hands, an unscrewed tube of dental cream, the squeezed-out paste snaking in a thick worm of white down her fingers.

It was funny. It was just not quite as funny as she had imagined.

On Saturday afternoon Dora knocked on Emmeline's door. She was wearing canvas trousers and carrying two lumpy-looking string bags. A loaf of bread wrapped in paper protruded from one, something green and leafy from the other. Emmeline was hazy about vegetables. Dora put the bags down. The handles of the bags had striped her palms with red.

'They look heavy,' Emmeline said.

Dora grinned. 'It's Oma's birthday today. I may have overdone it.'

'Are you having a party?'

'Not unless you want to come. Do you?'

Emmeline thought of the diary she had written as a schoolgirl in Switzerland, the elaborate fantasies she had spun about her glittering future in Berlin. Behind her in the kitchen the tap dripped, steady as a clock.

'Of course I do,' she said. 'Thank you.'

'We'll see you later, then. Seven o'clock?'

Emmeline was late. She had not meant to be, she had spent most of the afternoon lying on her bed playing patience, but it was only when it was time to go upstairs that she realised she had nothing to take with her and she had to run out to Veniero's, the Italian café on the corner of Möllstrasse, and persuade them to sell her a fat-bellied bottle of Chianti in a woven basket.

'Sorry,' she said, handing it to Dora. 'It was meant to be flowers.'

Dora grinned. 'Good choice. Flowers taste awful.' She stepped back to let Emmeline in. It was barely dusk but inside the little flat night had already fallen. A lamp burned in one corner and the table was bright with candles. The room smelled deliciously of herbs and slow-braised meat. Dora put the bottle of wine on the table, then held out a hand to help her grandmother up from the armchair wedged in by the bedroom door. With the three of them there was hardly room to move.

'Oma, this is Emmeline who lives downstairs,' she said. 'Emmeline, this is my grandmother.'

Dora's grandmother was small and bent and very wrinkled, her sparse white hair pulled back into a bun. Emmeline could see the liver spots on her scalp, a patch of purple like a birthmark near her right temple. A wiry tuft of darker hair sprouted from her chin. She peered at Emmeline appraisingly, her eyes sharp as a bird's.

'So you're the one who's been getting my granddaughter intoxicated?'

Emmeline glanced at Dora, who laughed. The old woman patted Emmeline's arm.

'Good for you,' she said. 'Dora's much more fun when she's tipsy.'

'What she means is I lose at pinochle,' Dora said.

'What I mean is she loses worse than usual. Last time I finished thirty-five pfennigs up.' The old woman grinned at Emmeline triumphantly, showing a missing front tooth, and despite the sunken cheeks and the wrinkles Emmeline could see exactly what she must have looked like when she was a little girl. Dora shook her head and kissed her grandmother on the top of her head.

'Pride comes before a fall, little Oma,' she said. 'By the time I'm finished with you those thirty-five pfennigs will be a distant memory.'

Dora gave Emmeline the corkscrew and asked her to open the wine. When it was poured they sat at the table and Dora brought out a goulash, its surface cobbled with herb-flecked dumplings. The meat was meltingly tender, the gravy rich with silky slivers of onion, sweet chunks of carrot and turnip and swede. Dora's grandmother leaned over her bowl, a wide linen napkin tucked into the collar of her dress. Her hands were bones wrapped in a purple-stained tissue of skin. They shook as she raised her spoon, spilling gravy down her chin.

'Hell,' she said, clattering the spoon against the side of the bowl.

'It's nothing.' Leaning over, Dora took a corner of her grandmother's napkin and gently wiped her mouth. 'Gone.'

The old woman shook her head at Emmeline. 'Don't get old. There's no dignity in getting old.'

'You're not old, Oma,' Dora said. 'You're just a messy eater.'

'Says the girl who goes to work with butter in her hair. Just this week, out of the door and off to work with a great yellow blob of butter in her hair.'

'I told you already,' Dora said, 'all the fashionable Berlin girls wear butter in their hair these days. It's absolutely the latest thing. Isn't it, Emmeline?'

'It is,' Emmeline agreed gravely. 'I put some in myself for tonight, only it melted on the stairs.'

'An occupational hazard,' Dora said.

'Not in this building, surely?' Her grandmother screwed up her face. 'That stairwell is so cold you'd chip a tooth on your soup.'

'Soup,' Dora said. 'Now that's a thought. I don't know about you, Emmeline, but I have a feeling butter's almost had its day.'

They laughed a lot that evening. When the stew was finished Dora produced an apple tart. The glistening slices of fruit spiralled out from its centre, each golden half-moon baked to a darker brown on its outside edge, as if it had been outlined in ink. There were tiny cups of coffee with cream and sugar like chips of smoky quartz. When they had finished Dora settled her grandmother in the armchair while Emmeline stacked the dishes in the sink.

'Leave that,' Dora said.

'Yes, leave it,' the old woman said. There was an edge of childish excitement in her voice. 'Come over here and sit down.'

There was nowhere to sit. Dora's grandmother patted the arm of her chair.

'Here,' she said. Dora was already sitting on the other arm, the arm closest to the wall, her feet inside the chair to balance herself. As Emmeline sat the old woman stroked her granddaughter's leg absently, as if she were a cat. 'Ready?' she demanded.

It was a habit they had got into, Dora told her later, when her grandmother grew too frail for the stairs. Every evening, after supper, the two of them would sit down and Oma would close her eyes and Dora would tell her what she had seen and where she had been, the taste of the air, the colours of the sky and the river and the window boxes, the clouds heaped up like whipped cream or the pink and gold streaks of sunset or the intricate pattern of dots on the pavement as the rain began to fall. The days when the wind chased leaves and bus tickets through the empty streets, or when the air was so warm and thick you could not tell where you ended and the city began.

Suddenly, Dora said, she found herself noticing things, little pieces of the city she could bring home to Oma. The child carrying a loaf so large it looked like the bread had legs. The labourers fifty feet above Alexanderplatz, strolling in their shirtsleeves along the arms of the cranes. The businessman battling with his umbrella blown inside out. The heat from the sausage stand rippling the air so that it was like you were looking through spilled water. The first snowdrops, the first fat stalks of white asparagus, the first glossy chestnuts in their prickly jackets. The woman singing 'Sempre libera' at an open window and the white dog with a little wheeled cart where his back legs should be. Fragments of days, of other people's lives, dropped or forgotten or thrown away, saved like scraps of fabric and tipped each evening into Oma's lap so that, for a few minutes, the walls of the flat disappeared and she strode through the streets with Dora, sharp-eyed and strong-legged and free.

When Dora finished talking her grandmother was quiet, her eyes closed and her hands folded in her lap. The light was low, the candles almost burned out. Somewhere in the building a man was shouting. There was the smash of something breaking. A door slammed. The old woman opened her eyes. Unfolding her hands, she patted Emmeline on the arm.

'Your turn,' she said.

Dora smiled and kissed her on the top of her head. 'Good try, but you know what the doctor said. It's late. Time for bed.'

'Not so late surely,' the old woman wheedled and Dora laughed.

'Careful, Emmeline. Any moment now she'll be demanding we take her dancing.'

'And why not?' her grandmother said. 'Emmeline looks like the dancing sort. Come now, dear, won't you tell us what it's like in one of those nightclubs?'

'Oma,' Dora protested, and rolled her eyes at Emmeline. 'Do you see now what I have to put up with?'

Emmeline smiled. She thought of Zanzibar and Mali und Igor and the Cocoanut Club, where the waitresses were slim-hipped and silky and all men, and she wondered if the old lady would be shocked if she knew what went on after dark in the blacked-out backrooms and cellars of Berlin. Somehow she could not imagine it.

'Next time,' she said.

The next time she remembered to take flowers. White hyacinths giddy with scent, their juicy stems leaking into the cone of brown paper. It was April by then and the trees along the Spree were foamy with blossom. She picked a branch and some tiny new leaves from the linden tree on the corner, curled and damp and a brilliant chartreuse green. She took her sketchbook. She could not describe things in words like Dora could, so that they lived in your head, but there were other ways to bring the outside in.

The evening was fine. Dora had thrown the window open as wide as it would go and the sounds of children playing and people calling to one another and a band playing something almost familiar on a distant wireless and the smells of other people's suppers drifted in on the faint breeze.

They sat over supper for a long time, Dora and her grandmother teasing one another and finishing each other's sentences. The strip of blue sky above the chimney pots turned pink and then lavender and finally indigo. Pots clattered and water coughed and thudded in the pipes. As the last of the children were shouted for and chivvied in, Dora's grandmother smiled a child's enormous smile and put her hand on Emmeline's.

'Show me,' she said and Emmeline settled herself on the arm of her chair as if it were something she had done all her life and put her sketchbook in the old woman's lap. The old woman gazed greedily through her lorgnette as she turned the pages. When they reached the Reinweiss lady with the toothbrush in her mouth she burst into laughter.

'My father would have approved of her,' she said. 'When my sisters and I were little girls he used to tell us that if we didn't brush our teeth every day we would end up like – what was her name, the famous woman, the one Napoleon Bonaparte had in his bedroom?'

Emmeline shrugged, baffled. 'Empress Joséphine?'

The old woman laughed so helplessly that Emmeline laughed too, even though she did not know why. 'Not Joséphine. The portrait. The famous portrait.'

'She means the *Mona Lisa*,' Dora said.

'The *Mona Lisa*. He told me that if I didn't look after my teeth, I would end up like the *Mona Lisa*. Obliged to smile with my lips shut even when I had my portrait painted by the most famous artist in the world.'

7

The office was warm and airless. Balz spread Emmeline's drawings over the milk-scummed coffee cups on his desk and studied them thoughtfully.

'It wouldn't have to be these ones,' she said. 'It could be any portrait, any artist. Whatever they wanted.'

Balz put down the *Mona Lisa* with her wide white smile and picked up the self-portrait of van Gogh at the easel. Emmeline had copied him from the front of Rachmann's catalogue, applying the paint in van Gogh's swirling style, but instead of a paintbrush he brandished a toothbrush. Froth spilled from his mouth and into his beard and his palette was dotted with curls of white dental cream.

'No one looks at the Reinweiss posters,' she said. 'It's as if they're not even there. But these are funny. People would notice them. Isn't that what they want?'

'Of course.'

'So why won't you show them?'

'Because that's not how it works. We draw the ideas our clients commission us to draw. We don't come up with our own.'

'And what if ours are a million times better than theirs?'

Balz shrugged. 'Then we still draw theirs. That's what they pay us for. Besides, Reinweiss dental cream is not one of our clients.'

'All right. Then I'll do it.'

'Do what, exactly?'

'Take my ideas to the Reinweiss company.'

'Reinweiss is a product, not a company.'

'But a company must make it.'

'Hoesch-Lorenz. In Hamburg.'

'Then I'll go to Hamburg. And if they don't like it I'll take it somewhere else. It's not as if Reinweiss is the only dental cream in Germany.'

Balz watched her leave, her cheeks flushed, her drawings clutched under one arm. They both knew she would never go to Hamburg. Emmeline supposed that was the end of that, he would want nothing more to do with her, but two days later she received a letter. Balz had an idea. He asked her to come back.

Cigarettes, Balz said. A simple substitution: cigarettes for toothbrushes, smoke for foam. He had a client who had been trying unsuccessfully to woo the Wahr cigarette company for months. Perhaps this would be the idea that seduced them.

Emmeline was unconvinced. Dental cream was funny. Cigarettes were not. There was a reason why film stars were always photographed smoking, not brushing their teeth. Balz only shrugged. Ideas were free. If she did not want to draw up the concept there were plenty of other artists who would.

'Who knows?' he said. 'This might be just what Wahr has been waiting for.'

'And if it isn't?'

'If it isn't I'll buy you a third-class ticket to Hamburg.'

*

He gave her five days. An idea was like a head cold, he said, somehow it got into the air and before you knew it everyone else had caught it too. For the first two days Emmeline stalked the Nationalgalerie, jotting down every possibility that occurred to her. On the third day she started to paint. She worked late into the night, her world shrunk to a foot-wide circle of light.

It was very late when Dora banged on the door. Frightened, Emmeline hurried to open it, but Dora shook her head.

'It's not Oma, she's fine. She's sleeping. Can I come in?'

She did not sit down. She stood in front of Emmeline's easel, arms crossed, her fingers twitching against her elbows. 'Smoke rings – inspired,' she said distractedly.

'Dora, it's the middle of the night. Do you want to tell me what's going on?'

Dora frowned, and bit her thumbnail. Then abruptly she sat down. The newspaper had sent her to cover a late-night party at the Opera, thrown in honour of Diaghilev and his Ballets Russes. The room was crowded and halfway through Dora slipped outside, taking refuge in a darkened doorway to scribble down some notes. The two men in dinner jackets who emerged from a side door to stand beneath a streetlamp did not see her. Dora recognised the art dealer Zeckendorf, a fixture of the Berlin scene who featured regularly in her column. The other one was slight and sandy-haired, with a distinct Dutch accent. They spoke urgently, their voices low, but Dora could hear every word. They were talking about a deal, a painting sold to a gallery in Amsterdam that was suddenly going to New York instead. The Dutchman was agitated, he kept repeating himself.

'A month ago, Arendsen was so desperate to acquire the painting he had Rachmann bring it to him in Amsterdam in person,' he said. 'A fortnight later he summons de Vries to an emergency meeting. They are seen together at the Rijksmuseum, looking at the van Goghs. Two days after that the deal's off and the painting's going to Stransky in New York. You don't find that suspicious?'

Zeckendorf was expansive, most likely a little drunk. At the parties Dora covered he was usually a little drunk. He waved away the Dutchman's concerns. Stransky was a dogged little bastard with money to burn, he said, he must have outbid Arendsen, made Rachmann an offer he could not refuse, but the Dutchman shook his head.

'Or perhaps Arendsen heard about the Cornelius paintings and got cold feet. They say Rachmann did the decent thing and took all four back without a murmur, but four canvases, all of them his, doesn't that worry you?'

Zeckendorf snorted. 'What worries me is that you would walk away from a deal like this on the strength of idle rumours. Our painting has five expert authentications, five! What more do you want? Köhler-Schultz and Ruthenberg, de Vries, they've all signed on the dotted line.'

'Köhler-Schultz and de Vries authenticated all four of the disputed Cornelius paintings too. It didn't stop the gallery sending them back.'

Dora did not hear any more. A couple came out of the theatre and the two men stopped talking abruptly and hurried away, but Dora stayed where she was, in the doorway, her notebook forgotten in her hand. She did not know exactly what she had heard but she knew what it meant.

What if some of Matthias Rachmann's van Goghs were fakes?

Emmeline and Dora talked for a long time that night, sprawled side by side on Emmeline's bed, sharing a bottle of wine Dora had smuggled out of the party.

'Medicinal,' Dora said. 'For the shock.'

They drank it out of teacups because there were no clean glasses, and smoked the packet of Wahr cigarettes that Balz had given Emmeline because an artist should feel an emotional connection with her subject. Emmeline thought he was joking until she smoked one and nearly coughed up her lungs on the first puff. Dora smoked rapidly, breathlessly, hardly able to contain her excitement. If she could prove that some of the most expensive and sought-after paintings of modern times were forgeries, well, it would be the scoop of the century.

'If I can just get someone at the Cornelius to speak on the record—'

'Except they never will,' Emmeline said flatly. 'Even if the gallery's right and the four paintings they sent back *are* fakes, the art world is like the Freemasons without the funny handshakes, it looks after its own. No one talks.'

'But the Cornelius Gallery have done the decent thing; they're protecting the market. Why wouldn't they want people to know that?'

'Because they want to protect the market. If some of the most expensive pictures in history turn out to be forgeries, buyers will run a mile.'

'As well they should. These paintings go for seventy, eighty thousand marks.'

'Exactly! Why would the Cornelius risk losing sales like that? Besides, they took six of Rachmann's paintings for the show. They only rejected four.'

Dora was silent, twisting round to lie on her back. 'So if they won't talk, then who?' Upside down, her chin suddenly a clumsy nose, her face looked slack-jawed and adenoidal. 'Don't laugh. I'm not giving up before I've even started.'

'I'm not laughing, I'm thinking.'

'What about this de Vries? He's not a dealer, so he won't be worried about sales.'

'Except people like de Vries broker sales all the time. They authenticate paintings, then put buyers and sellers together and take a fat commission.'

'Isn't that a conflict of interest?'

'Absolutely, but it's how it's always worked. Who knows which of those paintings de Vries has made money from? Which, by the way, would have to be returned if he admitted that they were fakes, which he won't. He authenticated all four of them in the first place. And included them in his *catalogue raisonné*, which has taken him a mere decade to complete. So any admission of error—'

'Fine,' Dora said, frowning. 'Not him. What about Köhler-Schultz?'

Emmeline shook her head. She had told Dora about dancing with Matthias at Julius's house, though not what happened afterwards. 'I can't see him talking either. He and Matthias – let's just say I spent that whole evening trying to work out what was going on between them.'

Dora blinked. 'You're not saying they were—'

'Lovers? I don't think so. But there was something in the way Julius watched Matthias, that dazed, naked look people have when they're in love.'

'Naked?'

'Exposed. You know, like they've forgotten to put their outside face on.'

Dora smiled. 'Sometimes I think you notice everything.'

'God, I wish. Most of the time I'm blind as a bat.' Squirming on to her stomach, Emmeline took two cigarettes from the pack and put them between her lips. She lit them with a single match, sucking redness into the tips, and handed one to Dora. For a moment they smoked in silence. Dora closed her eyes to think better. Suddenly she opened them and sat up.

'What about the Russian prince, the one who smuggled them out of Moscow? The only reason no one knows anything about where these pictures came from is because Rachmann won't say who he is. So if we could find him—'

'How? I mean, where would you start?'

'He has to be somewhere. A fugitive prince can't just disappear into thin air.'

'He can if he doesn't want to be found.'

'And why would he want that, unless his famous van Goghs are actually forgeries? In which case we have to find him. It's in the public interest.'

'Or perhaps he's just afraid for his family. Horrible things are happening in Russia. What if exposing him puts innocent lives at risk?'

'Seriously? You'd let someone rip off the art world for hundreds of thousands of marks, just because he has a family?' Dora upended the wine bottle into her cup but it was empty. 'Oh God, it's so late. How late is it?'

Emmeline peered at the clock. 'Quarter past three.'

'No, it can't be, I have to be up at half past seven.' Grimacing, Dora fumbled for her shoes. Her dress was rumpled, and her hair, and there were smudges of mascara under her eyes. Emmeline's heart was suddenly too big for her chest. She wanted to slide her hand on to Dora's thigh, to feel the softness of her skin against her mouth, but though her body was liquid with wanting she did not move. Whatever it was, this full-up dizzy drowning feeling, it could not be reduced to that. She could feel the throb of her pulse in her throat.

'I don't even know why I'm going,' Dora said. 'I won't sleep.'

'You're going so I can.'

'So selfish.' Smiling, she bent down and touched her lips lightly to Emmeline's cheek. 'I'll see you tomorrow.'

'It's tomorrow now.'

'Don't say that. If you don't say it, it's not really true.'

Curled in her bed, Emmeline hugged her pillow, listening to Dora's footsteps, the creak and click of the front door. All this time she had been only two floors up. Even the blindest bats were not as blind as that.

Dora tried everyone but, though they had all heard the rumours, nobody would talk. No one wanted to admit that forgeries even existed. The Cornelius Gallery had expressed doubts over a few paintings, so what? Rachmann had done what any respectable dealer in the circumstances would do and taken the pictures back. That was the end of it. Besides, who was to say that the Cornelius was right? The Rachmann paintings had all been properly authenticated, most of them several times. There were plenty of experts willing to swear that they were absolutely genuine. That was the business of art. There were always more opinions than anyone knew what to do with.

Pieter de Vries did not answer Dora's letters. His office in the Netherlands told her to direct any questions about the *catalogue raisonné* to his publishers. His publishers insisted that she talk to his office. Julius Köhler-Schultz was on a lecture tour in the United States with his wife. Emmeline could not imagine tiny Amelia Köhler-Schultz in America, where everything was ten times the size it was in Germany. Even Julius would be small in America.

'She was an absolute dragon, the housekeeper,' Dora said. 'Wouldn't even tell me when they were coming back.'

'I can ring and ask her, if you like?' Emmeline offered. 'She knows me.'

'You'd really do that? I thought you disapproved of my journalist's ethics.'

'I approve of you. We'll cross your ethics when we come to them.'

But Dora's letter to Matthias made Emmeline uneasy. Typed on purloined *Merkur* headed writing paper, its tone was both sycophantic and faintly threatening. She had recently been approached by an art world insider, Dora wrote, with a startling story. Her newspaper was not in the business of publishing unsubstantiated allegations but, given Herr Rachmann's public profile, it would surely not be long before another, less scrupulous rag splashed them all over the front pages. The subsequent scandal, however riddled with inaccuracies, would cause irreparable damage to his reputation. Would he not prefer to put his side of the story, exclusively, to the readers of the *Merkur*?

She received a two-line reply signed in his absence by his assistant. Herr Rachmann was unable to grant her request for an interview. Any requests for publicity materials should be directed to the gallery's press office.

As for the Russian, there were rumours, but Dora could not find anyone who had ever actually met him or knew of anyone who had. Certainly no one knew his name. Among Anton's coterie of gallery assistants it was generally agreed that he and Rachmann were lovers but, as Anton was the first to admit, that was always their explanation for everything.

8

Emmeline opened Balz's letter reluctantly, expecting a third-class ticket to Hamburg. Instead she was summoned to his office. The Wahr people loved her idea, they wanted it everywhere, on posters and cigarette cards and displays in tobacconist shops. They wanted to start straight away.

The man from the advertising agency was pale and twitchy, with a rabbit's pink eyes.

'What kind of a person is your product, that's the question,' he said, and when she looked at him blankly he nodded in satisfaction. The Wahr cigarette, he said, was a sophisticated man about town. Suave, rich, cosmopolitan, young but not too young, accustomed to the finer things in life. He was not a melting Norwegian madman screaming on a bridge. And he was most definitely not a Dutch madman who cut off his own ear.

'But van Gogh's one of the best,' Emmeline protested.

'A suicidal self-mutilating lunatic. Does that sound like the Wahr man to you?'

'No, but then it doesn't sound like van Gogh. That madman stuff, it's a myth. If you read his letters, you'll see—'

He cut her off with a shrug. 'If the Wahr customer thinks van Gogh's a madman then he's a madman. And it isn't good for business.'

Women were not good for business either. He turned down the *Mona Lisa* and Vermeer's *Girl with a Pearl Earring* with her toothbrush in her headwrap, and, though he hesitated over the Velázquez *Venus*, it was plain his curiosity was not commercial. The six he finally settled on were, in Emmeline's opinion, the dullest of the lot. But when he left and Balz handed her the envelope containing her advance, she discovered she did not give a fig. Just having the money in her pocket made her giddy.

At home she went straight to Dora's flat. 'Dinner's on me,' she announced triumphantly. 'A table for three at Veniero's.'

'Veniero's? But we can't, not with Oma, what about the stairs?'

'Not there. Here. Tonight the mountain comes to Muhammad.'

Or the mountain's sons, at any rate. Marcello Veniero, seventy years old and at least as wide as he was tall, got out of breath climbing the one step from the street to his restaurant. But he sent his boys, both grown men, who brought platters of scarlet tomatoes and creamy mozzarella, rose-pink slivers of Parma ham, dark red radicchio leaves stuffed with goat's cheese and herbs, balls of saffron arancini. They brought garlicky spaghettini with breadcrumbs and anchovies, bowls of green beans and spinach, flattened fillets of chicken striped black from the grill, the hot dishes wrapped in towels to keep them warm. Squeezing into Dora's tiny flat, they covered the table with a starched white cloth and set it with tall glasses and heavy silver cutlery, with white napkins and red candles and bottles of pale vinegar and green-gold olive oil. When everything was ready Emmeline poured the wine and the three women raised their glasses and toasted the Veniero family and Wahr cigarettes.

They ate until their bellies groaned, licking the oil from their fingers and wiping their plates with chunks of warm bread studded with rosemary and crystals of salt.

'In parts of Italy they still harvest the salt like the Etruscans, in pans cut into the rocks beside the sea,' Oma said. 'They call it white gold.'

Dora laughed, her cheeks flushed with wine. 'You wait. One more glass of wine and she'll be telling you that even the poverty in Italy is beautiful.'

'Italians know how to be happy, Dodo. They have the sun in their bones.'

'And Germans?'

'Coal dust and potatoes.'

Emmeline smiled. It made her happy to see Dora laugh. Since the disappointment of the Rachmann story she had grown smaller somehow, like a doll whose sawdust had leaked. She had tried to talk to her editor, had begged for an apprenticeship on the news desk, she had ideas, plenty of them, but he smiled, shaking his head, cutting her off before she could tell him even one.

'Do you know the secret of your success, my dear?' he said. 'You don't attract attention. No one sees you. Invaluable on the social pages, catastrophic in news.'

She would have resigned there and then but she thought of the bills and the queues outside the unemployment office and the hours and hours she had spent failing to persuade anyone to talk to her about Matthias Rachmann and she went back to her desk before he could decide to cut her pay. Stuff the moral high ground, she told Emmeline later with a weary laugh. By the end of each day she could barely make it up the stairs to the flat.

'Have you ever been to Italy?' Dora asked Emmeline.

'Never.'

'Me neither. We'll go together, shall we, when you're a

millionaire advertising tycoon and I've used up every adjective ever invented to describe a party dress?'

'Surely we don't have to wait till then? We'll be ancient.'

'Speak for yourself. According to my calculations I'll be done by next week.'

The candles burned low. Oma was falling asleep. Her head nodded forwards, then jerked up again. She blinked, rubbing her eyes with her knuckles, but before her hands found her lap her eyes were closing again, her mouth falling open. Dora smiled, rolling her eyes at Emmeline, and slid her chair sideways till it touched her grandmother's. When she put her arm around her the old woman murmured something, lifting her face towards Dora, but she did not wake. Dora kissed her forehead and she softened, tucking herself into the crook of Dora's shoulder, one gnarled hand against her cheek, the other abandoned in Dora's lap.

Reflexively Emmeline reached for the paper that had wrapped the bread. It was crumpled and pearly with oil but she used it anyway, the moment so strong in her that the pencil moved fluidly over the paper without thinking, the marks already familiar before they were made.

'Show me,' Dora asked quietly but Emmeline shook her head. Without looking at it she tucked the drawing into her pocket.

'It's nothing,' she said.

Dora made a face at her, resting her cheek lightly on her grandmother's head. 'It's not nothing. It's us. I'm sure that gives us some kind of rights.'

'None whatsoever.'

'You could still let me see it.'

'Not yet. When it's finished.'

'That's what you always say. You never show me anything.'

'What are you talking about? I show you things all the time.'

'Only your advertisements. I mean, they're funny and brilliant, of course they are, but they're not yours. They're not real.'

Emmeline was silent.

'Show me something of yours,' Dora said softly.

'I can't.'

'Why not?'

'Because there's nothing to show!' The exclamation made the candle flame gutter. Emmeline watched it as it steadied, the dark hollow at its heart. 'I haven't done anything for months. I – I don't seem to know how.'

'So all this time—'

'Nothing. Nothing good, anyway.'

Dora looked at Emmeline. Then, careful not to wake her, she detached herself from her sleeping grandmother and leaned across the table, putting her hand on Emmeline's. 'Then you just have to keep going.'

Emmeline did not answer. She kept staring at the candle flame, burning the glare of it on to her eyes as Dora ran her thumb over the back of her hand, tracing the fan of bones beneath the skin. She did not want to talk about her failures. She wanted to take Dora in her arms and kiss her until the stars sang.

Dora squeezed Emmeline's hand lightly, then held hers out, palm up. 'Give it to me,' she ordered. 'Give me the drawing.'

Emmeline wanted to take Dora's hand in hers, to put against her cheek, but the fear was too strong. Instead she put the folded paper in her outstretched palm and bowed her head, covering her face with her hands. She did not want to see Dora look. Behind her closed eyelids the candle flames gleamed, bright stripes of scarlet in the blackness.

'Oh, Em,' Dora murmured. 'You can't give up, not ever. I won't let you.'

Emmeline looked up. Dora was staring at her, her eyes fierce and bright. 'It's just a scribble,' she said.

'But it isn't, that's the whole point,' Dora insisted. 'There's something about it, I don't know, something raw—'

'Olive oil?'

'Not olive oil, you idiot. Love.'

9

The Berlin season was almost over. One of the last of the parties was the opening of an exhibition of photographic portraits, *Faces of Our Time*, at a ritzy modern gallery on Unter den Linden. Dora found Matthias Rachmann hanging between Max Reinhardt and a naked Josephine Baker, sleek and glossy as an automobile. He leaned unsmiling towards the camera, his chin cupped in one hand, his long fingers against his cheek. Despite his youth he looked imposing, even distinguished. In black and white his eyes were driftwood silver.

'Photography isn't art,' Dora told Emmeline sourly. 'It's propaganda.'

A week later the newspapers reported the acquisition by the Nationalgalerie of several van Gogh drawings for their modern collection. The seller? None other than Matthias Rachmann. At the same time, in New York, the painting Dora had overheard Zeckendorf and his Dutch friend discussing, the self-portrait Rachmann had sold to the American dealer, Stransky, had gone on public display: the *New York Times* declared it an indisputable masterpiece. According to the Berlin newspapers the painting had sold for thirty-two thousand dollars, over one hundred and thirty thousand German marks.

June was stifling, overcast. Swags of grey cloud sagged over the city and the famously invigorating Berlin air clung stickily to the skin, soupy and over-breathed. When the sky finally cleared, it was dizzyingly hot. The roads melted and the milk turned and along the wincing glare of the Spree the railings were too hot to touch.

Oma coughed incessantly. They propped open the window as wide as it would go but it only let in more heat and the fetid stink of drains. Dora wanted to send the old woman away to the country, to find a sanatorium with white sheets and breezes, but the doctor was reluctant to move her, he said that the upheaval was too much, and anyway she knew that the sanatoria were not like that, not the state-funded ones where the women slept in wards of twenty and there was never any silence, even in the middle of the night.

Not that there was much silence in the tenement building either. The weather made people argumentative. The nights were ragged, frayed with shouts and sudden smashes. Babies wailed. It was only in the heat-bludgeoned afternoons that a stunned quiet overtook the building. Oma slept a little then. Dora and Emmeline sprawled in the sitting room where they could hear her if she woke, Dora reading or writing, Emmeline with her sketch-book on her lap. She drew everything in the room that summer but mostly she drew Dora, the curves and the planes of her. Line by line, she learned her.

It's looking at things for a long time that matures you and makes you understand more deeply, van Gogh wrote to his brother. Emmeline marked the page with a linden leaf. In Arles van Gogh had painted the same subjects over and over again, until he no longer knew where he finished and they began, until they were a part of him. In the same letter he wrote *The time will come when I'll have someone.*

Oma grew impatient with the two of them. She said she was tired of them always worrying over her, that they should go and have fun. Why were they not picnicking in the Tiergarten or going to the cinema on Alexanderplatz where it was cool and matinée tickets cost only sixty pfennigs? The more they resisted her the more ambitious her suggestions became: the cycling races at the Sports Stadium; the roller coasters at Luna Park; the Rhineland Wine Terrace at Haus Vaterland, where an artificial river flowed indoors and every hour a mechanically operated rainstorm swept through the room amidst a barrage of thunder and lightning. She wanted them to climb to the top of the radio tower, to bathe in the lake at Wannsee. Dora was afraid of heights but she liked to swim and, stubborn as she was, she was not as stubborn as Oma. She told Oma she would bring her some sand in a jam jar.

The beach was very crowded, a jostle of parasols and deckchairs and picnic rugs spread possessively over the sand, their corners fortified with baskets and discarded shoes. The lake was crowded too. Children squatted in the brown shallows, solemnly emptying buckets into holes. Further out, gaggles of girls shrieked and splashed, and men showed off their strokes, kicking up water in glittering wings. Vendors picked their way through the crush with baskets of strawberries and sugary *Pfannkuchen*.

Dora and Emmeline walked along the water's edge, tiny waves licking their feet. The sand was a collage of bottle tops and sweet wrappers and cigarette stubs and dark ribbons of washed-up weed, and the sun was very hot. Dora wore a pair of Emmeline's sunglasses, black and pointed like cats' eyes. Beneath her faded black bathing dress her legs were long and milky-white.

Near the fence that marked the boundary of the beach the

crowd thinned. There were no deckchairs this far along, no parasols. Couples sat close together on towels spread out on the sand. In the water two men hit a rubber ball back and forth with wooden bats. Dora and Emmeline walked up the splintered wooden walkway towards a patch of pine woods where the shade was deep and dark. The woods behind the main beach had already been hacked down. A vast new restaurant was being built there, complete with swimming pool and open-air theatre. On the churned-up earth huge steam-diggers drowsed in the sun.

At the end of the walkway a group of young men in bathing trunks lounged on the sand, cigarettes pinched in their palms, drinking from a bottle they passed from hand to hand. Their shoulders were burned red from the sun. As the girls approached one of them drained the bottle, then hurled it towards the woods. There was a muffled smash. The youths laughed.

'Maybe we should go back,' Dora murmured but Emmeline only tucked her arm through Dora's.

'We'll go round,' she said. The sand was sharp with shrivelled pine needles. As they passed, one of the youths reached out and ran a hand down Dora's thigh. Dora yelped.

'What?' he said. 'Nice pussies like to be stroked.' The other youths sniggered. Flustered, Dora pulled off her sunglasses and turned, trying to steer Emmeline back the way they had come, but Emmeline took a step closer to the blond man, raising the middle finger of her right hand.

'Fuck you,' she said in Russian. 'And fuck your mother.'

'Em, please,' Dora pleaded, tugging at her arm, but it was too late, the blond man was already on his feet, two of his friends dropping their cigarettes to circle behind him, boxing them in. Emmeline could smell the shrivel of the sun on them, the sharp reek of their sweat.

'Get out of our fucking way,' she said coldly, this time in German, but the blond man only stepped closer, so close she could see the sharp yellow points of the pimples that pressed up through his skin. His eyes were raw-looking, the irises bluish-white like skimmed milk.

'Filthy-mouthed little whore, aren't you?' he said.

'Foreign, sounds like,' one of the other men said and the blond man nodded.

'A dirty little Jewess,' he agreed.

'Please,' Dora said in a strangled voice. 'She didn't mean it.'

'Oh, but I did,' Emmeline said. 'And if you don't step aside this instant I'll scream blue buggering murder. Have you ever heard a dirty little Jewess scream?'

'Scream all you like, bitch,' the blond man hissed. 'No one listens to your kind,' and, lurching at her, he pushed her hard with both hands. Caught off guard, Emmeline staggered backwards. The blond man watched her as she righted herself, a smile curving the edges of his mouth. Emmeline looked at him. Then, opening her mouth, she screamed.

Immediately the two men in the water stopped their game. Couples on their towels looked round. A man carrying deckchairs put them down. Emmeline went on screaming, her arms raised in front of her face like a shield. The men splashed out of the water and started up the beach. The blond man hesitated, rigid with hate, then jerked his head at his friends. Snatching up their bags, they headed for the woods, the blond man behind them. As he pushed past Emmeline he grabbed her hand, pressing it against his groin. His cock was semi-hard, a fat bulge in his bathing trunks.

'Filthy Jewish dyke whore,' he spat and stalked away.

They were quiet on the train on the way home, caught up in their thoughts. It was early, too early for the day-trippers, the sun still hot as metal through the dirty windows. They had the carriage to themselves.

'I'm sorry,' Emmeline said at last.

'What for?'

'For spoiling things. It was my fault, I should have walked away.'

'You're right. How dare you be a pretty Jewish girl on a public beach?'

Dora had caught the sun. Beneath the wide straps of her sundress her shoulders were the soft pink of strawberry ice. Emmeline looked out at the high embankment, the dry bleached stands of grass. 'I'm Catholic, actually.'

'Then why did you let them—'

'They were morons. There's no point in arguing with morons.'

Dora laughed softly. Or perhaps it was a sigh. 'I'm the one who should be apologising. I – I froze.'

'No, you didn't.'

'I thought I was brave but I'm not. I'm a coward.'

'Not poking sticks in wasps' nests isn't cowardice, it's common sense.'

'You think common sense is worth anything?' Dora demanded. 'I'm twenty-four and I still live with my grandmother. I'm stuck in a job I despise, with no money and no prospects. I've never been anywhere or done anything of the slightest importance and I never will.'

'That's not true. You're a brilliant writer. You haven't been lucky yet, that's all.'

'And what if I never am? What if I spend the rest of my life staying away from wasps' nests and nothing ever changes? It's not just work, it's everything. I'm halfway to being an old woman, Em, and I've barely lived. I've never left Germany. I've never danced all night or drunk champagne from my shoe or had a wild, impossible love affair. I've never even been kissed!'

'Then kiss someone.'

'It isn't that easy.'

'Of course it is. You're not Sleeping Beauty waiting for her prince to come and wake her. This is a republic and we have alarm clocks. If you want to kiss someone you should just kiss them.' The words prickled on Emmeline's tongue. She looked at Dora, at her disconsolate frown and her strawberry-ice shoulders and her cat's-eye sunglasses pushed up into her hair, and suddenly she could not hold it any more. Half-rising from her seat, she kissed her. Dora's lips parted, the tips of their tongues touched, and for a moment there was nothing else, nothing but her mouth and Dora's and the streaking flash of blood like light through her veins and her heart so huge in her chest it closed her throat.

'Tickets, all tickets please.' With a sharp little mew Dora twisted away, fumbling her rucksack on to her lap. Dazed, Emmeline leaned back in her seat.

'Nice day out, ladies?' the ticket inspector asked cheerily and Dora flushed, not meeting Emmeline's eye. He punched their tickets with a wink. 'Be sure to let me know next time, I'll come with you.'

As he slid the carriage door closed behind him Dora stared fixedly out of the window, her knuckles against her mouth. They were nearing Berlin. The buildings chopped the sunlight into slices that flashed across her face like strokes of paint.

'Dora, look at me,' Emmeline said softly. She kissed me back, she thought, and her heart swelled, throbbing like a bruise. Leaning forward, she stroked Dora's sun-pinked shoulder, tracing the angle her pencil knew by heart.

'Don't,' Dora snapped, jerking away. 'You win, all right? You've made your point.'

'My point? I don't understand.'

'Don't you? Just kiss someone, Dora, see how easy it is.'

'You think that was easy?'

'Wasn't it?'

Emmeline exhaled, a high choked laugh. 'Do you have any idea how long I've been waiting to kiss you, how I've thought about it and thought about it, only every time I just couldn't, I didn't dare, because I was so afraid I was wrong, that you weren't like me, that you wouldn't want – that somehow I'd manage to fuck everything up?'

There was a silence.

'Well, then, I'm sorry,' Dora said at last.

'Sorry for what?'

'That I can't – that you were right. I'm not like that. I'm just not.'

'But you kissed me back.'

'No. I'm sorry.' She stared out of the window, hugging her rucksack against her. 'Let's forget it ever happened, all right?'

They walked in silence through the station, one behind the other. The tobacconist's kiosk by the ticket office had an advertisement pasted on the side, Rembrandt at his easel, his head tipped back, blissfully exhaling, an open packet of Wahr cigarettes on the palette in his hand. Whoever had pasted it had been slapdash. The poster was askew and there were bubbles of air beneath the paper. It looked as though Rembrandt had a tumour on his jaw.

Another train must have come in because suddenly a flood of harried passengers streamed through the station. Humping bags, chivvying children, they hustled across the hall, around Emmeline and the tobacconist's kiosk and out through the arch that led out of the station. Nobody looked at the poster.

I've been wrong about everything, Emmeline thought numbly, and she let the tide carry her out into the glass-and-metal dazzle of the street.

10

Dora refused to talk about what had happened on the train. Emmeline still went upstairs for supper, but Dora was different, shut up inside a glassy shell she could not penetrate. Everything was too loud, the clatter of the plates, her remarks to her grandmother, the way she laughed at her own jokes. When the old woman patted the arms of her chair, summoning them to sit with her, Dora crossed her arms tight around herself, folding her legs emphatically against the wall so that there was no possibility she might brush against Emmeline accidentally.

One evening they ran into one another in the street outside their building.

'We need to talk,' Emmeline said but Dora shook her head.

'There's nothing to say.' She sounded angry. 'Look, I know you can't help how you are, it must be very hard, always going against the world like that, and I'm sorry, I hope you find a way to be happy, but you can't expect me to be like you because I can't help how I am either and I'm just an ordinary girl. And that's that.'

Emmeline did not go up to Dora's flat that night. She went for a walk. She walked for a long time. The next day she met Anton at their usual place outside KaDeWe. She had not seen him for weeks. He was preoccupied, in a hurry, he only had time for one drink, but when she asked him about studio space he agreed to ask around.

The place he found was part of an old warehouse tucked behind a railway line in the north of the city, a large room shared by several artists. It was cold and noisy but the light was good and it was very cheap. Sometimes one of them sat for the others but mostly they worked alone. Emmeline searched back through her sketchbooks, looking for ideas. There was both pain and comfort in it, like picking a scab. Sometimes, late in the evening, walking home, she stopped to draw something that caught her eye. She did not show the drawings to anyone. She tucked them into the books that lay scattered around her flat, pressing them between the pages like flowers.

It was early September when, crossing the river to Museum Island, she bumped into Julius and his wife. She smiled briskly and tried to walk on but it was too late, Julius was already introducing Amelia and then, before Emmeline could make her excuses, Amelia had started on a story about the tour of America from which they had just returned.

'Julius suffered horribly at the hands of overfriendly natives,' she said, laughing. 'They worshipped him, hung on his every word, but they did insist on calling him always by his first name. Poor darling, you could see him bristling from the other side of the room.'

The tour, she said, had been exhausting, a ceaseless round of lectures and dinners and exhibitions in Julius's honour. 'Though it was only me that was exhausted, of course, Julius loved every minute of it, but then Julius is the master of the whirlwind court-ship. Look at us, ten weeks from the day of our first meeting to marriage. I should have realised. I couldn't keep up with him then either.' She smiled fondly up at Julius, then abruptly tapped his arm. 'Wait a minute, that girl who wrote to you about Matthias Rachmann, wasn't she a friend of Fräulein Eberhardt's?'

Julius's face snapped shut. 'I don't remember, darling. You know, we really do have to be going.'

'Julius thought he might have known her father,' Amelia went on, undeterred. 'Flora someone. What was her last name, darling, the girl? It began with a K.'

'Dora,' Emmeline said dumbly. 'Dora Keyserling.'

'I really must get back,' Julius interrupted. 'Why don't you give Amelia your telephone number, Emmeline? Perhaps you could come to tea one afternoon.'

'I'm not on the telephone,' Emmeline said. Dora, Dora, Dora. Her mouth was dry.

'Your address, then,' he said. 'It's been so long, I'd like to be able to tell your mother we'd seen you.' He took a notebook from his inside pocket and handed it to her. Reluctantly Emmeline scribbled her address.

It was only after they had turned to leave that Emmeline called after them. 'You never did write back to her, did you, to Dora?' she demanded. She did not know why it mattered, not now, but she knew that if Dora had been there she would not have had to ask and that that, somehow, was Julius's fault.

Julius stopped. 'And why would I have done that?' he asked coldly.

'Because she wanted to help Matthias and Matthias is your friend.'

'Help him how, exactly? By printing malicious gossip masquerading as news?'

'By giving him a chance to tell his side of the story first.'

'My dear girl, are you really so naïve? When did the newspapers tell anyone's side of the story but their own?'

'She won't give up, you know. If Matthias has been swindled—'

'No one has been swindled, least of all Matthias. Your would-be journalist friend can abandon her little investigations because there is nothing to investigate. The paintings are genuine. There is nothing else to say.'

The next morning, very early, Julius came to the tenement building. It was raining, a persistent low drizzle, and in the courtyard the damp gleamed black-green against the stained grey concrete. He must have spoken to the caretaker because she sent one of her boys up to bang on Emmeline's door.

The boy was the youngest, red-headed and sharp-chinned. He could not tell her who the man was or why he had come, only that he was old and very rich. When she hesitated the boy shook the coins in his fist and told her to get a move on. In the street a black car was idling at the kerb. As soon as she came out of the building the passenger door swung open and Julius gestured her inside.

He did not say where he was taking her. As the car drove towards Alexanderplatz, he closed the glass screen that separated them from the driver. Then he handed her a pen and a cheap cardboard notebook from the briefcase on his lap.

'A source close to de Vries,' he said. 'If she names me I shall deny everything.'

Beyond the window people hurried along the wet pavements, their heads lowered and the collars of their coats turned up. Julius told Emmeline to tell Dora Keyserling that Pieter de Vries planned to publish a supplement to his *catalogue raisonné*. Having included all of Rachmann's van Goghs in his original list, he had now inexplicably changed his mind. All thirty-two of the works that had passed through Rachmann's gallery would be excised from the catalogue.

Emmeline stared at him. 'I don't understand.'

'The pre-eminent Dutch expert no longer considers Matthias's paintings to be genuine. No doubt he believes that by saying so publicly he is acting in good faith. But I would ask your friend this: what manner of expert asserts one day that more than thirty paintings are indisputably the work of van Gogh and the next that they are categorically fakes? The paintings have not altered. All that has altered is de Vries's personal opinion. Surely, then, it is not the veracity of the work that this volte-face of his calls into question but the man's professional competency, the soundness of his so-called judgement. Write that down.'

'You don't agree with him?'

'I consider his views beyond the pale.'

'And Dora can quote you on that?'

'Categorically not.' Reaching again into his briefcase he took out an envelope. 'This is my statement. Everything else is off the record.'

Emmeline took the envelope. It was addressed to Dora at the *Merkur*. She frowned. 'Why Dora? Why not one of your high-up editor friends?'

Julius did not answer. He looked out at the street, his fingers drumming his leg. 'Tell your friend to speak to Clovis Hendriksen in The Hague. The man's a self-aggrandising windbag but he knows van Gogh.'

'And if she has questions? Should she telephone you? Write?'

'I have never met or spoken to Fräulein Keyserling. I issued a statement in response to a written press enquiry. I have no further comment to make.'

'And if de Vries is right and the paintings are fakes, what then?'

'I've said all I have to say.' Leaning across her, he turned the handle, pushing the door open. 'Good day, Emmeline.'

'And what about the Russian, the collector? Isn't it time he was called to account?'

Julius smoothed his tie, his eyes fixed on the back of the driver's head. 'Matthias gave his client certain assurances. Naturally he considers himself bound by their agreement.'

'And what about you?' Emmeline demanded. 'You've been his champion right from the start. This isn't just about him, it's about you, your reputation—'

'Which is exactly why he went to Switzerland yesterday and why I will be meeting with the man in question myself in due course. And no, before you ask, she cannot quote me on that.'

Emmeline considered him. Then slowly she climbed out of the car. Julius leaned over, slamming the door. The car swept away, sending up an arc of dirty water from the gutter. Swearing softly, Emmeline looked down at her wet feet. A sodden cigarette card clung to the kerb. Henry VIII, his legs astride, enjoying a Wahr cigarette.

A sharp glance of lightning froze the street like a photographer's flash. A pause, then thunder, dark and low, and, beneath her feet, in answer, the subterranean rumble of the U-Bahn. The rain began again, this time in earnest. Pushing Julius's letter into her pocket, Emmeline started for home.

When Emmeline told Dora about Julius, Dora gave a high little cry and flung her arms around her before she remembered herself and backed stiffly away. When she thanked Emmeline for her help she sounded like a lady mayoress opening a new hospital ward.

Two days later the *Merkur* ran the story. The editor gave it a paragraph on the fifth page. Several other Berlin newspapers picked the story up, in particular the claim that Köhler-Schultz and de Vries had agreed jointly to re-examine all thirty-two of the Rachmann paintings, but when both men refused to comment the story rapidly ran out of steam. When Dora told Toller she had contacts, she might be able to find out more, the editor shook his head. The news desk would take care of things from here, he told her. Summer was over and everyone who was anyone was coming back to Berlin. Dora had work to do.

Work, Dora told Emmeline resentfully, that she could do standing on her head. She had taken once again to dropping by in the evenings, the way she had when they first met. Emmeline wished she would not. Dora was unable to sit still, unable to talk about anything but Rachmann and his van Goghs.

'The vast majority,' she said, again and again. 'That's what the statement said, that he believes the vast majority to be genuine. Not all. And Köhler-Schultz is on Rachmann's side.'

She did not care what Toller said, she knew the news desk would not investigate the story, not properly anyway. She had no choice, she told Emmeline, but to do it herself. Her old despondency had evaporated, burned out by a harsh, humming freneticism. In her lunch hours she met Anton's gallery friends and pumped them for information. In the evenings she grilled Emmeline. What did Emmeline know about Rachmann's habits, his family? She made her go over every one of her encounters with him, and with Gregor, again and again. She wrote it all down. When at last she went upstairs to her own flat she took the stairs two at a time.

'Oma's asking for you,' she told Emmeline one evening. 'She wants to know why you don't visit any more.'

'And what have you told her?'

Dora shrugged. 'The truth. That I ask you and you don't come.'

'Is that the truth?'

'Isn't it?'

The next evening Emmeline went upstairs for supper. Everything was different. Even Oma was smaller somehow, shrunken, her bones like teeth beneath her papery skin. Her voice was rough, as though her coughing had scratched away the varnish. Her laugh was a saw rasping through wood.

She was still stubborn. She scowled as Dora told Emmeline about her refusal to allow Frau Becker to bathe her or get her dressed, her insistence on using the lavatory across the landing even though she did not always make it in time. Dora, always so patient, had grown snappish. She scolded the old woman as she ran water into the sink, demanding to know how she was supposed to take care of her when she would not take care of herself.

'I can't do this any more, Oma, not like this!' she cried, exasperated, crashing together dirty pots and pans.

She apologised later, when Emmeline was leaving, but there was something in the way she spoke, the lines around her mouth, that suggested she did not think she was the only one with something to be sorry for.

Emmeline lay awake for a long time that night. The next day she came back from the studio early, while Dora was still at work. She still had the key Dora had given her in case of emergencies, tied with a green ribbon so that it would not get lost in her bag. It was easy enough to let herself in.

'Why are you here?' Oma asked suspiciously but Emmeline only smiled and made her a cup of tea. Two days later she went again. Before long she had slipped into the habit of it. They talked, or Emmeline read aloud. Dora still brought books from the library but Oma's eyes had grown weak and reading tired her. She closed her eyes as she listened. Sometimes she fell asleep. Once, waking confused, she thought Emmeline was Dora. She held Emmeline's hand and would not let it go.

Emmeline did not tell Dora about her visits. It was not exactly a secret, if Dora had asked Emmeline would have told her, but she never did, not even when she came to Emmeline's flat after work. She was too busy asking questions, writing the answers down in her notebook. When she stopped asking there was nothing else to say. In the end Emmeline had to ask her to leave. She said she was tired, but the truth was it was too hard to bear, Dora there and not there, their conversation filled with gaps like the delays on a long-distance telephone call.

When Dora banged on the door at almost midnight she was in her party dress. Her eyes were shining and her face was red. 'Oh my God,' she said excitedly, pushing her way in. 'It's happening, it's finally happening.'

Two days ago, she told Emmeline, she had met with a friend of a friend of Anton's, a man called Walther. Another Berlin dealer had grown suspicious about a van Gogh he had acquired from Rachmann. If Walther knew the man's name he was not saying, but he told Dora that when the dealer tried to return the picture Rachmann had refused to take it. Livid, the dealer had talked to other gallery owners. People were jittery. Since coming to Germany, Rachmann's pictures had passed through many hands. The sums of money were eye-watering. If buyers lost their nerve and demanded the galleries buy them back, the losses could be ruinous. The only recourse then would be to demand that Rachmann reimbursed them in his turn or, if he would not or could not do so, to threaten legal action. A civil law suit, Walther said, was a matter of public record. There would be no way to keep something like that under wraps.

'Poor Matthias,' Emmeline said.

'Poor Matthias my foot,' Dora retorted, her eyes shining. That afternoon she had received a telephone call from another contact. A modern art gallery in Hannover famous for its provocations was considering a completely new approach for their van Gogh show in November: they proposed hanging a selection of Rachmann's paintings alongside a group of undisputed van Goghs so that visitors might compare them directly and decide for themselves if the Rachmanns were fakes. There was even a rumour that de Vries had been invited to discuss his doubts about the pictures at a special event. When Dora contacted them, both de Vries and the gallery responded with emphatic and carefully worded denials.

'Which means lawyers, which means it's true, or parts of it anyway. Toller's dragging his feet, he says it's not enough, that we'd risk a libel action, too much money and vested interests – which means his own friends, knowing him – but he has to publish now or we'll lose it. I mean, it's a huge story. If another newspaper gets hold of it . . . '

Emmeline said nothing. In this mood Dora was like a wind-up toy, she would not stop until she ran herself down. She supposed she should be glad for her, Dora had worked indefatigably, she deserved her scoop, but she just felt very tired. When Dora said that she should go, she had to prepare for the editorial conference, Emmeline nodded.

'Of course,' she said, forcing a smile. 'Well, good luck. And congratulations.' She started to close the door but Dora caught her arm.

'Wait,' she said. For a breathless moment Emmeline thought she meant to kiss her.

'I just wanted to say thank you. You've been a brick and I – well, you know. Thank you.' Pecking a hard, dry kiss towards Emmeline's ear she clattered away upstairs.

Emmeline sat in the dark on the broken-down sofa, staring up at the ceiling. Dora was right. The scandal was coming. You could almost see it darkening the horizon, thickening like a storm out at sea. Perhaps it would be Dora who broke the story, perhaps it would be someone else, but sooner or later it would hit and there would be nothing Matthias or anyone else could do but endure it. Julius already knew it, it was why he had leaked the investigation to Dora, he was trying to mitigate the damage, but there would be damage. To Julius, to de Vries and all the others who had staked their reputations on Matthias's van Goghs, and most of all to Matthias. Everything he owned, everything he was, could be destroyed.

And yet he kept his word and refused to divulge the identity of the Russian. Dora believed they were lovers. She suspected blackmail but what did Matthias have to hide? Surely nothing as ordinary as a male lover, not in unshockable Berlin where police turned a blind eye to the scores of openly queer bars and clubs and left the rouged-and-powdered boys on Friedrichstrasse to go about their business. Maybe if Matthias were married or a politician, but he was an art dealer. Homosexuality was almost a job requirement. Matthias would have to fuck his Russian on the front steps of the Reichstag before anyone in Berlin would be roused to arrest him.

The light from the streetlamp spilled its sulphurous glow across the floor. Amidst the jetsam of books and shoes and dirty cups was a drawing Emmeline had been working on, a sketch for a linocut. Black ink, a few lines, no more. An old woman, her head tucked into the curve of a young woman's neck. Emmeline turned away, her throat burning, scrubbing angrily at her eyes with the heels of her hands.

Love. It was the only possible explanation. Matthias was doing it for love.

11

The news that the Nationalgalerie had bought their first van Gogh made headlines across Germany. That the work was unquestionably a masterpiece attracted less interest than the quarter of a million marks they paid for it, more than the gallery's acquisition budget for the entire year.

Toller summoned Dora. He could not run her story, he said, not as it was. Rumour was another word for libel. He needed facts, names, statements, people willing to go on the record. 'Talk to Stubbig on the news desk,' he said. 'Tell him everything.'

Stubbig was short and bald with a stomach like a coal sack and fingers stained with nicotine. He sucked his yellow teeth while Dora told him what she had and scrawled a single word on a piece of paper. He pushed it across the desk to Dora. SOURCES, the paper said. Go back, he told her. Push harder. Sooner or later, something will give. When it does, we'll talk.

Dora pushed. She went to the office before it was light and returned again after the parties were over. She arranged for the caretaker to bring her grandmother a hot supper at night. Frau Schmidt's rates were exorbitant, Dora could barely afford her, but she did not care. What mattered was Oma – and the story.

The caretaker was slapdash and always in a hurry. She came late or much too early, slopping down a stew of fat and gristle, potatoes radish-raw or boiled to floury glue. She forgot to stoke the stove, to refill Oma's water jug, to take her to the lavatory. Dora did not notice but Emmeline did. She saw how rough she was, yanking and pulling at Oma as if she were a rag doll.

Oma told Emmeline not to fuss. Frau Schmidt was a little rough around the edges but she was not unkind, she said firmly, and she pulled her sleeves down over her wrists, hiding the marks that stained her skin.

'You're not to say anything to Dora, do you hear? I won't have her worrying over nothing.'

And so Emmeline bit her tongue, she knew anyway which one of them Dora would choose to believe, but she tried to be in the flat when the caretaker came. With a witness present Frau Schmidt was obliged to be more careful.

'You should be working, not up here with me,' Oma said sometimes but Emmeline pretended not to hear. She was glad to be away from the studio, away from the paintings she was making. There was something false about them, something sugary and shallow. They laboured for simplicity, for sincerity, and managed only mawkishness.

She preferred to sit with the old woman, drinking tea. Without Dora there to hush her Oma told stories, stories about Dora as a girl, about Dora's mother, about her own long-ago childhood. They bled into one another until it was hard to know where one ended and the next began, but in all of them the girl was funny and fidgety and fierce. Emmeline drew as she listened, Oma laughing, thoughtful, exhausted, asleep. She drew herself also, over and over, a mirror propped in her lap. She seemed to be seeing herself for the first time.

One night, returning late to her own flat, she wrote to Matthias. *We never knew each other well,* she wrote, *but I want you to know that even after all this time I think of that evening when you danced with me and, for a few minutes at least, I believed I could do anything.* She almost added a line from one of van Gogh's letters, *what's done in love is done well,* but there was too much of Vincent the preacher in it and she did not want to preach. She wished him happiness and signed the letter with a handshake. She sent it to the gallery, it would reach him that afternoon, but as she slipped it through the slot of the post box she felt like a child dropping a corked bottle into the sea, dispatching a declaration of friendship to whoever might chance to pick it up.

Something gave. A little after eleven on a bright autumn morning Dora received a telephone call from Walther. The proprietor of the gallery where he worked had received a letter from de Vries in The Hague. After months of re-evaluation, de Vries wished to inform him that he was to excise a number of paintings from his *catalogue raisonné.* The excisions would be listed in a supplement to the catalogue, to be published on 10 November: a complimentary copy would be provided to all those who had purchased the original. He did not apologise.

Dora went to Stubbig. Within the hour the *Merkur* had a copy of the letter. Within two they had confirmation from de Vries's office. More than thirty paintings included in the original van Gogh *catalogue raisonné* were no longer judged to be genuine. No further details were given but, when pressed, the office was unable to deny that the discredited pictures might include the four Rachmann paintings rejected by the Cornelius Gallery and the self-portrait acquired from Rachmann by the Stransky Gallery in New York.

VAN GOGH PAINTINGS ARE FAKES! the *Merkur* blared

the next day. They were not alone. Three other newspapers led with the same story. News, it seemed, travelled even faster than delivery boys. Dora was furious. If Toller had only published when she first brought him the story, she raged, but no, he had to wait, had to sit there swinging his legs until the rest of the country caught up with him, until her scoop was no longer a scoop at all. His lack of nerve was contemptible.

Worse still, he flatly refused to authorise her to go to The Hague to interview de Vries. He had a man in Holland, he said, who was more than capable of handling the story. The way he shook his head, Dora raged to Emmeline, she might have been a child wheedling a sip of her father's whisky. Three days later, with the press in Paris and London and Amsterdam gleefully seizing on the scandal, de Vries granted an exclusive interview to a prestigious Dutch newspaper. The dubious canvases, he said, had been released on to the market through a dealer in Berlin, Matthias Rachmann, who claimed to represent a Russian collector. He now considered all thirty-two of Rachmann's pictures to be fakes.

Rachmann himself had gone to ground. Dora talked to everyone she knew but no one seemed to know where he was. The story was almost a week old when his lawyers finally issued a statement to the press. The claims made by Pieter de Vries were baseless and malicious. Steps were being taken to block their publication. In the meantime, any iteration of his libels would result in punitive legal action.

The refutation only fanned the flames. Outside the Rachmann Gallery reporters crowded the pavement, hoping to catch a glimpse of him. Newsreel crews brought vans that blocked the street. The boutique proprietors called the police and the fur-swaddled ladies let their little dogs lift their legs on their boxes of equipment, but they still came back. The story was irresistible, an intoxicating cocktail of money, celebrity, chicanery, humiliation and homosexual intrigue. According to Moscow's Museum of Artistic Culture, none of the Rachmann van Goghs had ever been in Russia.

Toller sent Stubbig. Dora had made a valiant start, he said, but it was time for the big guns. Klaus Stubbig had thirty years' experience. He was a heavyweight.

'Oh, he's a heavyweight,' Dora seethed to Emmeline. 'A bloated old hack who's never sober after noon. The most inventive writer at the paper? For Christ's sake. The only inventive pieces of writing that bastard's come up with in the last decade are his bloody expense claims.'

An apprenticeship, that was all she asked, but Toller would not listen. Stubbig's story meant Stubbig's way and Stubbig was adamant. Apprentices were a millstone around a reporter's neck, that was Stubbig's view. Toller's hands were tied.

'Then he dares to tell me journalism's no career for a girl like me, as though I'm a child in petticoats, as though it wasn't me who broke the story in the first place! He's insisting I give everything I've got to that bastard Stubbig so the two of them can take all the glory. I swear to God, I'd rather burn every last page . . . '

Emmeline said nothing. She sat in silence as Dora raged, shouting at phantoms like the drunk in his ragged greatcoat on Bülowplatz.

'It's my story, Em,' she ranted, again and again. 'Mine.'

'Except it's not, is it?' Emmeline said at last. 'Not any more.' She was not sure why she said it, except that she was exhausted and it happened to be true.

Dora stared at her. 'I don't believe it. You're on their side.'

'Of course I'm not,' Emmeline protested but perhaps she was. She knew how unfairly Dora had been treated. It was bitter that Toller refused to reward her for her efforts, worse still that he expected her to go back to the social pages without complaint.

And yet Emmeline could not help being glad. Perhaps if Dora went back to her old job then everything else would go back to the way it had been before too. Perhaps she would talk to Emmeline as she used to, when Emmeline was her friend and not just an audience for her obsession with Matthias Rachmann and the injustices of the Berlin press.

She avoided Dora after that, or perhaps they avoided each other. She stayed late at the studio and tried not to read the newspapers. She was experimenting with woodcuts. The technique was new to her. She had tried it briefly as a student and disliked it, dismissing it as craft rather than art, fit for book illustrations perhaps but lacking the great depth and grandeur of paint. But she no longer trusted paint, the confident gloss it gave to ideas that were commonplace or shallow or only half-thought. It was like a rich sauce, she thought, disguising tainted meat.

Prints hid nothing. Her progress was slow, she was clumsy and inexperienced, she made many mistakes, but she liked the ritual of it, the slow acclimatisation of the wood as it settled in the studio, the sizing and the sanding and the smoothing with alcohol to remove the dust. There was something in the simplicity of the images, the reduction of line and shadow to its most essential parts, that made her feel like she was peeling off the winter layers of herself, letting the light touch her skin.

Exaggerate the essential, van Gogh wrote to Theo. *Leave the obvious vague.* She was not sure why it had taken her so long to understand what he meant.

One night, she found Dora waiting on her doorstep. There was a raw patch at the corner of her mouth. She picked at the rough skin with her fingernail as Emmeline fumbled for her key. Anton's friend Walther had come to see her, she said, he had information but he wanted money, he would not talk until she paid him.

'I thought you might lend it to me,' she said. 'I'll pay you back. As soon as I sell the story I'll pay you back.'

Emmeline took out her purse. Dora mumbled a thank you and tucked the money into the waistband of her skirt. Emmeline glimpsed a brief pale gleam of skin. 'I wish you'd stop,' she said quietly but Dora shook her head.

'How can I stop? I have to show them, don't I? I have to prove them wrong.'

'And then what?' Emmeline asked, but Dora only glared at her.

'There's something else I have to ask you,' she said. 'A favour.'

'What favour?'

'I need you to persuade Köhler-Schultz to talk to me. On the record.'

Emmeline gaped at her. 'Jesus, Dora, when are you going to understand? There's no chance he'll ever talk to you, no chance at all.'

'You don't know that. I mean, you could at least ask, couldn't you? He trusted me before. Why not now?'

Emmeline bit her lip. She wanted to shake Dora. Why could she not see what was right in front of her eyes? Julius knew every newspaper editor in Berlin. He had not come to Dora because he trusted her. He had done it because she was a nobody and no one would ever trace the leak. He saw the way the wind was blowing, that his best – perhaps his only – chance of defending his own position lay in undermining de Vries's. Julius knew quite well that de Vries had never agreed to a joint re-examination of the paintings, but he also knew that if de Vries then refused to go through with it his decision to discredit more than thirty paintings would be judged not as a confession, a courageous *mea culpa*, but as arrogant and one-sided. Julius had not trusted

Dora. He had trusted she would be naïve enough to play into his hands.

Dora clutched Emmeline's arm. 'Please?'

Wearily Emmeline shrugged. The thought of trying to explain made her heart ache, and anyway Dora would never listen. 'Fine. I'll try.'

The next morning she woke to find a note slipped under her door. *Any news from JKS? D x* She put the note in her pocket and did nothing. She did not write to Julius. What would be the point? The next day there was another note from Dora. *Surely he's come back to you by now?* Two days later, there was a third.

Where are you? Come to supper tomorrow. Oma misses you, she says you're not allowed to say no.

'Well?' Dora said to Emmeline as soon as she opened the door, and when Emmeline shook her head she glared at the wall and banged her spoon furiously around the stewpot on the stove.

Oma took Emmeline's hand. 'Dear Emchen,' she said softly, smiling up at her, and Emmeline bent down, gathering her bones in her arms. There were towers of Dora's notebooks and folders stacked on the tiny table. They had to move them on to the floor to make room for supper.

'When Dora was very little her governess put a pile of books on her chair so she could reach the table but Dora refused to sit on them,' Oma said. 'Remember, Dodo? You thought you would squash all the people who lived inside.' She smiled at Dora, but Dora was not listening. She eyed the piles of papers, nudging them pensively with one foot. After supper, as Emmeline carried the dirty plates to the sink, she took a manila folder from a pile and leafed through it. Oma looked up from her armchair.

'Enough work for one day,' she coaxed. 'Come and sit down.'

Emmeline sat. Dora frowned, turning a page.

'Dora, we're waiting,' Oma said more sharply but Dora did not look up. Emmeline took the old woman's hand.

'Why don't I start?' she said. 'When I walked through Alexanderplatz today they were setting up the Christmas market. The air smelled like cinnamon and, behind a stall piled with oranges, there was a man with a huge moustache all tucked in on itself like the bow on a present.'

'The brother, Em,' Dora blurted. 'We forgot the brother!'

'Don't interrupt,' Oma scolded but Dora waved a hand, batting her words away.

'Gregor Rachmann,' she said. 'He liked you, didn't he? He liked you a lot.'

Emmeline shrugged. 'What's that got to do with anything?'

'Think about it. He and Rachmann are in on this together. They both went to Holland to see that Dutch expert, Hendriksen. So he'll know what's going on, the inside story. All you have to do is send him one of your letters full of charming sketches, you're lonely, you've been thinking of him, how about a little private dinner, a drink or two in an intimate bar where we can be alone? A silk dress, a few glasses of wine, a hand on his sleeve when you laugh—'

'Stop it,' Emmeline hissed. 'Don't say another word.'

'But it's perfect, don't you see? He was the one to start it so he—'

'You're my pimp now?'

'Oh, come on, it's not like that. A favour, that's all, and you never know, you might like it . . . ' Dora grinned, baring her teeth, and it was like grasping something on fire, Emmeline snatched up all the rage and the pain before she could feel it and threw it as hard as she could.

'What the fuck is wrong with you?' she shouted. 'You think you can pimp me out for a paragraph in your stupid fucking newspaper? Well, fuck you, Dora. Fuck you.'

'Emchen, please!' Oma said, distressed, but Dora only rolled her eyes.

'Oh, please, don't be so melodramatic. I'm not asking you to – you know – just to soften him up a bit, make him think he's in with a—'

Emmeline stood up. Her legs were shaking. 'What the hell happened to you, Dora?' she said and each word was something breaking inside her. 'When did you stop being you?'

Dora's bewildered frown made her want to scream and smash something. Instead, snatching up her bag, she slammed her way out of the flat. On her own landing she rummaged for her key, scrabbling and raking until in a fury she upended it, hurling its contents out on to the landing. The key skittered on to the floor, a bright glint of silver, and Emmeline bent her head and wept, only there were no tears, just the sharp corners of something she could not swallow. She pressed her fingers into her eye sockets as though she could push the tears out but instead, in the darkness, there was only the flicker of burned-down candles, the white gleam of paper translucent with oil.

We'll cross your ethics when we come to them. And here they were.

12

She went to the studio. She wanted to be where she was no one, where the work was all that mattered. Beyond the tram window the city floated in the darkness, its lights gauzed in fog. The studio was freezing. She kept her coat on as she worked but the cold still made her clumsy. When she came to cut the block she gouged too hard. The gashes gaped white in the pale wood.

Slowly a grey dawn leaked in. Some of the other artists arrived. When it grew dark they went away again. Emmeline did not want to go home but she could not think where else to go. It was snowing when she got off the tram. At the shop on the corner she bought a bottle of cheap Russian brandy. She hugged it against her as she pushed open the door to her building. Frau Schmidt was in the lobby, talking to a woman in a flowered apron. She looked round as Emmeline came in.

'You seen your friend, the one from 11C?' she asked and when Emmeline shook her head she shrugged, turning back to the woman in the apron. 'Well, I ain't goin' up there. I told her, a hot dinner, that's all, not nurse-maidin' while she's out all hours.'

The flat was colder than the studio but Emmeline did not light the stove. She climbed into bed with her coat on and drank the brandy out of the bottle. The snow was getting heavier. She watched it swirl and swarm, black against the light-stained sky. She could see her breath. She wondered if Frau Schmidt had remembered to stoke the stove for Oma. She did not always remember.

The brandy burned her throat. She drank more. She should have expected it. You found someone you thought was special and, sooner or later, when the newness wore off and they turned out to be like everyone else, you woke up and they were gone. You expect too much of people, her mother used to tell her, but Emmeline did not listen because who listened to someone who thought what mattered was to know the right people and wear the right clothes and always remember the right knife and fork, who believed that as long as your life looked perfect to other people it did not matter if everything was wrong inside?

It was her own fault, she knew that. She should have left before, while it was still her choice to do the leaving. She had forgotten to be careful. The pain of it shimmered behind the brandy, bright as a migraine.

The brightness faded. Time slipped. The building made its evening noises. People shouted. Infants wailed. The clank of the lavatory cistern banged through the pipes. Dora would be home from work by now. The snow was seething outside the window, the air solid with it. Emmeline thought of Oma alone and ill, the stove out. She could not get the picture of her out of her mind. Jamming the brandy bottle in her pocket, she went upstairs.

The stove was still warm. Oma was in her armchair, a rug over her knees. Her brow burned with fever. Berlin was unbearable in summer, she muttered to Emmeline, so hot, there was never enough air to breathe, but she shivered violently as Emmeline helped her to bed and tucked the blankets around her.

'There you go,' Emmeline said, slurring a little. 'All settled now.'

The old woman's face softened as she drifted back into sleep. Emmeline's own head was heavy, it was an effort to keep her eyes open. Kicking off her shoes, she lay down next to Oma.

The slam of the front door woke her. Shivering, she sat up, dry-mouthed and gritty-eyed, wiping the drool from her chin with the back of her hand, half-remembered dreams clinging to her like cobwebs, Julius and Gregor Rachmann, his hand on the small of her back. In the bed beside her Oma murmured something in her sleep. Emmeline put a hand on her forehead, checking her temperature. Beneath her downy hair her skull was as fragile as an egg.

In the other room all the lights were burning. Emmeline squinted in the brightness. Dora stood beside the stove, scrawling in a notebook. She was hatless and there was snow in her hair, on her coat, clumped on the soles of her boots. Her nose was pink with cold. When she saw Emmeline in the doorway she grinned at her and Emmeline could not help it, her heart turned over. Dora turned back to her notebook.

'Oma's not well,' Emmeline said.

Dora frowned. 'What kind of not well?'

'She has a fever. I – Frau Schmidt said someone should stay with her.'

Dora's frown deepened. Still reading her notebook, she walked past Emmeline and into the bedroom. Her boots left white petals of snow on the linoleum. A moment later she came out again. She turned a page. 'She's fine. She's sleeping.'

'You don't think we should fetch the doctor? She was so hot.'

'She's fine,' Dora said again. She took a pen from the table and scribbled rapidly. 'Thanks for coming up.'

It was not coldness as much as indifference. If it was not in the notebook it did not concern her in the least. Suddenly all Emmeline wanted was to smash the hard, heedless shell of her, to make her sorry.

'Julius Köhler-Schultz said no,' she said. 'He wants nothing else to do with you.'

Dora shrugged. She did not look up. 'No one cares what he thinks anyway. What people want is the inside story, don't you see? A personal portrait of Matthias Rachmann by the woman who knows him best in the world. I've got him this time, Em. I think I've finally got him.'

'What are you talking about?'

Dora put down her pen. She looked up at Emmeline, a small hard smile on her lips, and suddenly she was talking, the words coming faster and faster, tumbling over one another. Stupid with sleep and brandy, Emmeline could barely follow her. She thought of Irina, her eyes glittering with cocaine as though she was dazzled by the brilliance of the lights in her head. As though nothing that had happened before that moment had ever really happened.

'There it was, tucked away in this tiny magazine no one's heard of,' Dora gabbled. 'No one else seems to know she exists, certainly no one's talked to her, but once I saw that Rachmann wheeled her on Sundays by the lake it was easy. Name, address, everything. And, best of all, she's on the telephone.'

'Who is?' Emmeline said.

'Rachmann's mother, you blockhead. Haven't you been listening at all?'

Early in the morning was best, she said, people were less guarded when they had only just woken up. Besides, the woman was old and frail and almost certainly lonely, she would not refuse a distressed young mother with a sick child. She would let Dora inside to use the telephone and Dora would cry and they would talk about their sons. An exclusive: *VAN GOGH CHEAT, A*

MOTHER'S HEARTBREAK. Nils had even lent her a tiny camera, small enough to hide in her sleeve. This was a story of pictures, after all, a photograph would be worth—

'Shut up!' Emmeline cried, unable to endure another word, and she swiped at Dora's notebook, knocking it on to the floor. 'Shut up or I swear—'

Dora's lip curled. 'You're drunk.'

'I am. Unfortunately it doesn't seem to help.'

'I don't understand you.'

'You don't understand me?' Emmeline laughed bleakly. 'Jesus.'

'Why do you always have to be like this, why can't you just be happy for me for once? This is my big chance—'

'To do what? To break into an ill old woman's home?'

'It's not breaking in. It's—'

'Lying and cheating? Well that's all right then. As long as you don't have a shred of decency or conscience. Anything for the story.'

'People have a right to know the truth.'

'The truth?' Emmeline shouted. 'For Christ's sake, Dora, don't you see? All this, it's – it's shit. Twisted delusional muck-raking shit.' Seizing a pile of folders, she hurled them on to the floor. Papers scattered.

Dora stood very still. Her eyes were chips of ice. 'Get out.'

'How long before this is all you are, Dora, till there's none of you left?'

'I said, get out.'

Emmeline looked at Dora, the lines of her so familiar she could feel the movement of them in her fingers. Then silently she squatted, gathering up crumpled handfuls of papers, shoving them back into the folders, piling the folders in a stack. There were chalky marks on Dora's boots where the snow had melted. When she stood, the folders in her arms, Dora reached out for them, but Emmeline did not give them to her. Turning her back, she yanked open the door of the stove and rammed them inside. Dora screamed. She clutched at Emmeline's arm, thrust her hip against her, struggling to push her out of the way, to grab at the burning papers, but Emmeline pushed back, bracing herself against the sink as she snatched up the poker and pushed the folders deeper into the stove. The papers darkened, then caught, a bright surge of flame before Emmeline kicked the door shut.

Dora stared at her, her eyes stretched, the flesh shrunk tight against the bones. Her lips peeled back from her teeth like an animal's. Then with a sharp cry she set upon Emmeline, scratching, slapping, snatching at her hair, raining down blows with her fists. Emmeline hunched her back, covering her head with her arms, then, twisting round, struck out as hard as she could with her elbows. There was a sickening crack as bone met bone.

Dora fell backwards. Her hands were over her face, blood running between her fingers. Emmeline stared, frozen, mesmerised by the glossy redness of it. She put out a hand, her fingers brushing Dora's, touching the slick warm blood.

Dora scrabbled backwards, her hands still over her face. 'Don't touch me,' she hissed. The blood ran down her pale wrists and into the cuffs of her coat. Dark patches glistened stickily on the black wool of her lapels.

Emmeline looked at her outstretched hand, smeared with Dora's blood. It seemed to belong to someone else. 'You're bleeding,' she said helplessly.

'Get out!' Dora screamed and when Emmeline did not move she kicked out at her hand, catching the knuckles with her boot. 'I said, get out!'

13

Frau Schmidt knocked at Emmeline's door early the next morning. She had a letter of authorisation, carefully signed, instructing her to take possession of the key Emmeline held to Dora's flat. When Emmeline asked why Dora could not collect it herself, the caretaker frowned. Fräulein Keyserling has been called away early, she said haughtily, urgent newspaper business. Emmeline imagined Dora weeping on Matthias Rachmann's mother's doorstep. The bruises on her face would help, Emmeline thought, she had done her a favour. She wanted to laugh at the heart-ripping joke of it, to throw her head back and howl like a dog.

Authority made Frau Schmidt officious. When Emmeline reached out for the letter she stepped back, holding it above her head. Her blouse was stained yellow under the arms and her neck was red and flaky.

'The key, if you please,' she said.

Emmeline hesitated. Then, taking her bag from the back of the chair, she rummaged inside. 'Sorry, I don't seem to have it.'

'Let me see.'

'Be my guest.' She handed Frau Schmidt the bag, watching as the caretaker dug through it. 'It may be in my satchel at the studio. Or somewhere in the flat. I'm not sure, it's a while since I used it. Can I bring it to you when I find it?'

Frau Schmidt glared at Emmeline. Both of them knew that the caretaker could not enter a flat without the tenant's permission, not if the rent was paid.

'Six o'clock latest,' she said, tapping the letter against her hip like a nightstick. 'Keys is the lawful property of the occupant.'

The cobbler cut the copy while she waited. Emmeline put it on a piece of string and hung it around her neck.

She walked. It was a bleak grey day but she walked fast and little by little the cold key took on the warmth of her. Everywhere the city was being dug up, metal teeth biting through asphalt, pipes poking from the broken earth like tubes from a pig's liver. She felt stiff and hollow, a mannequin copy of herself. She passed the men with shovels and wheelbarrows, the steam pile-drivers thundering steel posts into the ground, the people hurrying along the planks set up where the pavements should have been, and it was like the old films in the days before the talkies: they jostled and thundered and opened and closed their mouths but there was no sound, nothing but jerking shapes, a roll of light and dust. Even the headache that thrummed against her skull seemed to belong to someone else.

Near the Tiergarten she stopped on a bridge and stared down at the canal. The water was black and still as a photograph. Beside her, on a dirt-streaked plinth, a naked Hercules battled with a lion. His first labour. Dora had told her that. Afterwards, when Hercules had choked the lion to death, he skinned it with its own claws and wore it as armour, his face framed by its huge jaws. Near here Rosa Luxemburg's waterlogged corpse had been dragged from the canal, months after she had been tortured and shot. Dora told her that too.

A horn blared. Startled, Emmeline turned to see a motor car roaring past a horse-drawn cab. The horse reared, sending the cab skewing across the road. Tyres squealed. The cabby was shouting. There was a scream, a shriek of brakes, then suddenly a rip of air tearing away and a sickening smash that ricocheted through her legs, punching the breath from her chest. Perhaps a foot away, the car's bonnet was crushed against the bridge's stone parapet. Shards of silvery glass glittered on the ground. A man in a dark overcoat grabbed her elbow. He was pale, out of breath, his hat askew.

'You're not hurt,' he said. 'Thank God.'

She looked at him and then at the motor car. Smoke hissed from the crumpled bonnet. There was a smell of engine oil, burned rubber. As the driver's door swung open a sudden swarm of people crowded around the car, voices raised. In the middle of the hubbub the cab horse hunched in its traces, its head low, its thin withers frothed with sweat. When Emmeline had first come to Berlin half of the city's cabs had been horse cabs but these days you hardly ever saw them. That was the way with Berlin. Nothing ever stayed the same.

'You should sit down,' the man said. 'The shock—'

'No shock,' she said and, touching the lion's foot with the tips of her fingers, she turned and went back the way she had come.

It was dark by the time she reached home. The wind cut through the cloth of her coat, biting at her ears, her calves. In the shadows near the street door three boys clustered together, passing round a cigarette. One of them whistled as she passed, a two-fingered shriek, and the others laughed. As she pushed her way into the building she held up one finger behind her and let the door slam.

Frau Schmidt sprang from her room like a rat from a trap. The tip of her nose was white, the knuckle of cartilage sharp against the skin. Emmeline handed her the key on its green ribbon. 'Fräulein Keyserling's grandmother,' she said. 'You'll take care of her, won't you?'

'What I do or don't do for another tenant is no business of yours,' the caretaker said primly, fishing in the pocket of her apron. 'Here, this came for you.'

Emmeline took the telegram without looking at it. She supposed it was from Balz, he had told her the last time they met that he was working with a new client, that there might be something in it for her. The thought of another commission, the exacting emptiness of the work, was strangely consoling. The stairwell smelled of boiled cabbage. She could hear the clatter of pots and dishes, shouts, the squeals of squabbling children. Each cramped flat crammed with lives, the centre of their own stories.

Her own flat was silent and very cold. The cup from her breakfast sat unwashed in the sink. She fumbled open the telegram, then stopped in surprise. Not Balz after all. Julius Köhler-Schultz.

IMPERATIVE WE SPEAK STOP
PLEASE TELEPHONE EARLIEST

Emmeline's heart sank. She thought of Dora and of Julius, who loved Matthias Rachmann in a way that Emmeline thought she might finally have come to understand, not as a friend or a lover, not even as a son, but as an unimagined and infinitely better piece of himself. But if he wanted it this way, if he wanted Dora, that meant he was lying. Lying or betraying someone else's secrets. Saving his own skin.

The tears came unbidden. Emmeline rubbed them away and thought of a story she had read as a girl, a letter written in snake venom that killed the recipient as they read it. She could feel it already, the poison on her fingers, burning itself into the tiny cracks in her skin. She would not be a part of it. Tearing up the telegram roughly once and then again, she dropped the pieces of paper on to the floor. Then, hoisting her bag on to her shoulder, she turned and went back down the stairs.

She went to Anton's gallery on Wilhelmsplatz. He would let her stay, at least for a night or two. She felt a sudden sharp longing for his waspish jokes, the way he took her troubles like a magician's balloons and twisted them into something amusing and absurd, but he was busy with a client, he could not talk. He gave her the address of a bar on Friedrichstrasse, told her to meet him there at seven o'clock.

He arrived at half past eight. The bar was loud and very busy. He had changed out of his suit into a billowy chiffon shirt that might have been purple or blue, the lights made it impossible to tell. When she hugged him she could feel the stripes of his ribs.

'I thought you were dead,' he shouted over the blare of the band. He told her he was happy, that life was good, that he was talking to a gallery about an exhibition of his work, that he had moved out of Schillerstrasse to a place in Dahlem, a first-floor flat with French windows and a balcony.

'You're officially grown up,' Emmeline said and he laughed but he winced when she asked if she could stay with him for a while.

'I'm not sure . . . Willi – I don't know. It's his place.'

'Willi? What happened to Kurt?' but Anton shook his head and did not answer.

'Please?' she begged him. 'I wouldn't ask if I wasn't desperate.'

Anton sighed. 'Tonight, all right? Tomorrow you find somewhere else.'

She slept on the sofa. When she woke Willi was sitting at the kitchen table in his shirtsleeves, reading the newspaper. He was wide-necked and heavy-jowled, his thick curls touched with grey.

He glanced up at Emmeline and then back at his paper. He did not smile. At the stove Anton was making coffee.

'Police finally got their hands on that van Gogh forger,' Willi said through a mouthful of buttered roll. 'Is that coffee nearly done?'

Anton brought the pot to the table and poured. 'They've arrested him?' he asked.

'Chap gave himself up. Says here he rang the police from the Netherlands and agreed to help with their enquiries. They must have been on to him. Man's clearly guilty as sin.' Gulping his coffee Willi stood up, pulling on his jacket. He put a proprietorial hand on Anton's backside. 'I'm late. I'll see you later. And no more waifs and strays, all right?'

He spoke just loudly enough for Emmeline to hear. Anton smiled awkwardly.

'Have a good day,' he said. He did not look at Emmeline. They listened in silence to Willi's footsteps tapping down the hall, the click of the front door closing behind him.

'I should go,' Emmeline said and Anton nodded.

'So they got Rachmann,' he said as she put on her coat. 'Dora must be beside herself.'

Emmeline did not answer. She hugged him tightly. 'Thank you for letting me stay.'

'That's all right.'

'I'm sorry if I got you into trouble.'

'It's not like that.'

'No. Well, see you soon, then.'

'Right. So long. Good luck.'

Emmeline hesitated, biting her lip. 'Be happy, Anton Dumier.'

'I'm doing my best.'

14

They were selling the *Merkur* at the station. When the vendor waved a copy at her Emmeline pretended not to see. At the Zoo station she got off the train and went to the bank. Once she had money she could find lodgings, somewhere to stay while she decided what to do. She waited at the counter as the bank clerk examined her cheque and paged through the ledger to find her account. His finger ran down the columns, then stopped, tapping something she could not see.

'I'm sorry,' he said, frowning. 'There are insufficient funds in your account to cover this withdrawal.'

'Then there's been a mistake. What about the monthly deposit from Jacob Visler, surely that's cleared by now—'

'According to our records the last deposit to this account was in November.'

'Then you must have made a mistake. The money is wired on the first of every month. Always. My stepfather does it personally. He wouldn't have forgotten.'

'As I say, the last deposit was made in November. I'm sorry.' He held out the cheque. Emmeline stared at it dizzily. She could not believe Jacob would do that, just stop the payments without a word. Had her mother found out and stopped him? But he could have written to her, surely, had the decency to let her know. How did she think she would live?

She had to wait almost ten minutes to use the public telephone on Prenzlauer Allee. The booth smelled of hair oil and other people's breath. She heard the operator speaking to someone on the other end, asking if they would accept the charges, then the click as the line connected.

'Fräulein Eberhardt, is that you?' It was Streicher, Jacob's habitually unruffled private secretary. He sounded strained.

'Yes, it's me. I need to speak to Jacob, it's urgent.'

'He's not here, he's at the hospital. I – I'm so sorry.'

'The hospital, why? What's happened?'

'He didn't tell you?'

It was a terrible connection. She could hardly hear what Streicher was saying. They had been trying to reach her, no one seemed to know her address or how they might find her, not until Julius Köhler-Schultz telephoned, and then when he offered to break the news—

'I'm so terribly, terribly sorry,' Streicher said. The line crackled as he said something about a weekend with the Metzes, bad weather, ice, loss of control, a tree, the words like pebbles on a frozen pond, skittering out of reach. Emmeline thought of Elvira, who only liked to ski on the flat, her legs scissoring backwards and forwards like a wooden puppet.

'Skiing,' she said stupidly.

'A motor toboggan,' Streicher said. The driver had broken his leg but Frau Visler— Emmeline heard only some of the words. Thrown. Impact. Skull. Seizure.

'She's dead,' she whispered.

'No, God, no, absolutely not – unconscious, but the severity of her injuries, they can't, that is, they don't know yet if – I'm so sorry. May I tell Herr Visler you'll come immediately?'

Emmeline's legs were shaking. A motor truck rumbled past and it echoed in her head, the sickening smash as the car hit the parapet of the Hercules bridge. She leaned against the side of the booth.

'Fräulein, are you still there?'

'I – I don't have any money.'

Streicher seemed relieved to have something practical to do. She was to leave everything to him, he would arrange a train ticket, a place in the dining car, an automobile to collect her in Munich. There was a train leaving Berlin in two hours, all she had to do was go to the station. When the call ended, Emmeline stood where she was for a long time, listening to the soft disconnected hum of the empty line. At least if her mother died she would not have to worry about money, a voice in her head whispered, and she closed her eyes, her throat burning as if she had swallowed tiny shards of glass.

She knew she should take clothes but when she looked into her wardrobe nothing made sense, so she took what she could see, yanking blouses from hangers, balling up sweaters and slacks. At the back of the wardrobe she found a clot of scarlet wool, creased and musty. Irina's scarf. She pressed it to her face, inhaling, but all she could smell was dust and raw wood. She dropped it, then picked it up and wrapped it round her neck.

They were talking to the caretaker as she came downstairs, two of them in helmets and greatcoats with gleaming gold buttons.

'That's her,' Frau Schmidt exclaimed and they turned. The older one wore wire-rimmed round spectacles and a sorrowful expression. He looked more like a professor than a policeman.

The younger one was lanky, with bulging blue eyes. He jerked his head at the bag on her shoulder.

'Leaving, are we?' he asked.

She told them her mother had been in an accident, that she was needed urgently in Munich, but the older man only tutted regretfully. There was no need to be alarmed, he told her, she was not under arrest, but Munich would have to wait. They had some questions, that was all, they hoped she might assist them with their enquiries.

The police car smelled of something rotten, it made Emmeline feel sick. She stared out of the window, her stomach coiling up into her throat. They would not tell her where they were taking her. She wanted to ask what they knew, what Dora had told them, but she was afraid to speak, afraid of incriminating herself, so she sat in silence, her hands pressed against her stomach to keep it steady. They drove her to the police headquarters on Alexanderplatz. She had not noticed before how like a prison it was. It hulked over the square, its walls studded with tiny windows. When they took her out of the car she was sick in the gutter. They waited until she had finished, then they took her to a room with two chairs and a table and a barred window too high to see out of. The clang of the iron door made her teeth sing.

She wanted to call Streicher, Streicher would know what to do, who to call, but though she hammered on the door no one came. She sat on one chair and then the other. Her mouth tasted sour. She spoke Dora's name under her breath, she cursed her in Russian, she wanted to be angry, but all she could think of was her mother's smashed-up body, all the poems and the songs inside her leaking out. She thought of the rose-and-jasmine scent of her in the lamplight of her childhood bedroom, the gleam of silk and diamonds, the untouchable going-out otherness of her. The knot in Emmeline's heart as she blew her a kiss, the same smile, the same words, always on her lips. 'Darling, you won't even know that I'm gone.'

The light turned duller, grittier. When she stood on the chair she could see a triangle of leaden sky, snowflakes, grey on grey. Once, when she was about seven, she had poured flour-and-water paste into her mother's evening shoes so that she could not leave the house. No one had ever said anything about it. No one had ever said anything about anything. Somewhere, a long way off, she could hear the muffled bleat of a telephone.

The darkness ran into the room, grain by grain. Emmeline put her head down on the table and closed her eyes. She did not know what time it was. In her mind she laid her mother on a bed, held her hand, dropped it, held it again, and there were either too many words or none at all. On her pillow her mother's face stiffened and cracked like drying clay. Again and again it played, like a reel of film, and each time she wanted the ending to be different and the ending was always the same.

It was very late when they came for her. A policeman took her to another room with another table. This time there was no window, only a mirror along one wall. An unshaded bulb threw a thin, stark light. Two men sat on one side of the table. They rose as she entered. The taller of the two men introduced himself as Kriminalkommissar Gans, his colleague as Leutnant Kufalt. Unlike Kufalt, Gans wore civilian clothes. He was smooth, placatory. There had been a misunderstanding, he said. He had not meant to keep her waiting, he hoped she had not been too uncomfortable. He offered her a glass of water, asked if she would prefer tea. His kindness was too much for Emmeline. She began to cry.

'You have to let me go,' she pleaded. 'Please, Herr Kommissar. My mother has been in a terrible accident. They don't know if she'll – I have to go to Munich.'

Gans smiled at her and shook his head. He was sorry, he said, but that would not be possible. There were matters that had to be cleared up, he was sure she understood. Until his questions were answered she would not be going anywhere at all. There was a folder, fat with paper, on the table in front of him but he did not open it. He leaned back in his chair, his fingers steepled at his lips. Beside him the uniformed Kufalt sat like a chaperone at a dance, a notebook and pencil in his hands, a large portfolio propped against the wall behind him.

'So, Fräulein,' Gans said in a friendly voice. 'You're an artist, I understand.'

Emmeline shook her head. 'Please, sir, I don't think you understand. My mother, she's unconscious. They think she might – they think she might die.'

'I'm sorry to hear that, Fräulein, I am, but the law must be followed. So, are you or are you not an artist?'

Steel glinted under the friendly tone. Emmeline felt a quiver of fear. She swallowed, wiping her nose on her wrist. 'I suppose so. Sort of.'

'Come now, I understand you're a graduate of Berlin Academy of Art. That's no small achievement for a woman.'

'I was not considered a very promising student.'

'Is that so? But you make a good living from your work?' He reached into the pocket of his coat, pulled out a packet of Wahr cigarettes. Flicking the bottom of the pack, he extracted the cigarette card and slid it across the table towards her. It was Jakob Muffel with his domed forehead and sucked-in lips, exhaling twin plumes of smoke from his nostrils. Emmeline stared at it, confused. What had her work to do with Dora?

'Not really,' she said. 'It's not very well paid.'

Gans glanced at Kufalt. Then, sliding an envelope from the folder in front of him, he tipped it out on the table. The other cigarette cards, a full set. He laid them out face up on the table as though he were playing patience. 'Your employer, Wilhelm Balz, tells us you painted all of these portraits yourself, is that right? No assistance from friends, from fellow artists?'

'I don't understand,' Emmeline said. 'What has Balz to do with anything?'

Gans's eyes narrowed. 'Answer the question,' he said, snapping the words like a whip. Emmeline flinched.

'I painted them all,' she said. Her mouth was dry.

'An impressive range. And there were others, I think, paintings you worked up but which the Wahr people decided not to use?'

'Yes. Herr Balz wanted to show them lots of options. So they could choose.'

'Can you tell me some of the ideas they turned down?'

'The best ones. All the women. They only wanted men.'

'What about this one? This is one of yours too, is it not?' Gans nodded at Kufalt, who took a large square of cardboard from the portfolio behind him and put it on the table. Van Gogh at his easel, a packet of Wahr cigarettes on his palette. There was something stuck in Emmeline's throat, she could not breathe.

'A very impressive imitation,' Gans said. 'I'm something of a dolt when it comes to art but, from what Herr Balz tells me, the resemblance to the original is uncanny. Were it not for the cigarettes, of course.'

'I hope that is true of them all.' Her voice was strange, high and tight. 'That's why they're funny.'

'Oh, they're funny,' Gans said. 'This one in particular is very convincing. But then you've made something of a practice, haven't you, of the work of Vincent van Gogh?' He held out a hand to Kufalt, who rummaged again in the portfolio and passed him a battered-looking book. A cold clamminess spread over Emmeline's skin as Gans placed it on the table. Her sketchbook.

The one she had left at the Rachmann Gallery. The one they had never found. Gans opened it, turning the pages. Pages of sketches from the drawings in Matthias's exhibition. Pages of van Goghs.

'This one,' Gans said, tapping a sketch with his finger, and he turned the book around so she could see. A sower in a wheat field, a basket in his arms. 'This one I find particularly interesting. Do you know why that is, Fräulein?'

Emmeline shook her head, not trusting herself to speak, but Gans nodded as though she had answered. 'That's right. This sketch is almost identical in composition to a painting that was sold by the Rachmann Gallery to a Herr Zeckendorf several months ago for seventy thousand marks. A painting that the gallery owner, Matthias Rachmann, claims was purchased thirty years ago from the widow of van Gogh's brother but for which the widow's son holds no record. A painting that has recently been dismissed as a fake. Naturally, this sketch caught my eye.'

'It's not what you think.' Fear screwed her voice tight.

'And what do I think, Fräulein Eberhardt?'

'I want a lawyer.'

'There'll be plenty of time for lawyers in due course. For now, you are not under arrest, you are simply here to help us with our enquiries. It would be better for you if you made as little difficulty about that as possible.'

Emmeline hesitated. Gans smiled at her blandly but his eyes were hard. Shakily she took a breath. 'Artists copy,' she said. She forced herself to speak calmly, civilly. 'At the Academy it was what we were taught to do, how we learned. It's how we get better. Go to the Nationalgalerie, go to any gallery, you'll see artists in every room. Just because I copied a few drawings at the Rachmann Gallery doesn't mean – I mean, the show was open to the public. Anyone could have—'

'Perhaps. But only your sketchbook was found in a locked drawer in Matthias Rachmann's office. Would you like to tell me how it got there?'

'Because I left it behind by mistake! I went back to get it, I wanted it back, but they said it wasn't there. The young man, the assistant, I don't remember his name, but if you ask him he'll tell you—'

'Herr Zedler? Oh, he has been very helpful. Very helpful indeed.' Closing the sketchbook, Gans clasped his hands on the table. 'I understand you were a frequent visitor to the Rachmann Gallery, Fräulein, often at times that it was not open to the public. Why did you visit Herr Rachmann after hours?'

'I didn't.'

'You're denying you went to the gallery?'

'No, but it was to see the drawings, not to visit Rachmann.'

'Even though he is your friend?'

'He's not my friend. I hardly know him.'

'And yet you wrote to him just the other day, expressing your sympathy for his situation in most affectionate terms.'

Emmeline's stomach turned over. She had forgotten the letter. 'I felt sorry for him,' she whispered.

'You felt sorry for him. And why is that?'

'Because of how he's been treated by the newspapers.'

'But, despite the warmth of your letter, you do not consider him a friend?'

'No. He's an acquaintance.'

'And a business associate?'

'Of course not. I've never had any business with Matthias Rachmann.'

Gans considered her. 'I see. Is it true, Fräulein, that you have known Herr Rachmann for some years?'

'I was introduced to him when I first came to Berlin, yes.'

'And who was it who effected this introduction?'

'A friend of my mother's.'

'This friend's name?'

'Julius Köhler-Schultz.'

'Julius Köhler-Schultz, the art critic who since has issued certificates of authentication for – let's see – twenty-six of Rachmann's thirty-two questionable van Goghs?' His eyes bored into her. Emmeline clamped her hands together under the table, holding them steady.

'I don't know,' she said. 'I don't know anything about that.'

'But you met Rachmann when? I assume you remember.'

'Yes. It was the summer before I started at the Academy. 1924.'

'1924. Almost exactly a year before Rachmann's first van Gogh came on to the market. Fascinating, the ins and outs of painting. I'm told that when oil paint is very thickly applied it can take months and months to dry.'

There was not enough air in the room. Emmeline dug her nails into her palms. She felt dazed, dizzy. 'I want a lawyer,' she said desperately but Gans only looked at her, his head on one side.

'I understand there was some awkwardness at your bank this morning,' he said. 'That you attempted to cash a cheque for which you had insufficient funds. That must have been an unpleasant surprise. Until now the money's been coming in so regularly, hasn't it, anonymous cash amounts every month for three years now, or is it four?'

'That money is an allowance from my stepfather,' she protested. 'He never used his name, he didn't want my mother to know, but he made the payments himself, every month. Jacob Vidler, he's a businessman in Munich, call him, he'll tell you, every month, so I could pay my rent . . . '

Gans nodded slowly. 'It must have felt like a good deal at the beginning. Not a fortune, perhaps, but enough to live comfortably, if you were careful. But then you aren't very careful, are you?

264

Perhaps you hoped that a rundown tenement in Berlin-North would allow you and your associates to come and go without attracting attention. A shame for you that your caretaker keeps a log. A very thorough woman, Frau Schmidt. Descriptions, times in and out, names when she has them. Automobile registration plates. Not that automobiles are common in your part of town, a fact it might have behoved Herr Köhler-Schultz to remember.'

Emmeline stared at him, her heart racing, as he drew the cardboard folder towards him. His nails were square and neatly manicured.

'So,' he said. 'I understand you speak Russian.'

Some time in the afternoon Gans left the room. Kufalt followed him out. Emmeline was left alone. She could hear the heavy thud of footsteps along the floor above her, the distant roar of the traffic on Alexanderplatz. The shriek of a motor toboggan as it veered out of control. She counted her breaths, in and out, in and out. In her empty teacup the dregs were a brown smear.

It was her choice, Gans had said with a shrug. She could make this easy or she could make it hard. No one blamed her. She had been an impressionable young art student in a city still reeling from the inflation. No wonder she had been tempted by the offer of easy money. It was not illegal to buy and sell approximations of other artists' paintings, there was always someone flogging something or other for a few marks in the city's market halls. How could she have known the swindles Rachmann intended? He had cheated her at least as much as the dupes who had paid tens of thousands of marks for her forgeries. He had made a fortune, had lived like a king on her talent, while she scraped by in a worn-out coat and a tenement building that was not worth the cost of demolition. Now, at last, she had the chance to put things right. If she cooperated, deals could be struck, arrangements made.

And if she did not cooperate? Gans did not trouble to say. It was all there in the cheerless cell, the knuckles tapped lightly but insistently against the palm of his other hand. There had been no space left for her denials, no option of innocence. The choice was simple: either an informer or an accomplice.

'One thing you should know,' Gans said as he left the room. 'We have Rachmann. Do you really want him to be the one who talks first?'

It grew late. The driver would be waiting for her at Munich station. Emmeline wrapped her arms around herself, squeezing herself tight, but the pain was too deep in her, she could not reach it. She thought of the drawings she had made when she was small, the same drawing over and over, her mother as tall as the paper and Emmeline beside her, her hand in hers. She had always coloured it so it looked like their dresses were the same.

She had never imagined there would come a time when her mother was not there to be angry with, when the chances to renounce her would have all run out.

The door opened. Emmeline looked up blearily as Gans entered, followed by a baby-faced policeman who stood expressionless by the closed door, his hands behind his back. Gans took something from his pocket and put it on the table. Julius's telegram from that morning, the torn-up pieces stuck together on a sheet of card. It felt like it had been sent from another life, a hundred years ago.

'Perhaps you'd care to tell me what this is?' Gans said.

'You broke into my flat?'

'A civil action has been brought today against Herr Rachmann. The police have been granted the authority to search all suspicious premises.'

Emmeline was silent. She could feel her heart in her chest,

a dull throb like a punched face. This is not going to end, she thought suddenly, this nightmare is going to go on unspooling, one incriminating coincidence after another, and at some point it will be enough. 'I demand a lawyer,' she said.

'And you will get one. Just as soon as you are under arrest. For now we are only asking questions, so I would suggest you answer this one. What is this?'

'It's a telegram,' she said wearily.

'From Herr Köhler-Schultz, who first introduced you to Rachmann.'

'Yes.'

'And what was so urgent that he had to speak to you immediately?'

'I told you, my mother has been in an accident. Why won't you let me see her?'

'And what exactly has that to do with Herr Köhler-Schultz?'

'My stepfather cabled Julius. He wanted him to tell me.'

'He did not think to cable you himself?'

'He couldn't. He doesn't have my address.'

'Your own stepfather doesn't know where you live?'

'My arrangements are none of his business.'

'And yet he pays you a monthly allowance. An interesting accommodation. But Herr Köhler-Schultz, you are willing to do business with him?'

'Julius lives in Berlin. He knew where to find me. That's all.'

'Is it? Is it not true that Köhler-Schultz wished to alert you to Rachmann's return from The Hague, that his cable was a warning to get out of Berlin?'

'No. I told you, he wanted me to telephone him so he could tell me about my mother. He thought it would be kinder.'

'And yet according both to his secretary and his housekeeper no such telephone call was placed.'

'I didn't telephone him because by then I already knew.'

'And how exactly did you know when nobody had been able to reach you?'

'I rang Jacob's office. When he didn't deposit my money I—'

A loud knock on the door interrupted her. Gans glared at the policeman, who opened the door and stepped out. When he returned his face was apologetic.

'Herr Kommissar?' he said.

Gans's frown deepened. Taking the room in three strides, he slammed the door behind him.

'I need to use the lavatory,' Emmeline said to the policeman, but he only stared blankly at the wall, his hands behind his back. Pushing back her chair, she stood up. Her legs felt shaky but there was something emboldening about the small rebellion, the assertion of her own will.

'Sit down,' the policeman ordered but she only shook her head. There was a smear of dried blood on his cheek where he had nicked himself with a razor.

'I mean it,' she said. 'I have to go. Or would you rather I did it here, on your boots?'

The policeman looked at her warily. When the door banged open they both turned round. Gans stood stony-faced in the doorway, a man in a civilian's wool overcoat and wire spectacles behind him.

'Fräulein Eberhardt,' he said through gritted teeth. 'The Berlin police would like to thank you for your cooperation with our investigation. We have no further questions at this time.'

Emmeline blinked stupidly at the man in the overcoat. He had a kind face.

'Alfred Böhm,' he said. 'Let's get you out of here.'

15

Böhm wanted to take her to the Köhler-Schultz house on Meierstrasse. The Köhler-Schultzes could give her a hot bath, dinner, a warm bed, he said, she could travel to Munich in the morning, but Emmeline had wasted too much time already. She asked him to take her to Anhalt station. As she stepped out of the car he pressed a fifty-mark note into her hand.

'Call me as soon as you get back,' he said.

At the ticket counter the clerk shook his head. He had no ticket in the name of Eberhardt. Perhaps the police had taken it. She bought a third-class ticket. The clerk held Böhm's banknote up to the light and reluctantly counted out her change. The last train for Munich would leave in one hour.

She walked across the deserted concourse, her feet ringing out beneath the vast glass vault. It was very late. Most of the kiosks were closed. According to Böhm the police knew very well that they could not hold her, that what little evidence they possessed was circumstantial at best and quite insufficient to justify an arrest. The newspapers were making them look foolish, that was the problem. They were clutching at straws. They might clutch at them again, Böhm warned her, if their investigations foundered. He wanted her to see him when she came back to Berlin. Damage limitation, he called it. Courts were required to adhere to legal procedure. The gutter press took a different approach.

The cafeteria was still open, its windows milky with steam. A woman in a grease-spotted apron brought her liverwurst and a buttered roll. The smell made Emmeline think of the *Zuerst* offices and fat, diligent Olga, wiping her fingers carefully on the napkin she kept in her desk drawer, Olga with her cardigans and her kindness and her blurry daughters with their sharp knees, squashed inside the borders of their snapshot.

It was before dawn when she arrived at the Hauptbahnhof in Munich. The streets were blank with snow, the shops and houses shuttered and dark, but as they drove towards Würnsee the sun rose behind the black cut-outs of the mountains, painting the low clouds with orange and rose gold, and the frozen lake shone like beaten copper. The beauty of it peeled away the last of Emmeline's courage.

The clouds thickened, blotting out the sun. By the time they reached the Metz house, it was snowing. As the car drew up Jacob came out to meet her. His face was grey and creased, salted with stubble, and there was an unsteadiness in his step that might have been weariness or drink or both. Taking her hands he looked at her and shook his head. He smelled ashy, of burned-down fires and dead cigars.

'Just before dawn,' he said and he began to weep. Emmeline said nothing. There was nothing to say. She let Jacob hold her hands as the snow fell silently around them. Nadine Metz came out of the house. She touched Emmeline's cheek lightly with her fingertips, then put an arm around Jacob's shoulders.

'Come inside,' she said.

*

Elvira was laid out upstairs in the room where she had died. Emmeline kept saying the word in her head, *dead*, *died*, but the numbness did not go away. The bandage on her mother's head looked too white to be real. Her face did not look real either. She did not look the way Emmeline remembered her. She was not sure if that was death or the wrongness of her memory. She had never seen her mother without her characteristic chignon, her immaculate daytime face. Someone had plaited her hair and laid it over one shoulder, tied with ribbon like a schoolgirl's. She would never have allowed that when she was alive, Emmeline thought, and the dryness in her throat was an ache that could not be swallowed.

Her mother's gold watch was on the bedside table. Emmeline touched the face with one finger. It had stopped. The time was wrong. Picking it up she shook it, holding it to her ear, listening to the tiny tick, and suddenly she was five again. Gently she opened the case.

'The time is sad stuck in there, it wants us to let it out,' she said but Elvira only took her hand away and shook her head.

'We can't do that, my dear. If you let time go, it will never come back.'

The tears burned behind her eyes but they had been unshed too long, all that was left of them was the dried-out scrape of salt.

She sat with Nadine in the winter garden. Elsewhere in the house people hurried through the stunned spaces, their voices low and urgent. Elvira's body was to be taken back to Munich for the funeral. Otto too was to be moved to a private hospital in the city where an orthopaedic surgeon could operate on his smashed pelvis. It was Otto who had been driving the motor toboggan when it crashed.

'He wants to see you,' Nadine said. 'I've asked him to wait. You have both endured enough.'

Emmeline was silent. She stared at the fountain, the water twisted in the air like a rope of ice.

'Regret is a heavy burden,' Nadine said. 'It counts for nothing, changes nothing, but it cannot be put down.'

The water curved and broke into glittering chips. The same water, cycled round and round, and every time different and new. Nadine poured coffee.

'My husband has a son, Klaus,' she said. 'His daughters are sweet and dull like their mother but Klaus is Otto all over again, impetuous, excitable, stubborn as a donkey. He lives in Chicago now. Otto has two grandsons he has never met. For a long time I puzzled over it. But now I wonder if it is the ones we understand best that we find it hardest to be kind to. The ones like us.'

Emmeline wished she would stop talking. Nadine put down the coffee pot and handed her a cup. When she took it, it rattled on its saucer.

'Otto has been angry with Klaus for a long time,' Nadine said. 'He thinks he should have been a better son and he is right, but it's Otto who bears the greater responsibility. He is the father and Klaus the child, however old Klaus is and far away.'

Emmeline took a sip of her coffee. It was strong and too hot, it burned her tongue.

'You thought there was always tomorrow,' Nadine said softly. 'Of course you did. Your mother thought so too.'

Jacob returned to Munich with the coffin. As the hearse drew away, Emmeline thought of all the times she had stood with one nursemaid or another on the steps of the house in Frankfurt, waving a handkerchief as her mother's carriage clattered away down the drive, and she put her hands in her pockets and drew out the only thing she found there, a page torn from a sketchbook, folded several times. Shaking it out she waved it once, twice, until the foolishness of the gesture undid her.

'I'm sorry,' she whispered to the disappearing tail lights and the words were like spider's silk, all of her weight was in them.

She and Nadine were to return to Munich that evening. Late in the afternoon she went upstairs. The bed where Elvira had died had been neatly made. There were freshly folded towels on the wooden rack, a vase of flowers on the chest of drawers. The furniture gleamed. Nothing might ever have happened there, except that the windows were thrown wide open and the smells of lavender and beeswax were cut with the metallic tang of snow.

Emmeline crossed to the window and looked out, her arms wrapped around her for warmth. Above the black lace of the trees the moon was a pulpy half-circle with a white rim like the peel on a slice of lemon. The first stars were coming out. It was very quiet.

Then, as she watched, a cloud of starlings rose and filled the sky. Hundreds, thousands maybe, a vast rippling cape of them, surging and wheeling, stretching into swooping curves, twisting in helixes, rising in streamers on the wind, the whisper-roar of their wings like the sea or the thrumming of a thousand fingers on a thousand paper drums. There were so many of them, Emmeline thought stupidly as they banked steeply, spiralling into a figure of eight, and yet they all knew exactly what to do.

'I thought you might be here.' Nadine stood in the doorway, her shadow sharp-edged in the spill of light from the corridor. 'It's time to go.'

Emmeline looked back towards the window. The figure of eight unrolled into a pointillist veil that drifted for a moment in the air.

Then, with a rushing noise, it coiled downwards like bathwater, disappearing into the fretted blackness of the trees.

'She's still here, isn't she?' Nadine murmured. 'I feel it too,' but Emmeline shook her head.

'It's much too cold in here for Elvira,' she said, and she walked out on to the bright landing without looking back.

16

In Munich there were letters, visitors, funeral arrangements to be made. The same words: *deepest regrets, sincerest condolences, rest in peace.* Emmeline answered the letters, received the visitors, ordered food and flowers and service sheets and suitable clothes for Jacob's stunned and solemn children. She looked away from Jacob as he stumbled through the house, his grief clutched around him like a blanket. Sometimes Emmeline found him standing in the middle of a room, blind-eyed as a sleepwalker, not knowing where he was or how he had got there. Sometimes, passing his study, she heard him weeping.

Nadine came every day to help.

The caretaker forwarded her mail. Balz wrote to her, he said he had work for her, asked her to get in touch. She did not reply. The day before the funeral the Köhler-Schultzes arrived from Berlin. Emmeline was surprised, she had not expected them. Julius did not look well. His skin had a yellowish pallor and his expensive suit sagged on his large frame. Even his bones looked too big for him. Amelia fussed around him as though he were an invalid or an idiot, but he made no protest. If anything, he seemed grateful.

His eyes followed her around the room, as though he was afraid to let her out of his sight.

He shook his head when Emmeline thanked him for Böhm. 'You should never have been caught up in that circus. They released Matthias, of course, that same day. The whole episode was shameful. They hadn't a shred of evidence against him.'

Matthias was a fine man, Julius said, a man of courage who esteemed the principles of honour and loyalty more highly than he esteemed himself. Such men were rare. He deserved the country's admiration, not its censure. He spoke emphatically, almost angrily, jerking his head, and when he gestured his hands shook like an old man's. Germany had been full of such men once, he said, and his eyes were full of tears. Amelia put her hand on his arm and he clasped it.

No one mentioned Otto, not even Nadine. He was still in hospital but, though it was too early to know if he would walk again, he was out of danger. Soon he would return home. He would open the book on the bedside cabinet that still had the silk ribbon in it to mark his place, he would pick up the hairbrush with his stray hairs still caught between the bristles and fasten his watch and put on the clothes in the wardrobe that carried the smell of him, and everything would go back to the way it was before. Everything that had not been said would go on not being said.

Emmeline did not want his remorse. She wanted to see what he had seen, every glass-shard, scalpel-blade detail of that day until it finally sliced through the numbness and she could weep.

Scores of people attended the funeral. She walked to the cemetery behind the coffin, Jacob by her side, silent and stiff-faced in his expensive black overcoat. They were standing at the graveside when she saw her. She stood apart from the other mourners, a slight figure half hidden by a lichened headstone, her shoulders hunched against the wind. A man was with her. He was tall, much taller than her. He stooped to murmur something in her ear. Then he turned, and Emmeline saw that it was Julius. As the priest raised his hands he walked slowly back towards the mourners and took his place beside Amelia. She tucked her arm through his.

There were words, handfuls of frozen earth against the polished wood. She was wearing Emmeline's cat's-eye sunglasses and a black hat that Emmeline had never seen before. She looked like someone pretending to be a film star.

'May her soul, and the souls of all the faithful departed, through the mercy of God rest in peace.'

'Amen.'

Emmeline touched Jacob's arm and he put his gloved hand on hers, squeezing it in the crook of his arm. There was solace in it. 'I'll be back in a moment,' she said.

People were dispersing, walking back to their motor cars. Their voices caught on the wind. There were clumps of snow in the grass between the neatly kept graves and bright flowers in metal vases like splashes of paint. Behind her, beside the stone gateposts, a row of cypresses cut dark gashes in the sky. Emmeline stopped on the path, her arms crossed.

Behind her sunglasses Dora's cheeks were whipped pink with cold. She held out her hands to Emmeline. Her gloves were shabby, frayed at the fingertips.

'Em, I'm so sorry,' she murmured.

'Why would you be sorry? It's the perfect opportunity to catch grieving mourners with their guard down. What could be better?'

'Don't.'

'You're right, of course, you came out of the goodness of your heart. The chance for an exclusive interview with Julius Köhler-Schultz was just the cherry on Elvira's funeral cake.'

Dora opened her mouth, then closed it again. 'I shouldn't have come. I'm sorry. It was a mistake.'

'I'm sure it wasn't a completely wasted journey,' Emmeline said. 'You're a journalist, or you pretend to be. You can always just make it up.'

Dora said nothing. She did not look at Emmeline. She kept her eyes on the fringe of untrimmed grass at the base of the headstone. Down in the road the automobiles were starting their engines.

'I have to go,' Emmeline said and Dora nodded. She did not try to stop her as she picked her way back through the long grass to the path. Emmeline did not look back. As the loose gravel crunched under her feet she thought of the beach at Wannsee, of Dora's white shoulders in her black bathing costume. She stopped. Then she turned around.

'You should know, I'm moving out of the flat. Turns out one of the advantages of a dead mother is not having to live in a rat hole any more.'

The tide of voices and laughter and chinking glasses surged through the house. Emmeline went upstairs. She sat on the lavatory for a long time, looking out at the bare trees, the sloping slate roof of the villa beyond. She wondered where Dora was, if she was already on her way back to Berlin.

Someone knocked at the door.

'Just a moment,' she said. When she stood up her legs had gone to sleep. She leaned on the basin as the water tumbled in the cistern, and as she caught her reflection in the mirror it was her mother she saw, her mother's grey eyes and full, amused mouth. *Darling, you won't even know I'm gone.*

Amelia Köhler-Schultz was standing by the landing window, looking out. She turned when she heard the door open. 'Hiding?' she asked Emmeline.

'Something like that.'

'Me too. Julius's found some old friends. I'm not sure I can bear to be told yet again how much better everything was before the war.'

Emmeline managed a smile. It was the closest she had ever heard Amelia come to a criticism. 'Is Julius all right?' she asked. 'He looks so thin.'

Amelia shook her head. 'These last few months have been a terrible strain. He's working too hard, of course, but it's this Matthias business – I suppose you saw the piece in the *Vossische Zeitung*? It seems that this isn't the first time Matthias has been picked up by the police for handling forgeries. There was a Corot, apparently, six or seven years ago. They didn't prosecute, they couldn't prove he knew it was a fake. I'm sorry, listen to me rattling on, you don't want to hear all this.'

'Actually it's nice. Talking about something else. I'm sorry about Julius.'

'Yes, well. It's been very difficult for him. He believed in Matthias. Loved him, even. The idea that Matthias deliberately took advantage of him—'

'You don't think Matthias might have been duped himself?'

'Not even slightly. Personally I wouldn't trust Matthias Rachmann further than I could throw him. But Julius? Darling Julius still believes doggedly in the imaginary Russian.' She sighed. 'I think believing is the only way he can endure it.'

'Is that why he was talking to Dora Keyserling, to give her his side of the story?'

Amelia frowned. 'You didn't hear? She left the newspaper.'

'Did she? When?'

'I think it was after she found the police searching your apartment, when she telephoned Julius and asked him to help you. She didn't tell you? Anyway, her editor demanded she write a piece about it, made quite a song and dance about it by all accounts, and when she refused he fired her. Either that or she resigned. You'd have to ask her. She's here, isn't she, or has she left? I know she had to get back to Berlin – Julius offered our driver to take her to the station.'

The Munich Hauptbahnhof was crowded. Heavy snow had caused problems on the lines, many of the trains were delayed. Emmeline pushed through the crowds, past men with briefcases and mothers with bundled-up children and pinched-looking women in mothy fur collars and jumbles of piled-up boxes and grips. Platform 7 for Berlin, the conductor said when she reached the gates, but there was no need to hurry, the train was delayed, they would not be boarding for half an hour at least.

'Buffet's over there,' he said. 'You've time for a cup of coffee.'

She saw her as soon as she pushed open the door. A slight figure in a black hat at a corner table, her head bent, her chin resting on her clasped hands. Emmeline stood in the doorway, tracing the familiar shape of her.

'You going to stand there all day?' snapped a slab-faced woman in a brown tweed coat behind her, and, as Emmeline stepped aside to let her through, Dora turned her head. She had a dark scab across the bridge of her nose and a black eye that was not black so much as purple and red and yellow-green. When she saw Emmeline her arms jerked upwards, her hands covering her mouth, and then she let them fall and she smiled, a smile so full of hope and apprehension that Emmeline's heart turned sideways, pressing itself against her ribs.

The slab-faced woman reached the table first.

'This seat free, is it?' she demanded, slamming her handbag down on the table, but Dora shook her head. She looked up at Emmeline, her teeth catching the corner of her smile, her hands clasped together against her chest as though she were praying.

'I'm sorry,' she said and the smile broke free, creasing the skin around her bruised eye into a green and purple fan. 'I've been waiting for my friend.'

Dora went back to Berlin. She had to get back to Oma. The woman she had found was kind and competent, but she already had her piecework and a family to take care of, it was not fair to ask any more of her. When she told Frau Schmidt she would no longer be needing her help, the caretaker had protested and then cursed, muttering under her breath about criminals and their associates. The police who came to search Emmeline's flat had not brought the proper warrants, but Frau Schmidt had shrugged and let them in anyway. Dora had seen her in the hallway, picking her teeth with a match while they turned the place upside down. Doing her civic duty, she called it. She had even showed them the trick to opening the wardrobe with the lock that stuck.

'You're right,' Dora said. 'The place is a rat hole. Perhaps we should all move out together,' and Emmeline smiled and closed her fingers around the thought of it, a stone still warm from Dora's pocket.

She stayed in Munich for another week. She did not want to leave Jacob alone with Nadine. Besides, someone had to sort out the mountains of clothes in her mother's wardrobes. Jacob could not bring himself to go into her dressing room.

'Take whatever you want,' he said. 'I'd like to think of you using her things.'

Elvira's clothes were arranged on rows and rows of matching silk-covered hangers. There were dozens of evening dresses, some of them achingly familiar. It occurred to Emmeline that she knew them mostly from the back. She laid them on the bed. She would ask the housekeeper to arrange for them to be given away.

A different house, a different husband, but the dressing table was arranged just as it had been when Emmeline was a child: the bevelled mirror with its three panels, the silver-backed hairbrushes engraved with a curling E, the same flower-painted porcelain pots with rosebuds for handles on their lids. She opened the drawers to find neatly folded handkerchiefs, a pot of pins, her mother's leather manicure case. Nothing else, no letters or photographs, no clumsily crayoned drawings. Elvira had disapproved of clutter almost as much as she disapproved of sentimentality.

Emmeline took out the manicure case and opened it, touching the nail files in their little compartments, the silver scissors with their curved blades. As a child she had been sure that if you just followed the curve of them you would cut out a perfect circle but her mother had put them out of reach, she had said that they were not a toy, that paper would blunt them.

It was harder than she had imagined. The scissors were sharp but small and the silky fabric slipped, cutting not in a single smooth line but in jags, like teeth. The curve of the blade was difficult to follow. The hole was a rough oval the size of a child's palm. It got easier with practice. By the time she had finished she had a pile of almost-circles of different textures and colours, and a heap of dresses, each one with a hole cut out of the back of the skirt. For the first time since coming to Munich she thought of her corner of the studio beside the railway line, the long high window with its white Berlin light. She thought of van Gogh writing to his brother. *In spite of everything I shall rise again: I will take up my pencil, which I have forsaken in great discouragement, and I will go on with my drawing.*

She wanted to go home.

She tucked the circles inside the manicure case and bundled the case and the cut-out dresses into a trunk. She would take those ones with her, she told Jacob's housekeeper. The rest of the clothes should be disposed of in whatever way she saw fit.

On the day Emmeline left Munich, Rachmann's name was once again splashed across the newspaper kiosks. She did not stop. In the first-class dining car she bent her head over her book of van Gogh's letters but there was no escaping it. The loud-voiced man across the compartment talked of nothing else. The police, he told his companion, had insisted that Rachmann return to Berlin from The Hague for further questioning. Rachmann had agreed. Moreover, as evidence mounted against him, he had promised at last to reveal the name of his Russian collector and to arrange a meeting between the mysterious Muscovite and the Kriminalkommissar in charge of the case.

Only he had not returned. On the morning he was expected in Berlin he had been found unconscious and with a broken arm at the bottom of the stairs in a hotel in Leiden. He remained much too ill to travel. His official statement blamed a heart attack but the German newspapers were sceptical. There were rumours that Rachmann had been poisoned, that he was the victim of a plot by the mysterious Russian collector who wished him dead, or else by vengeful art dealers, that the doctors themselves were part of the conspiracy. The loud-voiced man said that was what happened when you mixed money and art and he made a noise like an explosion, showering the table with spittle.

'Still, if you had an original right now you'd be sitting pretty,' he added as his companion blotted his face discreetly with a napkin. 'They say prices are going through the roof.'

Emmeline closed her eyes. In Munich, on the platform, Dora had hugged her and when Emmeline tried to pull away she held her closer, her gloved hands against the curve of her shoulder blades.

'Not yet,' she said and Emmeline had felt the chill of Dora's ear against her cheek, the narrow leanness of her body, and a tremor had gone through her. Certainty. That for as long as she stood there, for as long as Dora's arms were around her, she was where she belonged. She stood very still, her eyes closed, feeling the warmth of it spreading through her, softening her bones. Slowly Dora pulled away. Her eyes were dark and deep, and she looked at Emmeline as though she could see right to the bottom of her. She put her hand against Emmeline's face. She had taken her gloves off, her fingers were cold, cold enough to make Emmeline jump. Dora smiled. Then, standing on tiptoe, she kissed her very lightly on the corner of her mouth.

'Do you think we could start again?' she said quietly and Emmeline nodded, not trusting herself to speak. *Do you think we could start again?* She had not known what the words meant then, did not know now, but the thought of them was like a candle flame guttering inside her, provisional but very bright. She breathed slowly, a hand against the tilt beneath her ribs. The muddy fields were giving way to factories, houses, lines of washing. Whatever was going to happen next, it was coming. All she had to do was be there and tell the truth. Or as much of the truth as she dared.

In Berlin the sun was shining, the blue sky bright and hard like the glaze on a bowl. After the long journey the cold air tasted almost fresh. Emmeline walked to the U-Bahn, feeling the rumble of the trains under her feet. At the station there was a long queue, people were complaining, cursing the ticket seller, the train tracks, the earliness of the hour. Someone jostled someone who asked them if they were blind as well as stupid.

'You going to let me live my damned life?' the first someone growled back. The Berlin accents were unmistakable.

Emmeline looked at the queue, the restless, dissatisfied faces.

Her luggage had been sent on, she had only a small holdall. Taking it in both her arms like a baby, she began to walk up towards Potsdamer Platz.

At the corner she stopped. On Bellevuestrasse, where there had been the Grand Bellevue Hotel, there was now scaffolding, some twenty metres high, and on it an enormous advertising hoarding. Beneath a narrow billboard promoting the forthcoming department store, a single vast advertisement had been pasted.

REINWEISS DENTAL CREAM, it blared above a picture of Vincent van Gogh with a toothbrush jammed between his teeth, white froth spilling down his chin, and underneath it, in huge letters, *THE ORIGINAL*.

FRANK

Berlin 1933

Friday 31 March

We eat breakfast in silence. Gerda picks her roll into crumbs. I drink my coffee and I think of the expert witness at Rachmann's trial who talked for an hour about the distinctions between different shades of white. I used to think all silences were the same. It's late, I say, I have to go, and she nods. We both know it's the same time it always is.

I put on my coat and hat. In the kitchen the maid clatters pots. The silence is louder. I should tell Gerda not to worry, that everything will be all right, but the words stick in my throat. Don't tempt the devil, our grandmother always used to say, glaring at Stefan and me as though she saw him standing there behind us. She was furious if anyone was rash enough to remark favourably on the weather or the punctuality of the trains, dooming her to downpours and delay. Gerda was the only one who ever teased her. Don't you look well, she used to say, and the old woman would huff and tut and tell Gerda she would be the death of her, as if Gerda was not always her favourite, the one she liked better than any of her own. Her gloomy pessimism made Gerda laugh. She didn't believe in the devil, not then.

At the station kiosk I buy a newspaper. All week people have been saying that the Nazis will back down. They may have crushed their communist opposition but moderating elements remain. The Catholic Zentrums, the Social Democrats, the right-wing conservatives: they may have made their own shameful accommodations with Hitler but they surely still have influence, and there have been shocked remonstrations from abroad. Someone, we agree, will do something. They have to. I scour the paper but all I find is a restatement of the order. The boycott of Jewish shops, goods, doctors and lawyers will begin at exactly ten o'clock tomorrow morning. It will continue until the Party leadership orders its cancellation.

It is another beautiful day. As I walk to the office the sun warms my back and the sky is a perfect blue. Perhaps my old grandmother was right after all. Since they burned down the Reichstag I've barely noticed the weather and the result is a March that is more like May. The streets are busy. People walk in and out of the Jewish shops, baskets over their arms. The last ordinary day, I think, but then I have thought that every day for months.

I see the girl out of the corner of my eye. She is on the other side of the road, a tall girl in a blue coat, her right leg twisting as she swings her crutches. I stop. Everything stops. Her brown hair catches the light. Then a tram rattles past too close and, startled, I step back and by the time it is past me she is gone.

There will never be another ordinary day.

I cross the courtyard and hurry up the stairs to my office, but as I reach the first-floor landing Böhm is standing in his doorway.

'I thought it was you,' he says. 'Might I borrow you for a moment?'

Is Böhm Jewish? I don't know. He and his partner have been in this building almost as long as I have but, before the Rachmann trial a year ago, we had never exchanged more than a polite nod on the stairs. Still wouldn't have, most likely, if it had not been for the critic Köhler-Schultz, who requested his lawyer be present at our interviews. His lawyer, it turned out, was Alfred Böhm. I told Köhler-Schultz there was no need, he was a witness, not a defendant, but he insisted and Böhm seemed happy enough. Two flights up is not unduly onerous, as client demands go.

Böhm and his partner have carved two offices and a narrow waiting area out of a single first-floor room. The office Böhm ushers me into is hardly as wide as it is tall, with a window divided in half by a plasterboard wall. A man and a woman are sitting in the chairs squeezed in beside his desk. They make a striking couple, him blond and square-jawed, her dark and slender. Böhm introduces us. He says that they are engaged to be married, that they wish to agree a prenuptial contract. It is a condition of the arrangement that both sides take independent legal counsel before the contract is signed. He asks me if I would consider representing Herr Dumier. I smile and nod and offer my congratulations to the happy couple. I'd prefer my new client not to know how badly I need the work.

'This is ridiculous,' Dumier says impatiently. 'Why can't I just sign now?'

Böhm considers him coldly. 'You will consult with a lawyer as stipulated. Herr Berszacki will ensure you understand the implications of the agreement.'

'I understand just fine. If anything happens I get nothing, it all goes to Ivo. I don't need a lawyer to tell me that. So why can't I sign?'

'Because you have contractual obligations, Anton,' Böhm snaps. 'I wouldn't have thought it was in your interests to make difficulties.'

The young man grimaces at his fiancée. There are lines around his mouth, he is not as young as he looks. She shrugs and twists the ring on her finger. Her nails are dirty, her fingers stained with black ink. Somehow I can't imagine her as a blushing bride. Dumier sighs and rubs his face.

'Fine,' he says. 'Tell me what you need me to do,' and Böhm nods at me but I don't see it because I'm looking at Fräulein Eberhardt, at the way she looks at Dumier, not with ardour but openly, steadily, as though there is nothing about her he doesn't already know. When I ask Dumier to follow me upstairs, my voice sounds hoarse, as though I've used it all up.

Gerda passed a school playground yesterday. The children were singing a skipping song in their piping child voices: *Juda verreke, Juda verreke. Perish the Jews.* The same five notes over and over, she said, like birdsong.

Saturday 1 April

I should work. I brought papers home. Instead I sit on our narrow balcony and write in this diary. Gerda worries, she says these days it's better not to write things down, but I can't stop now, not when things are changing so fast. I don't want to look back when it's all over and find I no longer remember. In the dark days after the election, drunk on triumph, the SA terrorised this neighbourhood, beating up anyone who looked at them the wrong way – Jewishly. We thought things were getting better. Most of the shops in our neighbourhood are closed for Shabbat but that has not stopped people daubing yellow and black Stars of David on their doors. From where I sit I can see a brownshirt standing outside Corlik's hardware store and posters pasted over the windows: *GERMANS, PROTECT YOURSELVES! DON'T BUY FROM JEWS!* and *THE JEWS ARE OUR MISFORTUNE.* The shop is still open. Arni Corlik would open if the world was ending.

Families walk together along our street towards the synagogue on Oranienburger Strasse. As they near Corlik's they cross the road. No one wants trouble. Corlik's wife comes out of the shop with a broom and sweeps the step. The brownshirt says something to her. She goes back inside. A moment later she comes back with a cup of tea and, as he takes it, she smiles and I am filled with a sudden and violent rage. I want to know how it is possible that this is happening. It cannot go on, we have all been saying it for months, someone will stop it, and yet no one stops it and it goes on. It gets worse. April 1 and who exactly are the fools?

I go inside. In the kitchen Gerda is chopping onions. She wipes her eyes. The girl Lena has not come today. She told Gerda it wasn't safe. Next door the Orlowitzes' baby is screaming. It screams day and night, it is like an alarm clock that can't be turned off. Usually it drives me to distraction, but not today. Today I'm glad there are still Jews who refuse to be silenced.

A was a contented baby, she seldom cried. Sometimes I would come home to find Gerda sitting by her cot. You worry too much, I said once, she won't stop breathing the moment you leave the room, but Gerda only smiled and traced A's cheek with her fingertips.

'Do you think the day will come,' she said wonderingly, 'when nothing about her stops my heart?'

Monday 3 April

The boycott has been called off. Naturally the newspapers declare it a success, the editors who would have dared to say otherwise are long gone, but it is plain that the Nazis have been forced to back down. It is one thing, inciting the rabble to hatred during an election, quite another for a government to order its citizens to turn against their friends and associates. In Berlin, at least, they could not make it stick. Yes, some students at the university picketed the classes of Jewish professors but students have always been hot-headed, it's part of the job. Most ordinary people were appalled and embarrassed. One of Else Schwarz's patients left a bunch of irises at her surgery. The card said *For Hope*.

When I get to the office the caretaker's door is padlocked. I'm surprised, recently he has been uncharacteristically assiduous, monitoring comings and goings in a large ledger he keeps on his desk, but today he is nowhere to be seen. And then I turn into the courtyard and I understand. Someone has smashed the window beside the door. Bits of broken glass jut from the frame like teeth. On the wall the line of brass nameplates is slashed with gouts of black paint. *LAWYER, ACCOUNTANT, NOTARY,* all blacked out and instead, daubed above them in uneven capital letters, *DRECKIGE JUDEN* – filthy Jews. Not all of the occupants of this building are Jewish but what does that matter? In their zeal they have obliterated us all.

Wednesday 5 April

I read the Dumier papers, the contract Böhm has drafted for him to sign. *In the event of divorce or death, Anton Dumier and Emmeline Ursula Eberhardt waive their right to share in the property of the other, whether currently held or hereafter acquired.* Not so unusual, not these days, not when one or other of the signatories has children or a vast fortune, or both. What's curious is that neither of these two appear to have either. Neither of them has been previously married. According to the financial statements she has an apartment in Kreuzberg and a modest income from various investments. He has a small salary. It was plain to me that Böhm judged the benefit all on Dumier's side, but why, if the fiancée is better off than he is? Is Dumier hiding something, assets salted away somewhere he's not letting on about? And if so, why would she let him get away with it? She didn't strike me as a pushover, quite the opposite. I had the impression of someone who was in no doubt about what they were doing.

Then, going down the stairs, I pass her coming up, Fräulein Eberhardt, and suddenly I am eight years old and convinced I can conjure people out of thin air just by thinking about them. I had forgotten the jolt of it, the shocking lurch of power. She glances at me strangely and I nod and hurry away. In the courtyard the cherry tree is starting to blossom, the sticky buds splitting to show ruffled pink tongues. I am thinking about the blossom when I pass a man in dirty canvas trousers smoking in a doorway. I hardly glance at him, then he turns away from me and, though I do not see his face, there is something sharply familiar about the bulk of him, the way he moves.

It is only when I return to my office and the Rachmann boxes stacked in labelled towers against the walls that it drops like a coin into a slot. Rachmann's brother, Gregor. He sat across from me every day of both trials, his shoulders hunched in just that way, but why? He lives in Düsseldorf, or he did then. Is he here to see me? I peer out of the window but I cannot see that part of the street from here and anyway, when I came back past the doorway he was gone. I sit down, pick up my pen. Then I put it down. I go out on to the landing, look down the stairs. There is no one there. Of course there isn't, I'm being foolish. Yes, families sometimes take it badly when it goes the wrong way and, yes, the Rachmann brothers were close, unusually so, I thought, but Rachmann has been in prison for nearly a year. If his brother had scores to settle, he would have settled them long ago.

And yet. A week ago an old (Jewish) colleague who lodged a complaint against his (Jewish) client's illegal arrest was paraded through the streets of Munich, barefoot and bloody-nosed, a sign around his neck that read *I will never again complain to the police.* Berlin is not Munich, but the SA is still the SA. If Gregor Rachmann thinks now is the time to take matters into his own hands, who exactly is going to stop him?

When I get home I go straight to our bedroom. I am being alarmist, I know, but I take this diary from the night table and put it in the drawer. The drawer locks. I put the key on the ring I keep in my pocket. I tell myself it is a kindness to Gerda, that she worries too much as it is.

The door to A's room is open. Gerda is sitting on the bed, A's worn-out toy rabbit on her lap. Philip, A called him, after Fidgety Philip in the *Struwwelpeter* stories. A's toys were never well-behaved. When Gerda sees me she puts the rabbit back on the pillow and stands up. It's Wednesday. She meets the other mothers for coffee on Wednesday mornings, she never misses it. Wednesdays are usually one of the better days.

'Everything all right?' I ask but she doesn't answer. She straightens out the creases in the bedspread, then reties her apron.

'Right,' she says. 'I'll put the potatoes on.'

Thursday 6 April

Dumier is late for his appointment. His mouth is split and swollen, he has a black eye. Immediately I think of Gregor Rachmann. Since yesterday I have seen him three times at least, except that each time, when I looked again, it wasn't him. The bruise around Dumier's eye is dark purple, smudged greenish round the edges.

'Ouch,' I say. 'What happened?'

'Wrong place, wrong time.' He twists in his chair to look at the boxes stacked around my office, squinting a little to read the labels.

'Someone attacked you?'

He shrugs. 'People don't like my face. I don't suppose they like yours either.'

I am silent. I know how I look. I look Jewish in precisely the way that Joseph Goebbels looks Jewish, because I am short and dark and puny; but blond, blandly handsome Anton Dumier, surely he's the archetype, the ideal Aryan *Übermensch*. Unless he's a Communist? It's not my concern, I'm not defending him in court, but I feel it still, the slither of ice down my back. The fear. When did I become so afraid?

'So,' I say. 'Before we start, is there anything you want to ask?'

Dumier looks at me curiously. 'The Rachmann trial, that was you?'

'I defended Matthias Rachmann, yes. But I meant about your case.'

'Small world. You should have won.'

I shrug, not sure whether he means it as a compliment or a rebuke. Everyone has an opinion about the Rachmann trial. It dominated the newspapers for weeks, the public fascination voracious and inexhaustible. Even now, a year later, people remember. Two days ago there was a cartoon in the newspaper, a drawing of an art gallery with van Gogh's self-portrait with the bandaged ear on an easel in the window and a notice pasted on the glass: GERMANS, DEFEND YOURSELVES: BUY ONLY GERMAN VAN GOGHS! Pretty funny, I thought, especially if you're not a Jew.

I take Dumier through Böhm's contract. When I ask him if he understands that the contract is binding, that it takes no account of any change in circumstances in the future, he laughs bleakly.

'Nothing's going to change,' he says.

I try a different tack. 'Do you have a will?'

'Do you mean legally or existentially?'

It's a good joke. Perhaps there's more to Anton Dumier than meets the eye. 'I would urge you to be as open with me as possible,' I say. 'As your lawyer, I am bound by a duty of secrecy: anything you say is strictly confidential.'

'And all the things we can't say, what about those?'

He looks at me and I look back at him and the scab on his mouth is like a thick black stitch, sewing it shut. Then, pulling the contract towards him, he picks up my pen and signs.

Tuesday 11 April

We celebrate Passover with Erich and Erna Büttel and their sons. The boys laugh and shout and rag each other in their usual way but Gerda is very quiet. She barely touches her food. This morning she told me that this year there are no matzahs on display in any of the Jewish bakeries. They sell them secretly, sneaked out from under the counter like dirty photographs.

Thursday 13 April

I knew it was coming but it's still a shock to see it in black and white. The German Bar Association is required to inform me that, as a non-Aryan and further to the ratification of the revised Law on the Admission to the Bar, my licence to practise has been revoked. There are too many of us, that's the Nazi line, too many piglets at too small a trough. When there's not enough to go around – and the truth is there isn't and hasn't been for years – the German people must come first.

Thank God, at least, for Hindenburg, who grasps that some of us are German at least as much as we are Jewish. His intervention has ensured that non-Aryans who fought in the war will be exempt. Those of us who are eligible are required to reapply in person. I will have to swear an oath of allegiance. Not to my country or its constitution, but to a political party who'll be lucky still to be in power by Christmas. If they were not so frightening they would be preposterous, this brutish band of bigots who behave as though they are a cross between the Sicilian Mafia and the Boy Scouts.

I arrive early but already the queue snakes round the block. It is raining. I do not have an umbrella. I see Urschel, Böhm's partner, ahead of me in the line. We wait for a long time. It is mid-afternoon before a man comes out of the building and tells us to come back on Monday.

Urschel and I walk together back along the river. When we

pass a bar he stops. We need a drink, he says. I order a glass of beer, Urschel a large brandy. He downs it in a single swallow and asks for a second. Neither of us can think of much to say. I finish my beer. I have to go home, I tell him, my wife is expecting me. Urschel nods and gestures at the barman to top him up. I don't know much about his private life but I do know he's not married. I think perhaps he's a homosexual. Poor bastard. The Campaign for a Clean Reich is gearing up and arrests are on the rise. Two weeks ago they picked up Hiller, Hirschfeld's right-hand man at the Sex Institute, and sent him to the new concentration camp at Oranienburg.

Queer and Jewish and a legal aid lawyer in a city where Jews are now forbidden to act for the state. No wonder Urschel wants to get drunk.

Friday 14 April

I go into the office as usual. What else is there to do? I can't stay at home with Gerda. I've had enough of her anxiety, the way her eyes dart to my face when she thinks I'm not looking. I've had enough of my own. It goes round and round in my head, the bills and our dwindling savings account and what happens when we can no longer pay the rent. I sit at my desk and move bits of paper until it is time to go home.

Saturday 15 April

You should have won. Anton Dumier's words merge with the image of Gregor Rachmann smoking in the doorway to create one of those animated neon advertisements in my head, it repeats itself ceaselessly and I can't make it stop. Am I to blame? Could we have won if I had only done things differently? Not everyone agreed with my approach. I argued about it with my old friend Ernst Liffmann before we went to trial.

'People think criminal trials are a matter of plot, who did what when and to whom, but that's just housekeeping,' he said. 'Criminal trials are all character.'

I disagreed. Coherence, I said, that's what wins cases. The shaping of the jumble of the things we know for certain, the things we know and cannot prove, and the unknowable spaces in between, into a story with a beginning, a middle and an end, a story that makes sense.

What made sense to me with Rachmann was anger. Everything about it made me angry: the grasping dealers, the idiot police, the so-called experts who turned out to be as ignorant as everyone else. If Rachmann was guilty, his pictures not only had to be fakes, he had to have known they were fakes when he sold them. But how could he, when a dozen so-called experts assured him they were genuine? Rachmann never pretended to be a connoisseur. He paid for, and accepted, the assurances of others better qualified than himself. So why was it Rachmann who ended up in the dock and not the men whose defective judgement had put him there? For days in that dark courtroom I raged about scapegoats, about injustice, about the bitter unequal battle between the masters and the men. Anger is simpler than grief and I was very angry.

The experts were angry too. By the time the case finally came to court, and it took years, they all had scores to settle and reputations to salvage and not one of them was going down without a fight. With the exception of the mumbling Köhler-Schultz, they declaimed from the stand like evangelists competing for souls. They disagreed fervidly on everything. One man's blatant forgeries sent another into raptures. The Stransky *Self-Portrait* that the

Dutch expert Hendriksen declared van Gogh's greatest master-piece was, for Stemler of the Nationalgalerie, probably the worst painting he had ever seen. While even Rachmann conceded that some of the paintings he had sold were probably forgeries, no one could agree on which ones or how many. Even the ranks of technical experts, the paint analysers and the fingerprint people and the purveyors of all-seeing X-rays whose testimony I feared might prove our undoing, served up nothing but contradictions.

De Vries was the cherry on the cake. When the man who had started all this took the stand and solemnly informed the court he had changed his mind for a third time, that he now consid-ered five of the Rachmann canvases to be genuine after all, I was certain we had it. So were the journalists. On the morning of the judgment, almost all of the newspapers called it for us. We were wrong. The judges agreed that some of Rachmann's paint-ings were indeed van Goghs, though they didn't say which, but Rachmann was convicted of fraud, thanks mostly to some very dodgy bookkeeping. His story about the Russian, while never disproved, was dismissed by the bench as entirely implausible.

And at appeal it happened all over again, in pretty much the same order and with stiffer penalties. Rachmann got nineteen months in prison, with an extra three hundred days to cover the thirty-thousand-mark fine he couldn't pay. The sentence was harsh, unreasonably so, but by then the winds of change had become a hurricane and the judges were terrified, the world was breaking up around them. They made an example of Rachmann and he paid heavily. Until he settles his bills, so have I.

Did I misjudge the case? I didn't think so then. There was a sour mood in Germany at that time, a sense of reckoning. Hard-working people had struggled for too long. A new age was dawning and the little man's time had come. Rachmann's best chance was for the court to see him as a victim, the stooge of a privileged elite intent on protecting their own. Besides which the judges were right, his story about the Russian was implausible. We had to create a distraction, to make it someone else's fault.

I have changed my mind since then. I've come to think Ernst was right. The story I told the court was logical enough, but it forgot what every child with a picture book knows, that a good story needs more than a villain or twelve. It needs a hero.

Thursday 20 April

Today is the Führer's birthday. They're calling it the Day of the Nation. There are parades in the streets and rousing radio broadcasts and vast swastikas rippling from every lamppost and flagpole in Berlin. At the Criminal Court in Moabit proceedings were adjourned for two hours of singing and sycophancy for a leader who flagrantly flouts the rule of law.

Nothing sticks. That's what we tell ourselves. If recent years have taught us anything it is that nothing sticks. Soon it will be another party making all the promises. Hitler's strongest opponents have fled abroad, he cannot silence them there. The pendulum will swing. It must. Someone will make it swing. But who? When?

Tuesday 25 April

My readmission to the Bar is confirmed. I will no longer be listed in Berlin's justice administration directory – a separate guide will be issued for non-Aryans – but I have my licence, I can still work. The relief is shameful and exquisite. My limbs prickle with it. I can't stay in the office, I need air. In the courtyard a sharp breeze shakes the cherry tree, swirling the blossom into drifts of pink snow. I open a new pack of cigarettes and smoke one. I keep the card for the Büttel boy. It has the boxer Walter Neusel on it, the one they call the Blond Tiger. They used to print famous portraits smoking on the back of this brand, during the trial it amused people to buy me the van Gogh one, but it is all sportsmen now.

'Down, me down!' a piping voice cries out behind me and I turn to see Fräulein Eberhardt, a small boy wedged on one hip. She doesn't see me. The boy squirms, kicking his heels against her. He's at that solid, silky-haired stage, not a baby any more but not yet quite a child.

'Down?' she asks him. 'You don't want a horsey ride?'

'Horsey!' he crows and, hoisting him higher, she starts to gallop round the courtyard. The boy squeals with delight. As she rounds the cherry tree she sees me and smiles but she doesn't slow down. The two of them complete another round of the courtyard before she staggers to a stop. They are both laughing.

'Again, again!' the boy cries and she hugs him closer and kisses his cheek. The ring is still on her left finger in the traditional way, she is not married yet. The boy clasps her neck, fitting himself against her, and stares at me. His eyes are dark and fierce, like hers.

'Horses have to rest between races,' she says. 'This is Herr Berszacki, Ivo. He's a friend of Anton's.'

I smile. 'Hello, Ivo,' I say and, suddenly shy, he twists away from me, burying his face in Fräulein Eberhardt's shoulder. 'How old is he, your son?'

'He's three but he's not mine. His mother is my oldest friend. When she – when it didn't work out with Ivo's father, they came to live with me.'

'He's a fine boy. She will stay in Berlin, I hope, your friend?'

She frowns at me. I've confused her.

'When you're married, I mean. She won't move away?'

Fräulein Eberhardt turns her head, her lips brushing the boy's forehead, and it's like catching the smell of a long-forgotten perfume, something about the shape they make together twists my heart. I look down at the ground, at the brown-edged blossoms strewn about my feet.

'She'll stay with me,' she says. 'With us. They both will, it's their home.'

I leave the two of them in the courtyard, a last horsey ride. As I cross the road towards the station I see a man at the newspaper kiosk and my stomach drops. Gregor Rachmann, I could swear it, only it isn't him, it never is. I know that if I turn around the man will be someone else, someone who looks nothing like Rachmann, so I don't turn around, I won't let myself. I keep walking and my neck is stiff with not looking, with not being afraid.

Thursday 27 April

Every day brings more letters from clients who no longer require my services. Künel apologises, he hopes I appreciate the difficulty of his position. Hildebrand seems to think I am Jewish just to vex him. He returns my bill with *VOID* scrawled across it in red ink. I tear it up. My hands are shaking. This is the problem with not having enough work to do. Your anxieties loom over you like a bore at a party: *I'm Impending Ruin, let's talk about me.* So I do what I would do at a party. I flee. I shove the letters in a drawer and I get up and I tear open boxes. I lay the Rachmann papers out on the floor. What, I ask myself, if I had made that trial about Rachmann the man? In that courtroom, surrounded as he was by braggers and blusterers of the first order, could I have made a hero of him?

He didn't look like one. By then we Germans wanted heroes in the Aryan mould, muscled Blond Tigers with square jaws and manly eyebrows. Matthias Rachmann, as several newspapers cattily observed, looked like a girl. As Berliners fought pitched battles in the streets and kicked the last shreds of life from the limp-wristed Weimar experiment, no one was on the side of the queers and the dancers.

I should have remembered that Rachmann was a performer, that he knew how to hold an audience. On the last day of the trial, when the final arguments had been delivered, he rose and asked the bench if he might be permitted to say a few words. I was horrified, he had said nothing to me, but the judges acceded. Gravely he waited for silence. When at last he spoke you could have heard a fly blink.

'The last four years have been the hardest of my life. My belief in many of the paintings I sold has been shaken, my faith in many of those I trusted to help and advise me shattered. But in the darkness a light still burns, a beacon to guide me. I gave my word of honour to a man of honour. If I was deceived, so was he. My trust in him remains absolute and true.'

For a moment no one moved, and in that moment I believed in him completely. Not in the shadow-puppet Russian prince but in Rachmann's faith in him, whoever he was. For eleven days I had heard nothing but a cacophony of brass, trumpets thunderously blowing themselves. Then suddenly this, clear and pure like a single flute.

It changed nothing. How could it? It was too little, too late. A snatch of birdsong, sweet enough to give you pause, but brief and easily forgotten. If you want to make a melody stick, as any two-penny songster will tell you, you have to let all the instruments have it, then get them to repeat it over and over again, forwards and backwards and upside down until the damn thing hatches in your head, a maggot squirming ceaselessly in the folds of your brain.

Ernst Liffmann was right. I should have seen it coming. I should have kicked off the trial with that statement of Rachmann's and built a bloody great symphony out of it. I should have listened to my client and not my own anger, the raging in my head that I stoked and stoked, louder and louder, so I wouldn't hear the sound of my heart splitting in two.

Sunday 30 April

For days now I have been rolling an idea around in my mind like one of the coloured glass marbles my brother Stefan and I used to fight over as boys, looking at the patterns in it. A way to make some money, yes, but also to set the record straight, to settle the past more squarely on its axis.

When I first met Rachmann all I knew about van Gogh was what everyone knew, that he was a suicidal madman who cut off his own ear and never sold a single painting. It was Rachmann who told me that was rubbish, that in his last years van Gogh was widely admired, both by critics and by fellow artists who traded their work for his. He might have only sold one or two canvases but, for a man who had been painting for less than a decade, whose style broke every rule in the book, he was well on the way to success. It was Julius Köhler-Schultz who wrote the other story, the one everyone knows, and because we liked it better than the real one it stuck.

So this is my idea: why not do a Köhler-Schultz on Matthias Rachmann? Germany is floundering, drowning. We throw in our lot with one bungling government after another and each time, for our own protection, they push us further under. What better time, then, for the story of a man lit not by genius but by decency? A man who bore ignominy and imprisonment rather than betray his conscience, who chose to save not his skin but his soul. When we no longer believe in God, we need more than ever to believe in men.

Of course Rachmann will have to agree. For a celebrity he has a surprising dislike of the limelight, but I am hopeful. What is the harm in being hailed as a hero? Especially since he really, really needs the money.

Monday 1 May

Urschel comes to see me. Urschel & Böhm is to be dissolved. Böhm is an Aryan, under the new law their partnership is no longer permitted. Böhm wants Urschel to keep their office, he says he will find another place, but they have only just renewed their lease and Urschel knows what Böhm earns, he can't ask him to pay twice. He frowns at me, twisting his fingers together.

'Would you swap?' he asks abruptly. Böhm's office is smaller than this one, he admits, but it is also cheaper. I hesitate. I like my privacy, I do not want to share. The money, though. I tell him I'll think about it. At the door he pauses.

'Perhaps we should go into partnership ourselves,' he says. 'Urschel and Berszacki. Berszacki and Urschel. It has a certain ring, don't you think?'

I laugh or try to. It is only when he is gone that I wonder if he didn't mean it as a joke. Urschel & Berszacki, the rocks in each other's pockets. Perhaps he is right. If we must go down, at least let it be fast.

I get home late. The parlour is dark. I think of all the Friday nights we sat together in this room when A was little, the long shadows from the Shabbat candles, the smell of roast chicken and warm bread. We no longer bother to observe the Shabbat. It does not seem worth all the trouble, just for the two of us. I switch on the lamp. Gerda is sitting in the wing chair by the window. She raises a hand, shading her eyes against the sudden light. She has a photograph album open in her lap.

I lean down and kiss the top of her head. A grins up at me. She wears a striped dress with a white collar and her legs are skinny and very straight. Gerda closes the album. I put my hand on her shoulder and she leans her face against my wrist, and just like that I am nineteen again and in the parlour of her parents' apartment on the Schönhauser Allee with its lace curtains and the huge mahogany sideboard with the glass-fronted display case that took up all the room. She used to catch my hand and press it to her cheek when her mother turned to pour the tea. I had forgotten but my body remembers. I don't say anything. I stand very still with my hand on her shoulder, back at the beginning.

Tuesday 2 May

I spend the morning at the *Kammergericht*. The sun streams through the high windows, lighting columns of silvery dust. I watch them turn. An eternity ago, studying for my Bar examinations in this same library, I used to imagine the dust as the residue of intense concentration, hundreds of thousands of tiny particles of thought. Now the idea unnerves me. These days we're better off keeping our thoughts to ourselves.

In the lobby I see Voigt from the prosecutor's office, a junior clutching a tower of files panting in his wake. Voigt is a man always in a hurry but when I nod at him he stops. The junior staggers gratefully to a halt.

'Berszacki,' he says. I wait for the crack – there's always a crack with Voigt, like a schoolboy, he considers insults the essence of camaraderie – but today he claps my shoulder and tells me I look well. I smile but I don't like it. I want him to ask me how the weather is down there, to tell me that the way my hairline's going, it won't be long before he can read my mind. I want things back the way they were.

Later a clerk telephones from his office. I shouldn't be surprised. Voigt's memory is arranged into faces and favours: whenever he sees one he matches it with the other. The clerk tells me that three months ago the prosecutor's office released the evidence from the Rachmann trial. However, and despite several legal notices, Gregor Rachmann has yet to claim the crates of paintings seized from his studio. Storage space is limited and unclaimed items will be destroyed. Would I accept responsibility for said items on Herr Rachmann's behalf and make the necessary arrangements for their return? I think of Gregor Rachmann ducking away from me in the doorway. I still think I glimpse him sometimes in a crowded street.

'Herr Voigt is grateful for your cooperation,' the clerk adds blandly and my scalp prickles. These days even the mildest remark sounds like a threat.

Wednesday 3 May

At breakfast Gerda is pale. Her shoulders sag. I ask her if she has one of her headaches coming on and she shakes her head. Just a bit tired, she says. Wednesday is her coffee morning day, she doesn't like to miss it, but today she says she thinks she'll stay at home.

'Another twenty years and the Orlewitz baby will move out,'

I say and she tries to smile. Neither of us slept well. When I got home yesterday evening there was a letter waiting. No stamp, it had been delivered by hand, but Stefan was still careful. There are changes at his bank in Hannover. He is considering a new job in Antwerp. There are arrangements to be made, he needs to come to Berlin. He asks if he can see us while he is here.

Did he really think we wouldn't understand? My brother, who has spent his whole adult life refusing to be a Jew, is bailing out. His bank has let him go and in turn he is letting go of the rest of us. He doesn't care that we have as much right to be here as anyone, that in leaving he plays into their hands. A business opportunity, he calls it. Of course he does. He's never going to admit that he's running away.

Last night I punched my fist into the wall. This morning I take Gerda's hand and I tell her we can leave too if that is what she wants, that there are places we could go until things calm down, there are firms in Amsterdam and The Hague that specialise in German law. I don't say that you could count the positions in these firms on the fingers of two hands, that I don't speak Dutch and anyway we haven't the money, that even without the emigration taxes and the forced exchange rates we wouldn't have enough to start again. I've promised myself that I will offer Gerda the choice, that if she really wants to go then I will see what can be done.

Fine words and finer sentiments. They might even mean something if I didn't already know she would never leave. They would have to burn our building to the ground before she would abandon this apartment, the rooms where we lived together, the three of us. She clings to the traces A has left here, the ink stain on the kitchen floor, the scuffs on the paintwork, the pencil marks on the cupboard door where we marked her height. I can't bring myself to tell her that, if things go on like this, we will have to find somewhere cheaper. She knows things are bad but she never asks what will happen to us. Gerda has no interest in the future. Everything she wants is already in the past.

Friday 5 May

Diefenbach has gone. He was scrupulous and widely respected, but someone has decreed that the Senior District Attorney must be a National Socialist so he's out. Not one judge in Berlin has raised an objection.

I go to see Böhm. I want to tell him he can have my office and his own, that I refuse to practise in a country where the law bends so readily to political ends, but I already know it isn't true. I'll swap with him and I'll go on, chicken that I am, squawking and scratching in the dirt for flecks of grain. The law is all I know, and we have to live.

Böhm is outside his office, fumbling with his keys. He's wearing a stand-up collar and a white rose on his lapel. May 5th, of course, Anton Dumier's wedding day. I had forgotten. I tell him he can have my office and when he asks if I'm sure I shrug.

'A change is as good as a rest, don't they say?' I say, and the shame moves through me like a fever, hot and cold. 'How was the wedding?'

'Official. I just hope Dumier's grateful,' and, just like that, the penny drops.

'She did it for him?' I ask. Böhm looks down at the rose in his buttonhole as though he's not sure how it got there. Extracting it, he drops it in the wastepaper basket.

'Happy days,' he says flatly and goes in.

Saturday 6 May

It startles me to discover that, in all the boxes and boxes of papers, I have only one document in Matthias's own hand. It is a statement Matthias gave to the Dutch police in February 1929. By then the police had let him go, there was not enough evidence to hold him, but the case against him was mounting: in a single month Moscow denied knowledge of any Russian collection of van Goghs, the Swiss police drew a blank on Russian émigrés, and the Nationalgalerie declared all thirty-two of his pictures to be fakes. Then a police raid on Gregor Rachmann's studio in Düsseldorf turned up a clutch of doctored canvases. They weren't van Goghs, only some anonymous nineteenth-century landscapes Gregor was 'improving' to sell on and not in itself illegal, but still it looked very bad. Beleaguered and desperate for allies, the Rachmann brothers smuggled nine of the contested paintings out of Germany to The Hague, where they showed them to Clovis Hendriksen, Holland's pre-eminent van Gogh expert. A week later, Matthias was in hospital.

I read the second half of his statement three times.

On Saturday 2 February I travelled to Amsterdam to visit the Rijksmuseum. Near the Nieuwmarkt I was approached by a man who spoke German. He was dark & of medium height with a strong beard. His German was good. He told me his name was Zima & that he was interested in buying art. He invited me to join him for a meal. We went to a small restaurant on the Damrak. I do not remember the name. Afterwards I returned to Leiden by train.

During the night I fell ill. There was
a stabbing pain in my abdomen, nausea &
dizziness. My vision was blurred. I went
out on to the landing, I wanted to call
for a doctor, but I must have blacked out.
When I came to I was in the hospital. My
arm was broken. Dr Haak told me I had
suffered a heart attack, that the attack
had caused me to fall down the stairs.
I told him I had been poisoned but he
refused to examine me. I demanded that
the nurse take samples of my blood &c.
for testing. I also asked to see another
doctor. Both requests were denied.

On Monday 4 February Dr Haak visited
me alone. He told me that I had not
been poisoned and that I should drop
the matter. His tone was very threatening. When I told him I wanted to speak
to the police Dr Haak left the room. I
knew then that I was in danger. At my
insistence my brother arranged for me to
be brought here.

I was both relieved and astonished when the prosecution didn't
use the statement at trial. I feared it would sink us, either the par-
anoia or the sheer unscrupulousness of it. Back then I was quite
certain that Matthias had poisoned himself. If he was to have a
chance he had to win support for his paintings from experts who
believed they were genuine, but he knew that would take time.
During the nine weeks Matthias was in hospital and beyond the
reach of the Berlin police, his new friend Hendriksen declared

seven of his nine van Goghs to be genuine and persuaded several of his influential clients to buy them. He even bought one himself. By the time Matthias finally discharged himself from hospital, most of the Dutch art establishment had taken his side. A happy accident? In Matthias's hotel room the Dutch police found a bottle of tincture of aconite root, a common treatment for tonsillitis. In large doses aconite root is poisonous.

But reading the statement again, what strikes me now is the terror in it. Matthias knew the police were closing in, but he also knew that the evidence against him was circumstantial at best. What if his fear was not of Kriminalkommissar Gans but of someone closer and more ruthless? In his testimony Matthias always insisted that he had given the Russian his word of honour, but everyone knows vows, like arms, can be broken. The hospital might not have tested for poisoning, but the wrist was real enough. I saw the X-rays.

What if Matthias did not admit himself to hospital to avoid arrest? What if he was simply trying to stay alive?

Sunday 7 May

I go to Tegel to see Matthias. I take sausage, cigarettes. The last time I was here we argued about money. I want him to know I come in good faith. When I hand the items in, I ask the warder how he is doing. Tegel is grisly for everyone and grislier still for men like him. The warder shrugs.

'Knows how to handle himself,' he says. 'No flies on him.'

I sign the book. No one has visited Matthias since the last time I came. If Gregor has been in Berlin he has not been here. I go through to the cell. Matthias is already there, sitting at the table. We talk about this and that. He stares at the table, asks

314

me how I am managing. I'm not the one locked in here, I say, but he shakes his head.

'Safer inside,' he says. 'You have been a good friend to me, Frank. I'm in your debt. We both are. And we will repay you, I swear it. As soon as we can.' He looks up at me, into me. His eyes search mine. 'Don't lose faith. We mustn't lose faith.'

I lost my faith a long time ago but I don't say so. There's something about Matthias Rachmann that makes me want to believe, for both our sakes. I take the book proposal from my briefcase and hand it to him. He reads it. Then he pushes it back across the table and shakes his head. He says he's sorry but that time is past, there's nothing to be gained from raking it up.

'We'd do it your way, however you wanted,' I say. 'Think about it, at least. You need the money. I know I do.'

'And you'll get it, I swear. As soon as it's safe. You have my word.'

After that there isn't much to say. I tell Matthias about Gregor's crates. Immediately he stiffens. He wants to know what the process is for returning them to Gregor, what address I have for him, that everything that was seized will be returned. When I tell him there's nothing missing some of the tension goes out of him.

'Right. Good. Only I gave Gregor my word he'd get it all back. Every last thing.'

'Then he needs to answer my letters. I can't send anything without his signature.'

'So until you have that the crates are your responsibility?'

'It would appear so.'

We are both silent then. I can hear Matthias breathing.

'Aren't you angry?' I blurt. 'That in all this time he hasn't once come to see you?'

Matthias looks at me. I can't read his face, I have no idea what he's thinking. 'They are still our brothers, aren't they?' he says softly. 'However many times they disappoint us.'

So much I told him in those dark days. I always thought it was the trial that saved me, that kept me from drowning in the darkness, but perhaps it wasn't. Perhaps it was Matthias himself.

Wednesday 10 May

Tonight there is a public burning of library books by students in Opernplatz, outside the University. The event is broadcast live on the wireless.

'I consign everything unGerman to the flames,' the leader of the students proclaims. He has to shout to be heard over the bonfire which roars like something alive. The crowd whoops. As the students throw the books on to the fire a band plays and the radio announcer lists the authors whose work is to be banned. Communists, yes, but Jews too, the names go on and on. Albert Einstein. Stefan Zweig. Erich Kästner. I bought a copy of *Emil and the Detectives* to give A for Christmas. It's still hidden at the back of the wardrobe, wrapped in its shiny red paper.

We do not stay up to hear Goebbels make his speech. It is late and there is nothing left to say. Just after dawn, while the light beneath the curtain is still grainy and grey, Gerda rolls over silently in bed, curving her back into the shape of me. The years and rough weather have eroded us until we fit against one another like the boulders of some primitive temple. In defiance of gravity, of memory, we hold each other up.

Friday 19 May

Our maid Lena left this morning. She has another job. She refused to work her notice. She told Gerda to watch her step, her new employer is a high-up in the Nazi party and he likes to keep dirty Jews in their place. Her rudeness was prodigious and exultant. After she was gone Gerda found she had taken the good tablecloth and the last of the silver teaspoons.

'Good riddance,' Gerda says but her eyes are red. My hand shakes as I unlock the drawer of my night table and find to my relief that this diary is still inside. I do not know which is stronger in me, the hatred I feel towards Lena or the relief that she has spared me the shame of admitting we can't afford to keep her.

Tuesday 23 May

Stefan is already at the apartment when I get home. It is a warm evening, he is sitting by the open windows. Gerda sits in the upright chair by the table. She is wearing her good blue dress. Stefan stands to greet me, a glass in his hand.

'Frank, a drink,' he says. The wine is French, he tells me, from the Loire valley. He says something about the year that means nothing to me and pours me a glass. Already he is the host. He gestures at Gerda with the bottle and Gerda gives me a look and covers her glass with her hand. I am late.

'A long day,' I say. The wine is a pale clear yellow. I take a gulp and Stefan coughs out one of his wry little laughs. Too late I see that he has raised his glass.

'You Berliners,' he says. 'Always rush, rush, rush.'

Five minutes and already antagonism sours my mouth. I don't want it to be like this, not today. Forcing a smile, I clink my glass against his.

'It's good to see you,' I say. 'Thank you for the wine.'

Stefan nods, touches the neck of the bottle. 'We can't take it with us.'

There is a silence. Gerda gets up and goes into the kitchen to see about supper. On the balcony her flowers tumble from their pots, a tangle of pink and white.

'I suggested a restaurant but Gerda wouldn't hear of it,' Stefan says. 'She said she'd already cooked.' He murmurs something about it smelling good but I know Gerda's refusal annoys him. He would have preferred a restaurant. Not for the food, Stefan doesn't care much for food, but because he likes to run the show, to patronise the maître d' and order the wine and insist on everyone having the steak because it is the speciality of the house and the only dish worth eating on the menu. His party, his rules.

We sip his wine and listen to Gerda clattering dishes in the kitchen. Neither of us wants to start the conversation he has come here to have. I see him looking at the shabby sofa, the walls that need repainting. Stefan's villa in Hannover is very large and very new.

'Gerda says you're no longer on the telephone,' he says.

'We decided we didn't need it. There's a public box on the corner.'

'So you're all right, you're not struggling too badly?'

I am not sure which infuriates me more, the remark or Stefan's faux-paternal tone. The last time we met my brother told me why the NSDAP offered the only viable future for Germany. He put them in. Now he is bailing out.

'We're terrific,' I say. 'Thank God you stood firm against those Commie bastards.'

Stefan sighs. 'Please, Frank, not tonight.' His voice is clammy with forbearance. Stefan is three years my junior but you'd never guess it. Since the age of fourteen, when our father died and he grew four inches, Stefan has determined to look down on me. Over the years he has honed condescension to an art form.

Gerda calls us through to the dining room. It is not yet dark but she has lit candles. The flames flicker palely in the blue air. We eat soup and rouladen. Even the soup sticks in my throat. Stefan opens a second bottle of wine and I set about drinking it while Gerda asks the questions I cannot. Stefan is taking his family to Belgium. His wife's cousin owns a small company in Antwerp that manufactures children's toys, demand is picking up but he needs capital to expand. With Stefan's money they can set up a second manufactory near Brussels. It will take everything he has but Stefan is determined. At his bank all the Jewish directors have already been dismissed and, though promises have been made for their reemployment, nothing has been done. Stefan says he cannot sit idly by and wait until the nightmare burns itself out. He is afraid he will be next. I wonder if he thinks he will be richer in Belgium.

'You are letting them win,' Gerda says. Her cheeks are flushed, with anger or with wine, I cannot tell.

'Dear Gerda, do you honestly believe that staying will change anything? You are a principled woman and I admire that, but principles won't protect you against thugs with rubber truncheons. Frank, surely you don't agree with her? You're not a fool, you know as well as I that anyone with any sense is getting out.'

'Is it only bankers who cannot tell the difference between sense and money?' I say sardonically to Gerda but Stefan only sighs.

'You're not a pauper, Frank. I know change isn't easy for you but you need to wake up, see the way the wind is blowing.' He shakes his head at me and I am fifteen again, I want to punch his patronising mouth.

'I don't understand you, Stefan,' I say angrily. 'Don't you see that if you run away now, you leave everyone else in the lurch? You are a Jew, whether you want to be or not, and as a Jew you have to stand firm. How do you think anything will change if we don't stand firm?' It startles me, how strongly I suddenly feel about staying.

'How can I stay? My responsibility is to my family, I have to think of my children.'

The word hangs in the air. Stefan looks at the table. He straightens his knife. When he looks up at me his face is very stiff, a mask through which his eyes burn.

'Mina has been expelled from school,' he says quietly. 'The new quotas, she's meant to be exempt but the head is a Party member, he doesn't care for exemptions. He says she is disruptive. Mina, the bookworm, who wants only to learn. The boys, they still go. They sit at the back of the classroom on a special yellow bench for Jews. They are no longer allowed to go on school outings or to sing the school songs. Last week Rudy was made to stand at the front of the class while his teacher pointed out his deceitful Jewish features. Now the other children call him *Schweinjude*, Jewish pig. Tell me, Frank, do you really think I can stay?'

The speech uses up all the air in the room. Gerda brings a cheesecake and I shake my head but Stefan takes a piece and makes a pretence of eating it. Stefan's children have not been raised as Jews. Their neighbourhood in Hannover has no synagogue. When Gerda rises to take the plates into the kitchen he puts a hand on my arm. I stare at the signet ring on his third finger, the elaborate pattern of his initials engraved in the green stone. Then I move my arm away.

'It is not yet as bad here as it is in Hannover,' he says. 'But it will be. You have to leave while you still can.'

I snort. 'You think we can leave now?'

'For God's sake, Frank, why must you be so stubborn? If you really don't have the money, and if you don't, God knows why not, I've been telling you for years, then maybe we can help. I'd have to talk it over with Bettina, of course—'

His sentence tails off but we both know how it ends. Bettina is not an uncharitable woman but she is a German in the Lutheran style, she believes that God helps those who help themselves. I look at Stefan and somewhere inside me, beneath the anger and the exasperation, I feel the ache of something old and deep. I wish we had made a better job of being brothers.

'Thank you,' I say and I almost mean it. 'But we aren't leaving.'

'Don't drag your damned pride into this, Frank. You have to think of Gerda.'

And just like that we're back where we started. 'What is that supposed to mean?' I snap. 'Gerda doesn't want to leave any more than I do.'

'Then it's your job to persuade her she's wrong.'

'Christ, Stefan, why do you persist in believing that what's right for you is right for everybody else?'

'Why do you have to be such a blind bloody fool?'

'Stop it.' Gerda stands in the doorway, a clean dish in her hands. 'Both of you, please. Just stop it.' She has put an apron on over her blue dress. We sit silently as she opens the sideboard and puts the dish away.

'It's late, I should go,' Stefan says. I nod but he does not get up. He interlaces his hands on the table. The green of his ring gleams between his fingers.

'When do you leave?' I ask. The question sounds so final. I know it's the wine and the worry and the bone-aching weariness of it all but I am suddenly afraid that I will never see him or his children again.

Friday 26 May

I don't recognise my office since Böhm took it over. You can see the floor. There are neatly labelled plan chests and framed watercolours on the walls, hills and lakes. All it lacks is a Persian carpet and a pianoforte.

I'm grateful really. The lower rent gives me breathing space for a few months. Perhaps things will have picked up by then. Some of my bills are still outstanding, I should chase them up. Then I think of Erna Büttel's cousin who was reported to the SA for levying an excessive rate of interest on unpaid bills and is now in a camp at Osthofen. The customer who accused him was a crook who had evaded repayment for years but who cares about the facts? The cousin is Jewish and therefore guilty.

As for the book, I've thought many times about going back to Matthias, pleading with him to change his mind, but since Opernplatz I've lost the appetite. The newspapers claim that only a handful of 'harmful and undesirable' books have been withdrawn from circulation but people say 20,000 books were burned here in Berlin that night and that the bonfires continue at schools and universities around Germany.

Just how big are these bastards' hands?

Thursday 1 June

It's been nearly three weeks and still no reply from Gregor Rachmann so this evening two men deliver his crates to our apartment. There's a tea chest too, heavy with books. Gerda doesn't want them here, neither do I, but there's nowhere else they can go. When I asked Scherek, the grizzled Polish superintendent of our apartment building, if I could store them in the cellar, he said it was forbidden. We both know he's allowed other tenants to do it in the past but he wouldn't budge. I can't blame him. It would mean bending the rules and these days who wants to take the risk?

It takes the men several trips to lug everything up the stairs. According to the docket the crates contain eight canvases and a display case. I remember the case, a deep box of a thing several feet across and painted to look like a garden. A Monet copy, someone claimed, though even Voigt wasn't stupid enough to try that in court. According to Matthias the case was a commission, only the customer who ordered it never picked it up. He said Gregor kept it as a warning, in case he was ever again stupid enough not to take payment upfront.

Gerda comes out of the kitchen as I am signing for them. I can hear the little exhalation she makes when she sees them stacked up in the hallway. The men have made it clear that this is as far as they go.

'It's only for a few days,' I say to Gerda. Beside her the delivery man raises his hand and I'm afraid he is going to salute, but he only tugs his cap and pockets the coins I give him. As I close the door behind him Gerda touches the wall.

'They've scraped the paint,' she says.

'I know. I'm sorry.'

Gerda traces the mark with her finger. She opens her mouth and I think she is going to say something but she closes it again and goes back to the kitchen.

The crates are awkward. Using one foot as a sort of runner I half-lift, half-slide one down the corridor. The wood is rough, splinters jab into my fingers. At A's door I hesitate, catching my breath. Then I push open the door.

The room is just as it was. Gerda insisted, she was mad with the need for it, the perfect precision of the pain. She wouldn't let me touch anything. Stefan said I shouldn't listen, he said it was morbid, but I couldn't talk about it with Gerda, it was like twisting a broken bone. I told Stefan the time would come.

Time passed but it never came. Gerda was right, it is a comfort to sit here, to see what she saw. It's not quite the same, of course, not any more. The foot of the green bedspread is bleached grey from the sun and the pictures we cut from magazines are yellowed and starting to peel. Gerda would not let us paste on to the walls, she said it spoiled the paint, so we made a frame from balsa wood and hung it above the chest of drawers. A said it was better than any painting in the museum. She said she would paste a new set of pictures on to it every year of her life for ever and ever. It would be like the Elba Sandstone Mountains at school, she said, one stratum laid down on top of the other.

As old as the hills. I can't think that. We managed three layers, two in the corner where Clara Bow smiles the secret smile A could not bring herself to cover up, but there is a topography to it all the same, rucks in the paper and air bubbles and lumps where A used too much paste. On some of the faces you can see the ghost of the person underneath.

I stack the biggest crates against the wardrobe, the small ones between the chest of drawers and the wall. The room is too small for a desk so I built a foldaway table on the wall which A could unlatch to do her homework. More of a shelf than a table really, but A liked it. I hung another shelf above the bed for her books. *The Call of the Wild* is at the end of the row, wedged by the sea urchin fossil we found on the beach at Rüden. A and I read it over and over again, that last summer, captivated by Buck, the dog who must summon the wildness in himself to survive. And then with a jerk I remember: Jack London is banned. Hurriedly I take the book to our bedroom and, as I hide it at the back of the wardrobe, I think of the picture A always turned to first, the colour plate of Buck facing the pale-eyed wolf pack and underneath the line that made her draw in her breath: '*It was to the death.*'

Gerda is in the kitchen putting away the last of the supper dishes. She looks round as I come in. 'We should charge,' she says.

'I'll add it to the bill.'

'He still hasn't paid you?'

'I'm trying.'

'I don't want those things here.'

'I know. I don't want them here either.'

Gerda sighs, staring down into the sink. I put my arms around her, my belly against her back. I am short but she is shorter. My cheek rests against the twist of her hair. She stands stiffly, her hands clasped, but when I pull her closer something in her goes slack. She turns her head, her temple against my lips.

'Just a few days?' she murmurs and, when I nod, she threads her fingers through mine and we stand there in the raw glare of the electric light, our shared shadow draped over the draining board like a cloth.

Tuesday 13 June

Anton Dumier writes to me. He apologises for not settling his bill, his employer has let him go and he has some temporary financial difficulties. He asks for more time. The sum is small, it shouldn't matter, but we both know it does, just as we both know I will accept whatever payment he chooses to give me. Thank God, then, that there is some good news at last. I have, wonder of wonders, a new client, a clerk in a printing company charged with embezzlement. The case is not entirely without hope. My client is Jewish but so are the company's owners so the disadvantage is equal on both sides. I meet with him at Zoo police station. He is a small, bald man with bad breath and a brusque manner but his eyes bulge with terror, he sings with it like a struck glass. He tells me again and again that he has been set up, that he never broke a law in his life. It will be all right, won't it, he asks again and again like a child, tell me it will all be all right, but I don't, I can't. I think of A's first day at the *Grundschule*, her grey coat and her shoes shining like horse chestnuts.

'Remember, there's nothing to be afraid of,' I said at the gate and she sucked in her cheeks and tugged her hand from mine.

'You don't know that,' she said and walked away without looking back.

Thursday 22 June

When will Gregor Rachmann answer my letters? I can't stand those bloody crates. I want things back the way they were, when I could open A's door and slip fleetingly, exquisitely, into the before. Now even the familiar smells of beeswax and unworn clothes have faded, routed by the reek of raw wood.

Saturday 24 June

Stefan is back in Berlin. He cabled yesterday, asked me to meet him tonight at his hotel. I'm late. Allied warplanes have been spotted over Berlin, according to the newspapers, and in response there is a 'spontaneous demonstration' along Unter den Linden. I have to duck into a shop to avoid giving the salute as it passes. The girl behind the counter eyes me suspiciously. I should buy something but I can't spare the money. I slink away like a thief, empty-handed.

Stefan is waiting for me in the bar. Aside from a group of men in loosened ties at the back, we are the only people here. The place is nondescript, a little shabby, a facsimile of a hundred other anonymous hotels in Berlin. A mirror emblazoned with the name of a brand of beer hangs from a chain on the wall. It is not at all Stefan's kind of place. It smells of cigarettes and sweat.

Stefan is awkward, solicitous and distracted at the same time.

He asks after Gerda and his smile flickers like a faulty light. His foot jerks. It makes me nervous. When he summons the tired-looking waitress I ask for a glass of beer.

'Two,' he says. Stefan has never liked beer. When she comes back with the drinks he takes a swallow and I wait for the grimace, the dismissive *I don't know how you drink this stuff*, but he puts the glass down carefully on its wet ring and frowns at it and suddenly I know exactly why he's come.

'Don't you dare say anything,' I say and, when he looks up, startled, I glare at him. 'Not now and not ever. You're going, I understand that, but it's too late. Nothing you say now will ever change that.'

Stefan's shoulders sag. 'Oh, Frank.' He sounds defeated.

'I mean it. I'm going to finish my beer and then I'm going home.'

'Wait, Frank, that's not – please. I have no right, I understand that, but I have to ask you something. A favour.'

Like sauce from a bottle it comes, slowly at first and then all at once. Bettina's cousin is impatient, Stefan is needed in Antwerp to get the new factory up and running. He has resigned from the bank or the bank from him, I'm not sure which. Either way they have given up their house. He'll send for Bettina and the children as soon as he's settled, but till then Bettina's friend Else has agreed they can stay with her. The two women are close, like sisters, and because Else's flat is nearby the boys can stay on at their old school. It's a good arrangement, except for one thing. Else's apartment is small. While the boys can bunk up with Else's son, there is no room for Mina. Of course Bettina would rather keep them together but they must manage the best they can and with no school Mina could go anywhere—

'You want us to have her.' My astonishment makes it sound like a question.

'I'm asking you to think about it,' Stefan says. 'It would only be for a month or two, just till things are settled. I'd help, of course, with her keep. She's a good girl, Frank. She wouldn't be any trouble.'

I haven't seen Mina since the funeral. Before that we used to visit Stefan and Bettina in Hannover perhaps once a year. The German holidays, not the Jewish ones. A looked forward to those visits for months. Once she even had Gerda make her a paper chart so that she could cross off the days until it was time to go. Mina was two years older than A, a goddess-queen, and A her willing slave. The last ever time we went Gerda went upstairs and found A so tightly wrapped in bandages she could hardly breathe. She would not let Gerda unwrap her. She was hurt, she told Gerda earnestly, Mina was making her better.

'Perhaps a different game,' Gerda said to Mina but Mina shook her head.

'She likes this one,' she said and it was true, she did.

'I don't understand,' I say now. 'Why us?'

'Because you're her uncle. And there's no one else.'

'Not even Bettina's mother? I thought you were so marvellously close?'

Stefan looks at the table. 'Bettina's mother wants us to divorce. She thinks it's wrong, that Bettina shouldn't have anything to do with Jews.'

'Christ,' I say and he shrugs. 'But surely the children, her own flesh and blood?'

'Apparently they're Jews too.'

I am silent. I don't know what Gerda will say. She never liked Stefan's children. She thought Bettina spoiled them. Every little thing they did was applauded and admired. Gerda hated that. She thought praise was like money, children needed to learn its value. A used to copy out her poems and stories in her best handwriting to show to Gerda. When Gerda praised one, which she did rarely, the pride on A's face was like a lamp coming on.

'Of course I know you can't agree to anything straight away,' Stefan says. His eyes zigzag the room like a fly. 'Not before you've discussed it with Gerda.'

If Mina comes she will sleep in A's room. It is not just the crates we will have to find somewhere else for but Philip the worn-out rabbit and the cup with the clown painted on it on her bedside table and her nightgown on the back of the door. The clothes in the wardrobe and in the chest of drawers. The room of a ten-year-old will, after three years and seven months, become the room of a girl on the cusp of being grown up.

Tuesday 27 June

Something terrible is happening in Köpenick. A Social Democrat shot two brownshirts and there have been reprisals. The papers take the party line, atrocity stories are lies and harshly punished, but we all know. Hundreds of political opponents of the Reich rounded up and tortured. Whips and chains, sulphuric acid, hot tar, heads smashed so hard the eyes pop out. They want us to know. They dump the bodies in the river, hang them from trees.

Here, twelve miles away, we're not sure what to believe but we all understand. The law is theirs now. We are completely in their hands. I take the key to the drawer of my night table off my ring and, lifting the mattress, hide it between the wooden slats of our bed. The key is tiny, you would never see it if you didn't know it was there. It still wakes me whenever I turn over.

Wednesday 28 June

I have been putting it off but I cannot wait any longer. I ask Gerda about Mina. I tell her I know it is a lot to ask, that the burden will fall on her shoulders.

'Think about it,' I say but she shakes her head. She doesn't need to think about it. There's so little we can do but we can do this, she says, and she looks up at me and she smiles, or nearly, and her face is so dear to me it stops my heart.

Thursday 29 June

When I told Stefan that we would have Mina I heard the breath go out of him. He could not stop thanking me. I was glad, I wanted his gratitude, but the weight of it took me aback. He will bring her next week on the train. I am surprised – at sixteen she is surely old enough to travel alone – but I let it pass. She is not my daughter.

My clerk's trial starts today. There is a new presiding judge, a sandy-haired boy from the sticks who looks about fourteen. All day he interrupts proceedings to direct the bench on specific points relating to non-Aryans. He even makes an impromptu speech about the meaning of the law counting for more than the letter. It is the sort of tripe a student would be failed for trotting out, but the other two judges stare at their hands and say nothing. I storm back to the office in a furious rage. Urschel is sitting at his desk. When I demand to know when that rabid spew of bile *Mein Kampf* replaced the Criminal Code, he looks stunned, appalled, like I have pulled out my cock and then punched him in the face.

'Outside,' he says.

By the time we reach the bottom of the stairs I am shaking. My recklessness frightens me. The caretaker has taken to loitering on landings and we've all heard the stories: intimidation, denounce-ments, groundless accusations that abruptly harden into fact. Only infants and the insane speak without thinking.

In the courtyard Urschel glances around, then tells me quietly that the state plans to bring charges against individuals in the SA for murder and bodily harm. The Interior Minister is to give a speech, publicly condemning the violence in Köpenick. The government wants political stability, public order. Their plans for economic recovery depend upon the rule of law.

'The madness is ending,' he murmurs. 'Don't go mad before it does.'

He goes back upstairs. I should be preparing for tomorrow but I need to be somewhere else, so I go home. Outside our building there is a removal van with SHANGHAI painted on its sides. A huge desk is being manhandled into the back of it. It reminds me of the monstrosity my father used to have, only this one's even uglier. I can't think why anyone would go to the trouble of ship-ping something so hideous halfway around the world. A brute like that must strain even the inscrutable politeness of the Chinese.

Gerda is in A's room. Her hair is tied up in a scarf. She has taken down the curtains and stripped the bed. The rag rug is missing.

'Everything needs washing,' she says. There is a smear of dust on her cheek.

'You shouldn't be moving things by yourself,' I say and she makes a face at me and I am struck by the strength of her, this woman who has been worn down and worn down by grief until she shines with it. Behind her the drawers of the chest are pulled out. They're all empty.

'Where—?' I say and she squeezes my arm.

'In the suitcases,' she says. 'Just for now.'

The suitcases live under our bed. It will be like the old days when we had guests, A in with us till we have the place back to ourselves.

Friday 30 June

The telephone is ringing when I reach the office. It's Stefan. Bettina is in hospital. Puerperal convulsions, he says, as though I'll know what that means. Bettina is out of danger, they delivered the baby safely, a little boy, but it is five weeks too soon, maybe more, no one knows yet if he will live. Stefan's distress crackles down the wire. I think perhaps he is weeping. He says he is sorry and, when I ask him what for, he says he wanted to tell me but he didn't know how.

'I didn't want to open old wounds,' he says and I want to rage at him for his stupidity, his blindness, but what good would it do? If the worst happens he will know soon enough. For now let him think that the heart repairs itself like the body, that it goes back to being nearly the way it was before.

Wednesday 5 July

Mina arrives on Friday. She will come alone after all. Bettina remains in hospital and Stefan has his hands full with the new business and packing up the house, he simply cannot spare the time. They have the baby in an incubator. Bake until risen, Stefan says, with a shrill laugh. His hope is unendurable.

Gerda has made up A's bed with clean sheets but she cannot sweep the floor until the crates are gone. I promise I will get rid of them tomorrow, Friday at the latest. I have no idea where they can go. It is only in the middle of the night, unable to sleep, that

I think of Böhm's office, his plan chests and his watercolours and the marks on the walls where my boxes scuffed the paint.

Friday 7 July

The greengrocer Katzke agrees to loan me his cart and his sons for an hour when their deliveries are done. Gerda can't wait for us to be gone. She fusses around us, brandishing her broom. The boys are scrawny-looking and clumsy, when they dump the tea chest on the bed half of the contents spill out, but they hoist the crates like they are nothing.

When I asked Böhm he agreed straight away. I suppose he thinks he owes me a favour. The Katzke boys have almost finished when he comes back to his office. One of the crates blocks half the window. The tea chest is under the desk. Böhm glances at it, a tiny frown pinching his eyebrows, but he says nothing. I tell the boys to take it down to my office. I'll find room for it there.

'A week, two at the most,' I promise Böhm. The crates have G RACHMANN printed across them in black letters. It occurs to me that I've never talked to Böhm about the Rachmann case. I want to linger, to say something, but I'm already late. I mumble something about my niece, the train. Already the office smells of raw wood.

At the station the woman in the information kiosk sends me to the wrong platform. By the time I reach the right one the Hannover train is already disembarked. Mina is waiting at the gate, a small valise clutched in both hands. She is wearing a blue coat and a hat with a matching ribbon. I wave and she sees me but she does not smile. A porter is standing behind her with two enormous suitcases. I can't imagine what she has brought with her or where it will go.

'Mina, I'm so sorry, this place is a maze.' I kiss her on the cheek. She pulls away.

'Papa said you would be late,' she says stiffly. She has grown tall. With her pale hair and blue eyes she is the double of her mother.

'Did he?'

'He says you're always late for everything.'

'Your father thinks everyone is always late for everything. As a boy he used to leave for school before our mother had even gone to bed.'

She glances at me sideways. She does not want to be here. Who can blame her?

'He ate his lunch before breakfast,' I say. 'And his supper before lunch. Still, it meant he got to Sunday a whole day before the rest of us,' and she presses her lips together until she might almost be smiling. I take the valise.

'Come on,' I say, smiling back. 'Let's get you home.'

Monday 10 July

When I get home Gerda is chopping vegetables in the kitchen. I can tell from the bang of her knife that something is wrong. When I kiss her she frowns and asks why I'm so late. I am not late, but I tell her I am sorry anyway and she puts the knife down and leans against the table with her eyes closed. I put my arms around her and rest my cheek on the top of her head. I can feel the thump of her heart against the underside of my elbow. Her hair smells of onions. When she turns her head towards me I kiss the corner of her mouth.

When I look up Mina is standing in the doorway. Mortification stretches her face. I smile at her and she makes a little choking noise and disappears.

'Mina?' I say. Immediately Gerda shakes free of me and, snatching up her knife, starts once again to chop. A door slams. It's been another stifling day. I push the window wider.

'Stefan telephoned,' I say. 'The baby's doing well.'

She puts down her knife, reaches past me for a pot. 'That's good.'

'I should tell Mina.'

'You should.'

She turns away from me, turns on the tap. I can hear the water drumming in the pot as I squeeze past Mina's suitcases to A's room. I knock. There is a long pause. Then Mina opens the door. I stare past her. The faded green bedspread is gone. Instead there's a shawl with a paisley pattern over the end of the bed and on the chest of drawers, arranged on an embroidered cloth, a photograph of Stefan and Bettina, a pair of silver hairbrushes, a flower-painted porcelain pot with a lid. The familiar books on the shelf have been replaced with books in jackets of blue waxed paper. Mina has even draped a scarf over the bedside lamp. I wonder dumbly if it might catch fire.

'Aunt Gerda said it was all right,' Mina says. 'It looks nicer, doesn't it?'

She looks at me hopefully but I don't answer. Even with all her things the room looks strangely bare, I can't think why, and then I see that she has taken down the curtains, the ones Gerda washed and ironed specially for her. On the windowsill there is a framed photograph of Mina with her arm around another girl, who pouts at the camera like a young Ruth Weyher. I turn to look at A's collage of magazine pictures but it's gone, there's nothing there but the nail in the wall.

'Where is it, the picture, what have you done with it?' I cry and I see Mina flinch but I can't help it. Panic surges through me.

'I put it away, that's all,' she says, opening the wardrobe. In the space beneath her hung-up dresses I see the green bedspread bundled up with the curtains. A's collage is jammed behind them. I pull it out. Clara Bow is torn, her mouth severed from her nose. I want to weep.

'I can put it back up if you want,' Mina says in a small voice but I shake my head.

'I'll keep it,' I say, holding it tight. 'It can go back when you're gone.'

Friday 14 July

The window is wide open but there's nothing to breathe. I lie awake in the darkness, staring at the ceiling. Gerda is awake too but when I reach out for her she doesn't move. She lies stiffly on her side, away from me, rigid with the effort of not hurting.

On this day four years ago the fever came. A went to the lake with her class, a nature excursion, and when she came home she was sick. She told Gerda her legs hurt. The next day her temperature was 104° and she could not stand up. Dr Posen told us it was a summer cold and we believed him, or we tried to. When she could not hold a cup they took her to hospital. The man who strapped her to the stretcher wore rubber gloves, as though she was poisonous. We knew then. They put her in an isolation ward. We were not allowed to go in. There was a window on the side of the ward. They let us stand there on Sundays and look through. The nurses wore long white gowns and masks over their faces. They glided behind the glass like ghosts.

When they moved her it was autumn. The new place was outside the city, it took an hour to get there on the train. Gerda went every day. She massaged A's arms and legs, worked her unresponsive fingers around a toothbrush, a spoon, a pencil.

'Nothing in the world you can't do if you try,' she said. It was Gerda's unflinching faith that lifted A's spirits, Gerda's strength

336

that kept her strong. And Gerda's heart that was buried with A's at Weissensee when it turned out she was wrong.

Saturday 15 July

At breakfast there are letters from Stefan, one to me and one to Mina. Two stamps, I am struck by the extravagance. I check the flaps of the envelopes reflexively. Mina brought an envelope like this from Stefan when she came. No letter, just money. I wanted to tell her to keep it, that we didn't need it, but pride is one of the many luxuries I can't presently afford. Mina puts her letter in her pocket and drinks her tea. I suppose she wants to read it later when she is alone.

I remember Mina as a rather noisy and self-important little girl. She is not noisy now. She speaks only when spoken to and excuses herself after meals to spend time in her room. She does not want to read with us or listen to the wireless. I might forget she was here if it were not for the discarded cardigans and books she strews around the flat. When Gerda suggests coffee with Anna Büttel, who lives on the floor below and is almost her age, Mina shakes her head. She says she has homework to do, that she has to keep up or she will be behind when school starts again. Last night I asked Gerda if we should not find a school for her here in Berlin, but Gerda only looked at me strangely and told me that it's the summer holidays.

'Good news,' I say. 'Your mother's going home.'

Mina shakes her head, her eyes fixed on her plate. 'That's not true.'

'Of course it is. Your father says the baby should be home soon too.'

'How can they go home when we don't have one?'

'Mina—' I say but she is already pushing back her chair,

stumbling out of the room. When I try to follow her Gerda puts a hand on my arm.

'Let her be,' she says.

I hear A's door slam. I drink my coffee and read the rest of Stefan's letter. They are feeding the infant with a dropper, like a baby bird. Stefan does not want to leave them but he can delay his departure no longer, he travels to Antwerp on Sunday. His reluctance is in every word.

Sunday 16 July

At last a little coolness. On the balcony, Gerda's flowers nod in the breeze. There are other reasons to be cheerful. Urschel has a friend who may be able to give me a loan. And yesterday a new American ambassador arrived in Berlin with instructions to protest the treatment of Jews in Germany. They say the order comes directly from the President.

A walk, I suggest when breakfast is over, it's high time Mina saw the city, but they both make excuses: Gerda has a pile of mending a foot high and Mina mutters something about algebra. Fine, I say, I'll go alone. Half an hour later I bang on Mina's door and push it open. She is lying on the bed. She fumbles something hurriedly under the pillow.

'Come for a walk,' I say. 'Aunt Gerda says you haven't been out all week.'

Mina shrugs. I want to ask her what's under the pillow. 'A whole new city awaits you,' I say instead. 'Don't you want to know what you're missing?'

'You think I don't already know?'

A low blow but not entirely unjustified. I make a face at her. 'Come on, Mina. Just to the corner. Then you can come home.'

Home. I watch Mina chew her lip, considering the word. Then slowly she uncurls her long legs and stands up.

'That's my girl,' I say without thinking and instantly I want them back, the words that are A's still, not mine to give away. Mina slides her feet into her sandals, then squats down on her haunches to buckle the straps. A used to do up her shoes the same way, her chin on the sharp juts of her knees as her fingers found the fastenings. A was gawky, all jolts and corners, but Mina has the easy grace of a cat.

I grab my hat and together we go downstairs. We pass the shuttered butcher's shop. A For Sale notice is pasted to the door. It's no surprise, the Nazis banned kosher butchering months ago, but I can't help thinking of the pick-up-sticks game A used to like, each one pulled out makes the pile that is left more precarious. I pause at the corner but Mina keeps walking, so I walk too. On Oranienburger Strasse she stares up at the buildings. The green and gold domes of the New Synagogue gleam in the sun and the tables outside the Weiss café are crowded with couples and families. Waiters in white aprons weave between the umbrellas.

'Shall we?' I say and Mina hesitates, then nods. It is an extravagance, but you can't be careful all the time. We are given a table set back from the street.

'Do you like cake?' I ask. 'Because the plum cake here is famous.'

'Is this where you used to come with Anke?'

All this time and still it knocks the breath from me. I nod.

'I thought so,' she says. 'Plum cake was always Anke's favourite.'

I am glad when she says it's too hot for cake and asks for a strawberry ice. I don't want to talk about A with Mina, who says her name as though it were a word like any other. Instead I ask her about her schoolwork. What is her favourite subject? If she thinks the question dull she's too polite to say so.

'Science,' she says firmly, running her spoon around the outside of the glass where the ice cream is melting. 'It's the only thing that matters.'

'The only thing?'

'I think so.'

'We learn nothing from history, from literature?'

'Only that human beings have always told themselves the stories they want to believe. But what is important is how things are, don't you see? How they really are, whether we want to believe them or not.'

'You think only scientists tell the truth?'

'I think at least scientists understand that nothing is true until they prove it.'

'And yet scientists through the ages have believed a great number of things to be true that turn out to be mistaken.'

'Yes, but when they are shown to be wrong they change their minds. Do you think priests change their minds, or politicians?'

'That will do,' I say sharply. The man at the next table is looking at us. The brim of his hat shades his eyes, I cannot see his expression, but I am filled with a sudden apprehension.

'Finish your ice cream,' I say, dropping coins on the table. 'It's time to go home.'

Thursday 27 July

Having Mina in the flat changes everything. It is not just the trail of her discarded belongings. It is not even the atmosphere when I get home, though it is plain Gerda is finding it a strain to be so little alone. It's how it alters things between the two of us. Before Mina came Gerda and I had reached a kind of peace. Perhaps we didn't talk as much as we used to, without A and her chatter we lost the knack of it, but our silences were companionable, tender even. When I put my arms around Gerda, all the words we didn't say moved through us like invisible threads, stitching us together. But with Mina here the silences are solid, sharp-edged. They squat between us, defying us to ignore them. And so we talk, stumbling through courtesies and platitudes like actors in a bad play.

Mina notices. I watch her at dinner as she chews on her lip and waits for us to finish. Sometimes I see her looking from Gerda to me and back again as though we are pieces in a puzzle she's trying to fit together. I suppose it was different in Stefan's house, Bettina reeling off lists of improving admonitions, the boys nudging and giggling and pinching each other under the table. What I would give for some peace and quiet, Stefan used to say when we visited, the pride coming off him like heat.

When supper is over Mina helps bring the plates into the kitchen but it is too crowded with three.

'It's all right,' Gerda says. 'You can help tomorrow.' Mina doesn't need to be told twice. When she is gone Gerda closes her eyes and leans against the sink.

'That bad?' I ask but when I put my hand on her shoulder she straightens up and sets to scrubbing the roasting pan. She tells me Mina has taken to pacing the flat, along and round and through, the same circle again and again like a sleepwalker or the dead-eyed bear at the Zoo. Gerda has tried sending the girl on errands, giving her chores, but, though Mina never refuses, she forgets what she has been sent for or does the work so poorly that it is less trouble for Gerda to do it herself.

'Not stupid, is she?' I say and the look Gerda gives me could turn milk.

The light is on in A's room, I can see the stripe of it under the door. I knock. There is a pause before she answers. When I open the door Mina is sitting on the bed, her hands folded in her lap. Books scatter the bed. She looks at me cautiously.

'I thought we might have a talk,' I say and immediately her face snaps shut. It would be better to sit but the only place is beside her on the bed so I stand, one shoulder awkwardly against the wardrobe. 'Aunt Gerda is worried about you. She's afraid you don't like it here.'

Mina stares at her lap.

'I don't know what you've heard about Berlin but it's quite safe to go out so long as you're careful. Most Berliners don't hold with this Nazi nonsense and, besides, no one would think to give you trouble, you don't look Jewish in the least.'

'Because I'm not.'

'Well. The thing is, you mustn't be afraid to go out. It's not good for you, cooped up in here all day.'

'Aunt Gerda never goes out.'

'That's not true, though, is it? Yes, there's the housework and so forth but she goes out every day to shop, she meets her Wednesday friends for coffee—'

'What Wednesday friends?'

I sigh. 'Look, Mina, I don't want to argue with you. I understand you don't want to be here and I don't blame you. No one wants what is happening at the moment. But this is how things are, for now at any rate, and locking yourself away in here won't make it any easier to bear.'

Mina is silent. Then she shakes her head. 'You don't understand,' she says.

'Don't I? Then perhaps you should explain.'

She glances up at me quickly, as though she suspects a trick, and says nothing. Perhaps she thinks I'll lose patience, but I am a lawyer, I know how to wait.

'There's no point,' she says at last. And then, 'I need to go back. To Hannover.'

'You miss your family, I know you do, but as soon as your father is settled—'

'I can't go to Antwerp, don't you see? What about the *Abitur*, what about university? It's all right for the boys, what do they care if they're some place no one wants them, where they don't understand a word anyone says, all they care about is playing football and stuffing their faces with sausage, but I can't just leave, I have exams, if I go now I'll lose a whole year, maybe two, I'll have to start all over again. How can Papa ask me to do that?'

'Because he wants what's best for you all. Because he thinks it isn't safe here any more.'

'Not safe for Jews, maybe, but I'm not a Jew! My mother's a Protestant and my father's nothing, he doesn't believe in any of it. I don't even know what Jews do except not eat pork, we've never bothered with any of that, and Papa agrees with me, religion is just a bunch of superstitions, a primitive social mechanism invented to frighten people and keep them in order, I mean, the idea of some old man with a long white beard presiding over some invisible kingdom with flaming pits of sulphur in the cellars and up in the sky angels in white nightdresses, how can anyone still believe in fairy stories like that? Why is it so impossible to accept that once someone is dead they're dead and that's that!' She breaks off sharply, bites her lip. 'I'm sorry, I didn't mean—'

'I know.'

'You don't believe it, do you? That Anke's sitting on a cloud somewhere, playing a harp?' Her name cast carelessly as a fish hook, tearing my throat.

'No,' I say quietly. 'I don't think that.'

'So you don't believe in God either?'

'Not in a God who would give Anke a harp. It was bad enough having to listen to her sawing at a violin.' I don't know how long it is since I said her name out loud. The taste of it lingers in my mouth. 'What good would it do to return to Hannover? Haven't you been expelled from school?'

'That wasn't my fault. The headmaster was a Nazi. He said only Germans could excel in German schools.'

'I'm sorry.'

'I told him I wasn't even a Jew, that I had finished top of my year three years in a row, except for Hans Meier there was never anyone who did better than me, but he didn't listen, he said Jews like me set a bad example to the rest of the class, that I could never be a scientist because there were two kinds of science, German science and Jewish science, and German science was the only one that counted. He said Jewish science was nothing but fakery and lies, that Einstein made up his theories so he could be famous.'

I rub my face. I think of Bettina's mother, who considers it her duty as a good German to deny her grandchildren a father and a home. 'The man is plainly a fanatic,' I say. 'Most people in Germany do not think like that.'

'Which is why you have to talk to Papa for me. I've written to my friend Margarete, her parents will let me live with them, I know they will, they've known me all my life. Please, Uncle Frank, he'd listen to you.'

I sigh. 'I'm sorry, Mina, but your father's made up his mind. It's all decided.'

'But it isn't fair, why didn't he ask me what I wanted? He's ruining everything and for what? I mean, if things were actually as terrible as he says they are, you and Aunt Gerda would be leaving too. Wouldn't you?'

I don't answer. I walk over to the window. When we moved in we were told that the rooms on this side of the flat looked on to a light well, which is true only if you choose to spell 'well' with an a. The bricks are streaked with damp and almost close enough to touch. Among the scatter of books on the bed is an open exercise book, its square-ruled pages busy with equations. I have no idea what they mean but the way they dance across the page makes me think of music. Idly I pick it up. There is another book open underneath it, a sketchbook, and I catch a glimpse of a drawing, a man's face, before Mina snatches it and snaps it shut.

'I didn't know you could draw,' I say. Mina hugs the book against her chest and says nothing, only chews her bottom lip. It won't be long till there is nothing left to chew. 'Won't you let me see?'

She hesitates, then lets the book slide into her lap. She doesn't meet my eye.

'It's not mine,' she says. 'I'm sorry, I – it's Anke's.'

She looks at the sketchbook, then holds it out to me. The cover is worn and bruised with ink. I think of A at the kitchen table, a piece of butcher's paper in front of her, her face furious with concentration. She couldn't understand why her pictures never came out the way they looked in her head.

'It was behind the bed,' Mina says. 'I was going to tell you, only – I'm sorry.'

I open the covers. *BERLIN*, someone has written in large capitals on the flyleaf, and underneath, *November 1927*. The first drawings are all of hands. Whoever drew these, it wasn't A. Sometimes A pressed so hard her pencil went right through the paper. I turn the pages and the hands give way to people, a fat woman on a balcony, an almond-eyed girl with cropped hair and an impatient expression. Some people in evening dress. I stop, look more closely. The drawings are sketchy but the likenesses are strong, there's no mistaking them. On the left-hand page, Julius Köhler-Schultz and his very young wife. On the right, in a too-tight collar, Gregor Rachmann.

'I never knew Anke was so good at drawing,' Mina says and I frown, closing the book.

'Why didn't you say you'd found this?' I demand.

'Why do you never talk about her?' she demands back and I

345

say nothing and the silence is like holding a seashell to your ear, a whole ocean roars inside it.

Friday 28 July

It is Gerda who works it out. A couldn't have hidden anything behind the bed, she says when I suggest it, Gerda would have found it, she pulls the bed out every time she changes the sheets, but what about those crates, couldn't it have fallen out of one of those, and immediately it comes back to me, the Katzke boys and the tea chest tipped over on the bed, and my stomach lurches as if I have stepped up a step that isn't there.

Furious at my reckless stupidity, I order Mina out of A's room and yank the bed from the wall. I tear off the sheets, upend the mattress. I don't know what I am looking for, only that I have to look. I signed for those crates, if anything goes missing it's me they'll come after. I know it's only a sketchbook, but you hear about it all the time, the shopkeeper arrested for short-changing a customer, the tailor accused by his debtors of harbouring communist sympathies and imprisoned without trial. A few pfennigs or a vengeful fiction, it doesn't matter. For Jews trouble comes down like the executioner's axe, swiftly and without pity.

I find nothing in the bed but the fear is in me, I dare not stop, so I haul the chest of drawers into the middle of the room and empty the drawers. I yank open the wardrobe, dragging Mina's clothes from their hangers, scrabbling among her shoes. I am on my hands and knees when I look up and see her standing in the doorway. Her face is white.

'Mina,' I say but she is already gone. The front door bangs. I sink my head to the floor and close my eyes.

346

They have done nothing to us, not yet. I am going mad all the same.

Saturday 29 July

All of Mina's things are put back as they were. It is not so easy with Mina. At breakfast she passes the butter when I ask her but she does not meet my eye. I pretend not to notice. In a bright voice I don't quite recognise I tell Mina that the sketchbook she found came from the Rachmann case. The prosecution never disclosed it, which was why I'd never seen it before, but it must have been one of the articles seized from Matthias Rachmann's brother's studio.

Mina shrugs. Apparently she has never heard of Matthias Rachmann. Of course she'd have been too young for the newspapers then, but I'm surprised Stefan never mentioned it. So I tell her, anything to fill the silence, and as I explain about the paintings and the inability of the art experts to agree on what is real and what is fake I see I have piqued her curiosity. She has never seen a van Gogh, she says, but she has heard of him. She knows his pictures have sold for hundreds of thousands of marks.

'Not now though, I suppose,' she says and when I tell her that, on the contrary, in the years since the Rachmann scandal broke the prices for van Goghs have almost doubled, she nearly chokes on her milk.

'The Nationalgalerie acquired three in 1929,' I say. 'The most expensive, *Daubigny's Garden*, cost them nearly a quarter of a million marks.'

Mina gapes. 'How can a picture be worth that much money?'

'Perhaps we should go and see for ourselves,' I suggest, and to my astonishment she agrees. We walk together to the Kronprinzenpalais, where the Nationalgalerie keeps its modern paintings. Though it's still early it is already uncomfortably hot. It is a relief to reach the river, the faint stirrings of a breeze.

'So if half of Rachmann's paintings were real and half were fake,' Mina asks, 'who painted the fake ones?'

'No one knows. The prosecution had Rachmann's brother in their sights for a while but they dropped that long before the trial – their evidence didn't stand up.'

'You must have an idea, though. Who did you think did it?'

'Rachmann always insisted that all thirty-two paintings came from his Russian.'

'And you believed him?'

'A criminal lawyer must always believe in his defence.'

The foyer of the gallery is cool. A large photographic portrait is displayed prominently at the bottom of the stairs. The man in the portrait shares both the Führer's bank manager moustache and his air of suspicious irritation. The plaque beneath the photograph reads *Gerhard Hanfstaengl, Direktor*. So Gustav Stemler has gone. I shouldn't be surprised, it's happening all over Germany, but I still don't understand. It is one thing to fear the Communists and the foreigners, but what kind of government is afraid of art?

Mina and I stand in front of *Daubigny's Garden* for a long time. The picture gleams, in this light-filled space there is a just-licked freshness to the colours that the paintings in the gloomy court-room never had, and though the paint is applied in thick slashes it gives off a feeling of enormous calm. When I ask Mina if she likes it she frowns and says she isn't sure. 'But I don't want to stop looking at it,' she adds.

'So is it worth a quarter of a million marks?'

She thinks for a moment. 'I don't know. Maybe. It's difficult, isn't it, when there's only one of something in the world? How can you say what it's worth?'

'Especially when there's a chance it might actually be a fake.'

348

'What?' Mina looks at me and back at the painting. 'Seriously?'

'There was something of a to-do about it after the Rachmann trial. It seems this isn't the only *Daubigny's Garden* in the world, after all. There's a second one in a Swiss collection, which shouldn't matter, van Gogh painted plenty of his pictures more than once, except that apparently in this case he didn't. According to a Dutch expert, a man called Teuling, the Swiss painting is the real thing and this one here is a copy, made by a friend of van Gogh's after he died.'

'And the Nationalgalerie, what do they say?'

'They dismiss Teuling's claim completely. They assert that, if a forgery was made, it's the Swiss picture, not this one.'

'So how will they prove who is right?'

I think of the experts at the Rachmann trial, their contempt for conclusions that differed from their own. 'I'm not sure they will. Both sides have threatened to sue but so far nothing's come to court. Ultimately, it seems, it's just a matter of opinion.'

Mina frowns. 'But there must be ways of proving it, scientific ways.'

'It's not that simple. There are tests, X-rays, chemical paint analysis, that sort of thing, but even the scientists admit they're not foolproof. They could dismiss some of the Rachmann pictures because they found a hardener in the paint that van Gogh never used, but it's much more difficult if the paintings were made forty years ago, with the same paints and canvases the artist used himself. And that's assuming you can run the tests in the first place. Under German law no painting can be scientifically examined without the consent of its owner. In this particular case both sides refuse. They claim the risk of damage to the paintings is too great.'

'You'd think the risk of doing nothing was higher.'

'If they do nothing they can't lose. Staking two hundred and fifty thousand marks on a test tube is a serious gamble.'

Mina is silent as we leave the gallery, gnawing away at that poor lip of hers. I suggest a walk in the Tiergarten, it is always cooler there than anywhere else in Berlin, and she nods but she's not really listening. We take the double-decker bus along Unter den Linden. Mina sits at the front of the upper deck and stares out of the window. All down the wide boulevard the buildings are hung with swastikas. I suppose I should be pointing out the sights as we pass them, the Zeughaus, the Berlin State Opera, but instead I look up at the trees. The sunlight plays through the leaves and makes patterns on the seats of the bus, it is like being underwater. Someone told me that the Nazis mean to cut the lindens down to make more room for their goose-stepping parades. I wish I could believe it wasn't true.

The bus slows as it approaches the Brandenburg Gate and, as it squeezes between the central pillars, I suck my stomach and my elbows in, I cannot help it, the gap seems too narrow to pass through, and when I look at Mina she is sucked in too, her arms folded tight over her chest, and I laugh.

'Breathe in,' I say and she looks down at herself and back at me, and as the bus shudders forward it's as if something has broken open inside me, I cannot stop it, the laughter spills out of me until I am helpless with it and Mina laughs too, astonished, she can hardly believe what she is seeing, and her laughter makes me laugh again, and it is only when the conductor rings the bell that we see that we have reached our stop and, still laughing, we stumble down the steps and out into the bright hot noon.

Monday 31 July

I go to the office early, the sketchbook safely tucked inside my briefcase. I slept poorly last night, I was afraid I would find other things missing from Rachmann's tea chest, but, thank God, everything's there. I put the items back carefully, one by one, marking them off against the docket.

I pause at a large photograph in a cardboard mount. I remember it. A print of a van Gogh self-portrait, it was the only piece of evidence directly pertaining to van Gogh that the police found in Gregor Rachmann's studio. It was never shown in court. The idea that the self-portrait Matthias sold to Stransky might have been copied from the print was scuppered the moment the police saw a print of the Stranksy painting. The two portraits were quite different.

Gregor Rachmann told the police that the self-portrait in the photograph belonged to Köhler-Schultz, or, more accurately, to his son, part of a trust set up for the boy when Köhler-Schultz divorced his mother. According to Gregor, the photograph had been a present from Köhler-Schultz to Matthias, but when I mentioned the photograph to Köhler-Schultz, just to tie up loose ends, he knew nothing about it. Most likely, he said, Matthias had arranged the photograph for insurance purposes. When Julius finally convinced his ex-wife that the painting should remain in his collection until his son was of an age to inherit it, it was Matthias who had arranged to have it brought back from Munich to Berlin.

'My ex-wife didn't want me to have it, she wanted it locked up in a vault,' he said. 'We had to make sure Matthias did everything by the book.'

I never thought to doubt Köhler-Schultz's explanation. The photograph had no bearing on the case, I was content to account for it and move on. It is only now, as I slip it into the tea chest, that I wonder why an insurance company would require a photograph enlarged to sixteen inches by nine.

I run my pen down the docket, checking off the ticks. It's all there. Only one thing puzzles me. The sketchbook is not listed. I go through the docket again more slowly but it's not there. Is it possible that Mina was right all along, that it was A's and she hid it where Gerda would not find it, but if so who gave it to her, where did she get it?

I open the book, look once again at the flyleaf, but there is no name, only BERLIN and the date. I turn the pages, looking at the faces. It's stupid, I know, but I want to see them as Mina saw them, through A's eyes.

Halfway through the book, the style changes. A series of heads, rough peasant faces with noses like potatoes and wise, weary eyes. A woman in a scarf with her hands in the earth. A cluster of tumbledown cottages. Some of the pages have been cut out, only the narrowed strip of paper remains. Then, near the back, on a loose sheet tucked between the pages, haystacks under a roiling sky. I stare at it. The sketch is boxed by pencil lines and divided by a grid, four pencil lines up and down and diagonally, all intersecting in the middle, like looking through a window, and there is no colour in it, but I would know it anywhere. I spent the whole of the first trial staring at it when I was trying to think.

The knock startles me. I push the drawing hurriedly into a drawer. 'Yes?'

It's Böhm. 'I'm sorry to bother you,' he says. 'I was just wondering when you thought you might be able to move your crates.'

His civility shames me. He's had those crates for almost a month. When I apologise and tell him that I'm still waiting to hear from Rachmann he nods.

'Of course,' he says. 'Just as soon as you can.' It's only as he turns to go that I think of the sketchbook. Köhler-Schultz and Böhm have been friends for years.

'A quick question,' I say, paging through the sketchbook for

Köhler-Schultz's portrait. 'I don't suppose you have any idea who might have drawn this?'

Böhm stares at it. 'Good God. Where did you get this?'

'You know it?'

Böhm is silent. He doesn't deny it. I explain about the tea chest.

'I don't know how it came to be among Gregor Rachmann's things, but I think it might shed some light on the case,' I say. 'There are copies of van Goghs in it: I'm pretty certain one of them is a sketch of a painting Rachmann sold. If I could just find out whose it is, where it came from—'

'No,' Böhm says firmly, putting the sketchbook on my desk. 'I'm sorry to disappoint you, but this has nothing to do with Rachmann.'

'How can you be so sure?'

Böhm is silent. 'Because it belonged to a client of mine,' he says reluctantly.

'But that's impossible. How did it get into Gregor Rachmann's box?'

Böhm sighs. He is bound by his duty of secrecy. The sketchbook was discovered at Rachmann's gallery when the scandal first broke, he tells me. When allegations were made about his client's relationship with Gregor Rachmann, she was arrested.

'They were lovers?'

'Of course not. The allegations were malicious and without foundation.'

'The police files didn't declare any arrests.'

'My client's arrest was unlawful. The police agreed to strike it from the record.'

I raise an eyebrow. Böhm looks at me blandly. He must have threatened the police with a formal complaint. Those were the days. Even so, it is still quite something to have magicked Gregor Rachmann's maybe-lover into thin air.

'I'd be happy to arrange for its return,' he says but I shake my head.

'That's kind but you know how it is. Safer to go through the proper channels.'

He nods. I can tell from the way he looks at the sketchbook he wishes he could take it with him. I spend the afternoon studying the drawings more closely. I can't believe Böhm succeeded in suppressing it, a book containing copies of van Goghs made by a woman alleged to be Gregor Rachmann's lover. If the prosecution had got hold of it Matthias wouldn't have stood a chance.

I look for a long time at the sketch of the haystacks, its grid of careful lines. It is like looking through a window. *Haystacks* was one of the paintings smuggled to The Hague in 1929. Hendriksen declared it genuine, then bought it for himself. No one knows how much he paid. I remember very little of Hendriksen's testimony – when taken together, pretension and self-importance are a powerful anaesthetic – but what I do remember is the expression on his face when de Vries took the stand and declared five of Rachmann's van Goghs to be genuine after all.

One of those five was *Haystacks*.

Wednesday 2 August

More scraps and peelings of work. The blessedly irresolute Frau Craemer is changing her will again. We will not starve, or not yet. At home I'm hardly through the door before Mina is tugging at my sleeve. She has something to ask me, she says, it cannot wait. I kick at a pair of discarded sandals.

'I'll break my neck on these things one day,' I say and Mina sweeps them up by the straps and kisses me on the cheek.

'Don't be cross, Uncle Frank,' she says and I glance at Gerda but she only smiles a little and goes into the kitchen. She used to smile at me like that in the old days when she had a secret. I want to go after her. Instead I roll my eyes at Mina.

'So what's all this about?' I ask and she's off, the words running so fast her tongue can barely keep up with them, something about a competition at her school, how the students must make an argument for a particular area of scientific discovery that would bring great honour to Germany, something that has not yet been done, and the best idea will win a prize and if hers was the best they would have to change their minds and let her go back, they'd just have to, so all summer she's been trying and trying to think of something, not just curing diseases or faster trains because that's what everyone will do, but then she found out about the paintings and about how the Dutch wanted to humiliate Germany by telling the world they wasted quarter of a million marks on a picture that wasn't even by van Gogh and there was no science Germany could use to prove them wrong, and she realised that this was it, this was something science had to work out how to do, so she went to the library, the big one on Oranienburger Strasse, she went through everything they have, even the never-looked-at books they keep in the basement, and there wasn't a single one on the science of pictures, but it didn't matter because the woman there told her about the library at the Nationalgalerie that keeps every art book ever written, or almost every one, and anyone can go there, as long as there's no other library that can help, so the librarian wrote a letter for her and all they have to do is to telephone for an appointment.

'So can we?' she asks breathlessly and, before I can reply, she says she has the number, the librarian gave it to her, and she could go tomorrow, she remembers the way and anyway everyone in Berlin knows where the Nationalgalerie is, and she's so fizzy with excitement that she can't keep from bouncing up and down. I smile lopsidedly. Her eagerness is agonising.

'All right, all right,' I say, holding up my hands. 'We'll telephone them tomorrow.'

'Tomorrow?' Her face is stricken. 'Why not now? Please, Uncle Frank? Please?' She holds her hands up to me as though she's praying, and I laugh. She must be putting something in my coffee. Gerda is standing in the doorway.

'Isn't it supper time?' I ask and she smiles.

'It'll keep,' she says.

Mina scrabbles her sandals on. We walk together to the corner, Mina straining like a puppy on a lead, but when we reach the kiosk there is a man inside and we have to wait. Mina grimaces and squirms. I have to take her arm to keep her from knocking on the glass.

He leaves at last and I dial the number Mina gives me. The telephone mouthpiece is unpleasantly warm. The woman who answers offers me an appointment for the following Wednesday. She tells me students under eighteen must be accompanied by an adult. I hesitate, I don't want Gerda missing one of her precious Wednesdays, perhaps another day, I say, but Mina is frowning at me through the glass, her face screwed up with anxiety, and I tell the woman Wednesday will be fine and give her my name.

Perhaps I should stop drinking coffee. Less than a month and already I cannot bring myself to disappoint her.

Saturday 5 August

I wake to find Gerda sitting on the floor, her knees pulled up against her chest. It is very early, or very late. Moonlight gleams through the thin curtains, touching her with silver. She has pulled the suitcase out from under the bed. The lid is open, clothes spill out. In her hands she holds A's lop-eared rabbit.

Pushing myself up on to one elbow, I stroke her hair. She closes her eyes, stretches her neck, pushing against my hand like a cat. I lean down, press my lips lightly against her temple.

'Do you remember that picnic in the Düppel forest when Philip got left behind?' she murmurs. The words make tiny movements under her skin. I close my eyes and read them with my lips like braille.

'I remember,' I say. 'Anke made a home for him in a hollow tree. The next day, when we went back, every other tree was absolutely definitely the one, do you remember? It took the whole morning to find him.'

When Gerda smiles her cheek presses against mine. 'I remember.'

'And when we finally found him she cried because it wasn't fair, that Philip had camped out a whole night in the woods and she never had?'

Gerda's soft laugh is almost a sob. I slide my hand over her shoulder and ease her towards me and she turns, her arms reaching up to fold around my neck, and though the embrace is awkward we hold each other tightly and neither of us lets go.

Wednesday 9 August

Mina insists on leaving before I have finished my coffee. Punctuality is the politeness of kings, she says loftily, and it's not just the proverb that is Stefan's but the angle of her voice. And Germany is a republic, I almost say, but the words die in my mouth. A *res publica*, a public thing, a state where power rests with the people and their elected representatives. A month ago the NSDAP became Germany's only legally recognised political party, the Nazi-controlled DAF the only trade union. It's getting harder to see where it ends.

In the tram Mina gets out her notebook. She has a list of questions, she wants to know if there is anything she has forgotten. From her place by the door, a middle-aged woman glares at us. She looks worn and exhausted and I rise and offer her my seat but she recoils, clutching her bag against her chest.

'I'm not sitting where one of your kind's sat,' she hisses. The other people on the tram look at their laps or out of the window. Nobody says anything. Mina and I travel the rest of the way in silence.

When we get there the Nationalgalerie is not yet open.

'About that woman—' I start to say but Mina scowls at me.

'I don't want to talk about it,' she says and stamps away towards the river. I sit on a bench in the shade. It's already stickily hot, the air thick with all the things we can't say. Perhaps I should ask Mina why she cares so much about a competition she'll never be able to enter but I know I won't. Not when I already know the answer.

When the gallery finally opens we show our papers and go downstairs to the basement. The library is low-ceilinged and crowded with metal stacks pushed in too close together. There's no one else here. The wired-glass windows run in narrow strips along the tops of the walls like sliced-out cornices. When Gerda said she would bring Mina, that I would be needed at work, I told her that I wanted to come, that I hoped the library might know who the sketchbook belonged to. I don't imagine she believed me – it's a library, not a detective agency – but though she hesitated she didn't protest. Her Wednesdays with the other mothers mean more to her than she is willing to admit.

I have given Mina the names of the experts who testified at Rachmann's trial but beyond that she doesn't want my help. I'm sorry, she said, but it has to be mine. She shows the list to the grey-haired librarian who studies it, then takes her over to a wall of narrow wooden drawers. As they leaf through the index cards Mina looks over her shoulder and frowns at me to go away, so I turn and walk away through the stacks. Some of the shelves are newly emptied: in the dust I can see the ghosts of the books that have gone.

At the end of the room there is a door with LIBRARY DIRECTOR painted on it in neat white letters. I'm only a few feet away when it bangs open and a man in shirtsleeves strides out, pushing his way past me into the stacks. He is greyer than when I last saw him but I know him immediately: Gustav Stemler. Through the open door I see a jacket slung over the back of a chair, a curl of smoke from a half-smoked cigarette in the ashtray. So that's what happened to him. They did not boot him out. They buried him alive.

I wait for him to return. 'Herr Direktor, might I have a quick word?'

He frowns at me. 'Have we met?'

'Frank Berszacki. I defended Matthias Rachmann last year.'

And just like that his face changes. His gaze slips uneasily around the library. 'Berszacki, of course. Don't tell me there's to be another trial?'

'No. I'm afraid that ship has sailed. For him and for me.' A different kind of look passes between us. He's Jewish, I know it now for certain. 'Do you have a moment?'

He shows me into his office. As I tell him about Mina and her project I can feel his impatience, he is waiting for his moment to refuse me, so I do what I would do with a recalcitrant witness, I sigh and then I shake my head. There are times when you want a witness to believe you have a brain like a box of knives. Mostly, though, bafflement is better. Witnesses like to explain. So I ask him how it was that the experts in the Rachmann trial could change their minds as they did, how some of the most expensive pictures in the world could be reduced overnight to worthless daubs and then, just as suddenly, magically restored to masterpieces.

'How can it be,' I ask, mystified, 'that science, objective technical analysis, remains so approximate that even today there is no definitive means to prove those paintings genuine or fake?'

And Stemler bites. 'You think it was a failure of science?' he scoffs. 'It never occurred to you that the technical experts might have had other reasons to be judicious with their testimony?'

'They were under oath.'

'They were under pressure.'

'Are you saying they lied?'

'I'm saying they made bloody sure no one knew the more uncomfortable facts. Did you know your Dutch experts ran tests on Rachmann's *Sower* in 1930? Of course you didn't, because the results were never published. By the time the police finally ordered Rachmann to submit the canvas to us for tests by our people it was too late. The picture was already sold and halfway to Chicago.'

'And no one thought to mention this in court?'

'You never asked. And neither did the prosecution.'

I am silent. It's true. I never asked.

'Apparently they ran the same tests on *Haystacks*.' Stemler spits a bitter laugh. 'No one's ever seen those results either.'

'But these experts were independent.'

'Independent? You have to be joking. The art world is tiny, and tinier still in Holland. Who do you think these men work for? Without Hendriksen and his millionaire clients they'd be out of a job.'

'Are you saying they withheld information to protect Hendriksen?'

Stemler looks at me as though I am something on his shoe. Since we last met his arrogance has hardened into something harsher and more hateful. 'Clovis Hendriksen made a mockery of that damn trial. You danced to his tune, the whole bloody lot of you, and you didn't even have the wit to see it.'

'With respect, Herr Stemler—'

'With respect? With respect, it would have behoved the court to consider why, out of the blue, in the full and certain knowledge that the press would eat him alive, Pieter de Vries was willing to testify that five of the Rachmann paintings that he had categorically dismissed as forgeries were van Goghs after all. And which five? The Dutch ones, including Hendriksen's *Haystacks* and at least two acquired by Françoise Jacob-Bakker who, with Hendriksen as curator, has amassed a collection of some one hundred and fifty van Goghs she is considering donating to the nation. The Dutch needed those paintings to be genuine, and you? You handed them the whole stinking lot on a plate.' Stemler's eyes are bulging, spittle blooming in the corners of his mouth. A once-eminent man of culture, reduced to spinning conspiracy theories like an embittered spider. I think of the old saying, *Art holds fast when all else is lost.* An adage for a different time, another Germany.

'Or perhaps de Vries just changed his mind,' I say mildly.

'The night before de Vries's testimony Hendriksen spent an hour in his hotel room. No one else, just the two of them. The next day all five paintings are back in the van Gogh oeuvre and the outcast de Vries restored to favour. Have you seen Hendriksen's latest self-aggrandising slab of pseudo-scholarship? Introduction by de Vries, dauntless champion of Dutch van Goghs against the German unbelievers and curator of next year's monster show in The Hague. Come back, Pieter, all is forgiven.'

Stemler is trembling now, the loose flesh on his neck vibrating like something electrified. Anger, perhaps, or something deeper and more desperate. I remind myself that it was Hendriksen who publicly accused Stemler of blowing a quarter of a million marks on a fake van Gogh. Whatever his legacy at the Nationalgalerie, Stemler will always be remembered for that. But then I remember de Vries on the stand, his face rigid, the words like knives in his mouth.

'These are very serious allegations,' I say. 'Without proof—'

'Hendriksen threatened me too.'

I stare at him. 'What? How?'

'He told me that if I told the court I believed *Haystacks* to be a forgery, he would tell the German press that *Daubigny's Garden* was a fake. I told him to go fuck himself, that no amount of petty intimidation would induce me to perjure myself. Six months later he did it anyway. Nothing in it for him by then, except the pleasure of it. That jewel for his worthless piece of shit. A barely there sliver of decades-old gossip against an avalanche of greed and wilful blindness.'

'But if you knew Hendriksen was perverting the course of justice, if you had evidence, why didn't you report him to the authorities?'

'Report what, exactly? His word against mine and another stinking shitpot for the press to upend over the Nationalgalerie, over Germany. I couldn't do that. All I could do was tell the truth. Not that it counted for anything in the end. We still lost. All of us, we all lost.'

The rage leaves him so suddenly you can almost see him shrivel. He doesn't look up as I walk out of his office. He sits like a monk at prayer, his hands folded and his head bowed. If one didn't know better, one might mistake it for humility.

The ceiling of the library presses down on me and the dusty books swallow up all the air. My head spinning. I tell Mina I'll wait for her outside.

Friday 11 August

They have come for Urschel. I arrive to find his office smashed up, the window broken and drawers pulled out and upended, files all over the floor.

I go upstairs to see Böhm. His face is white. He locks the door behind us. There were three of them, he whispers. I have to strain to hear him. He saw the caretaker take them upstairs and let them in with his key. Afterwards Böhm went to the police station but Urschel was not there, he'd been taken to Oranienburg, so Böhm went to his house. The landlady was crying. She told him they had come before dawn and taken him. They hadn't allowed him to get dressed. When they put him in their van there was blood all over his pyjamas.

But why? I ask and Böhm shakes harder and puts a hand over his mouth. He says Urschel was one of the lawyers who advised Hirschfeld during his campaign for homosexual emancipation. When they smashed up Hirschfeld's Institute they burned the library, but not before they'd taken all the files. They've been working their way through them. Two months to get to U.

I go back to Urschel's office. I slide the drawers back into their slots, pick up the files and the bits of broken glass. Nobody talks about Oranienburg but everyone knows what happens there. They have smashed his ink bottle, ripped his books from their spines. A wanton ecstasy of destruction. I set his chair back on its feet and suddenly I am seized with a boiling fury towards Urschel, who knew what he had done and did not tell me, who let me move into his office and never said a word. I think of Gerda, sleep-creased, waking to the crash of a broken-down door, of Mina rigid with fear. I think of Anke, my darling girl whose sobs I still hear sometimes in the dead hours of the night, and I hate Urschel with a hatred so poisonous that it shrivels my scalp, because I cannot keep them safe and I never could and none of it, none of it, is his fault.

Tuesday 15 August

I tell Gerda I have a headache, that I will go late to the office. When she and Mina go to the shops I take a chisel and prise up a floorboard in our bedroom. I wrap the chisel in a cloth, I don't want the blade to mark the varnish. There is a space under there, between the pipes, big enough for *White Fang* and *Emil and the Detectives* and this diary. I should stop writing, I should burn them all, but I can't. There is nothing I can do to stop what is happening, but I can write it down. I pull the rag rug back over the floorboard, it creaks a little when you step on it but then all the floors creak in this flat. I haven't told Gerda. If anyone should come it's better that she doesn't know.

I haven't told her about Urschel either. What good would it do? She never met him, he is a name to her, no more, and the list is long enough already. At night I hold her as we wait for sleep and I do not want to let go, when she murmurs and shifts away from me the emptiness in my arms is a fresh grief. Do not go mad before the madness ends, Urschel said to me, but I am, I can feel myself unravelling. When I close my eyes the darkness spins me in circles.

I am afraid for Böhm. Afraid of him too. Yesterday he showed me a letter he had written to the camp commander at Oranienburg, pleading Urschel's case. He wanted my opinion on some points of law. I asked him if he had lost his mind and then I burned it, but I'm afraid he'll try again. Urschel was his oldest friend. Was he more? There was a kind of abandon in the way Böhm looked at me, as though pain was the only thing left in the world worth anything at all.

Oh Anke, my darling, darling girl. It was you I saw in Böhm's eyes. He wants to know where it all ends, just like you did. And I want to tell him, not here, not yet, not while there is a sliver of hope. *Isn't it a blessing really, an end to all the pain and the suffering?* Stefan's words hot tar in the wound of my heart. *Because, think about it, Frank, what kind of life was she really going to have?*

Our life, together.

Sunday 20 August

It's hotter than ever today. The apartment is stifling. My thoughts jostle around me, pushing and jeering: Urschel with his split mouth plum-purple, the caretaker on the landing, Stefan and Böhm and the brownshirts in the streets and money, money, money. Eighty marks in the bank and no hope now of Urschel's loan. I am like Stemler brooding in his underground prison, I have to get out. Out of the city, into the woods and the meadows where you can hear the birds sing and the grass grow and the air smells of more than brick dust and dirty bodies. But when I suggest it to Gerda she shakes her head.

'Next time,' she says, and she smiles at Mina, a secret smile that tucks itself into her cheek. 'Today Mina has plans for you.'

Something has changed between them. Yesterday I came home to find Gerda sitting on Anke's bed, Anke's collage in her lap and Mina cross-legged beside her.

'I was just telling Aunt Gerda how we used to play at film stars and Anke was always Clara Bow,' Mina said and I waited for Gerda to get up, to say something brisk about dinner, but instead she went on looking at the collage, her hands clasping the frame as though she was afraid of falling in. Later Gerda told me that Mina writes every week to her friend Margarethe in Hannover but Margarethe never answers. Mina thinks her letters must have been opened or lost in the post.

'The Berszacki optimism,' Gerda said and her eyes were furious with pity.

Mina and I walk together along Friedrichstrasse. The hot sun hacks between the high buildings, jack-knifing off windscreens and shop windows. Mina carries a satchel on her back and a hand-drawn map. She won't tell me where we're going. There are brownshirts everywhere. They look at Mina and then at me and my toes curl in my shoes but they let us pass. There is to be another parade today, another spontaneous demonstration at the Lustgarten to celebrate some victory or other against enemies of the state. Victory, as though we are fighting a grand war. As though any war is grand. I wish we had gone to the country.

Some way north of Wedding station Mina stops, turning her map upside down. I take out my handkerchief and mop my face. A year ago there were violent clashes here between the reds and the police, the streets ran with blood, but today swastikas hang from the windows of the rundown buildings like rugs put out to air. On the other side of the street two gossiping young women fan themselves with their hands, their cotton dresses already limp from the heat, and I think of the damp-winged butterflies I watched as a boy, nosing out of their chrysalises. They are barely older than Mina and suddenly quite grown up.

I follow her down a cobbled street. The shops are shabby. A few are boarded up. Some boys are throwing stones at a row of tin cans on a wall. There is a summer stink of canal. I am hot and thirsty and about to lose my patience when Mina points towards a small shop on the corner. The sign has been painted over but shadowy letters push up from underneath the white: *SCHILLER CAFÉ*.

'This is it,' she says. I follow her inside. A man, a boy really, sits reading at the back of the empty room. He nods as we come in but he does not get up. The white walls are hung with pictures. Some are splashy, abstract splodges of colour, but most are lithographs, black and white. Mina gestures at one. Two heads very close together, an old woman and a young one. The old woman has her eyes closed. The young woman gazes into space, her chin on her hand, the back of her fingers brushing the old woman's cheek. The picture is austere and fiercely tender.

'Do you recognise her?' Mina asks.

'Which one?'

'Not the women in the picture, silly, the artist.' She looks at me eagerly, her bottom lip caught between her teeth, and when I shake my head she grins. 'This is her. The sketchbook woman. That's my surprise.'

I am so startled that I laugh out loud. 'I don't believe it. How did you find her?'

Her grin widens, creasing her eyes into half-moons. 'We worked it out, me and the librarian at the Nationalgalerie. You know how you said you wished you could know who'd done the drawings, how you thought it might have something to do with your Rachmann trial? Well, I said to Aunt Gerda that you should ask when we went to the library, only she said you could be stubborn about things like that and wouldn't it make a better surprise if I did it myself, so I showed the book to the librarian and at first he said he couldn't help but then I showed him the little pattern hidden away in some of the drawings, the one like a tiny four-pronged comb broken in the middle, and just like that he said, oh, so EE are her initials, which of course it was, though I didn't see that till he said it. So he looked up all the EE artists in this big book and there were three but only one woman, because I'd remembered you saying it was all you knew, that she was a woman artist, so the librarian found this catalogue with some of her pictures in it and one of them was the woman with short hair who's in the sketchbook so we knew right then it was her and then when we found out her work was in this show right here in Berlin – are you pleased?'

I laugh again. I don't know how she does it, all those words without a single breath between them, but I am learning to like it.

'Pleased? Mina, I'm in awe,' I say and I put an arm around her shoulder, kissing her clumsily on the side of her head before it occurs to me how sweaty I am, my face damp with perspiration, my shirt sticking to my back, if it was me I'd pull away in disgust. Hurriedly, awkwardly, I let her go. 'So who is she, what's her name?'

'She's called Emmeline Eberhardt. She was born in 1907 in Frankfurt and she studied at the Berlin Art Academy.'

It comes out of the blue but somehow it isn't a shock. When I think of Fräulein Eberhardt in Böhm's office, the ink stains on her fingers, the only real surprise is how I could have missed it. How stupid of me, I almost blurt, and then I look at Mina, her eyes shining and her spine pulled tall with pride, and instead I punch her gently on the shoulder.

'You, Wilhelmina Ursula Berszacki,' I say, 'are a bona fide genius. Those scientists are going to have to look to their laurels.'

Mina shrugs, affecting nonchalance, but it doesn't work, her grin is too wide. 'And you know what else? She lives here in Berlin. In Kreuzberg. She's on the telephone. The operator looked her up for me in the directory.'

'What can I say?' I shake my head admiringly and take the piece of paper she holds out to me. 'You've thought of everything.'

'You could say thank you.'

I laugh. 'You're right. Thank you. Thank you squared. Cubed. To the power of n.'

'That makes no sense. But you're still welcome. I liked it, it was interesting.'

We drift slowly around the room, looking at the pictures. The abstracts are by someone else. His work is showier and more expensive but the Eberhardts are the ones you can't stop looking at. Is it possible that she was Gregor Rachmann's lover? There's something both intimate and opaque about her portraits, a closeness of gaze that, for all its tender intensity, cannot pierce the essential otherness of her subjects. They belong to themselves, and, sometimes, like the women with their heads together, to each other, but not to her. The young man looks up from his book as I pass his desk. She's finally starting to attract the recognition she deserves, he says, nodding towards some newspaper clippings pinned to the wall. The reviews are short, no more than a paragraph each, but someone has underlined selected phrases in ink: *a raw quiet power*, one says, and another, *simply and strikingly her own*.

'I'd be interested in seeing more of her work – does she have a studio?' I ask and the young man nods and offers to make an appointment for Tuesday week. I give my name as Frank, Herr Frank. I tell myself it hardly counts as a lie.

Mina has returned to the picture we saw when we came in. I cross back and stand beside her. We stand there for a long time, in silence, just looking.

'Apparently when I was a little girl I told my mother that when I grew up I wanted to marry my grandma,' she says. Her face is pinched. When I put my arm through hers she stiffens, I'm afraid she'll pull away, but she leans closer, her hand finding mine, and we stand together, our fingers twined, looking at the young woman and the old, at everything that once was and will never be again, and it is as though all the love and the faith that we've lost is there in the faces of two people who never knew us at all.

Monday 21 August

I should stop reading the newspaper but I can't quite bring myself to do it. It is still possible, away from the news reports, to catch glimpses of the old world, shadows moving between the lines like fish under ice. Not today. Today there is a long editorial supporting the establishment of a Reich Chamber of Culture. The Chamber would supervise and regulate all facets of German culture, from filmmaking and theatre to literature and the visual arts, under the presidency of Joseph Goebbels, Reich Minister for Public Enlightenment and Propaganda. Once it passes into law, only those artists officially approved by the Chamber will be permitted to work in their field, to have their work exhibited or published or performed. The Reich Minister will not only decide which books are burned but which are written. He will control every painting, every poem, every symphony, every film, each and every line uttered on a German stage.

Who was it who said 'Art is a line around your thoughts'? When this law is passed, it will be Herr Goebbels who wields the pen.

Tuesday 22 August

I need to talk to Böhm. I have to tell him I am moving out, that I can no longer sub-let his office, but when I go upstairs he's not there, and anyway how can I leave him in the lurch now, after all that has happened? The last time I greeted him on the stairs he stared at me blankly, as though I was speaking in a foreign language.

At supper I'm relieved when Mina rattles on about her project. The Nationalgalerie librarian has arranged for her to meet with one of the gallery's picture restorers, she wants to ask him how long it will be before scientists can guarantee the provenance of every painting in the world. I nod absently. It's nearly the end of the school holidays. What will happen to Mina then? The city schools are not safe for Jews and the Jewish ones cost money we don't have. And at Christmas the lease on the apartment is up and we will have to find somewhere cheaper. Somewhere with just one bedroom.

I don't have thoughts any more. I have columns of numbers, zeros like looming faces on the credit side and debits that grow bigger every day.

Wednesday 23 August

As I cross the courtyard this morning the caretaker beckons me over and asks me to step inside. Closing the door behind me, he asks me what I know about Alfred Böhm's political affiliations. I tell him I know nothing, it's the truth, but he shakes his head as though I am a botched repair. We all have a part to play, he says, and he jerks his head towards the wall behind me. I turn. A new set of cubbyholes, labelled by number, each one with a file. I feel sick.

'Vigilance, that's what counts,' he says with satisfaction. 'Steady drops wear away stone.'

At supper, as if she reads my thoughts, Gerda asks about Urschel.

'How are you getting along together, you two?' she asks and it is only in that moment that I see how much I have left unsaid, how narrow the distinction between omission and betrayal. I look at Gerda and it is as though I am on one bank of a stream and she is on the other, only it is not a stream any more but a rushing river and I cannot see how I am going to get across.

'I like him,' I say weakly and I turn to Mina before Gerda can ask anything else. 'How was your day? What did you do while Aunt Gerda was out this morning?'

'I went with her. We went to the market. You wouldn't believe the kittens we saw, Uncle Frank, they were so small, truly, they would have fitted in my hand.'

I look at Gerda, surprised, but she quickly looks away, adjusting her knife and fork on her empty plate. 'You took Mina to meet your friends?'

Gerda is silent. Then, standing, she begins to pile the plates. 'Actually I didn't see them today. Mina, the glasses, please.'

'Really?' I ask, concerned. 'But you've hardly missed a Wednesday in years.'

Gerda looks at me helplessly, then picks up the plates and takes them out to the kitchen. Mina follows her with the glasses, the water jug with its chipped spout. I hear Gerda say something, the cough of the pipes as water gushes into the sink. Her shoulders hunched, Mina walks back across the room towards the corridor.

'Where are you going?' I say but she doesn't stop. I hear the click of the bedroom door closing. When I look round Gerda is standing in the doorway.

'I should have told you before,' she says. She stares at her hands as, in a flat voice, she tells me she has not had coffee with the other mothers since January. After the Nazis took power she thought it best not to go, she did not want to put her non-Jewish friends in an awkward situation, but then she bumped into one of the women out shopping and she told Gerda that they all missed her, that she must come again, they would not dream of letting her stay away, and so the next Wednesday Gerda went to the café as usual, only the little table that was always reserved for them in the corner was empty. Not one of them had dared to come.

'I understood,' she says. 'They have families to think of, they couldn't take the risk. I should have told you but I knew how you would worry if I did. I thought it would be better for you—'

I stand up and take her in my arms. She presses her face against my chest as I tell her about Urschel's arrest, about giving up the office. I tell her I'm afraid we will have to move out of the apartment. I have not wept for years but I weep now, I cannot help myself. Gerda tightens her arms around me and I weep quietly into her hair.

'I'm so sorry,' I say and she shakes her head.

'Hush,' she says and she holds me as she used to hold Anke, when everything that mattered in the world could be contained inside a single pair of arms.

Tuesday 29 August

I go by myself. Mina wants to come but I tell her it's work and she doesn't protest. The studio is in what must once have been a factory, a hulking building in a weedy stretch of waste ground near the docks. I pick my way along a cracked path. Mina asked to look at the sketchbook again last night. She knows it isn't Anke's and never was, but somehow knowing hasn't altered her attachment to it. I understand that well enough. When facts shift their shapes to suit the times it's only our faith that holds us steady.

The metal door is open. Inside, a hangar-like space is divided between eight or ten artists, barricaded by metal shelving units and rusting bits of machinery. A shop mannequin painted in wild patterns presides over one corner, a foot-wide paper smile glued to her blank face. Light bulbs dangle from the ceiling on fraying cables. The vast windows are grey with dirt and cobwebs but the sunlight still spreads itself in tiled sheets over the cracked cement floor. It must be bone-shrivellingly cold here in winter.

She is arranging prints on a table. When she sees me she crosses her arms. She wears oversized canvas trousers and paint-spattered work boots, and her hair is tied up in a scarf. 'Herr Frank?'

'I know. I'm sorry.' I look down at the prints spread out on the table. A series, a woman and a child, the two of them fitted together like jigsaw pieces. They summon memory like a familiar smell, instantaneously. The impermeable oneness of mother and child, the sense, always, of being on the outside. My heart bursting and aching at the same time.

'What's this about?' she demands. 'Why have you come here?'

I open my mouth to answer. Then I close it again. The truth is I'm no longer sure. If she did do it, if she was the painter of Rachmann's fake van Goghs, what exactly is her crime? She only did what our esteemed Reich Minister for Propaganda will soon require all artists in Germany to do: to produce work to an approved form that can be relied upon to elicit the desired public response. It's already happened to the newspapers; we all know the rules. In February a story would be tolerated provided it observed strictly specified parameters and arrived at the correct conclusion. Six months later the only acceptable news story is a faithful regurgitation of the Party line, untainted by interpretation or imagination, a bundle of stock phrases repeated until the words lose their meaning. If Herr Goebbels has his way every artist in Germany will be a forger or finished.

'I'm sorry, Fräulein, or is it Frau Dumier now? Congratulations, by the way. Look, I should never have – the name, it was stupid. I'm not here to cause trouble.'

'Right.' Her gaze is unnervingly direct. 'Or to buy, I suppose.'

'No. That is, I would if I could, one work in particular in your show, I mean, *Upstairs IV*, I thought that was remarkable, really, but no. I'm sorry.'

'Me too.'

I watch helplessly as she gathers up the prints. 'How's Ivo?' I say.

'He's fine. But I don't imagine you came here to discuss him either.' She looks at me, her arms crossed, and her dark eyes seem to see straight through me to the shadows beneath, to pierce skin and bone as if they were water. 'Then why have you come here, Herr Berszacki? What do you want from me?'

'Frank, please,' I say. I mean it as an apology, a sign that I have come in good faith, but when she glares at me I remember Herr Frank, and, flustered, I shake my head. I'm getting this all wrong. 'Look, I'm sorry, I'm going to leave now. I just wanted to return this to you.'

I put the sketchbook on the table. I somehow expect her to flinch but she only gapes. 'Where did you get this?' she says, opening it. 'I thought it was lost.'

'It was. Someone at Alexanderplatz must have misfiled it. It was found among the items seized from Gregor Rachmann's studio when the state finally released them.'

'Gregor asked you to give it to me?' Gregor, the first name summoned without self-consciousness. The speaking of it alters the shape of her: her voice is sharper, shriller, and her eyes scan the room as though she might see him hiding there. Perhaps they were lovers after all.

'Gregor Rachmann has not been involved. I'm holding his property on his behalf until we can track him down. This turned up when I checked the crates.'

Fräulein Eberhardt pauses at the drawing of the girl with the cropped hair. In the silence I can hear birdsong, the muffled whistle and clatter of a passing train.

'Herr Böhm would have given this to me, you know,' she says. 'I know.'

She studies me. 'I suppose he told you what happened?'

'Böhm? Of course not, he told me nothing, he's your lawyer,

he can't discuss your affairs with me. He's bound by professional secrecy.' I'm protesting too much, I can hear it, I know quite well that if Böhm had thought for a moment that I might find out who owned the sketchbook he would never have said what he did, but Fräulein Eberhardt says nothing, only turns the pages. The early drawings touch her, I see the way they move across her face like clouds, changing the light. The van Gogh sketches she flicks through, but when she finds the loose sheets tucked into the back she frowns. Shuffling through them like playing cards she sorts them into two piles on the desk. Most of the drawings go on to the left-hand pile.

She has almost finished when abruptly she stops. Her eyes widen and her ears go back like a cat's. I glance over her shoulder, the drawing is the haystacks one with the ruled grid. She puts it down, finger and thumb calipering a diagonal line. Then, turning to scan the metal shelves behind her, she pulls out an oversized book and hefts it on to the table between us. There is a painting of van Gogh on the cover. Gaunt and grey, his orange hair cropped almost to his skull, he stares at his easel like a prisoner with no hope of reprieve. Fräulein Eberhardt flips through the pages until she finds what she is looking for.

'Shit,' she says.

The book plate shows a pen-and-ink drawing of two poplar trees by a path, a rocky outcrop rising behind them. Someone has marked up the drawing in pencil. A grid of four lines, horizontal, vertical and two diagonals, dividing the drawings into eight equal segments.

'Was there a *Two Poplars* among the paintings Matthias sold?' she asks. 'Because there was a *Haystacks*, I've seen it. A reproduction, anyway.'

I think of the five paintings de Vries changed his mind about, the day after Hendriksen got to him. Three of the pictures were in the courtroom. One showed two poplars by a path, a rocky outcrop rising behind them.

'Yes,' I say. 'There was a *Two Poplars*.'

Fräulein Eberhardt closes her eyes. Her face is stiff, her lips pressed into a line, when she puts a hand to her temples I'm afraid she might cry, and suddenly I wonder if she is playing me, if she has been playing me all along.

'But then I think perhaps you knew that already,' I say.

Fräulein Eberhardt is silent. She rubs her forehead, then looks at me steadily, wearily. 'You're wrong. I didn't know. I didn't know any of it. I thought Matthias . . . I thought he was the scapegoat, but he knew they were fakes. He knew all along.'

'What possible evidence do you have for an allegation like that?'

'Because I drew this.' She picks up the haystacks. 'See here, along this edge where it's been cut out from the book? I copied it in the Rachmann Gallery, I remember doing it. But the grid, that's not mine. Someone else drew that in afterwards.'

'And why would they have done that?'

'People use grids to break down a picture, to fix line, perspective. Van Gogh did it himself. He had a frame made when he was teaching himself to paint, two stakes and four wires just like this, intersecting in the middle, and he'd set it up outside and draw the same grid on his canvas. He said it made sense of what he was looking at, that it gave him the courage to make marks.'

'You seem to know a lot about it.'

'I've read the letters. Of course I know about it.'

'And you're asking me to believe that it was Matthias Rachmann who added these grids to your drawing, to this book, and not you, the artist who just happened to have read all about them?'

'Jesus Christ, are you serious? We've been through all this, ask Böhm if you don't believe me. Ask Matthias, for Christ's sake. Why would I have done it? I didn't have this sketchbook, Matthias did, and anyway I've never drawn with a grid in my life, it's not the way I was taught. Someone took my drawing and used it and whoever it was Matthias knew, don't you see? This was Matthias's exhibition catalogue, he lent it to me, I was supposed to give it back, only – this was his copy. From the gallery. My sketchbook, his catalogue. It can't be a coincidence. Whoever made the fakes made them with his blessing. He knew.'

There are two spots of colour on her pale cheeks. Her eyes blaze. If this is an act, Fräulein Eberhardt is in the wrong profession.

'If he knew, he's never said so,' I say quietly. 'He always insisted he sold them in good faith.'

'Protecting his Russian to the grave.'

'Or his brother.' An unguarded and inflammatory remark, I regret it as soon as the words are out of my mouth.

She frowns at me. 'You think Gregor Rachmann—'

'I don't think anything. I have no evidence, as you so ably demonstrated. And anyway I'm not so sure it matters any more. A man's behind bars. Justice has been seen to have been done. What else can we hope for?'

'That the law will protect the innocent. That people who break it will be caught and punished.'

'You're right,' I say. 'We should hope for that.'

We stand together silently, lost in our own thoughts.

'I should go,' I say and she nods.

'Thank you for returning my sketchbook.' She hesitates. 'You should ask him, you know. Gregor, I mean. You should ask him what you asked me.'

'Yes, well. Perhaps I will. If I ever find him.'

When I leave she doesn't walk with me to the door. She stands where she is, grave-faced behind her table, a slight figure in her oversized clothes beneath the wide white grin of the painted mannequin.

A letter on the breakfast table. The address on the envelope is typed, stamped URGENT in red ink. I open it reluctantly but it's not a bill. It's a letter from Stefan's lawyer. The letter is couched in business jargon, it refers to the consignment, but I know what it means. Stefan is ready. He wants Mina to return to Hannover. In two weeks they will leave for Antwerp. I hand Gerda the letter and she looks at me. It is a blessing. Of course it is. Mina will be with her family. I put my hand on Gerda's and she threads her fingers through mine, her wedding ring a hard ache against my skin.

'She'll be safe there,' I say and she nods and does not look at me.

'She must miss her family,' I say and she nods again and tries to smile.

'It's for the best,' I say and she turns to look at me, her eyes hard and full of tears.

'No,' she says and she pulls her hand away. 'None of it is for the best.'

In her room Mina is making her bed. She looks up as I come in. I tell her about Stefan's letter. I tell her that the plans have been made, that we will miss her. I do not tell her it is for the best. Gerda is right. Everything is getting worse and there is nothing I can do to stop it. We stand together side by side in the room that is hers and Anke's, by the chest of drawers with the embroidered runner and the silver hairbrushes and the porcelain pot with its painted flowers. I have grown accustomed to them there.

'What about my project?' Mina says. 'I can't just leave my project.'

'You still have two weeks,' I say. 'And if you have to you can finish it there. Surely if Belgium's good enough for Albert Einstein it's good enough for you?'

She does not smile. She looks up at me, her bottom lip caught between her teeth. 'But what about you? What about Aunt Gerda? What will you do?'

'We'll be fine,' I say and she looks at me for a moment, her gaze fierce, and then she sighs and turns away and it tears at my heart because I love her, this girl of my brother's, and all I have to give her are my lies.

Saturday 2 September

Böhm comes to see me. I haven't seen him for more than a week. He looks ill. He checks the landing before he closes the door. His hands are shaking, it makes the paper he is holding rattle. He tells me he is sorry but the Rachmann crates will have to be moved. The caretaker has issued a warning, he says that the storage of crates contravenes a term in the lease, he has given Böhm a week to get rid of them. They both know there is no such term, but the caretaker is a Party member and a block warden, and Böhm would prefer to avoid trouble. When I promise that they will be gone he apologises for being a bother. His politeness leaves me shame-filled and appalled.

As I am putting on my coat the telephone rings. It's Frau Dumier, she asks if I will meet her tomorrow. She doesn't say why and I don't ask. No one trusts the telephone any more. The Floraplatz in the Tiergarten, she says, four o'clock. As soon as I agree she rings off. I realise as I hang up the receiver that it's the first time I've heard her use her married name.

Gerda and I go to bed early but I can't sleep. The moon is full, or as good as, and the light slices through the gap in the curtains and lies like a knife across the end of the bed. I wonder what Frau Dumier wants to see me about. Rachmann, I suppose, or her husband. I hope to God it isn't Böhm. I can still hear it, the rattle of the paper in his shaking hand.

Gerda sleeps beside me, her breath catching in soft snores at the back of her throat. I nudge her and for a moment she is silent, then the snores start up again. Sighing, I slide out of bed and walk to the kitchen for a glass of water. Coming back I see a pale stripe of light under Mina's door. Knocking softly I push it open. She lies curled like a prawn on one side, reading a book.

'You should be asleep,' I say.

'So should you.' She does not close her book.

'Want to talk?'

Mina hesitates, then nods. I sit down on the bed beside her. When I got home yesterday she told me flatly that she was abandoning her project. We ate our supper in silence. Later Gerda told me that the restorer at the Nationalgalerie had been kind, enthusiastic even. He had spoken with passion about the potential of new scientific means of examination and analysis: microscopy, paint dating, infrared and ultraviolet radiography. But when Mina asked him, her eyes shining, how long he thought it would take before German science stamped out forgeries completely, he sighed. We never will, he said. All we can do is to make it harder to get away with it, to find better and better ways of proving that a painting is fake.

'But one day surely there'll be different science, science that can prove what's real?' she protested but the restorer only shook his head.

'How?' he asked. 'The best forgers don't make any mistakes.'

Gently I take the book from Mina's hands and put it on the night table. It is one of the blue books she brought with her, *Algebra IV*.

'Not exactly bedtime reading,' I say but Mina picks it up again and opens it.

"'It was the masterful and incommunicable wisdom of eternity laughing at the futility of life and the effort of life,'" she reads and hands the book to me. Not algebra but *White Fang*. 'Papa and I made the covers before I came. So I could bring it and not get you into trouble.'

'*White Fang* was Anke's favourite.'

'Papa said. He said she knew whole parts of it by heart.'

I smile, my throat tight. Stefan is right, she did, but I didn't know he knew. There is an inscription on the frontispiece, above the drawing of the sun rising like an explosion of fire over the frozen Yukon. *In loving memory of Cousin Anke, your Papa*.

I close the book. We look at the blue paper cover. *Algebra IV*.

'Life is an effort,' I say. 'Often a great effort. But it isn't futile.'

'It is sometimes. When you try and you try and it makes no difference, nothing changes at all.'

'But something does change, don't you see? Not the things you want to change, maybe, but you. You change. You learn what it means to try.'

'To try and fail.'

'To try and fail and try again as all scientists must. To go on.'

'But what's the point? What's the point of any of it when nothing's for certain, when the only things we can prove are the things that aren't true?'

'Because it's not the truth that undoes us.'

Mina is silent. Sleep is closing in on her, her eyes are heavy. I rise and, leaning down, kiss her lightly on the top of her head.

'Sleep tight, darling girl,' I murmur and I switch off the light.

Sunday 3 September

In the Tiergarten the leaves are starting to turn, there are splashes of orange in the green, and despite the glazed blue sky there is an edge of coolness in the air. Summer is nearly over. Nursemaids in starched caps push perambulators along the paths and stout ladies tug impatiently at little dogs on leads. In the woods horses glimmer between the trees like fish.

The Floraplatz is a large circular garden with flowerbeds and low privet hedges and a bronze statue in the middle of an Amazon astride her horse. I see Frau Dumier as I come out of the woods. She has the child with her, they are playing with a ball. On the lawn, a woman with a picnic basket is sitting on a rug watching them, her arms wrapped around her knees.

When Frau Dumier sees me she puts the ball down. I can hear the boy's shrill protests, he tugs at her skirt, but she only murmurs something to him and takes his hand. There is something different about her, I can't put my finger on it, and then I realise that she is wearing a dress, a green dress with a white collar and white buttons down the front. She is wearing stockings too and neat brown shoes with a heel. There is nothing remarkable about the outfit, I see scores of girls every morning setting off to work dressed just like she is, but on her the effect is disorienting, wrong somehow, like the cats in the picture book I used to read to Anke, trussed up in starched pinafores for tea. I have never seen Frau Dumier in anything but trousers. I'm glad when I see that there are still ink stains on her fingers.

'Frau Dumier,' I say and she sighs and shakes her head.

'My name's Emmeline,' she says and, turning, she raises a hand to the woman on the rug who claps her hands and calls out Ivo's name. The boy pays her no attention. He leans against Emmeline's leg and stares at me, his face screwed up against the low afternoon sun.

'What is it?' I ask her. I look around me. It is not possible to be overheard here, there is no cover for thirty yards in any direction.

I wonder if that's why she asked me to come here. 'Why did you need to see me?'

Emmeline strokes the boy's head, then gives him a little push. 'Go on, Ivo darling, go to Mama.'

'No,' Ivo says firmly and puts his thumb in his mouth, stopping it up like a bottle. Emmeline bends down and sweeps him into her arms. He squirms furiously, pushing at her with his dimpled hands.

'We need to find the zookeeper,' she says. 'A monkey like you belongs in the monkey house, not at home with Mama and me.' She moves towards the rug but the other woman is quicker, she comes forward, taking the wriggling child in her arms. 'This is Ivo's mother, Frau Keyserling. Herr Berszacki.'

'Frank, please,' I say quickly.

'Hello, Frank. Dora.' Smiling, Dora untangles the child's fingers from the chain around her neck. From the chain hangs a little golden key. Then, shifting the boy round on to her back, she canters him back to the rug. 'Come on then, Ivo, where do you think Mama might have hidden that gingerbread?'

Emmeline watches as the two of them upend the picnic basket on to the rug. 'I've been wrong about so many things. When Dora met Ivo's father, when she got pregnant, I was so sure it was the end of the world. That nothing good would ever happen again.'

'He's dead, your friend's husband?'

'He was never her husband, but no, not as far as we know. He doesn't exactly stay in touch.' She shrugs, biting the inside of her cheek, and twists her wedding ring on her finger. 'It's good of you to come.'

'Is this about Anton?'

She stares at her ring, then slowly nods. 'He's gone. He asked me to tell you.'

'What do you mean, gone? Gone where?'

'After he was sacked, we thought that would be the end of it but it wasn't. They came to the house, they said he was a Marxist spy, Anton who never had a political thought in his life. They didn't find anything, there was nothing to find, but they took him anyway. When they finally let him go he knew it wasn't over. He said they'd never give up, they'd just keep coming back and back until – he said if he stayed it would only make trouble for us, for Ivo. So he left. He didn't say where he was going, just that he'd send a postcard when he got there.'

She's crying. I put a hand on her shoulder.

'Have you heard from him?' I ask and she shakes her head. 'You should have telephoned me when they took him in. I might have been able to do something.'

'Like what?' When I don't answer she leans down. I hadn't noticed the battered leather bag propped against the statue's plinth. Unbuckling it, she pulls out a small folded envelope and hands it to me. 'I want you to have this.'

The envelope has been opened, its edges are torn. 'What is it?'

'I was going to burn it. I burned the others. It didn't change anything. It's my fault, don't you see? What happened to Anton—'

'Is happening every day,' I say. 'It's vile and vindictive but it's not your fault.'

She shakes her head fiercely. 'You're wrong. When I – I never thought – I was a mess. I thought it didn't matter, that none of it mattered any more.'

'I don't understand.'

She is silent. Then she looks at me, the bag cradled in her arms. 'Nearly four years ago I screwed Gregor Rachmann. September 1929. It was stupid, meaningless, but Dora had just told me she was pregnant and I – he was in Berlin and, I don't know, it happened, I let it happen. I barely remember it, it lasted a week, less, I was drunk the whole time, but after that he wouldn't leave me alone. I changed my telephone number but he still wrote to me once or twice a month even though I never answered, right up until Anton and I got married. Then he stopped. I thought he'd finally given up. And then this came.'

'From Rachmann?'

'I thought I saw him, you know. A few weeks ago, outside our flat. Watching us. Only when I looked again he wasn't there.'

I think of the man smoking in the doorway in the street beside our office. 'He was following you?'

'Em-em!'

Emmeline turns. The little boy is waving. The other woman, Dora, has her hands round his waist, she is trying to make him sit down.

'I have to go,' she says. 'Look, all this time I've wanted to forget the Rachmanns but that sketch, the grid, I can't just let it go, not now, not any more. It's too late for Anton but perhaps – I don't know. Here, take it. And take this too.' She pulls the sketchbook I returned to her out of the bag and holds it out. 'You're the lawyer. You decide.'

I take the sketchbook and the letter. I am not sure I want either. There is no address on the envelope and no stamp, just EMMELINE EBERHARDT scrawled in large capital letters. I turn it over.

'Not here,' she says quickly. 'Later. When you're alone.'

I want to give it back. Instead I put the envelope in my pocket. It's all I have left to offer her. 'You'll let me know, won't you, when you hear from Anton?'

'If.' She tries a smile. 'He's always been hopeless at keeping in touch.'

'It's better, you know, that he's away from here,' I say. 'It's a terrible burden, having to hide who you are.'

Emmeline is silent. She looks down at her green dress with its white buttons. There is a smear of mud on the skirt. She does not try to wipe it off. We stand there together in the bright afternoon sunshine. Then, holding out her hand, she smiles crookedly. 'Goodbye, Frank. And thank you.'

I walk back to the path. When I reach the trees I stop and look back. The two women have the boy between them; he's holding both their hands. They smile at each other, then swing him high into the air. His shrieks are giddy with delight.

At a café near the Reichstag I go to the lavatory. Locking myself into a cubicle I take the envelope from my pocket and slide out the letter. There is no address, just a place name. I know it, one of those once-villages at the end of the U-Bahn line where the fields are now planted with factories.

My dearest E

How many times have I taken up my pen to write to you & yet never with so sure a hope as I do today. Today the darkness & its demons have been cast out, there is light at last. The world sees clearly & the chains that bound you are broken. You are free.

I want you to know I forgive you. I have reason enough for anger, God knows, but I am not angry, not with you. How could I be? I love you today as I have loved you always, with all my heart. Remember what Vincent said, though I fall 99 times, the 100th time I shall stand? When he fell the 100th time he broke himself into pieces but I shall go on standing. We cannot fight what must be, any more than we can fight the rising & setting of the sun. I must not, will not, cannot live without you, as an artist or a man. You are my beginning & my end, the sky above me & the earth beneath my feet. You are my she and no other.

Come, my darling. Come to my Yellow House.
Everything is ready.
Your G

Monday 4 September

I take the train to the end of the line. I know it may turn out to be a fool's errand but, as we rattle past the factories and the bleached yellow fields, my spirits lift. I have the papers in my briefcase, I will knock on every door if I have to. The stationmaster shakes his head, he doesn't know any Rachmann, but when I show him the drawing I've cut from Emmeline's sketchbook he whistles through the gap in his teeth. He knows that face sure enough, though his man's not Rachmann but goes by the name of Gelb. He points past the raw new houses scattered like boxes along the unpaved road. The old Schmidt house, he says, backs on to the woods. I nod. *Gelb* means yellow. The Yellow House.

Outside the station two skinny boys squat beside a patch of weeds, one of them is poking a dead bird with a stick. The other one stares at me without curiosity as I walk towards the woods. I wish I could say that I intend to confront Gregor Rachmann, that I will press him about his role in his brother's frauds, that as Dumier's lawyer I will demand to know his part in Dumier's systematic harassment by the SA, but I know already that I won't. The Rachmann case is over. Art, despite the proverb, does not hold fast. In Germany anyway, it is coming to an end. As for Dumier, Rachmann may have stirred the pot but it was still my client who broke the law. While Paragraph 175 stands, unnatural fornication remains a crime punishable by imprisonment. Provoking Rachmann will not change that.

No, my sole purpose is to have him sign the necessary papers that will authorise his crates to be returned. That is all that matters now, I tell myself, to execute my duty under the law, but still my soul squirms. Every day, across the country, these same accommodations, the same justifications for doing nothing. The politicians, the judges, the medical establishment, the professors, all of us with our fingers in our ears and our eyes squeezed shut. I tell myself I have to be careful because I am a Jew with a wife and a niece to think of, but I know I am a coward. Someone will do something, we have said it all along. But we are all of us too careful – too cowardly – to be the someone who does.

Where the new houses peter out there is a jumble of decrepit stone cottages. Most of them look abandoned. The one I take to be Rachmann's is set back from the road behind a cluster of gnarled fruit trees choked with weeds and brambles. It is only as I lift the sagging gate that I see a kind of path has been trodden down. Thorns snag my trousers as I pick my way along it to the wooden porch that runs along the front of the house. The porch is rotten, soft and mossy with damp, and piled with empty bottles and rusting tin cans. A decomposing wicker chair slumps against the wall.

I bang on the door. When no one comes, I peer in through the dirty window and like a reflection another face looms back at me, pale, dark holes for eyes. I gasp and step backwards, sending bottles clattering across the porch. A bolt scrapes. The warped door creaks open.

'Berszacki, well, well. You took your time.' It's Gregor Rachmann all right, beneath the unkempt hair and the thick black beard. He grins at me and, as I nod back, baffled, I catch the sharp smell of sweat and stale alcohol. Perhaps he is drunk. I fumble in my briefcase for the papers but he kicks the door wider and jerks his head. 'Come on then, man, what are you waiting for? Come in.'

My dreams are like this, restless and unsettling, cleaving to a logic that I can't grasp. Uneasily I follow him inside. There is no hallway, the door opens straight into the main room. The light is dim, the shutters are closed, but I can see it is crowded with junk. Bundles of cloth and old newspapers, broken bits of furniture, more empty bottles, rusted tools, a rickety table heaped with dirty plates and pots and pans, mountains of dog-eared books. It smells of unwashed clothes and turpentine and the sharp sweet smell of rotting rubbish.

'I'm sorry it's taken so long,' I say feebly and I hold out the papers. Rachmann snatches them from me, ripping open the envelope. I take a breath, draw myself taller. 'Herr Rachmann, I am here on behalf of the state in my capacity as guarantor for the safe transfer of items seized from your premises by police on 18th January 1929—'

Rachmann drops the papers on the floor. 'Jesus, Berszacki, you and your legal bullshit. None of that matters now. Where's my painting?'

The floor seems to tilt as I fumble the papers up. 'That's what I'm trying to tell you. Just as soon as I receive the necessary funds for—'

'Funds? What the fuck?'

'As detailed in the original confiscation order, the owner of any property seized is responsible for meeting the cost of its return.'

Rachmann's eyes narrow. He takes a step towards me. Instinctively I step back. 'You extorting little shit. You're holding me to fucking ransom.'

'Of course not. I'm simply asking you to meet your legal responsibilities.'

He leans closer, his breath hot on my face. 'My legal responsibilities? Your business was with Matthias, Berszacki, not me. If you want funds, get my brother to settle his fucking bills. That painting is mine and you'll give it to me, you hear me, or, I swear to God, I'll break you in two.'

I am cringing, I can't help myself, I'm afraid he will hit me. 'That's what I'm saying. Everything that was taken from your studio, it's all there, every last item, just as it was. All I'm asking is that you meet the cost of the carter. Or make your own arrangements, I don't care, as long as you sign. I've been trying to get them back to you for months but we had an address in Düsseldorf, then Matthias told me you were in Frankfurt, so when you never answered my letters—'

'Why would Matthias tell you I was in Frankfurt?'

'I don't know. But he wrote it down, look.' Tugging my notebook from my pocket I flip through the pages till I find it, a Frankfurt address in Matthias's handwriting. Gregor's face hardens. Then he laughs.

'Then how the fuck did you find me, if he didn't tell you? There's no Rachmann here, Berszacki. Matthias is the only person who knows where I am.'

The sketch is folded inside the notebook. I take it out, hold it out to him. 'You can find anyone, Herr Gelb, if you know who to ask.'

Rachmann takes the drawing. The white paper dances in the dim light. 'And my painting? What did my brother tell you to do with that?'

'I told you, he made me promise I'd keep everything until you sent for it,' I say helplessly. 'Everything the police took from your studio. He said he'd given you his word you'd get it all back and you will. Pay the carter and you can have it tomorrow.'

'And the painting in your strong room?'

'My what?'

'I don't know what that bastard told you, but that painting isn't his. It's mine. It's always been mine. Yes, we agreed it was safer with you till the craziness was over, you were his lawyer so you couldn't talk and it would be safe in the strong room, no one could touch it there, but the arrangement was very clear, when things died down you'd find a way to get it back to me. It's my painting, Berszacki, whatever he told you, and I want it.'

Confused, apprehensive, I shake my head. 'I'm sorry but I don't know what you're talking about. Matthias never entrusted me with a painting.'

'Right. So what exactly are you keeping in your strong room?'

'I don't have a strong room.'

With a roar of fury Rachmann turns from me and slams a fist against the wall. A bottle falls from the table and smashes on the floor. 'Christ, Berszacki, how much longer are you going to lie for him? Don't tell me you're still holding out for your money? Jesus, don't tell me you still believe he'll pay?'

I don't answer. I can think of nothing to say that will not provoke him further.

'What did he tell you, that he and his phantom Russian would see you right?' He barks a laugh. 'His imaginary lover with the priceless collection of paintings no one's ever heard of? Jesus, Berszacki, wake up! Aren't your lot fucked enough these days as it is?'

Your lot. It is as though all the hatred and intimidation we have endured are pressed into that little phrase. The anger mixes with the fear to choke me, my breath is noisy in my ears, but I clench my fists and stay silent. Rachmann's eyes are fixed on mine, they gleam in the gloom.

'You blind fucking fool, don't you see the way the wind is blowing?' he murmurs, leaning closer. 'Whatever he's told you, he won't sell that picture, he can't, it's too well known, no one's going to touch it. And even if he did, even if he could, he wouldn't give you a fucking pfennig. He wants your kind out, don't you get that? He means to chase you out.' His face is so close to mine I can smell the sour tang of his breath. I hold his gaze but I say nothing. There might not be truth in silence but there is dignity or something that passes for it. If I start speaking I will not be able to stop. Rachmann can't stop.

'Since May last year my brother Matthias, your client, has been a paid-up member of the Nazi Party,' he says. 'His birthday present to himself, he called it, he said it was the best thing he'd ever done – I'm surprised he didn't tell you. But then perhaps he'd given a rather different impression of himself to you. Of course back then it was different, politics was a matter of principle, and there was nothing to be gained by jeopardising his appeal. No doubt he was afraid you wouldn't understand his position, as a Jew.'

My jaw is clenched so tight it might be bound with wire. I shake my head. 'The law exists to judge a man's actions, not his conscience.'

'You honestly still believe that? Matt thought there should be a boycott of outstanding Jewish bills, just as there had been a boycott of their shops. Non-payment as punishment for centuries of hoarding, of profiteering, of screwing the German people out of their rightful share. Time to screw them back, he said. Let them see what it feels like to be owed. He never intended to pay you, Berszacki. And who's going to make him now?'

'He gave me his word,' I say, or I try to, but the words have thorns, they catch in my throat. Is there a line, a marked point where hopefulness becomes dishonesty, where faith shrinks to nothing but a resolute determination not to see? All I know for certain is that I have been on the wrong side for a long time. There is a weight in my chest, a heavy emptiness. Only a child believes that wanting something hard enough can make it so.

He leans closer, so close I can see the pores around his nose, the flecks of dandruff in his beard. 'So here's the deal. You give me the painting and I'll settle your bill. All of it, with interest. In cash.'

My heart jolts. I stand straighter, refusing to look down, but it is too late, the vertigo is already in me. If I had this painting of his I would do it, I know it absolutely. I do not know who I have become.

'You could pay me ten times over,' I say. 'It doesn't change the facts. This well-known painting Matthias intended to sell, what was it, a forgery? Stolen? Either way, he would never have entrusted it to me. Your brother knew the law, Rachmann. He knew that a lawyer's professional duty of secrecy does not extend to unlawfully obstructing justice. How do you think that would have played to the bench, the defence counsel called as witness for the prosecution?'

Rachmann stares at me, his face moving as though there is something crawling under the skin. I shrug.

'Whatever this painting is, wherever it came from, I don't have it.'

Rachmann closes his eyes. His laugh is harsh, a bitter soundless exhalation. 'He told me to be patient, to bide my fucking time. He said you'd expressly instructed us not to make contact, that the police were watching you, that it wasn't safe. And I believed him. Jesus. My whole life I've watched him do it, watched him screw himself into whatever shape he had to be to slip through keyholes and into people's heads. I never thought the fucker would do it to me.'

I say nothing. There is nothing to say. It is over. We stand in silence. Then, bending down, I pick up the envelope from the floor and open it.

'Sign by the cross,' I say flatly, holding out the letter. 'You'll have the crates on Friday.'

Rachmann takes the paper. Slowly he tears it into two, then two again. He lets the pieces drop. Then, turning, he walks up the stairs and out of sight.

Tuesday 5 September

The telephone is ringing as I arrive in the office. When I lift the receiver there is a dull clunk as coins are deposited. The line crackles.

'Berszacki, is that you?' It's Gregor Rachmann. He sounds agitated. 'Listen to me. I have to see you. I need a lawyer.'

I'm so startled I almost laugh. I gathered up the torn strips of paper yesterday, evidence in case it was needed, but a shadowy Voigt still stalked my semi-dreams last night, slapping my shoulder and bantering about baldness and betrayal. 'If this is about the crates—'

'Fuck the crates. Just get back here now. I'll pay you up front. On arrival. A hundred marks cash.'

I should ask him why he wants to see me. I should ask him if he understands that I am Jewish. 'You have that kind of money?'

'I wouldn't offer it if I didn't, would I?'

I think of Gerda, the lines cutting silently into her face. 'Two hundred. And you sign for those fucking crates. No signature, no deal.'

'All right. Fine. I'll sign.'

It's done. I want to put my head down on the desk and weep with relief. Instead I nod. 'Good,' I say. 'Then I'll see you in an hour.'

Rachmann greets me at the door. Fishing in his pocket he pulls out a thick wad of banknotes. There must be two thousand marks there. He peels off two hundred and hands them to me.

'So that's it, you're my lawyer, it's official?' he says, and when I nod he looks at me very hard, as though he wants to memorise my face. Then, turning, he leads me upstairs.

The staircase opens on to a narrow landing. Someone has painted a sentence on the wall in black paint. *It left me feeling that I had seen it all before and that I will not remember it for long.* Rachmann walks ahead of me into a bright high-ceilinged room.

It is a working studio, there is an easel in the window, a clutter of brushes and rags and squeezed-out tubes, half-finished canvases stacked against the walls, but the walls are the walls of an art gallery. Paintings everywhere, hung in every space, only when I look closer I see that they are not paintings but photographs printed to the size of paintings, hand-tinted in brilliant colours and carefully framed, and every one of them familiar. It is like a dream, I have walked through a crease in time back into the courtroom at Moabit. The poplar trees, the haystacks, the bread rolls in their basket. The boats on the beach at Saintes-Maries. The self-portrait of van Gogh with his cropped hair and his death-mask stare. All of them crowded around the room and between them ribbons of words written in swoops directly on to the walls. *Considered by many to be the finest painting he ever made. The work of an artist at his incandescent, glorious best. An indisputable masterpiece.*

I stare. It is a museum. A shrine to Matthias Rachmann and his brief glorious career. I step closer. Each photograph is signed. Black against yellow, scarlet against blue, a single name, the letters neat and carefully spaced. Van Gogh's signature, only the name is not Vincent. It is Gregor.

'You,' I say.

Rachmann does not answer. He crosses the room, disappearing through a door on the far side. When he comes back he is holding an envelope. He slides a piece of paper out of it and hands it to me. It is a drawing in pen and ink, a young girl in a striped jacket, a ribbon in her hair.

'So here's what you're going to do,' he says. 'You're going to write to Julius Köhler-Schultz. A legal letter, all the formalities. You're going to tell him a drawing has come into your possession, a drawing that was originally assumed to be a copy of a work in his collection but which has been proven, after expert examination, to be the original. You have therefore been instructed to arrange for the safe return of the drawing to its legal owner. You assure him of your complete discretion.'

'And exactly how much of that is true?'

'Every word.'

I look at the drawing. The girl looks back, wide-eyed. The picture of innocence.

'You will tell him that you will hold the drawing securely until he is able to arrange for its collection. You'll enclose a photograph to prove it, a guarantee of your good faith. And when he writes back to tell you you're mistaken, that the drawing remains safely in his possession, you'll telephone him. You'll admit that some awkward discrepancies have recently been turned up and you'll ask him very politely if he is quite sure the mistake isn't his. Whether other similar mistakes might have been made. You can't be specific, you're bound by professional secrecy, blah, blah, but you'll admit to him confidentially that you've been shocked by what has been found under frames and stretchers, behind restorers' liners, even, using X-rays, under the layers of paint.'

'And what do you expect him to find?'

'I expect him to find himself suddenly very eager to return to Berlin.' Rachmann's smile is cold, savage. 'And when he does my brother better have a fucking good story.'

My hand finds my pocket, the soft edges of the banknotes. Then I shake my head. 'Perhaps I haven't made myself clear. My duty of confidentiality does not extend to acting as accomplice to a crime.'

'What crime? We're talking about returning property to its legal owner.'

'You bring me up here to this room, you show me all this, and you still expect me to believe this drawing is a genuine van Gogh?'

'I'm telling you it is.'

I think of Mina and her restorer and I shake my head. 'And I'm telling you that it isn't possible to prove beyond doubt that any work of art is an original. Any expert who tells you otherwise is mistaken.'

'Jesus, Berszacki, I'm the fucking expert. Matt gave me Köhler-Schultz's original drawing and gave him back my copy. Is that enough proof for you?'

I stare at him. 'So it's stolen? You stole it?'

'I borrowed it. And now I want to give it back.'

The room is electric with him, prickling and breathless like the air before a thunderstorm.

'Why?' I ask quietly. 'Why not take the money and run?'

'Because this isn't about money. Whatever my treacherous shit of a brother may believe, this has never been about the money. I want him here, where I can look him in the fucking eye. That bastard killed me, Berszacki. Köhler-Schultz and his band of hired assassins. Five minutes and three poisonous fucking sentences dashed off in a cab and years and years of dedication and every pfennig I could beg gone just like that, up in fucking smoke. Everything over. No dealer, no future, just fucking flower murals and fifth-rate restorations. He killed me. And the craziest part? Apparently it meant nothing. He doesn't even remember. Well, he's going to remember now. He's going to spend every fucking minute he has left remembering.'

His words are pure acid, they blister the air. I should walk away, I should give Rachmann back his money and I should walk out of here, but I think of Gerda and I stay where I am. This is our chance. I do not know when we will have another.

'We can't do it in writing,' I say. 'Letters aren't safe these days, they open everything, and this is unfinished business. Gans has always made that very clear. This gets out and you're going down. No, the only safe way is for me to go to France. I can take the drawing, talk to Köhler-Schultz in person.'

But Rachmann shakes his head. 'No fucking way. He has to come to Berlin.'

'He's a Jew and he's dying. Why would he come?'

'Because the one fucking thing he cares about in the world is here. And because he has to. He has to see.'

'See what? This?' I gesture at the photographs on the walls. 'And what will that change? There's nothing new here, Rachmann, he's seen it all already. He saw it in court.'

But Rachmann is already walking out of the studio. I hesitate. Then I follow him. The room on the other side of the landing is smaller, so plain as to be almost monastic. Whitewashed walls, rough wooden floor, a narrow bed. The window looks out over the woods, a tumble of trees beneath a brilliant sky, but I do not look at the view. All I see are the paintings. Three canvases, unframed, hung together on the wall. On either side, vases of sunflowers, brilliant yellow, their heads drooping beneath their weight. One has a yellow background, the other blue-green. The paint is so thick that the heads of the flowers bristle with seeds and the petals seem ready to drop from the canvas to the floor. The image is familiar, it was reproduced many times in the illustrated papers during the trial, but nothing I have seen has prepared me for the vividness of the canvases or their vigour. It is as if the paint is made of sunlight. All the warmth in the room seems to come from them.

And between them, lit by them, a portrait. A dark-eyed girl in a cobalt blue jacket against a pale green ground, a scarlet scarf around her hair. The colours are dazzling, they stain the air like coloured glass, but it is the girl herself that draws me. It is the girl in the drawing, the pose is the same, the way she sits very upright on the edge of her chair, a posy of white flowers in her hands, only it is not her. There is nothing fragile or childlike about this girl, nothing innocent. She leans forward out of her seat, her gaze fierce, so much impatience in her the paint can hardly hold her in.

She is not the girl in van Gogh's drawing. She is Emmeline Eberhardt.

A line comes back to me, a satirical piece at the time of the trial, Kerr, perhaps, or Tucholsky. *The dead Vincent keeps painting and painting.* I stare at the sunflowers, at the portrait of Emmeline Eberhardt. It is perhaps the most beautiful van Gogh I have ever seen.

Friday 8 September

I do it. I do what Rachmann asks me. I take the drawing and the photograph, and I write to Julius Köhler-Schultz. It is the first legal letter I have sent from our home address. I have agreed with Gregor Rachmann that, should Köhler-Schultz return to Berlin, I will arrange the necessary permissions to secure a private visit to Matthias in Tegel. Otherwise, once I have spoken to Köhler-Schultz, once the necessary messages have been passed on, my duties are done. Not bad for two hundred marks.

The money has saved us. For now, at least. Last night when Gerda asked where it had come from I told her to give thanks for that fount of undying motherly spite, Frau Craemer. It was not an answer and therefore not a lie, not quite. She smiled wearily. She hopes that one day I might coax Frau Craemer into kindness. I gave her enough to settle the reddest of the red bills. Tomorrow the engineer will reconnect the telephone. I have not paid the rent, not yet. I put what remains of the money in a shoe at the bottom of the wardrobe. When we leave we will need all the money we can get.

My wife believes me to be a finer man than I am. I should tell her the truth but I do not. I tell myself I am protecting her, protecting Rachmann, but I know that the person I am protecting is myself. I am afraid, afraid that if she knew she would pull away again, that disappointment would chill and stiffen her just as her grief did for so long, that I would lose her all over again. I cannot lose her.

And besides, what would I tell her? I have committed no offence. The guilty have as much right as the innocent to legal representation and in my dealings with Gregor Rachmann I have followed the letter of the law. I have not obstructed justice, nor have I aided or abetted a crime. I have Rachmann's assurance that the paintings he showed me will never be sold and I believe him. As for his business with Köhler-Schultz I have been frank. I advised him to think carefully, to consider the possible consequences of confessing to an offence that carries a significant penalty, a confession that risks the wholesale resurrection of the fraud case against his brother, only this time with him in the dock. He could spend the next ten years in prison, I told him, Matthias too, but Rachmann was blithe. Köhler-Schultz won't breathe a fucking word, he said, and he laughed. Personally I fail to see the joke but I cannot compel my clients to act in their own best interests. Gregor Rachmann's conscience, like mine, is his own affair.

He calls it justice. If a man can ruin another with the stroke of a pen he cannot protest when the pen ruins him in his turn. *It left me feeling that I had seen it all before and that I will not remember it for long.* A line Köhler-Schultz wrote some fifteen years ago about a young Düsseldorf painter named Rachmann, a line – an artist – he forgot as soon as it was written. But Gregor Rachmann intends him to remember.

It was Matthias's idea, he said, at first. But it grew and it grew and, when the problems started and they had to flee to The Hague, Matthias forgot their agreement, he told Gregor to be satisfied. Six paintings in respected international collections, considered by several experts to be among the finest of van Gogh's works: what was that if not justice? They argued, violently. The game was over, Matthias said, as though all they had ever been playing for was money. As if money had anything to do with it at all.

An eye for an eye. A reason as old as the scriptures. A one-line report neatly typed and filed in a cubbyhole. Perhaps it was true once, back at the start. The seed from which their great deception grew. But what comes back to me as I write this are the words Gregor Rachmann said to me as we stood together in that narrow whitewashed room, in the golden light of his sunflowers, when he told me that he would never sell them.

'They were his gift to me,' he said softly. He did not understand it, perhaps it was a kind of madness, but something had moved in him and suddenly he was himself and not himself, his paintbrush dancing to a melody he had not known he knew, a melody as certain and steady in him as his own breath. The meticulous preparations he had relied on, the pencil marks and the grids and the distinctive pattern of brushstrokes he had taught himself to master fell away and the colours took him over. They leaped and licked around him like brilliant flames, he was half-blind with the dazzle of them but his heart roared, he painted with his heart. He could not say how long he painted, the colours burned up time, days drifting from him like streamers of smoke. When the paintings were finished he hardly knew who had made them. He knew only that he had been shaken to the depths of his soul.

I felt the infinite, he said simply, with a child's simple awe. I hardly recognised him. As he fell silent, his face was a child's face. Even the bones seemed to soften. We stood together, looking at the paintings, and I felt it too, or the ghost of it, pulling at the knots in my heart.

Then Rachmann turned and clapped me hard across the shoulders.

'Time to get to work,' he said, and his smile was set hard as cement.

Saturday 9 September

Monday is my last day in the office. Everything is arranged. When the morning deliveries are finished Katzke will send his boys here to pick up Rachmann's crates. Gregor Rachmann signed the paper and, despite everything, I want to do what Matthias asked me to do. I want to be in some small way the man I once thought I was, the man Gerda still believes me to be. When the greengrocer's boys are finished with Rachmann they will come back here and collect my boxes and cabinets of files and take them to our apartment. There are a great deal fewer of them than there used to be, after all, and it is only paper, we must be able to find a place for it somewhere.

I go upstairs to tell Böhm, he will be relieved, I know, but his office is locked. I haven't seen him for days. As I rattle the doorknob I tell myself there is no cause for alarm, he is unwell or travelling for business or gone away on holiday. People do still take holidays, even now. I try to picture him drowsing in a deckchair, a straw hat over his nose, but all I can think of is the way the caretaker licked his pencil before he asked me what I knew of Böhm's political affiliations, as though he was savouring the taste. *Steady drops wear away stone.*

I do not know what I will do if Böhm is not back on Monday. The caretaker is the only other person who holds a key.

Sunday 10 September

I cannot sleep. I rise early. Mina's train for Hannover leaves at half past ten. As I wait for the coffee to boil I stand on our little balcony looking down on the street. Outside the apartment building opposite ours someone is sweeping the pavement. His brush swings in rhythmic strokes, like the hand of a clock. There is no one else about. Fingers of sun stretch over the roofs but there is a chill in the air. It is the last day of the summer vacation. Tomorrow school will start and the street will once again be full of children.

Last night we had dinner together, the three of us, for the last time. I wanted to buy steak, we had the money for it, but Mina said that she could have steak any time and all she wanted was Gerda's stuffed potato dumplings. They made them together, their heads bent close together as they shaped the dough into balls, and the murmur of their voices was a stone in my throat. At dinner I opened a bottle of red wine and poured a glass for Mina.

'Don't tell your father,' I said and she smiled and sipped and made a face.

'Wine tastes like mud,' she said. 'Mud and vinegar.'

'Don't tell your father that either. I'm pretty sure his wine tastes of neither.'

Mina smiled. Biting her lip, she looked into her glass. 'When will I see you again?'

I should have smiled too. Soon, I should have said. We will all see each other soon. But I did not. I just shook my head. In the end it was Gerda who rose and kissed Mina gently on the cheek and asked her to help with the plates while I sat with my heart and my throat and my eyes burning, unable to summon a single word.

The coffee pot whistles. As I go to turn it off I step over a pair of Mina's sandals abandoned in the middle of the hall. I pick them up.

'At least when I'm gone you won't break your neck.' Mina is standing in her nightdress in the passage. She does not smile. Her hair is tumbled and there are creases from her pillow on her cheek. I open my arms and she steps into them and I hold her, inhaling the sleepy warm biscuit smell of her as the coffee pot shrieks, forgotten, on the stove.

Darling girl.

Gerda and I take her together to the station. We walk down the platform together to her carriage. When I kiss her Mina pulls away first, too soon for me, and I see what she has not known or perhaps has been careful to hide, that, despite everything, she is excited. She waves from the window as the train starts to pull out of the station.

'Work hard,' I say, walking beside her. 'Become a famous scientist. Don't forget to write. And take care of your brothers. Be sure to take care of your brothers.'

Mina grins. 'I know, I know. The Berszacki law.'

The train is gaining speed. I break into a run. 'There's a Berszacki law?'

'Papa says there is. Hold on to your brothers or regret it for the rest of your life.'

Monday 11 September

I walk from the station to the office. The streets are busier than they have been for weeks, men in business suits and children in uniform. My last day. I have been making this journey for nearly fifteen years, I could do it in my sleep, and yet today I somehow manage to walk past my turning without noticing and it is only when I am almost at the church that I realise I have gone too far. A tired-looking woman in a black hat glances absently in my direction as I turn back and, as our eyes meet, her face stiffens, blankness slamming down like the metal shutter of a shop. A reflex. My own face stiffens too.

There is no sign of the caretaker as I walk through the courtyard. The iron gate in front of his door is locked, the chain looped through the post. I glance up at the cherry tree. Its yellow leaves are brittle. Soon they will fall. I take the stairs two at a time, my key already in my hand, but when I reach my office the door is already open.

'Hello?' I say. My voice sounds thin. I cough, my breath ragged, but no one comes. I can feel my pulse knocking in my throat. I push open the door. The office is empty. It looks as it did last night, like something dead, the boxes piled up for collection, the battered desk bare and desolate. I put the key down on a filing cabinet, one hand against the wall. I close my eyes. My legs are shaking but already my fear feels foolish. My mistake. I have been distracted, my mind elsewhere. I must have accidentally left the office open when I went home last night.

The Katzke boys will be here at two. My last day. I put the key in my pocket, move some boxes closer to the door. The solid weight of them steadies me. Mina has gone. Tonight, when this is over, Gerda and I will talk about what happens next. We will find another apartment, smaller, cheaper. There must be some kind of work I can do. Berlin is our city. We have never lived anywhere else. We speak only German. We are old, nearly, and we are tired. It must be better to endure, to put up with this kind of life than to try to start again, without money, without employment or friends, without words. In the courtyard a stray cat sleeps in a slice of sun. Germany is still our home, I say to myself. Then I go upstairs to see Böhm.

Someone has broken down the door. What is left of it lolls on its hinges, splintered and raw. I want to back away, to run, but I make myself go in. I can hardly step across the threshold. Böhm's desk is on its side, the drawers of his plan chest pulled out and upended around the room. There are files and papers strewn across the floor. Straw too. They have jemmied open Rachmann's crates and emptied them out. I pick up one of his canvases, a man in a nightcap holding a candle. Someone has put a boot through it, or a fist: there is a hole where his jaw should be. Beneath the window I see the painted wooden case with its riotous garden of flowers. A jagged spur of wood juts from one side of it like a broken bone.

A noise on the landing makes me turn. The caretaker smirks and lifts his arm in a salute. 'Heil Hitler. You got business in here, Berszacki?'

Panic surges through me. I know how it looks, what he could make of this. I shake my head as I put down the painting, raising my arm halfway like a tentative schoolboy. 'Heil Hitler,' I mumble. My abjectness sickens me.

'They arrested your pal this morning, did you hear?' the caretaker says. 'Dragged him from his bed, the traitorous bastard. Turns out he was a commie agitator. And you said you didn't know a thing.'

I think of the smash in the darkness as the front door gives, the thunder of boots in the hall, and my throat aches. 'I didn't. I don't. He's not my pal.'

'Come on, you and him and that other Jew, Urschel, in and out of each other's offices, you were thick as thieves. You expect me to believe you didn't know what he was up to, defending Commies openly in court?'

'If he did he was only doing his job,' I say weakly. 'He's a lawyer.'

'He's an enemy of the state,' the caretaker barks, his eyes

bulging, and I realise suddenly that it is not just a matter of the petty powers, the backhanders. He truly believes. There are block wardens in every office block these days, every apartment building. They know everything.

I look down at the painted case with its flowers and trees, the case Rachmann kept to remind himself that customers couldn't be trusted, and I see what I have somehow managed not to see until now, that it is over, that however impossible it is for Gerda and me to leave Germany, it is more impossible to stay. You can salute and keep silent, you can close your mouth and your ears and your eyes and your heart. You can become someone who kisses his wife only in the dark when she cannot see the truth of him and it will change nothing. They will make enemies of us all.

Close up the trees and flowers are just splodges, dabs and dots and strokes of different-coloured paint. The caretaker picks up the canvas of the man with the candle and throws it out on to the landing.

'Wait,' I say. 'These paintings, they're not Böhm's. Their owner was sending someone to collect them today. Gregor Rachmann, he's a Party member, you can check.'

He frowns. 'I thought you said you didn't know nothing.'

'I know that the state prosecutor signed an assurance that they would be returned. A man's possessions are still his, aren't they, under the law?'

The caretaker looks at the jemmied-open crates and something twitches in his cheek. Perhaps there are still people in Germany, ordinary people, who are not afraid.

'I can keep them in my office till they come,' I add. 'You'll need to sign the dockets. Proof of damage. You don't want any trouble.'

The caretaker's frown deepens. He rubs a hand over his head, tugs on his neck. Then he shrugs. 'Go on then.'

A small victory. It should make me feel better, only I am no longer sure why it matters or what I have won. I carry the canvases one by one to my office. The painted case is awkward and heavier than it looks. I put it on top of the pile of boxes by the door, then I sit at my desk, waiting for Katzke's boys. Perhaps this is how a snake feels when it is ready to shed its skin. When I turn to look out of the window, a bonfire is burning by the dustbins. The caretaker has a sack, he feeds fistfuls of papers to the flames. Black plumes of smoke smudge the sky.

And suddenly I cannot bear the waiting any longer. I throw open my window and, ripping open the boxes, I snatch up files and hurl them out. They burst open in mid-flight, scattering paper like white birds. The caretaker turns and looks up. I hurl another file and another. Paper fills the air, swoops of white against the grey. The tree is there, and the walls, but the shapes are gone, I see only the colours. The bonfire is a dazzle of orange. I am not weeping but the tears blind me, they fall and fall. Blindly I turn for another box but it is the painted garden that I see, the trailing willow and the lake and the flowers, that midsummer song of praise to mistrust and disillusion, and the implacability of it breaks something deep inside me and I grab hold of it, I lift it high with both hands, and I hurl it with all my strength against the wall. I want it to smash, to explode into fragments, but instead the wood cracks politely, softly, like someone clearing his throat. Sliding to the floor, I cover my face with my hands.

When the Katzke boys come the caretaker is with them. He is red with fury. He shouts at me and I close my eyes and say nothing. The Katzke boys hoist a crate between them and manoeuvre it out on to the landing. The caretaker follows them, growling at them to mind the walls. I open my eyes. The painted case is broken but the garden inside it is still bright with sunlight. I push it with my foot, turning it away from me, and that's when I see it, the narrow cavity between the back board and the case itself, except the cavity is not empty. There is something hidden inside, a flat parcel wrapped in brown paper. I yank at the back board with my hand to try to get it out but the case is too solidly built, it does not give, so I fumble in my drawer for the metal ruler and slide it into the split, prising the case open. The wood sighs, then gives. I prise again, working my way down until the back comes open and I can take out the parcel.

It is tied with string. I undo the knots, pull away the paper. Another layer underneath, like a child's game, this time soft cloth. I open the folds and he is there in front of me. Vincent van Gogh in a cobalt blue shirt, his hair flame-orange against a background of blue. The paint glistens, thick slabs of colour. The van Gogh in the photograph seized from Rachmann's studio, the van Gogh owned by Julius Köhler-Schultz. He gazes past me with a bleak calm as though this is exactly where he expected to find himself, as though no amount of joy or horror in the world could ever surprise him.

The Katzke boys are coming back upstairs. Hurriedly I slip the painting behind a pile of boxes and come to meet them at the door. They take the last of Rachmann's canvases. One of them whistles as they clatter down towards the lobby. I wait for the bang of the door before I take the painting out again. The frame has been removed, you can see the shadow of it, faint indentations in the paint, and I wonder where it is and then I realise that I already know. Gregor Rachmann told me. He told me everything. *You'll admit to him confidentially that you've been shocked by what has been found under frames and stretchers.* The drawing of the girl was just the lure. This is the hook.

The van Gogh that Köhler-Schultz took with him to France,

the painting his wife told me was the only painting in the world he could not bear to live without, is not a van Gogh at all. It is Gregor Rachmann's copy.

The Katzke boys and I load my boxes of papers into the cart alongside Rachmann's paintings. There are not so many. We put most of the papers we gathered up in the courtyard on to the bonfire. I cannot remember now why I thought it necessary to keep hold of them for so long. I look back at the building as the taller Katzke whips up the horse. I will not come back here. The caretaker is standing on the pavement. He does not salute. He watches us, expressionless, as we rattle away, his arms crossed over his chest.

I tell the boys there is a change of plan. We go to the apartment first. I carry the heaviest box myself, the boys protest but I insist on it. I ask Gerda to wrap some bread and sausage up for them, I ask them to take it downstairs, to wait with the cart. There is something I have to do.

The painting is wrapped in its cloth, concealed under layers of paper. I take it out. Gerda folds her hands and looks at it.

'This is blackmail,' I say. 'I will be a blackmailer.'

Gerda puts her arms around me. She holds me very tight, her fingers pressing hard into my back. 'Oh, Frank,' she says. I can feel the thump of her heart, the shudder of her breath, in and out. Her chin is sharp against my chest. Then she pulls away from me a little. She looks up at me, her hands sliding up to cup my face, and in her newly old face her eyes are soft and very young. For twenty years, I think, I have looked into those eyes and found myself. 'Thank you,' she says and she gasps, a choked sob of a laugh that stretches her mouth. 'Thank God.'

I give the Katzke boys instructions and send them on to Gregor Rachmann's without me. I give them the court paperwork, I tell them when they hand over the paintings to be sure to get a signature. I need to know that they have been delivered safely. I also give them a sealed letter. If they are quick, I say, I will make sure to give them a little extra. They are good boys and I am grateful.

Herr Rachmann,

I enclose a copy of the letter sent at your request to Julius Kühler-Schultz. As yet I have received no response to my enquiry but I will forward any reply for your consideration. Please find enclosed also the balance of the monies issued yesterday as fees in advance. As your lawyer, it is my duty to represent the best interests of my clients under the law. As a Jew in Germany, I am no longer confident of my ability to do so. It is with a heavy heart, therefore, that I have decided to retire from legal practice with immediate effect. I regret any inconvenience this may cause you and would like to reassure you that all business discussed prior to this termination remains entirely confidential. I would also be happy to provide recommendations for a suitable replacement.

I am taking this opportunity to return the property taken by police in Düsseldorf on 18 January 1929. I must inform you that during a search of our offices by police this morning, 11 September 1933, the crates were opened and damage sustained to at least one of the canvases contained therein. One item, a wooden case painted with flowers, was destroyed. I enclose the amended dockets, signed by Gunther Holz, building superintendent. Any application for *compensation should be made directly to the Prussian State Police Department.*

Sincerely,

Frank Berszacki

The case burns slowly, yellow flames licking over the flowers, the willow tree. I watch as the paint blisters and blackens, until the garden is gone. I do not think that Gregor Rachmann will miss it. He does not need a painted box to remind him that people don't always keep their word.

Later that afternoon Gerda and I walk to the telegraph office on Oranienburger Strasse. I send a telegram to Sanary-sur-Mer in the south of France.

CHANGE OF PLAN STOP V AND THE GIRL SAFE WITH ME AND EAGER TO RETURN HOME STOP ASSUME YOU WILL MAKE NECESSARY ARRANGEMENTS F BERSZACKI

Tuesday 12 September

The telegraph boy arrives early. Köhler-Schultz's cable instructs me to go to the offices of Alfred Böhm. I go instead to the public telephone box on the corner. Köhler-Schultz accepts the charges. When the call is put through he is shouting. I wait until he stops and then I tell him about Böhm. I set out my terms very clearly. I wish to be reasonable, to act as far as possible within the law, but I will not negotiate. He listens. Then he tells me he will do as I ask. He is grateful, I think, or as grateful as he is capable of being. He gives me his word but I tell him that will not be sufficient, I will require formal assurances, guarantees. He gives me the name of another lawyer.

Back at the apartment Gerda is waiting for me. When I nod slowly she holds out her hands to me and I take them in mine. I feel numb, like we have come home to find our house burned down and all we own with it. All we have worked for, everything gone, eaten up by the flames. The future too, burned away, nothing but a blank black void beyond the smoke, one could fall for ever into the fear of it, but in this moment none of it matters because we are alive. We can begin again.

Tuesday 7 November

The day is cold and damp, the grey sea and the grey sky blurred together beneath a glaze of drizzle. We huddle against a grey wind sharp with salt and the sting of disinfectant. People are still crowding out of the low sheds on to the quay. Stefan says something but I cannot hear what it is. Porters push past us through the crush, trunks balanced on their heads, their shouts drowned out by the blare of horns and engines and the rolling rattle of chains. Above us the ship from the Red Star Line looms, an unscaleable cliff.

They are all here to see us off, Stefan and Bettina and Mina and the boys, their caps abandoned who knows where and their wet hair plastered to their scalps as they chase one another, squeezing around the mountains of piled-up luggage, the coils of tarred rope. Even the baby, perched on Bettina's hip, his face round and pink beneath his tufted knitted cap. When he starts to wail Bettina embraces us quickly, one-sidedly, angling him away, but Gerda reaches out for him and takes him in her arms.

'Don't cry, little one,' she says, rubbing her nose against his and, startled, he stops crying and stares at her, his eyes shiny with tears. Softly she sings the snatch of an old song, a song she sang in the long-before, and the baby grins and lurches forwards, grabbing at her hair with his starfish hands. When she gives him back to Bettina there are strands of silver tucked between his fingers.

People are starting to move towards the gangplank. Summoned by their mother, the older boys sidle up to us and stiffen themselves to be kissed. The younger one tugs at his sleeves, wriggling and elbowing his brother. Standing still is a torture to them.

'Ten minutes,' Stefan says to Bettina. 'We'll meet you at the castle,' and, as she nods, the boys bound away, their skinny legs releasing like springs. They are Antwerp boys already, the Dutch words easy in their mouths. They never speak of Hannover.

We stand together in silence, the four of us. Mina chews her lip. She has started to learn English. Her Jewish school has ties with a Dutch chemical company, each year they fund two scholarships to America. Mina wants to go to Princeton.

'If it's good enough for Albert Einstein,' she said last night and no one else at the table understood why we laughed.

The rain is falling harder. Stefan pulls his scarf more tightly around his neck. He has lost much of his old bulk since he left Germany. A smaller man in a smaller life. He works hard, long hours, but he is cheerful. He has found them an apartment at the top of a tall thin house in the north of the city. On fine days, he says, you can see almost to the sea.

'We should go,' I say and Mina's face crumples as Gerda takes her in her arms, her hands reaching to clasp tightly around her back.

I hold my hand out to my brother. He takes it, squeezing hard. Without my reading glasses, the lines on his face are smooth. He looks almost like he used to, when we were boys.

'I'm so sorry,' he says softly. 'If you only knew how much I wish we could go back and start again—'

'Aren't we?'

He is silent. As his grip slackens I take my hand from his. The ship's horn sounds, a long sombre wail. I touch his arm lightly then, pressing my hand to his shoulder blade, I pull him towards me. His chin sandpapers my ear as he steps closer, his hands hard against my back. The crowd is shifting. In the crush I am pushed against Gerda. I feel the sharp wing of her elbow through the wool of her coat. Then, still holding Mina tight with one arm, she circles the other around me, pulling Mina into the curve between us. Head bowed, Mina tucks herself in against her father. His arm finds her back. We do not speak. We stand together, the joints and curves of us interlocked, as the rain falls and the ship's wail echoes over the grey sea.

Later, as we are herded on to the gangplank, I turn. They are standing where we left them. I think it is them. I take off my hat and I wave it. My face is wet. It tastes of salt. Towards the horizon the weather is lifting, a pale streak of light that turns the water to a beaten pewter. Gerda is crying. I take her hand and together we walk towards our next beginning.

Author's Note

I had been toying with the idea of a book about Vincent van Gogh's sister-in-law, Johanna van Gogh-Bonger, when I stumbled on the extraordinary story that inspired this novel. While the exploits of forgers like Tom Keating and Han van Meegeren, the Dutch artist who famously sold a 'priceless' (fake) Vermeer to Hermann Göring, have made them notorious, the van Gogh forgery case that rocked Germany in the 1920s and 1930s remains little-known. The tale of Otto Wacker, the dancer from Düsseldorf who turned to art dealing in the aftermath of Germany's devastating hyperinflation, planted a seed in my imagination. The book that grew from that seed is very much a work of fiction. I have not cleaved to the historical record, in so far as there is one. Most of my characters have no real-life counterpart. I have altered and invented at will. But Wacker's story, with its many contradictions and gaps, continues to fascinate me. On several occasions I considered drawing on the facts, only to realise how improbable or even fanciful they were. Instead I chose to make up my own. Fiction, unlike the truth, cannot defy belief.

Vincent van Gogh died on 29 July 1890. He left behind a

body of work that had never properly been catalogued, except perhaps by his brother, Theo, an art dealer, who died only a few months later.

In the years that followed, the artist's reputation grew rapidly and, as prices for his paintings rose, the fakes followed close behind. As early as 1899 a fake van Gogh was sold by the Ambroise Vollard gallery in Paris, and in 1901 another Parisian gallery had two paintings removed from an exhibition because they no longer believed them to be authentic. This did nothing to halt the demand for van Gogh's paintings, which grew more frenzied every year. In 1921, Germany's pre-eminent art critic, Julius Meier-Graefe, published a vividly imagined life of the artist, painting him as a madman genius and secular messiah. The purpose of the book, Meier-Graefe wrote, was 'to further the creation of legend. For there is nothing we need more than new symbols, legends of the humanity that comes from our own loins'. In Germany particularly, still reeling from their humiliating defeat in the Great War, the idea of a tormented hero unjustly spurned struck a powerful chord. The book was a bestseller.

Three years later, in 1924, Otto Wacker began to introduce his collection of previously unknown van Goghs. He refused to disclose the identity of the paintings' owner, asserting only that he was a Russian nobleman who had been forced to flee Moscow after the 1917 revolution. Several eminent Russian collectors were known to have collected Impressionist works, including the businessman Ivan Morozov who before the war had owned some two dozen van Goghs, and this lack of provenance did nothing to stem demand. Wacker was also careful to seek authentications of all of his paintings from a number of van Gogh experts in Germany and beyond. He sold the paintings to dealers and collectors in Germany, the Netherlands and the United States, gaining a reputation for humility and straight dealing. It was not until 1928 that a gallery in Berlin cast doubt on the authenticity of several canvases received for an exhibition. But even then the tight-knit art world kept its secrets. The story never reached the newspapers. That July Wacker sold a van Gogh drawing to the Nationalgalerie for nine thousand marks.

By December, however, things were starting to unravel. Jacob Baart de la Faille, the Dutch expert who had worked for a decade on van Gogh's *catalogue raisonné*, had re-examined the paintings and announced that he now considered all thirty-three of the Wacker paintings to be fakes. Wacker's friend and champion Julius Meier-Graefe was robust in his defence of the pictures. Ludwig Justi, the director of the Nationalgalerie, agreed with de la Faille, declaring them all fakes, and bad fakes at that. Experts across Germany and the Netherlands rushed to weigh in on both sides. Many of them were dealers or collectors with financial interests to protect.

The police struggled for years to put together a compelling case against Wacker. When he was finally brought to trial in 1932, the experts were no closer to an agreement. The prosecution was unable to prove that Wacker had knowingly and deliberately sold fake van Goghs. They also failed to identify the forger. In a dramatic volte-face, de la Faille changed his testimony in court, suddenly claiming five of Wacker's paintings to be genuine. Foul play was suspected (though never proved). Wacker was charged with fraud and falsification of documents, and imprisoned for a year. At appeal the sentence was upped to nineteen months and a fine of thirty thousand marks.

In the end the judges were as equivocal as the art experts. While they dismissed the story of the Russian as nonsensical, their judgment concluded that only eleven of the Wacker paintings could be considered definitively to be fakes. Several more they considered to be genuine van Goghs. This left open the possibility that there might be further authentic canvases among those paintings not produced at trial. It was not until 1984 that Wacker's *Self-Portrait at an Easel*, purchased in New York by the American industrialist and art collector Chester Dale, was finally declared to be a forgery.

These days there is not a single expert who is willing to speak out in defence of Wacker's van Goghs. None of the canvases survive but, as far as one can tell from grainy reproductions of photographs, many were unconvincing. It is hard to imagine how they could have deceived anyone. But van Gogh was, as Meier-Graefe himself admitted, a 'painter of weak moments' and, for many, the desire to believe was very strong. By the time Wacker was uncovered many of these experts were too deeply involved, professionally, financially, perhaps even emotionally, to be able to extricate themselves.

No one has ever proved who painted Wacker's pictures. Both Wacker's father, Hans, and his brother, Leonhard, were able artists. Leonhard contributed several times to the annual Düsseldorf art exhibition and, in 1922, exhibited in that city's international show. In 1929, the studios of both men were raided by police who seized paintings that, according to a Nationalgalerie curator, were unquestionably attempts to mimic the style of van Gogh. However, Leonhard claimed that these canvases had been given to him for restoration and the police were never able to prove that this was not so. He was never charged.

Otto Wacker joined the Nazi Party in 1932, some months before it became politically pragmatic to do so. After his release from prison he returned to dance, under the name Olinto Lovaël. There are indications that to promote himself he faked reviews of old shows, including a letter he claimed was from Julius Meier-Graefe, by then long dead, comparing his work to the paintings of Rembrandt, El Greco and van Gogh. In 1946 he performed

Zouave, a dance that he dedicated to van Gogh. He must have been disappointed that, unlike Vincent van Gogh, the myth of Otto Wacker never managed to ignite.

Even today the authenticity of many of van Gogh's works remains in doubt. Twenty years after he published his canonical *catalogue raisonné* in 1977, Jan Hulsker raised questions over forty-five of the works included in his original list. Among the doubtful paintings were *Dr Gachet*, owned by the Musée D'Orsay in Paris, and the Metropolitan Museum's *L'Arlésienne*. Since then, thirty-eight paintings and drawings have been downgraded by museum curators, though eminent British art historian Martin Bailey puts the number of fakes closer to one hundred. A 1998 Channel 4 documentary presented evidence that one of the iconic *Sunflowers* canvases, acquired in 1987 by Japan's Yasuda Fire and Marine Insurance Company for a record $39.9 million, was a forgery. As recently as 2016 the Van Gogh Museum in Amsterdam issued a statement strongly denying the authenticity of *The Lost Arles Sketchbook*, which purports to contain sixty-five previously unknown drawings by the artist.

Not that these scandals diminish our fascination with van Gogh. According to Bailey, the patch of floor in front of the *Sunflowers* in London's National Gallery gets more scuffed than any other part of the museum, and the postcard is their number-one bestseller. Despite all the questions, all the doubts, the work of Vincent van Gogh endures. The myths endure too. They are both too powerful to let go.

Acknowledgements

As always, I owe an enormous debt of gratitude to the historians and writers who have guided and inspired me during the research for this novel. It would take another book to pay tribute to them all but I want in particular to acknowledge two works that underpin all the others and without which I would never have been able to conceive of my story: *Solar Dance: Van Gogh, Forgery and the Eclipse of Certainty* by Modris Eksteins and *A Real van Gogh: How the Art World Struggles with Truth* by Henk Tromp. Among a huge number of articles, two by Stefan Koldehoff, 'Van Gogh and the Problem of Authenticity' and 'The Wacker Forgeries', published online by the *Van Gogh Museum Journal*, were another key resource, as were Martin Bailey's 'Van Gogh: The Fakes Debate', which appeared in *Apollo* magazine, and 'The van Gogh Fakes: The Wacker Affair' by Walter Feilchenfeldt, in the Dutch journal *Simiolus*. Feilchenfeldt's father, also Walter, was managing director of Cassirer's, the prestigious gallery in Berlin which first raised questions about the authenticity of Wacker's van Goghs.

Among the dozens, perhaps hundreds, of volumes I devoured about Berlin in the 1920s and 1930s, there were a handful I came back to again and again. *A Dance Between Flames: Berlin Between the Wars* by Anton Gill; *Before the Deluge* by Otto Friedrich; *Weimar Berlin: Playing on the Tips of the Waves* by Wayne Andersen; *Weimar Eyewitness* by Egon Larsen; and *Weimar Culture* by Peter Gay immersed me entirely in the world of interwar Berlin. The work of contemporary German novelists like Vicki Baum, Alfred Döblin, Gabriele Tergit and Hans Fallada provided the opportunity to step back in time, as did *The Weimar Republic Sourcebook*, edited by Anton Kaes, Martin Jay and Edward Dimendberg, a brilliantly curated collection of pieces by contemporary journalists, intellectuals and artists which encompassed everything from Bauhaus architecture to Jewish persecution and the rise of the New Woman. *Days of Masquerade: Life Stories of Lesbian Women During the Third Reich* by Claudia Schoppmann and Allison Brown, and *Lesbians in Germany: 1890s–1920s* by Lillian Faderman and Brigitte Eriksson offered insight into the challenges faced by gay women in Germany in this period.

When it came to life under Nazi rule, I relied heavily on *Life in the Third Reich* by Richard Bessel, *A Social History of the Third Reich* by Richard Grunberger, *In Hitler's Germany* by Bert Engelmann, and *Life in the Third Reich: Daily Life in Nazi Germany* by Paul Roland. Both *Jewish Daily Life in Germany 1618–1945*, edited by Marion A. Kaplan, and *Nazi Germany and the Jews* by Saul Friedländer provided me with detailed and often distressing first-hand accounts of the torments endured by Jews during the Third Reich, as did the personal diaries of Victor Klemperer.

There are many translations of van Gogh's extraordinary letters to his brother: *Letters of Vincent van Gogh to His Brother 1872–1886* and *Further Letters of Vincent van Gogh to His Brother 1886–89*, translated by Johanna van Gogh-Bonger (Constable, 1927–1929); *Dear Theo: An Autobiography of Vincent van Gogh from His Letters*, ed. Irving Stone (Constable, 1937); *The Letters of Vincent van Gogh*, edited and translated by Mark Roskill (Atheneum, 1963); *The Letters of Vincent van Gogh*, edited by Ronald Leuw and translated by Arnold Pomerans (Penguin Classics, 1997); and the latest and most complete, the magisterial six-volume *Vincent van Gogh: The Letters*, edited by Leo Jansen, Hans Luijten and Nienke Bakker (Thames & Hudson, 2009) have all left their mark on this novel. Among the innumerable biographies, I would particularly recommend *Van Gogh* by Steven Naitch and Gregory White Smith, and *Van Gogh: A Power Seething* by Julian Bell, as well as editor Kodera Tsukasa's fascinating collection of essays, *The Mythology of van Gogh*, which attempts to unpick a century of myth-making and what those myths tells us about ourselves. Martin Bailey's *The Sunflowers are Mine* (Frances Lincoln, 2013) is an enthralling study of what is surely van Gogh's most iconic image. Finally, this list would not be complete without the work of Julius Meier-Graefe, who, though much altered, remains the inspiration for the character of Julius Köhler-Schultz. His book, *Vincent van Gogh, A Biographical Study*, translated by John Holroyd Reece (Harcourt Brace, 1933), might not always stick strictly to the facts but it contains some of the most vivid and evocative writing about painting that I have ever read.

The excerpt in the novel from Dostoevsky's *The Brothers Karamazov* is loosely taken from the translation by Richard Pevear and Larissa Volokhonsky (Vintage Classics, 1992).

It is the writers in this list, and the ones I have not space to mention, who have shaped my world over the last three years. My sincerest thanks to them all. My thanks too to Clare Alexander, my agent and dear friend for two decades; to Lennie Goodings, my editor, whom I have been waiting to work with for almost as long; to Susan de Soissons and her wonderful team at Virago; to Ed Boydell for his advice on divorce law and Philip Watson for his guidance on van Gogh. And to Chris, Charlie and Flora, as always, from the bottom of my heart.

Charlotte Betts began her working life as a fashion designer in London. A career fol... ...design, ...worm, C... ...e discovered her pas... ...r three children and two stepchildren had gro...

Her debut novel, *The Apothecary's Daughter*, won the YouWriteOn Book of the Year Award in 2010 and the Joan Hessayon Award for New Writers in 2011. It was shortlisted for the Best Historical Read at the Festival of Romance in 2011 and won the coveted Romantic Novelists' Association's Historical Romantic Novel RoNA award in 2013. Her second novel, *The Painter's Apprentice*, was also shortlisted for Best Historical Read at the Festival of Romance in 2012 and the RoNA award in 2014. *The Spice Merchant's Wife* won the Festival of Romance's Best Historical Read award in 2013 and was shortlisted for the Romantic Novelists' Association's Historical Romantic Novel RoNA award in 2015.

Charlotte lives with her husband in a cottage in the woods on the Hampshire/Berkshire border.

Visit her website at www.charlottebetts.com and follow her on Twitter at @CharlotteBetts1 and on Facebook as Charlotte Betts - Author.

Also by Charlotte Betts:

The Apothecary's Daughter
The Painter's Apprentice
The Spice Merchant's Wife
*The Milliner's Daughter**
The Chateau by the Lake
*Christmas at Quill Court**
The House in Quill Court
The Dressmaker's Secret
The Palace of Lost Dreams

*ebook only